THE
CHRONICLES
OF AN
OUTRYDER

THE
CHRONICLES
OF AN
OUTRYDER

THE ETERNAL RIVALS

CONNOR OSWALD

THE CHRONICLES OF AN OUTRYDER
THE ETERNAL RIVALS

iUniverse books may be ordered through booksellers or by contacting:

iUniverse
1663 Liberty Drive
Bloomington, IN 47403
www.iuniverse.com
844-349-9409

Because of the dynamic nature of the Internet, any web addresses or links contained in this book may have changed since publication and may no longer be valid. The views expressed in this work are solely those of the author and do not necessarily reflect the views of the publisher, and the publisher hereby disclaims any responsibility for them.

Any people depicted in stock imagery provided by Getty Images are models, and such images are being used for illustrative purposes only. Certain stock imagery © Getty Images.

ISBN: 978-1-6632-3869-6 (sc)
ISBN: 978-1-6632-3868-9 (e)

Library of Congress Control Number: 2022907204

Print information available on the last page.

iUniverse rev. date: 04/27/2022

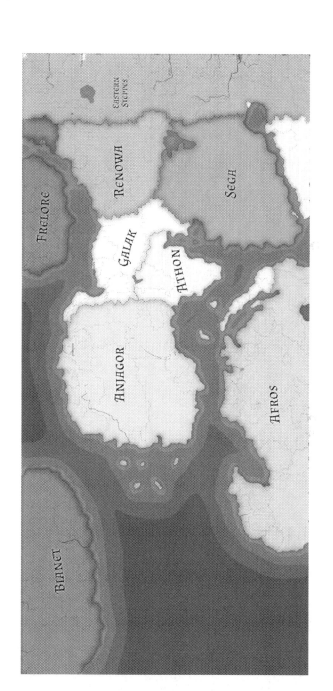

PROLOGUE

Haran looked up from his father's tattered satchel and into the bright sun above his head.

"Come on Haran," Lottie called from the far side of the courtyard as he began to jog out of the castle yard. "I want to get to the canyon before sunset hits."

"Relax we will get there with plenty of time to spare," Haran said back to him. Haran was eager to explore the canyon again since the last time when they found a small cave at the bottom. However, Lottie's eagerness was on another level entirely. In fact, he hadn't stopped talking about it since then.

Haran ran to catch up with Lottie in hopes that Lottie wouldn't take all the exploring for himself. "Slow down idiot," Haran said as he caught up with the boy, "You know for someone of your size you are pretty quick on your feet."

"Of course I am," Lottie said shuffling his feet back and forth to show their speed.

"Oh yeah." Haran scoffed, "Why don't we test your speed then." He took off into a sprint leaving Lottie in his wake.

"You little rat," he replied laughing as he took off running after the boy.

Haran arrived at the rocky canyon some fifteen minutes later utterly exhausted. He collapsed on the ground, his lungs writhing in pain. Lottie arrived a minute or so later wheezing just as heavy, "you are lucky I just ate," Lottie said in between deep breaths.

"Wait you were trying?" Haran asked with a smile. "I walked all the way here." It was an obvious lie as he too was breathing heavily and was doubled over in pain.

Lottie playfully punched Haran in the arm with a surprising amount of force. Haran took the punch like it was thrown by a baby, but he knew the spot would be bruised by the end of the day.

They sat basking in the sunlight for several minutes before they moved again. Lottie was the first one up, "alright, let's get going then."

Haran got up begrudgingly; his body still ached in pain from climbing out of the castle the night before. Sneaking out was heavily frowned upon by the Baron, but he didn't care. As long as he wasn't caught in the act he would continue the action.

He followed Lottie into the canyon below. There was a mostly natural walkway that went down the bottom of the canyon. However, the path down was narrow, just enough to fit one person at a time on it. Lottie took off running down the walkway without a care in the world. "Come on Haran," Lottie said as he stopped halfway down the path on a slightly wider part of the natural pathway.

Haran looked at him skeptically. Of course, they had been down this path many times before in their explorations of the vast canyon, but for some reason something didn't sit right in Haran's stomach. "Wait up Lottie," Haran said as he took off after the boy.

By the time Haran reached Lottie he asked, "Are you sure we should be down here? I mean Heide did say there were wolves sighted down here just yesterday."

"Heide's a worrywart," Lottie replied, "Plus I'm not too worried about wolves." He gestured to the sword hanging at his waist. The uneasiness in Haran soon faded. Lottie had been practicing with a sword since he could remember, and he was quite good. Even as good as many of the Battleschool boys.

"Now come on," Lottie said gesturing for Haran to join him on the wider platform. Lottie shifted to Haran's right and closer to the edge of the ledge leaving Haran just enough room to stand on the ledge.

Haran did as Lottie suggested and stepped onto the ledge. "Alright come on let's go," Haran said worriedly.

"What are you so stressed about?" Lottie asked, "Its not like anything bad is going to happen to us up here."

Almost as soon as the words came out of Lottie's mouth, the rocky ledge below his feet crumbled from under him from the sheer weight. Lottie's eyes grew wide as gravity took him with the broken piece of the ledge. "Lottie!" Haran called from above as he watched his friend slowly fall, grasping for anything he could find.

Luckily he found a small tree growing out from the side of the canyon just a meter or so below where Haran stood petrified. "You alright?" Haran asked.

"Of course I'm not alright idiot I nearly fell to my death," Lottie said as he looked down to see the twenty meter drop beneath him. "Here take my hand."

Haran looked down at his friend's extended hand and grabbed it with both arms. He pulled with all of his might, but the boy barely moved with his efforts. "What are you doing pull Haran," Lottie yelled as his grip started to weaken on the tree branch. Haran pulled harder, using his legs to drive into the rocky ground. There was a little bit of movement, but there was no way he could pull the large boy up.

"Hold on for just a minute longer," Haran said as he let go of the boy's free hand and took his satchel from around his shoulder. He grabbed a long piece of rope from out of the bag.

As soon as the rope cascaded down the side of the rocky edge of the canyon Lottie's hands slipped from the tree branch he was holding. Haran gasped as he saw his friend slide helplessly down the face of the canyon. He tried again to reach for anything that could help him, but he found nothing. His forearms simply raked against the rocky canyon walls.

After what seemed like minutes of Lottie falling he again found something to hold onto. Haran could barely see the boy now as he had descended fifteen meters down the rocky canyon. However, he could make out the visible red that now covered Lottie's arms. "Lottie!" Haran said as he pointed to his friends left. There was a small ledge just big enough for the massive boy to stand on.

Lottie saw what Haran was pointing to and swung himself over to it. As soon as he landed on the ledge he ripped off his shirt and used it to bandage his arms. Haran watched in shock as he saw his friend at work. It must have been excruciating to do any of those things, yet he did them with such composure. The boy seemed to be less shocked than Haran and Haran wasn't about to bleed to death.

Haran snapped himself out of his daze and said loud enough for the boy to hear, "I'm going to get help. Stay there."

As soon as he left he mumbled to himself, "As if he could move anywhere."

Haran arrived at a farm five minutes later. Luckily for Lottie the farm was so close otherwise—*never mind that,* Haran thought as he knocked on the farmer's door.

Thirty seconds later the door creaked open. In the doorway was a middle-aged man, maybe forty or so. He was tanned from the constant sun beating on his face. "Well, if it isn't the little nuisance. Come to apologize then?"

Haran was confused, then he looked to the man and then to the house. Haran recognized the blue porch and the farmer's scowl. *Of course, it had to be this guy,* he thought. It was only two days before that he and Lottie had snuck into the man's farm and tormented his chickens. They were eventually told off by the old man, but they didn't care too much. Now he cared. "I am so sorry sir for sneaking in here and messing with your animals, but I need your help now. My friend is in trouble, and you are the only one who can help him."

The farmer inhaled deeply, "Is it the one you were with earlier, the big boy."

Haran nodded.

"Then sorry I can't help you," the farmer said as he shut the door in Haran's face.

Haran threw his hands up in frustration and knocked on the door once more. The door opened once more and the farmer said, "What do you want boy?"

"Please sir." Haran fell to his knees, tears flowing down his face, "he needs your help, if he doesn't get help right away he's going to die."

The farmer looked down to Haran, "Stand up boy." Haran followed his instructions, the farmer patted him on the shoulder, "What do you need me to do?"

Hours later the two boys stood at the top of the canyon. Lottie's forearms were wrapped in bandages and every time he moved he grimaced in pain. "Hey Lottie," Haran said, Lottie craned his head in Haran's direction, but didn't meet his eyes, "I'm sorry."

Lottie nodded his head in acknowledgement of the apology, but then turned coldly away from Haran and began to walk south towards Castle Norhall.

CHAPTER

1

Haran woke up just before dawn in fits of sweat; he kept replaying the battle at Calcore over and over again in his sleep. The nightmares were the same as the battle but also very different.

The Outryder's arrived at Calcore. The Lupens came out of the canyon menacing and ready with Lyra, Shiva, and Scarlett alongside them as their captives. King Nigel and Doran spoke back and forth until eventually Doran asked for a fight to the death, a Shinoketto they called it. Orion revealed that King Nigel and Doran were in fact brothers and then they fought expertly for many minutes before King Nigel eventually killed his own brother in self-defense. Haran's biggest rival Lottie filled with rage from the loss of his father figure and attempted to kill Nigel. However, Haran intercepted his blow, and their fight began.

Haran and Lottie both fought valiantly with Haran barely being able to stop Lottie's unbelievable power. While this was happening Orion and Gilpin began their fight and Cassius, the Outryder commander, let Lyra and Shiva free from their bondages.

After she was set free, Haran's pet lion Shiva charged towards the struggling Haran only to be attacked by Lottie's wolf. Lupe as Lottie called him was a prophesized wolf god called Albalupius that would ensure the Lupen's victory. After Shiva attacked Lupe, Haran took advantage of the momentary distraction and turned the tables against Lottie knocking his sword from his hand and then performed Contrium, a move taught to him by Orion, to win the fight. Haran won, but Shiva was still being attacked by Lupe, and there was nothing he could do about it.

Orion threw a few knives into the back of the wolf, but they did no damage. The only thing that saved Shiva was Scarlett the fox, who knocked the wolf from Shiva, momentarily stopping the attack, but in the process, Scarlett sacrificed her life.

This point is where the dreams divulged from the truth; Haran told Lottie to call off Lupe. However, as Lottie did, Lupe didn't listen. Lupe went back to Shiva, killing her with one bite. Then the wolf diverted his gaze to Orion, then to Lyra, then to Cassius, then to the king, killing each of them with the force that could only be described as . . . godly. Finally, he turned his attention to Haran, who stood paralyzed in fear, the night grew darker and colder. Lottie got off his knees where he was defeated, but as he got up he wasn't Lottie anymore. He was a suit of black, spiked armor, designed to strike fear in everyone who sees it. The helmet was open, but there was no face, the only thing inside was piercing red eyes searing their ways into Haran's very soul. The spike figure kicked Haran off the canyon's edge and into a seemingly bottomless pit. Haran woke up from the dream sweating terribly. It was the same dream he has had for fourteen days straight since the battle.

He sat staring at the ceiling for several minutes. It was dark, maybe a few hours past midnight. Haran sighed; his eyes were heavy from his lack of sleep. A sound opened his eyes fully. No, it wasn't a sound, it was a feeling. Someone was watching him. He peered around the room to see nothing was there. He closed his eyes once more before he heard the creak of the wooden floors. His eyes shot back open; the black figure from his dream stood in front of him, dark swords hanging loosely from his steely hands. Haran tried to get up, but he was paralyzed with fear. The only thing he could move was his head. He picked it off the pillow and looked at the warrior. The spikes gleamed ominously off the waning moonlight. Blood dripped from the man's sword and onto the floor, soaking the wooden panels. "Who are you?" Haran asked. "What are you?"

Deep breathing came from the suit of armor, almost as if it were a task for him to do rather than a natural action. The thing did not respond, it simply moved its dark metallic body to Haran quickly. Faster than Haran could have ever thought possible. "Your worst nightmare," it croaked as it brought the gleaming blades high above its head and down onto Haran's chest.

Haran woke up again with a start, dazed and confused he looked to the wooden floor. *No blood.* He thought as he felt his chest where the swords struck. *No holes. Impossible.* He felt the pain as the swords were driven deep into his chest.

He sat up with a great effort as if his body were frail. Slowly he got up, his hands shaking from fear and exhaustion. He made his way quietly into the living room where he saw Lyra already awake beside a sleeping Shiva.

Haran came up to her and looked at her, tears rolled down her face, she was crying. There was a slight attempt to brush the tears away, but Haran stopped her, "Can't sleep either?" he asked, wondering if she was getting the same dreams as him.

"No, I keep thinking about what I could have done to stop it. Why'd I have to set them free Haran? Why'd I have to set them free?" She asked twice, almost choking on her tears the second time. Haran simply wrapped his arms around her, and they sat, staring into the smoldering fireplace.

"You know I don't think I am made out for this job," Lyra said after a brief moment.

"What do you mean?" Haran asked.

"Well, Outryders are people who live for danger, and I just don't think I am cut out for it," Lyra said as her eyes closed from exhaustion.

Haran shook his head, "You've got it wrong. We don't live for danger we live to protect people and save lives. The danger is just an unfortunate part of that."

"It sure doesn't feel that way," Lyra said, "it feels like everything we've done so far has only led to death and destruction."

"Maybe so, but that's only reason to try harder," Haran said as he felt Lyra relax in his arms. Minutes passed and Haran was about to fall asleep when she said, "Your right." He smiled to himself and fell asleep with her in his arms.

An hour later, Orion came out to see the scene, both of his apprentices cuddled next to the fire, sound asleep. He didn't want to wake them. They had been through a lot in the last month or so, and he knew they weren't getting any sleep otherwise. He walked out into the foggy yard. It had been relatively quiet the past two weeks which was unusual for the big fief of Norhall. There was always a drunken tavern fight, or farmer's animals being attacked, or even a bandit attack. However, there were none of those things in the past two weeks, everything was quiet. He really hoped something would happen soon, not because he wanted people to suffer, but to stop his apprentices' suffering. If only they had something other than training to distract them from the constant reminders of their losses. Something other than another attack from the Lupens.

KNOCK-KNOCK-KNOCK. Gilpin looked up from his pile of papers on his desk a little shocked. Who, other than him of course, would be awake at this time?

"Come in," he said to the door. He assumed it would be one of his apprentices, but no. As the door creaked open he saw it was Sylvia Frenger, Ella's mom, who entered.

"Hey Sylvia, what is the matter? Can't sleep?" Gilpin asked, Sylvia hadn't been there when Doran died, so it shocked her when they came back with his lifeless corpse on the doorstep.

"You know, Doran used to be up at this time too, never missing the break of dawn." Sylvia said, Doran was once the leader of the Lupens, but after his death the mantle had been passed to Gilpin. "Obviously, there is no sunrise down here, but if there was he wouldn't watch it. He would be too busy working to even care. Just as you are now," she said as she approached the window.

"Well, there isn't any rest for the wicked I suppose," Gilpin said. He hadn't really thought about how he took on Doran's mannerisms before now.

"Is anyone really wicked though? To me, you have done everything possible to protect the people you love. Tell me, is that wickedness or righteousness?" Sylvia asked, she hated the way Gilpin blamed himself for the death of her husband.

"Can't be righteous if you don't believe in gods, so I suppose the former. But Doran, now he was a righteous man to the core," Gilpin said, he loved his friend more than anything, and he knew he could never be like him.

"Oh, the most righteous indeed," Sylvia said, "How do you think Lottie has been holding up since? I know Doran was much like a father to him."

"To be honest," Gilpin said, "I really don't know. But I know his loss to Haran really didn't help. He's been begging for me to get him a shot in the military so he can sharpen his skills."

"Oh, so that was the reason for changing the nativity law?" Sylvia asked. Gilpin had recently changed the law that stated that only native-born citizens could be in the military to anyone willing can.

Gilpin smiled, "Well, that is what I told him, but I have bigger plans for that."

Sylvia smiled tiredly, "Just like Doran, always scheming. Hey, I know you've been looking for someone to take over the religion in Doran's wake, and I think I know someone who could fit the role."

"Sure, what's his name?" Gilpin asked.

Sylvia paused. "Have you ever heard of the man named Percival Woodberg?"

CHAPTER

2

L ottie woke up in his room in the giant mansion of Randint Cavern. As he got up and looked out the window he saw a bustling street of people moving from place to place. He still hadn't gotten over the fact that there was a whole civilization under his nose. A civilization with families, jobs, pets, culture, and religion, and all of it was under hundreds of tons of rock. The massive cavern was lit with the radiant crystals that lined the rock walls. Hundreds of houses lined the streets below. The slightly sloped hill of Randint led to the bottom of the cavern where there was rows and rows of crop fields. Springs popped up near the bottom also leaving a small lake at the very bottom right of the cavern that watered the crops around it. As he discovered weeks before, the Lupen military trained at the very bottom of the cavern past the crop field and in a training facility well hidden from the public eye.

Looking over, he saw his wolf Lupe sleeping soundly at the foot of the bed, deciding to let the wolf sleep, he got dressed. It was a big day for him today, for he would be officially admitted to the Lupen army. After he defeated the captain Tomas word of his skill spread like wildfire, and after a lot of begging, Gilpin eventually changed the law to allow him into the ranks.

His training was scheduled in just an hour, and he really didn't know what to expect from the Lupen procedures. Gilpin said that the training would be rigorous, much more than that of Norhall.

He walked down the marbled stairs of the mansion totally prepared for his day to come. As he was walking out of the door Ella stopped him, "Lottie, we need to talk."

He stopped dead in his tracks, he had been dreading this conversation. Ever since the battle, Ella has been trying to talk to him about what happened at the canyon, apparently something didn't sit well with her. "Listen, El, I really have to get going, it's really important," Lottie said, desperately trying to avoid the conversation.

"Fine, but we *will* talk tonight," Ella said. Lottie knew she hated how nonchalant he was about the whole ordeal.

"We will El, I promise." Lottie was many things in life, but a liar was not one of them. He would talk to Ella tonight.

He made his way down to the hidden area where the Lupen's trained. Sticking his pinky in the tiny hole that was, somehow, the way that the rock door slid open. Walking through, it closed behind him, "So weird," he said silently to himself. Looking around the training arenas he saw around fifty new recruits waiting for further instructions. He didn't recognize anyone except of course, Tomas. The captain was slightly older than him and had his brown hair pulled back into a tight man bun. He walked over to the captain who was talking to a few of his friends.

"Hey Tomas, long time no see," Lottie said as he approached the young man.

"Hey Lottie," Tomas said backing away from the boy, "You haven't come to beat up on me again have you?"

"No not quite. I was actually looking for where to go, I was supposed to be here for my first day," Lottie said jokingly confused by what he was supposed to do.

"Of course, you can just hang out with us until they call for you, they have to do an evaluation for all the newbies here so it might take a little while," Tomas said welcoming Lottie into the friend group.

"What kind of evaluation?" Lottie asked.

"You see, every member is separated into one of three different categories of ability. Blue being the best, yellow being the second best, and red being the worst. You, obviously will end up in the blue category with me, so you will have to train twice as hard as everyone else," Tomas said.

"LOTTIE, LOTTIE." Lottie whipped around to the sound of someone calling his name. A man stood at a door to his left with a clip board in hand.

"Looks like I'm up," Lottie said to Tomas as he walked to the person who called out his name. A ball of nerves sunk to his stomach, something about being judged by random strangers with keen eyes and a lifetime of experience didn't sit right in his stomach. Suddenly, Lottie really wished he had eaten that morning.

He followed the man that called his name into a room to the left of the big training area. The room had one long table where three men dressed in the regulation Lupen white sat. The men wore tons of pin and patches that marked them as high-ranking generals in the Lupen military. Other than the large table, the small room held only one fighting arena in it.

As he looked to the other side of the room he saw a giant man well over 2 meters in stature and at least one hundred and twenty kilograms. The man carried a giant club that Lottie realized could bash his brains to bits if he wasn't careful.

"Welcome Lottie," The man at the middle of the table said, "the name is Norman, I am the supreme general of the Lupen army. To my right is General Jaron, and to my left, General Feris. In front of you is your worst nightmare, so let's see what you got."

"You want me to fight that?" Lottie asked shocked, the general simply nodded, "Where are my weapons?" Lottie was hoping to get *something* to defend himself, anything.

"You get none," Norman said in response to the boy.

"No surprise," Lottie sighed and whispered to himself as he walked into the arena.

He lined up some three meters away from the giant and tensed his muscles waiting for the signal, "begin," Norman called from his table.

The giant man leapt into action, slamming his club right where Lottie had just been a second before. Thoughts raced through Lottie's mind, pondering what to do next. The giant man swung into action again swinging his club vertically down once more.

Lottie rolled out of the way as the giant picked up his club for another swing. This time the swing came horizontally at Lottie's head. Seeing the movement, Lottie hit the ground fast. If he hadn't he would have been easily decapitated by the debilitating blow. As the giant was finishing his swing Lottie swept the giant's feet from under him sending him crashing to the ground. The giant's club was ejected from his hand. Lottie got up off the ground quickly, picked the club up, and threw it out of the arena as the giant was getting up.

"Now let's play," Lottie said getting into his fighting stance as the giant rose.

Lottie launched into action, cutting two meters of distance in just a second; Lottie tucked his chin ripping punches to the body at will.

The giant pushed Lottie away from him as if Lottie was nothing but a minor nuisance, almost sending him to the ground. Lottie recovered himself and tried the same tactic again, but as he moved into range, he was clipped with a shot from the giant's surprisingly fast right. He flew two meters away, hitting the ground hard with a loud thud and limp limbs. "Ow." Lottie got up, blood running from his lip, and asked, "that all you got?"

The giant smiled and charged the boy, Lottie barely rolled out of the way of the charge and was up on his feet as the giant prepared for his second charge. However, Lottie was prepared for the charge now and slipped just far enough to the side and shot his right hand straight onto the giant's temple. The giant stumbled and crashed to the ground, unconscious.

"We done yet?" Lottie said looking at the generals and wiping his lip.

"Good work Lottie, come accept your mark for the blue group, we look forward to seeing what you do against our enemies. Same place same time tomorrow," Norman said as he held up a blue arm ring with the ends designed with wolf faces in them. Now that he thought about it, Lottie did notice one of these on Tomas' arm. As soon as he wrapped it around his arm a feeling of pride came over him. It was nothing but a piece of fancy metal, but he felt free, respected and protected all at once.

As he was walking out, the giant was getting up from his unconsciousness. "Hey, big man, it was nothing personal, just doing business you know," Lottie said trying to be as nice as possible.

The giant gave him a death stare, Lottie flinched, ready for another fight. But none came and a low, uncontrollable laughter came from the giant man, "No problem small man, the name is Tyson, welcome to the club." Tyson held out his hand for Lottie to shake, which he did, noticing the blue band around his arm as well. Tyson followed him out, Lottie assumed his job was done for the day.

"Well?" Tomas asked as they came out.

Lottie held up his arm, "Totally demolished him."

Tyson roared with laughter, "I let you win little one. Don't get too cocky."

"Whatever you say," Lottie said, "But last time I checked you were the one who was unconscious on the floor not me."

They all three laughed and he stayed all day talking to them both trying to get to know them better. Turns out Tyson had an unnatural affection for birds for the reason as he explained it, "They seem so maje- majest- majestation. Floating through the air with no care in the world."

Lottie also found out that Tomas had never seen a sunset before. It made sense; he has only lived underground his entire life, but the confession still shocked Lottie.

When the clock struck six Lottie decided it best to go home. He walked into the mansion and was immediately face to face with Ella. "Ready to talk?" she asked. There was only one answer to that question, and it was in any form that said yes.

"Sure, however, we might want to do it more privately," Lottie said knowing the conversation they were about to have.

She nodded and they walked up the stairs to Lottie's room. She closed the door behind her and sat on the bed, Lottie sat next to her with his head down analyzing the floor for ever speck of dust. "So," she said trying to find the words. "Listen, I know you saw Doran as a sort of father-figure, but don't you think you went a little overboard at the canyon?" She, of course, was talking about how he grew angry after the death of Doran, and attacked Nigel causing everything else to unfold.

"I do," Lottie said, "but I don't regret any of my decisions. I made the choices I had to make to stop the oppressive king from taking more lives." As he spoke he realized that he was no longer Anjagorian anymore. He was a Lupen through and through.

"But he did stop, and that's what I don't understand. Yes, he killed Doran, but he also killed his brother. He was grieving when you attacked, what would you have done if Haran hadn't stopped you?" Ella asked.

Lottie looked up from the ground, "Honestly El, I don't know. But I am glad that he did stop me. I know I became full of rage filled, and I think that's the reason I lost to Haran. However, I promise it won't happen a second time."

Ella was confused by the promise so, to clarify, she asked, "You promise to not get angry again, or you promise to not lose to Haran again?"

"They are one in the same. I lost because I was angry," Lottie said recalling how, when Haran was angry at him, Haran lost, and when he was angry with Haran, he lost.

Ella looked at him with a hint of confusion, "Why do you hate that boy so much?"

Lottie looked to the scars on his forearms, "I told you what happened at the canyon years ago. The boy was weak, and it almost cost me my life. I can't let him harm anyone else with his weakness."

"That's why?" Ella asked, Lottie nodded half-heartedly. "Oh, and one more thing."

"Yes?" Lottie asked skeptically.

"You have to *promise,* you won't go after them again. At least without their provocation," Ella said. Lottie's grimaced slightly. Seeing his expression she added, "For me."

"I promise." Lottie said, and he never broke his promises.

CHAPTER

3

Lottie woke up and went straight to training. It had been weeks since he had trained consistently. Between the battle at Calcore and the funeral, he just hadn't found the time. But now, he was pumped to get back to the training, especially with his new friends Tomas, Tyson, and the entirety of the blue group. After going through the weird sliding door Lottie found himself in the training facility of the Lupens again.

As he discovered yesterday, the door to the left was the evaluation room, and from the looks of it, the main area was for the red group seeing as it was the biggest and some Lupens with red arm rings on were already training in the area.

There were two more doors in the giant room. The first was straight ahead from the entrance and the second was to the right. Lottie saw a person with a yellow arm ring walk into the door on the right which meant that the one to the blue room must have been straight ahead.

He walked past those training basics in the red group and through the large oak door. He found himself in a rather simple training room with one large sand pit where some were already sparring. Lottie watched for a moment as he waited for training to start. He immediately saw that the blue group was no joke, they were fighting both smoothly and quickly with no hesitation in each stroke. They were also not using the practice weapons that hung on the wall, so if one slipped up it would spell out his immediate death. He watched for a little while before he eventually got bored and began to check out the rest of the blue group.

By his count, there were about 300 people in the blue group, the smallest by far. He knew the Lupen military consisted of about 2,500 in the standing army, very little in comparison to the Anjagorian army of around 15,000. However, as Gilpin put it when Lottie asked how he planned on taking Norhall. "The Anjagor army will take weeks to gather all of its troops from the different fiefs, so if we strike fast we just might be able to win the fief."

After a few minutes Tomas started lining the blue group up into ten rows of thirty each as they waited for Norman to come in. As the supreme general, he controlled the training of the blue group and he was the most intense, at least that's how he was described by Tomas and Tyson. Lottie fell into rank in the last line behind a boy roughly the same size as him with black hair. The boy turned around and asked, "What's the name?" Lottie looked into his eyes only to realize that they were jet-black like the color of his hair. It was almost as if the boy's eyes were searing into Lottie's soul as he spoke. To say that it frighted Lottie was an understatement, his eyes were terrifyingly black.

"Lottie." He faltered, avoiding eye contact with the boy, "how about you?"

"Theo but my friends call me Jet."

"Ahh because of the eyes. Not very clever, are they?" Lottie asked.

"Nope," Jet responded with a small smile, but before he could continue he was interrupted by Norman. "Alright boys it seems we have some new recruits in with us today, but they might not be by tomorrow because today we are going to show him how we train. How the blue group trains. Now, are you ready boys."

"Yes sir" shouted all the boys.

"I said are you boys ready?" Norman shouted at the top of his lungs.

"Yes sir!" The boys shouted louder.

"Then let's begin shall we," Norman said, "The first three rows grab your weapons and pair up with the person beside you and give me some good sparring. The next three rows, you are going to give me a run up to the top of the hill and back three times led by Tomas. And the last four rows give me two hundred pushups, three hundred sit-ups, and seventy pullups. Chop-Chop." Norman finished and the boys sprang into action each row doing exactly what they were told. It was at this moment that Lottie noticed the giant horizontal bars hanging from the ceiling. The bars spanned the entire room on either side, plenty of room for the roughly 120 people to cycle through it without the cycle being slowed too drastically.

Lottie cycled through the first three quarters of the circuit easily, but on about the 150th push up and 50th pull up he was definitely starting to feel the strain put onto his muscles. However, he persevered under the intense scrutiny of Norman.

He didn't have much time to watch the sparring from the first three lines but from what he saw they were all just as good as those he saw spar earlier. He figured they were all almost as good if not as good as Tomas. If these fighters were put head-to-head with any man apart from an Outryder, Gilpin, or himself, he was sure they would win. Lottie smiled after he finished his last pullup and looked over to Jet, "Quite good aren't they?"

Jet simply laughed at the rhetorical question. "Whatever you say."

About five minutes later, the runners came back through the door led by Tomas. "Alright boys, now that we are all back, you four that did the circuit get to running. You that just ran get to sparring, and you that just sparred get to the circuit. Chop-chop boys I want to be home in time for dinner."

The run for Lottie was easy enough, the hardest part would have been weaving through the crowd, but they took a way to where they ran into very little people on the street. They were only halfway through, and Lottie and Jet were already leading the pack significantly. "I haven't seen you around here. Did you just move here?"

"Yes not to long ago," Jet said.

"Oh cool," Lottie said as he picked up the pace slightly leaving Jet to catch up.

After they touched the mansion at the top of the hill the two went back down passing the main group of runners as they went. At the end of the run, they were waiting outside for the others to catch up. "Hey, you're pretty fast," Lottie said as they were waiting for the others.

"Yeah, you too, I'm surprised you beat me here," Jet said.

"I'm not," Lottie said casually.

"Huh, bet you couldn't beat me in a spar though," Jet replied.

"Why don't we just try it out when we get inside huh?" Lottie said accepting the boy's challenge. He was well known throughout the whole military as a fierce warrior after his defeat of Tomas a month or two back, but he had heard nothing from the boy called Jet.

After everyone showed up, they went inside and saw that the other boys had just finished their circuit. As soon as they walked in Norman yelled out, "Alright those who just ran its time to spar, those who just did the circuit get to running and those who just sparred get to the circuit lets go we haven't got all day"

Lottie and Jet paired up immediately. There was only one choice of practice weapon on the wall, a wooden sword. Lottie figured he'd best not grab two just in case. Norman seemed angry enough already, and he didn't want to incur even more of his wrath. Knowing nothing of the black-eyed boy, he figured he wouldn't need it.

The spar started slow, with each boy slowly circling each other, the tips of their swords moving slowly clockwise to keep their wrists warmed and ready for a parry. It was Lottie to strike first letting a side stroke go followed by a lightning-fast downward stroke. Each were parried with ease and returned with an underhand stroke and side stroke of their own. Lottie blocked them, but the sheer power and speed of the shots left his arm jarred. *Impossible*, Lottie thought, *he's stronger*. Lottie tried it once more sending a side cut at the black-eyed boy, but once again it was blocked, leaving Lottie's arm jarred once more. It continued like this for several minutes, Lottie would attack, Jet would counter, and the counter would leave Lottie's arms jarred. *How is he so good?* Lottie asked himself. He foolishly walked into a battle with an opponent he knew nothing about and was about to face the consequences. If the fight continued like this he would lose once more, and that sheer idea made his brain work in overtime to find a solution.

He thought to when Gilpin had mentioned to him how to beat someone stronger and faster than himself. He had never struggled with this problem before, no one could ever compare to him in sheer power, but somehow the black-eyed boy in front of him was. Lottie looked into the boy's dark eyes. An unbridled rage now took over from his once hint of charm. As he stared into the darkness of the boy's eyes seeing the determination he knew there was no win condition.

Or was there? Now that he thought about it, just before his fight with Haran during the tournament, Gilpin said, "If you are to come upon someone stronger than yourself, pick up the pace, make them tired. Fatigue makes cowards of even the most determined of men."

And that is what he did, he gave Jet no room to breathe in his relentless flurries of attacks, each were defended pretty easily for minutes but eventually he grew tired, his arms dipped just below where he was meaning to keep them, and Lottie struck him in the ribs. A devastating blow, but Jet didn't fall, in fact he barely even reacted to it at all. *He's a monster*, Lottie thought. The dark-haired boy was about to counterattack before Norman called out, "Alright boys that's enough."

Lottie looked up to see that they had a crowd watching them, admiring their skill. He threw down his sword and Jet did the same, a wave of embarrassment wash over his face and he knew Jet was feeling the same way. They had both wanted to win the spar so badly against the other. But there was no bad feelings, for each had earned them a brilliant new rival.

CHAPTER

4

Haran woke up again to the same nightmares he has had for the past fifteen days; however, he was getting accustomed to the dreams now that he knew they *were* just dreams. He even found that he was able to control them as opposed to simply watching the events from above. He was able to make decisions, decisions that he wished he had in real life. In his dream he tried to warn Lyra not to let Shiva out. He tried killing the wolf before the battle even started. He even tried to let Lottie win their fight. However, the dreams all ended the same; the black warrior would appear, everyone would die, and he would always fall into the bottomless pit until he eventually woke up. There was nothing he could do. Luckily, this time there was no apparitions of the black warrior. He hoped that the instance was a one-time thing because he didn't know if his heart could handle another occurrence.

He sat on his bed for a few moments silently staring at the wooden wall in front of him.

He wanted something to happen, anything, but nothing did, so he got up and walked out into the living room. Shiva was sitting patiently by the fire for their routine morning exercise. She recovered well from her injury received by Lupe even to the point where there was barely even a scar there now. She had also grown bigger in size since then, being just over two meters in length, a meter in height and two hundred kilograms in weight. He patted his leg motioning for her to followed behind. He always loved their early morning walks. It seemed to help relax his mind, especially since the battle.

After the battle, King Nigel and Outryder Commander Cassius returned to their respective homes in Anjagor Castle. The king took the death of his brother really hard, and he hoped to regain his composure while in the presence his family. Heide stayed a few days after the battle to simply comfort the two Outryders after their tragic loss at the canyon's edge. When she left the cabin, they agreed that they would meet at the first of every month to go on a friendly date. Tomorrow was that day for the two and Haran was hoping that they could relax after everything that had happened over the past few weeks. However, for now he had training to get to.

After his walk, he went straight to his training. He was getting rather good, even for Outryder standards. He had always been a natural with his axes and his silent movement was getting better, but his knife throwing had hit a plateau. He just couldn't seem to improve his throwing any more. He could hit the target, but it would be centimeters off his intended position. He went to practice his throw, but the effect was still the same, from every range he would still be slightly off. After a few hours of building frustration, he ripped his satchel off his shoulder and threw it on the ground.

"You alright?" Lyra asked worriedly from where she was practicing with her axes in the sand pit ten meters away.

"I'm fine," Haran said. "Want to get some sparring in?"

"If you want to lose," she replied. She was great with the axes, but it was her worst skill of her skillset, and she would never be as naturally good as Haran. They both knew it; however, that didn't stop her from poking fun at Haran exclusively.

"Whatever you say. Just let me know if I need to go easy on you that's all," Haran said.

"HA-HA-HA. So funny," Lyra said as she got into her fighting position.

Haran did the same and they began circling each other expectantly. Haran was the first to make a move by sending a lightning-fast downward stroke with his lead axe. Lyra blocked it easily and returned with a side stroke with her back axe. Haran was a little slow to block it from his hours of throwing practice, but he did barely. She backed off, "You know what, maybe it isn't smart to practice with our razor-sharp axes." She then threw her axes on the ground behind her and threw up her fists in a classic fighting position. Haran nodded his agreement and then did the same. They began circling again, each having their own rhythm that the other couldn't quite pin down. However, apparently Haran did first because he threw two stiff jabs at Lyra that were caught in her guard. Lyra retaliated with a right hook that would have sent Haran reeling if he hadn't ducked out of the way. As he backed away, Lyra swept Haran's legs sending him crashing on his back to the sand below. She then got on top of the now winded boy and whispered into his ear. "You may beat me with those axes of yours, but you can never beat me with your fists."

The sound of hoofbeats filled the clearing. Orion had returned from the market, and at the worst possible time.

"What is happening here?" He asked with a hint of laughter in his words.

The two got up instantly, knowing exactly what it looked like, "We were just uhm sparring and I lost," Haran said.

"Clearly," Orion said holding in his laughter. Haran and Lyra turned to each other, each redder than the other. And on that note Haran went to practice throwing his knives once more.

His throwing was still not as crisp and accurate as he would have liked it. He was performing all of the movements just as Orion had showed him, but something was off. Therefore, he decided that he would dedicate the next few days of training to improving his throwing skills, even if it would be the most repetitive and boring thing he had ever experienced.

By the time he finished his throwing and walked inside it was well after sunset. He wasn't very hungry even though he had been doing hard work for the past eight hours. Maybe it was due to building frustration in Haran's mind, or the lack of good sleep, but he simply walked into his room and lay on his bed.

He stared at the ceiling of his room long into the night, analyzing every flaw and every cut in the wood. He could see the small knot in the third board, its dark brown showing barely in the little moonlight there was. He stared at the painting of Heide on his wall, trying desperately to stay awake, but eventually the exhaustion overtook him, and he fell into a deep sleep.

He still dreamed, but surprisingly it was a different dream; he was alone in an unfamiliar woods. He heard leaves crunching around him, he glances around to see what made the sound. He found nothing. No one was there. He turned back to look straight ahead down the clear trail. The autumn hues showed visibly in the fading sun. He heard the sound again. He turned to his left to see nothing. He looked back straight and finally he saw a small girl running down the trail. He was visibly confused; it was as if she had just faded into existence right in front of his eyes.

The girl was young, maybe four or five, but she looked surprisingly familiar to Haran. She had Lyra's dark eyes, and her jet-black hair. However, the little girl's hair was beautifully braided and she was wearing an elegant white dress that matched her pearl necklace perfectly. "Daddy," the little girl called, "hurry up, I want to see the flower cove."

Haran looked around to see who the girl was talking to, but only to find out that he was the only one there. *She's talking to me*, he thought. He followed the young girl down the trail for a few hundred meters When he got to the end of the trail he found a small beach inlet.

It was breathtaking, daisies lined the fifty-meter field from the wood line that faded perfectly into the sand on the beach. Rock formations shot up from both the left and right sides of the inlet leaving the only real access to the inlet a ten-meter gap fifty meters from the beach. The gap was in the west because the sun was setting directly positioned within the two rock formations. The water shined brilliantly in the evening sun even so that Haran thought about taking a dive into the glistening water.

The girl ran out into the flowers, almost being swallowed by daisies. He looked off into the sunset and felt sheer bliss as the sun came down in between the jetting rocks.

He snapped awake in the shine of the rising sun outside, but he lay for a few minutes, closing his eyes trying desperately to go back to the dream. *What is the flower cove?* He thought. H*ow do I go back?* But soon he realized that it was just a dream, so he got up.

He walked out the house to meet up with Heide shortly after sunrise. He fed his horse Spirit a handful of oats from a stash in his satchel and saddled him up, "Good boy," he said as he got onto the horse. The horse shook his head in appreciation, *or maybe that was just a sneeze,* Haran thought. Whatever the case the two rode out of the dense woods and onto Castle Norhall.

He saw Heide standing on the drawbridge at the gate to Norhall Castle. She was as beautiful as ever, her red silky hair flowing in the wind; Haran couldn't help but to be mesmerized by her. She waved as she saw him approaching, snapping him out of his drooling daze. However, the look on her face wasn't one of excitement per se. It was more of a nervousness, like she had just been tossed into the sea with no ability to swim.

"Hey Haran," she said when he came up to her.

Haran got to the point immediately, standing in front of her with cross arms, "What's wrong?"

"Nothing," she said trying to play it off. Haran didn't even have to respond; he just gave it a minute until she finally cracked under his scrutinizing gaze. "Fine, listen I am sorry to do this to you today. I know it was supposed to be our date night, but I have been given a solo assignment. It's my first one, and I was hoping that you would join me on it as a bodyguard."

"Sure," Haran said relieved, "Where to?" He expected it to be to a neighboring fief like Dalhurst or Osmole.

"Randint Cavern," Heide said while visibly cringing.

"Randint Cavern? You mean where the Lupens live?" Haran said, he thought he had put all the Lupen stuff behind him after they won the battle, but now it seemed to follow him everywhere. Apparently even in his dreams. "Yeah," Heide said.

"No way," Haran said, "it's far too dangerous. The last time I was down there I got both myself and Lyra captured, and we were almost killed."

"While that is true," Heide argued, "you also went down there as spies, we will be going as diplomats to arrange a peace treaty between the two nations."

"Peace?" Haran asked, "Surely you can't believe that they can be anything but savage. I mean you were there at the canyon right?" He caught eyes with Lottie after Doran's death. There was nothing peaceful about them; the only thing that filled that man was rage and revenge.

"Yes Haran, but I don't think they planned to harm anyone," Heide said.

"Of course they did Heide," Haran replied, "Lottie tried to kill the king and me that night." He didn't know if Lottie would have actually killed him given the opportunity; however, even as he said it, a nagging feeling of worry washed over him. *What if he would have?*

Heide looked stunned that Haran would ever believe that about Lottie. She began to shift away from Haran, "If you really believe that, then I guess I will just have to go alone."

"Absolutely not," Haran said, "what makes you qualified for the job. And I mean no offense by it, but it is a daunting task, and one that could put your life in danger. I mean you have not even been a courier for a full year yet."

"You went down when you were barely six months in," Heide said making a very valid point.

"Yeah, but that's different," Haran said defensively. Haran had been trained as an Outryder for six months before and he was still captured almost immediately by Lottie and Doran. Even the thought of being in that cold and dark dungeon once more left chills down his spine.

"Oh, how is that? Because you're a big bad Outryder now?" Heide said a little aggravated by her friend.

"Heide, you know that's not at all what I meant," Haran said calmly. "Listen, I just don't want to see you hurt that's all."

"And you won't," Heide replied. "Because you will be accompanying me into the toils that are Randint Cavern."

Haran thought for a little bit, if he let Heide go into Randint Cavern alone then there was a much higher chance that she would get killed or worse, but if he went with her he might be able to stop the Lupens from doing something bad, "Fine, when is it?"

"We leave an hour past noon," Heide said.

"Okay, so we have six hours until then. Now can we please go on our date?" Haran asked as he gestured kindly to his horse.

"Of course, my good sir. Where are we off to?" Heide asked as she curtseyed to the boy in front of her.

"A graveyard my dear," Haran said matching the tone.

"Ooh sounds romantic," Heide said and then they both laughed uncontrollably as they got onto Spirit and headed towards Malen Plains for a peaceful picnic before they plunged into the toils of Randint Cavern.

CHAPTER

5

Lottie walked into Gilpin's office just after noon. He saw the man sitting at his desk looking over some papers. He glanced around to see that Gilpin had redone the office slightly in Doran's passing. The bookshelf was no longer behind him, but it was on the far-left wall. The giant windowed wall was no longer majorly covered in a blackout curtain, and the wooden desk was restained to match the darker color of the walls.

Apparently Gilpin needed him there for a meeting with a courier to discuss a peace agreement with Anjagor. Lottie didn't necessarily like that idea. Anjagor has proven in the past that they would break peace treaties at a moment's notice when it benefits them. The first example that popped into his mind was the longstanding feud between Anjagor and the Bianet people. In the foundational years of Anjagor, Bianet raiders raided the coastal fiefs of Anjagor for goods and supplies. Anjagor retaliated by sending Outin Ryder and the Outryders to frighten the Bianets into ceasefire. After the threat, the Bianet king agreed to a peace treaty which held strong for seven years. That was of course until Anjagor broke the treaty by supporting the nation of Galak in their war with the Bianets. Bianet won the war against all odds, and ever since then the nation has stayed strong and continue to return to pillage Anjagor. Whereas the Galak nation fell to power hungry lords and rebellions.

"Just so you know, I don't think this is a great idea, Gilpin," Lottie said. "We have the advantage with Lupe. We could fulfill Doran's goal and take over Norhall."

"I know," Gilpin said. He was looking at papers in front of his face totally absentminded to Lottie in front of him.

"So then why make peace with them then?" Lottie questioned.

"I don't plan to make peace with anyone. This meeting is just political jumping jacks designed to keep the king questioning what we are going to do next," Gilpin said revealing his thoughts to his apprentice. Lottie nodded and looked at the papers his master seemed so focused on. The papers had a picture of a man on it with a description of the man under it, Lottie read the name, Percival. "Who's that?" Lottie asked curiously.

"A very interesting priest who Sylvia thinks will fit the role that Doran once served," Gilpin said as he looked over the paper again.

"And what do you think?" Lottie said. He had never met this Percival guy before, but he also hadn't met over half the people in Randint Cavern.

"I think I don't trust any man who claims to be a saint," Gilpin said.

Lottie nodded his acknowledgment, "When do you plan to meet him?"

"I invited him over for dinner at the end of the week, I expect you will be there." It wasn't much a question as it was a demand, but Lottie didn't care, he too wanted to meet this

Percival character. There was a knock on the door. "Come in," Gilpin said. Ella entered the room.

"The diplomats have just arrived at the house," Ella said and turned her head to Lottie who was standing beside Gilpin, "but I am not sure you will be happy to see who it is."

Not even a minute later, Sylvia led a red headed girl into the office. Lottie immediately saw who it was and smiled at her kindly. Heide had always been very kind to him and a very good friend. However, when he turned to Ella and saw her death glare his friendly smile soon faded. The neutral face soon turned into a scowl as he saw the dark green cloak of an Outryder walk in behind Heide. Lottie immediately recognized the boy's light brown hair and sea green eyes. Both Lottie and Gilpin stood and reached for their weapons instantly. Haran did the same.

"Relax boys, there is no need to fight right now. Remember this is a peaceful discussion," Sylvia said, and the boys removed their hands from their weapons but remained standing.

"Heide." Lottie nodded to the beautiful girl.

"Hey Lottie, I trust you are doing well?" Heide said.

"I am, but what is he doing here?" he asked looking to Haran.

"My question exactly," Gilpin added, "Nigel said that he would send one delegate here to discuss possible peace." Gilpin sat back down on his soft cushioned chair. Lottie followed his master's movements, but he was still ready to strike at any moment. Ella and her mother exited the room quietly, leaving Haran, Heide, Lottie and Gilpin alone.

"I am here to protect the delegate in which is discussing possibilities of future peace between our two nations," Haran said trying to remember his rehearsed lines, but then he just had to add, "and its King Nigel to you Gilpin."

"He is no more a king to me than I am a king to you," Gilpin said, "so unless you would like to refer to me as King Gilpin, I shall not refer to him as King Nigel."

"Good point," Heide said as she looked to Haran, "and an *actual* diplomat would not ever ask such a thing of you. So, I think those who are not should try to speak as little as possible."

"But are you an actual diplomat?" Gilpin asked looking at the girl barely of age in front of him, "They sent a child to deal with a king. This is mockery. I demand they send an experienced diplomat. Now."

"No," Heide said plainly to the man.

"What do you mean 'no' girl," Gilpin said getting more and more hostile, "you are a child you've no right to be discussing such matters of peace between nations with me."

"I have every right to discuss peace," Heide said, "I am a trained diplomat under the excellent tutelage of Miss Anna of Norhall."

"You are nothing but a little scared girl. I bet this is your first mission isn't it," Gilpin said. Haran looked to Heide who seemed to not confirm or deny his assumption.

There was a slight pause as Heide waited for Gilpin to finish, "You keep referring to me as a child," Heide said, "but ever since I enter this room two minutes ago, you have threatened both myself and my companion, disrespected a national delegate, and complained obnoxiously to someone who really does not care. So, you tell me *Sir* Gilpin. Who is acting more like a child to you?"

Heide's words flowed out of her mouth smoothly and sharply. Haran looked at her starstruck, she had just sent chills down his spine. He realized he underestimated Heide, he thought he would be needed in this discussion. Turns out, this was her domain.

Gilpin looked embarrassed, realizing the girl was right, "Your right Miss Heide, I have disrespected both you and your companion, and I apologize. Now please, take a seat. We have much to discuss."

Heide took a seat as requested; Haran knew she was proud of herself for the small victory. Even though there was no outward change in appearance. Haran followed suit, sitting down in a way that he could get up easily if the need were to arise.

"Alright Miss Heide, what is it that Nigel sent you all the way down here for?" Gilpin said trying to test how good this girl really was.

"Heide is fine. And, *King* Nigel has sent me here to discuss possible options for a peace between our two nations," Heide said choosing her words very carefully.

"I didn't realize we were at war Heide, what makes Nigel think anything along those lines?" Gilpin asked feigning ignorance.

"Well, as you say," Heide said, sitting up even straighter in her chair, which Haran thought to be impossible, "there has not been a formal declaration of war between the two nations. However, as you are seemingly unaware, approximately two weeks ago the former leader of the

Lupens, a man by the name of Doran, captured two of Anjagor's finest Outryders. He then sent a threatening letter to King Nigel, in which the king answered with great poise. Unfortunately, after a battle between the two parties at the designated meeting point of Calcore Canyon there was loss of life on both sides."

"Oh yes, I do recall now. I also recall that these so called *finest Outryders* were sent to Randint Cavern as spies, even adopting new identities. Do you recall what they were Haran?" Gilpin said gaining a little bit of traction with his words.

Haran looked at Heide, she nodded her head, apparently there was nothing much to lose from the exchange. Therefore, Haran replied, "I believe the two went as Herald and Leida Lightfoot."

Gilpin smiled a little, "what a beautiful couple they were together." Haran saw Heide shift uncomfortably in her seat as Gilpin continued. "I also recall that we captured these two Outryders with relative ease. It would be a shame if their master realized what they were. Failures. I wonder what he would do? Maybe he would just get rid of them entirely."

The man's words nestled their way into Haran's head now as he shifted slightly and looked down. Would Orion replace him due to his failure? Could he even replace him? Who was he to be an Outryder anyway? He was Haran, the orphan boy that randomly showed up on the Baron's steps. He was a nothing, a nobody.

"Many people make mistakes Gilpin as I am sure you are very aware of," Heide said snapping Haran out of his own questioning daze, "However, that is not the point. I assume now, that we are familiar with the story. Now, what do you suggest would be best to rectify the atrocities on both sides of the altercation?"

"I believe that Anjagor should have to give up the fief of Norhall," Gilpin said, making his purpose all but visible.

Heide looked shocked. Haran had always known the Lupens were after Norhall, but apparently it had been a surprise to Heide. "Preposterous," she said after a slight pause, "Norhall is one of Anjagor's largest fiefs, it provides the most warriors to the military and its proximity alone to the capital could serve as a launching point for further Lupen attacks."

"Once we have Norhall there will be no desire to take the rest of Anjagor, so you shouldn't worry about that. And, after all that Anjagor has done to the Lupens, I think it is a small price to pay on your country's side," Gilpin said.

"That is a ridiculous request," Heide replied, "King Nigel would never give up Norhall fief, and I'm sure neither would you give away a part of your country."

Gilpin began to tap his finger on the hard wooden table. "Ahh, but the Lupens didn't even have the choice I am presenting to Anjagor. We simply just lost everything."

"How do you mean?" Heide asked confused by the phrasing.

"Do you know the history of the Lupens Heide?" Gilpin asked. "Or are you just as ignorant as your King Nigel wants you to be?"

"I am fully aware of what we have done to your people," Heide said, "and that is why I am here to fix it, but demanding reparations for something that happened a century ago is absolutely ridiculous."

"Is it really though?" Gilpin asked, "For a century our country's growth has been stunted due to your country's actions. For a century we have been religiously persecuted for worshipping a god just because your country doesn't believe in it. And for a century our country has had to hide underground in secrecy due to your country's desire for a claim to *our* land. So, you tell me is it more ridiculous. To want what is rightfully ours, or to deny someone of what is rightfully theirs?"

Heide was about to say something, but Haran interrupted. "Alright, that's enough. This is going nowhere. You demand something we cannot give, and you have disrespected our king egregiously. We will not tolerate this talk from an inferior nation such as yours." Haran got up walking towards the exit; Heide followed closely behind him.

But before they exited the door Gilpin called from his desk. "This isn't over orphan boy; you haven't yet seen the wrath of the *Order of the Wolf.*"

The words echoed through Haran's head long after he slammed the door to Gilpin's office. Words that reminded him of the last line of the prophecy that started the whole thing:

The order of the wolf will prevail.

CHAPTER

6

After the meeting with Haran and Heide, Lottie walked down to the training area to see if he could finish the spar with Jet. He found the boy training with Tomas. He looked around to see only Tyson watching contently against the wall. There wasn't a scheduled training day today, but they were there anyway to train. "Hey guys," Lottie said as he approached the three boys.

"Hey Lot, care to go for round two?" Tyson asked as he struggled to get up from where he was leaning against the wall.

"Actually, I came to finish what I started with Jet, but maybe next time," Lottie said. Tyson sat back down with a face that can only be seen as disappointed.

"Actually, that's going to have to wait too," Tomas said as he sheathed his sword. "Because we have been given an assignment by supreme general Norman."

Jet sheathed his sword also, "What sort of assignment?"

Tomas waited for the four boys to circle around him in the sand pit and eventually said, "There is a convoy of supplies and men going from Anjagor Castle to Norhall Castle at the request of the new Battlemaster of Norhall fief.

Our job is to disrupt the convoy and take out all the men who have been sent to aid Norhall."

"How many men are there in the convoy?" Jet asked.

"Twenty-five," Tomas replied. "However, we can take ten blue group troops with us, as well as the four of us, so that should even the playing field a little."

"The five of us," Ella's voice said behind Lottie as the other three boys turned to look at the source.

Without even having to turn around Lottie said, "Nope, no you are not coming El."

"That's cute that you think you are in charge of me Lottie, but I am coming whether you like it or not," Ella said with great conviction.

"It's far too dangerous, I can't keep putting you in situations like this," Lottie said sadly.

"I can handle myself just fine, would you like me to prove it?" Ella said as she went over to pick up a wooden practice sword from the rack.

"Really? You know I won't fight you right?" Lottie asked.

"Oh, I know, I don't want you, I want him," she said as she pointed her sword to Jet. "If I win I go. If I lose I stay."

Jet looked over to Lottie who just shrugged acceptingly, there was no stopping her now. "Deal," Jet said as he went over to grab a sword of his own.

They squared off in the center of the arena circling each other cautiously. Lottie noticed that the way Ella held her sword wasn't as natural as it once had been. And as soon as she made her first down stroke he knew; she was rusty. Jet blocked the labored shot easily, holding it there for a few seconds before she finally eased off. She struck again with a side stroke and followed it with an underhand cut, then a stab to Jet's stomach. He blocked them all with ease but did not once return with a shot of his own. He was holding back. However, what Lottie didn't know was why.

Ella continued to send strike after strike against Jet's unbreakable defenses until finally he did strike back, but the stroke was slow and labored and Ella blocked it easily. He then threw one labored strike after another, each one blocked with ease. At least until he sent a slow side cut. Ella parried it, and with great precision and speed followed it up with a shot to Jet's ribs.

Jet fell to one knee in surrender and Ella threw her sword to the sandy ground with great force. "Stop holding back," she said to the boy in front of her.

"It looks as if you have won," Jet said with a smile.

She turned to Lottie for approval who only sighed and turned to Tomas, "When do we leave?"

Lottie had to inform Gilpin of where he was going, but soon after that they gathered troops to leave. They left through the tunnels of Randint Cavern with a company of fifteen.

Tomas led the group out of the long, dark tunnels that eventually led him to a big circular room with five separate doors in them. Lottie hadn't seen the room before, so he turned to Tomas and asked, "What is this place?"

"I call it the Connection Point. Each of these doors leads to an exit from Randint Cavern," Tomas said.

"There's exits in the cavern though," Jet noted, "so what are the point of these?"

"I don't know, that's just how it is," Tomas said. "But it helps for our scenario." He then turned to Lottie. "What is the closest landmark in Norhall to the main road?"

"Fuestres Woods," Lottie said.

"Alright, then that's where we are heading," Tomas said as he began moving to the second door to the right of the door they initially came through.

They walked down the dark and damp tunnel for several minutes. Lottie hated these tunnels; they were so cramped, and he could barely move through them with his larger frame. He looked behind him to see Tyson moving sideways through the tunnel. The giant wouldn't fit moving regularly so he had to side shuffle the whole way through. *At least I don't have to do that,* Lottie thought.

By the time they reached the end of the tunnel Lottie's head was fixed in a permanent stare at the ground. They climbed a small ladder and pushed through a heavy wooden trapdoor to their freedom from the confining tunnel. By the time everyone had made their way up the ladder and had time to stretch in the densely packed woods, Tomas had already covered the trapdoor with a various assortment of leaves and sticks.

"Alright guys gather around," Tomas said, and the fourteen others moved to circle around him. "The convoy should be traveling on the main road from Anjagor to Norhall sometime within the next few hours, so all we have to do is be there to ambush them in time."

"How many carriages are there?" Lottie asked as Tomas' right-hand man.

"The spy says there are five, each loaded with armor, weapons, and most importantly for our sakes, food," Tomas said.

"What does the spy look like?" Jet asked. "How will we recognize him?"

"He said you will recognize him by the distinct scar on his cheek. Whatever you do, no one kills this man," Tomas said. To which everyone nodded.

"Are the men heavily armed? What fief are they from?" Lottie asked again. The fief where troops were from solely signified the skill of the troops they would be facing, so it was a great question to ask.

"The spy says that all of the men there are from Millstone," Tomas said.

Lottie thought for a minute then realized what fief he was talking about. Millstone. Millstone. Which one was Millstone? "Oh my," Lottie said.

"What?" Jet asked.

Lottie turned to the dark-eyed boy beside him, but he spoke loud enough for everyone to hear, "Millstone is one of the biggest fiefs in all of Anjagor. Their Battleschool program is known as the most rigorous, and their fighters are known as the most skilled."

There was a shift as many in the blue group started having doubts about Tomas' plan. It grew silent and Lottie felt the doubt fill the air, making it thick and hard to breathe. Moments passed until Ella let out a laugh of joy. All fourteen heads turned her way, "Sorry, I just really miss being in action again. The suspense is just so riveting."

She locked eyes with Jet who was the only one smiling, they stayed like this for a while until Lottie noticed the prolonged eye contact and shifted uncomfortably. "So, are you all ready to head out?" He asked clearing his throat in the process. Everyone shook their head and they moved toward the road to Anjagor.

"Look Lot," Tyson said as they were exiting the woods. He was pointing to a blue jay resting on the tree above his head. "Look at the majestation bird."

Lottie sighed and let out a short laugh, "Its majestic Tyson not majestation. Ma-jes-tic."

"Majest- Majesti- Majestic?" Tyson asked.

"You got it buddy," Lottie said with a smile as he walked out of the woods. "You got it."

They set up their ambush some ten kilometers out from Norhall Castle, Tomas figured that any closer would see them surely found out. Lottie sat away from the camp they had set up to plan with Tomas. It was a simple plan; one of the two boys would sit in the middle of the road pretending to be injured from a fall from their horse. When the leader of the convoy comes to help, the rest of the troops, who lie in wait, will surprise the convoy before they can react. They decided it best that Lottie be the one pretending to be injured because he already had a gash on his knee from knocking it against rocks in the narrow tunnels that led out of Randint Cavern.

When Lottie and Tomas got up to tell the rest of the group of their plan, Lottie noticed Ella and Jet sharing a laugh and sitting on a fallen log rather close for his liking. He stood there staring for a while, not moving.

"Hey, I am sure its fine, they are probably talking about the mission or something," Tomas said failing to comfort Lottie.

"Yeah, I'm sure," Lottie said as he moved towards the camp; Tomas followed behind quickly.

During the debriefing Lottie couldn't seem to keep his eyes off of Jet and Ella. Thoughts ran through his head at speeds he never thought possible for his brain. Why was she laughing so much with Jet? Why did she never laugh with him? Did Jet know they were dating? Jet was very handsome; how could he ever compete? Did Jet purposefully lose to get Ella to come with him?

He snapped out of it when Tomas said, "Sound good to you?" He was looking at Lottie, but they had already talked it over, so really it was the company he was addressing.

Lottie cleared his throat, "Sounds good."

The lead driver of the convoy was getting tired now, and he knew he would have to rest soon, but they only had a few kilometers to go until they reached Castle Norhall. He could hold out until then he thought. The soldiers hadn't given him much conversation on their trip, and he was glad for it, he had too many thoughts running through his head. He thought about his wife and children back at home waiting for him to come back. He thought about the animals, and how they would manage to take care of them by themselves. He snapped out of the deep thoughts when he heard a cry for help some fifty meters down the road. When he got closer, he saw a figure in the middle of the road. He signaled to stop the rest of the convoy and went to go check on the young man lying in the middle of the street; he looked to have an injured leg. "Hey," he called out, not trusting the young man, "Are you alright?"

The man didn't call back. He just laid there, groaning and clutching his leg. The driver got closer until eventually he was on the boy. The boy had blonde hair and blue eyes, and the driver noticed a gash in the leg he was holding. "What happened? Do you need help?" The driver asked as he moved closer to the boy to help him up.

"No," the boy said pausing and standing up unsheathing his previously hidden sword from his waist. "But you do."

In that moment the driver saw some twenty people come from the tree line on either side of the road. *An ambush*, the driver thought. The moment's hesitation in the boy's eye allowed the driver to quickly move out of reach of the boy's swords and ran swiftly to the edge of the woods. Luckily for him, the boy behind him was carrying a lot of weight. Otherwise, he would be dead.

He sat for a minute in the shadows to watch the battle unfold. The troops that were stationed outside the convoy had already engaged with the attackers, and even when they were caught by surprise, they were holding their own. That is until they came up across a kid with jet black hair. The boy didn't look like an Anjagorian in the slightest. Every Anjagorian he knew had light hair and light eyes. And even though the driver knew nothing of swordplay, he could tell the boy was a master of the craft. The way he weaved in between the guards, cutting them down at will was almost…graceful.

The driver scanned the battlefield, the attacker in most need of help was a girl with blonde hair. She was struggling to keep up with the two defenders in front of her. *Why would anyone allow a girl on the battlefield?* He asked himself. The boy with jet-black hair and the blonde boy who had pretended to be injured both hurried over to her aid. The black-haired boy arrived first and blocked a sword stroke from one of the two fighters on the girl. Then the blonde arrived, kicking the second attacker to the ground in sheer rage. He then pierced his heart with both his swords, killing him instantly.

The black-haired boy was still dealing with his man and somewhat struggling. He seemed to be distracted by the blonde boy's arrival. The blonde boy and girl stood by waiting to see what happened. The driver heard the black-haired boy call for help from the blond boy. But the blonde boy hesitated and didn't move to the black-haired boy's aid. Although he had no backup, after a brief struggle the black-haired boy finally got a killing blow on the man he was fighting. And just like that the battle was over, the attackers had won. The driver knew he could not stay around to watch anymore. He had to leave and fast before the attackers saw him.

CHAPTER

7

Orion walked into the cabin about an hour before noon. Haran and Lyra were eating lunch at the table. Their meal was simply salted meat and bread, but Haran was scarfing it down as if it were cooked by the chefs of Norhall.

"Finish eating you two. We have been called to talk to Baron Ligate," Orion said.

"For what?" Haran asked through his mouthful of bread.

"I don't know, but it seemed important so I wouldn't doubt it if it were the Lupens again," Orion replied.

Haran perked up with the mention of the name, he had just been in Randint Cavern the other day and there seemed to be no notion of future attack. "Maybe you made them mad when you went to negotiate Haran," Lyra suggested.

"Oh, I definitely made them mad," Haran said, "but that was rather quick don't you think?" He hadn't even been gone for two days and they had already launched an attack. It seemed unlikely. It had to have been preplanned.

"I think we should go find out," Lyra said as she got up from where she was eating. Haran followed, leaving Shiva sitting by the fire. He very rarely left the house without

Shiva for long trips, but he figured a chat with the Baron wouldn't take that long. All three of them walked out of the door and onto their horses to Castle Norhall.

They walked up the wooden stairs of the keep and to the end of the hall to Baron Ligate's office. Haran noticed that the door was slightly cracked and realized that it was because there was someone else inside already. When they walked Haran saw a man in his early thirties; he was well built, most likely a farmer. He had blonde hair and blue eyes; the signature looks of many Anjagor natives. Haran noticed he had a very distinct scar on his left cheek, he thought maybe it was a cut from a sword, but then he realized it wasn't long enough. A knife would definitely do it though. Haran nodded his greeting to the man.

"Welcome Outryders, nice of you to join us today," Baron Ligate said.

"Hey Baron, nice to see you too," Orion said, "So, what seems to be the problem here?"

Baron Ligate cleared his throat, "As you are well aware, there is war brewing with the Lupens, especially after your stunt at Calcore. So, as a safety net, the new Battlemaster Wesley asked me to send reinforcements to him. So, I requested a convoy of men and supplies from the capital. King Nigel obliged and sent me 25 Millstone warriors."

Orion cut him off, "Millstone has some of the best fighters. Is King Nigel really expecting something that bad?"

"Seems so, or maybe it's a personal thing," Baron Ligate said, "whatever the case, the Millstone convoy now lie dead some ten kilometers northwest on the main road. And this man right here is the only survivor." He pointed to the scarred man to Haran's left. Haran looked over to the man who looked terrified, but he was still skeptical, "wait so you escaped the Lupens."

The driver looked at him confused, "What is a Lupen?"

Orion interrupted his apprentice who was just about to answer the man's question. "Ok, we will take him to the scene and investigate then."

"Fine with me," Baron Ligate responded.

The man rode on the back of Orion's horse the entire way to the scene of the incident. Soon after leaving Castle Norhall Haran asked the man, "So what's your name sir?"

"Terence," the man replied.

Orion shifted on his horse to give the man more room, and without looking back he asked, "And can you tell us what happened?"

Terence mirrored Orion's movements and shifted his weight also, "Well I was driving the convoy when there was boy in the middle of the road, when I stopped to help he withdrew his swords on me. Then some twenty men came from the trees and ambushed the men guarding the convoy. I ran in the chaos, but I stayed to watch if my men would win. Now they lie dead."

"Do you know what the boy looked like?" Haran asked.

"Blonde haired blue eyed and muscular, but that's many Anjagor natives," Terence said.

"Did you notice scars on his forearms?" Haran asked pointing to his own forearms subconsciously.

"Uhm it's very possible. I don't know though; it was far too fast to tell," Terence said.

Haran looked to his master, "It could have been Lottie."

"Could have," Orion said, "but let's not worry about that right now. We just need to figure out what happened here first."

They smelled the scene before they saw it. The smell of smoke and charred corpses was abundant through the air. When they came up onto the scene they realized why. The Lupens had burned down the convoy and everything in it. Orion got off his horse and went to investigate; Haran followed suit, but Lyra decided to stay behind with Terence. Haran knew that dead bodies was one of the things that Lyra could not stand, so it only made sense.

There were no salvageable parts of the convoy, they were all burned to the ground. There were some thirty-five bodies strewn out across the battlefield, most of them wearing the crest of Millstone. However, Haran counted eight bodies that wore the Lupen crest of the white wolf. He also noticed they had weird blue rings with wolf heads around their arms, much like he had noticed on Lottie's arm when they visited days before. Now his suspicions were confirmed. Whatever the purpose of this attack was, he knew that Lottie was involved.

Haran approached his master who was carefully examining the bodies trying to piece together what happened. "What are you thinking Orion?"

"Well, there is nothing here that is going to help us," Orion said as he got up from his crouched position. "So, I am going to track them, let them lead me to where they came from."

"I don't understand though, if all of the entrances to the cavern were guarded, how did they get out?" Haran asked.

Orion shrugged his shoulders and moved back to where Lyra and Terence were standing by the horses. "That's what I am about to find out."

"Okay then, we are following you," Haran said.

"No, you are not," Orion replied as he hopped onto his horse Nova.

It was Lyra who responded this time, "What do you mean we are not, what are we to do then?"

"You are to escort this poor man back to his home in Millstone," Orion said.

Haran looked to his master with confused eyes, "Surely you can't be serious."

Orion met his eyes with a steely gaze, "Does it look like I am joking son?"

Haran bit down on his jaw and walked some five meters away from Lyra and Terence and gestured for Orion to follow. When Orion walked over he asked, "are you seriously benching us? We want to help not take this man take this man to his rundown farm three fiefs away."

Orion sighed calmly, "Listen Haran, this man has been through a lot today and I don't want him to be robbed on the road back home. It's called moral obligation, its what we have to do."

"But I want to help you find where they came from," Haran argued, the fire in his voice calming down slightly, "Surely that's a bigger obligation?"

"Haran," Orion said, "I know you want to go after Lottie after what you just saw, but you should always remember. You cannot change the decisions of others, but your decisions are entirely in your hands. Now please go, help the man, it's what we do."

Haran's anger completely subsided now, "I'm sorry, you are right. Where is Millstone anyway?"

"Shows how much you pay attention to what I teach you," Orion said, "However, I am sure he can show you; he did just make the ride all the way over here."

"Fine," Haran said again, still feeling a little sidelined by his master. He walked back over to Lyra and Terence, "Let's get going then."

They left the scene almost ten minutes after they arrived, and the smell of freshly charred corpses remained in their noses long after they left. Terence rode with Haran out of deference to the lady. It was only after they crossed the border onto Anjagor that Haran spoke, "Do you know how long it will take before we get to Millstone?"

"Well first we have to get through Anjagor fief which will take a day or two on its own," Terence said to which Haran rolled his eyes. The man seemed to notice the movement but still continued, "then we have to go through Serta fief, which is fairly small, and then we will be in Millstone, so I would say a week tops."

"A week? That's a long time," Haran said.

"Orion's orders," Lyra reminded him with a warning glare. She then turned to Terence and asked, "Do you have any family?"

"Yes actually, a wife and two daughters," Terence replied.

"Aww," Lyra said almost making Haran throw up in his mouth, "How old are they?"

"My oldest is ten and my youngest is eight," Terence said.

Lyra looked over to Haran who was siffling his frustration poorly, "Aww I am sure they are really adorable."

"Yes indeed, they are the loves of my life," Terence said with a warm smile.

Haran began thinking about what the man said about the attack and then realizing that there was still one piece missing he asked, "I'm sure your glad you got out of that fight alive then aren't you?"

"Haran," Lyra snapped. She must have found it rude to address something so traumatizing so soon, but Haran didn't care.

"Oh, it's fine young lady," Terence said, "Yes, I thank the gods that they save me from such a horrible death."

Gods? Haran thought. Haran brought Spirit to an abrupt stop in the middle of the road. "Haran what are you doing?" Lyra asked cautiously.

Haran didn't respond to her question, he simply got off of Spirit and took a knife out from his sash. "I wondered why Lottie didn't kill you, but now I know."

"I don't know what you are talking about," Terence replied staying on the horse.

"You see, you would have fooled me, but you made one mistake," Haran said.

"Oh yeah, what's that?" Terence asked his voice dropping the innocent tone. Lyra stayed on her horse confused as to what was happening.

"We Anjagorians don't worship gods, but good try I suppose," Haran said flatly. "Now, get off of my horse and I just might not kill you."

Terence took Spirit's reins and tried to run from the Outryder. Haran let him go for a little bit. "One…Two… Three." On three, he launched a knife to Terence's back, killing him instantly.

The lifeless body fell from Spirit's back as Lyra watched both horrified and confused. "What just happened?" she asked.

"That man was the Lupen spy that told them about the convoy. He led the twenty-five men to their deaths," Haran said plainly.

"And how did you figure that out on two words?" Lyra asked in awe.

"Well not really," Haran replied. "I was already skeptical when he first explained the story of him getting away. It just didn't make sense that Lottie let him go free like that, and when he thanked gods I immediately knew that he was working with the Lupens."

"And what if you were wrong?" Lyra asked.

"Then he wouldn't have run," Haran said and then added, "But I had intended to hit him to wound so we could question him further."

Lyra sighed, "Oh well. He got what he deserved after what he did on the road."

"Sure enough." Haran whistled for Spirit and when the horse came over he hopped on.

He began heading back the road they had just traveled down when Lyra asked, "Well what are we going to do with his body? We can't just leave it to rot in the middle of the road."

"Why shouldn't we," Haran asked, voice cracking with anger, "the man just led twenty-five men to their deaths and their bodies are still strewn across the road." Haran pointed down the road they just came from.

Lyra met his scrutinizing gaze, "I thought you were better than that Haran. We are better than that. If we leave him in the road to the vultures we are no better than the Lupens."

Haran relented and whipped Spirit back around. "Fine, we can bury it. Where's the nearest town? Or do you happen to have a shovel on hand."

Lyra was a little taken aback by Haran's sudden change in attitude, something was definitely wrong. "Haran," she said.

"What?" he asked coldly as he got off Spirit once more.

"What's wrong?" Lyra asked.

"I'm fine. Now, can we please get going?" Haran asked.

"Fine" Lyra said, "Well the nearest village is about fifteen kilometers down the road."

"Okay, let's get to moving then," Haran said as he moved to put the dead body on the back of Spirit.

They didn't speak the whole ride, neither of them felt it necessary. When they arrived at the village they saw just how small it was, with only five houses and a town square.

They set out to find the nearest person and after ten minutes they saw an elderly woman with platinum white hair hobble out of her home. Haran waved at her from the gravel path in front of the house and asked, "Do you know where we can find a shovel?" He noticed the woman's skeptical look at the two foreigners in green cloaks, so he added, "We have dead to bury."

He saw the old woman's face turn from skepticism to compassion in an instant. "Oh dear, I'm so sorry for your loss," she said, "is there anything I can do for you?"

"Yes. I need a shovel," Haran said coldly.

Lyra coughed and stepped on Haran's foot hard, "I'm so sorry for my friend here. I suppose he is grieving heavily for our loss, but that is no excuse for being rude."

"Oh no its fine," the old woman said, "I'm sure he meant nothing by it. Now, let me get you that shovel you needed." She shuffled slowly to the back side of the house.

While she was gone Lyra said, "Listen, I don't know what your problem is, but that type of insolence is unacceptable. Now, tell me what is wrong with you."

"Lyra I don't even know what insolence means," Haran said trying to change the subject.

However, his tactic didn't work as Lyra gave him a death stare, "What's wrong with you?"

"The Lupens are back Lyra," he snapped, finally revealing what he had been feeling ever since Orion sent then on this little side mission. "And so is Lottie and they are killing dozens at a time. Yet here we are. Benched. Burying an enemy spy's body while Orion is doing the real work. He doesn't trust us to do Outryder work anymore."

Lyra sighed, "Haran, did you or did you not just figure out that Terence was a spy on just two words?"

"I did, so what?" Haran asked not getting her point.

"Ok so Orion heard Terence's story as well and didn't see any problems with it right?" Lyra asked, but before Haran could answer she continued, "but you figured out that Terence was the spy. I would say that is more important than finding another entrance to a place we already know exists don't you?"

"Yeah, I guess you're right," Haran said.

"We weren't benched, we were just put on a different task. Get it?" Lyra asked. Haran nodded, surprised that although Lyra and himself were of the same age she was so much wiser.

"Good, now look here she comes. I hope you're in higher spirits," Lyra said as she watched the old woman come from around the house.

They graciously took the shovel for her and walked towards a lone oak tree at the top of a small hill. It took about an hour for Haran to dig the hole while Lyra talked to the old woman. The only thing that Haran heard from the conversation was that the old woman just lost her husband weeks ago to a sickness and she had been struggling to keep food on their table since. After shoving the body into the hole, he turned to Lyra, "There, now we really must get back home."

Lyra said her thanks and told the woman goodbye. However, they stuck around for a few more hours resting under the oak tree until night hit. Deep into the night when

Haran was sure the old woman was asleep he snuck into her humble home. Though it was dark Haran could pick out the outline of a dining table. He set a bag full of silvers on the table and snuck back out of the house with not a sound.

"You really didn't have to give her that much," Lyra said as she met him outside with their horses ready. "That was all of your money."

"Ehh." Haran shrugged, "She needs it more than I do. Plus, it only serves to make up for my. . . how did you put it? Oh yes *insolence*."

Lyra smiled and punched him on the arm as they began to make their way back to Norhall.

Fuestres Woods was as quiet as ever as they rode through it early the next morning. Well, as quiet as the sounds of birds chirping and scuttering animals could be. "Well, this was an eventful day," Haran said as they hopped off their horses and walked towards the cabin. Lyra just simply nodded at Haran's words; they were both far too tired for much more than that.

When they walked in they saw Orion sitting at the table looking over papers and covered in what looked like dust or dirt. "What happened?" he asked, "Why are you back so soon?"

"Well, it turns out the only way that Terence got free from the Lupens is that he was their spy," Haran said.

"And Haran figured it out off of just two words, can you believe it?" Lyra asked still slightly in awe.

Orion looked over to his apprentice with the hint of a smile. "Yes actually. I can."

Haran looked down to his shoes in embarrassment, but eventually looked back up to ask, "And what happened with the entrance? Did you find it?"

"Yes, it was here on the outskirts of Fuestres Woods," Orion said.

"Right under our noses?" Lyra asked.

"Yes," Orion said, "It seems that is a running occurrence with these Lupens."

"So why are you covered in dust then?" Haran asked.

"I explored the tunnels as much as I could, and it led me to a central room to where all the tunnels connected. It turns out there are five tunnels from Randint Cavern in all. The ones we know for sure are the one that lead here and the one that leads to the town. We can assume there is one at the Battleschool because it's how Gilpin got to and from without being seen. And one at Calcore seeing as they arrived from seemingly nowhere before the battle."

"And what of the fifth?" Haran asked.

"I don't know. I couldn't explore further without chance of getting caught," Orion said, and almost as if he knew the question was coming he said. "It's far too dangerous to explore those tunnels even so much that I was almost caught. So, no you two cannot explore the tunnels for yourselves."

"Ok, but if we can't risk exploring the tunnels what do we do next?" Haran asked.

"We find out how to kill that wolf god," Orion said.

CHAPTER

8

The day after the ambush Lottie met up the man who Gilpin had been researching, Percival Woodberg. Lottie walked into Gilpin's office where Percival was talking to Gilpin and was immediately starstruck by the man's appearance. He was handsome. Very handsome in fact. His brilliant blue eyes shined perfectly against his tanned skin. *How is he tanned?* Lottie thought. No one in Randint Cavern was tanned due to the fact that they spent all of their time underground. His sandy colored beard was trimmed to perfection, almost fading into his slightly darker blond hair.

The man turned his attention from Gilpin to Lottie, "And you must be Lottie, I've heard a lot about you."

Lottie picked his jaw up from the ground to say, "And I you."

In just a weeks' time he had converted more to Lupism than Doran could have done in six months. Lottie had heard that services were things of legends, people from all walks of life came to his speeches and were immediately converted to the religion. Promises of better lives and salvation were thrown out like candy to people still grieving from the death of Doran.

"I hope they were mainly good." Percival smiled, his teeth burning so ever brightly into Lottie's soul.

"Oh, they were," Lottie replied.

Percival caught a glimpse of Lupe who was laying at the door. "Unbelievable," he said giddily, "He's actually real. I can't believe it."

"What? Lupe?" Lottie asked.

"Yes, Albalupius here, in the mortal realm once more," Percival said standing up, "I mean I've seen him from a distance sure, but I have never been this close. Can I touch him?"

"Of course," Lottie said with a smile. It was like a child with a puppy. Or anyone with a puppy for that matter.

Percival bent down to touch the wolf's fur, a low growl came from the wolf warningly, "I know. I know," Percival said to the giant wolf. His knees touched the floors as he knelt before the god. He lifted his upper body up and down continuously in worship.

After a few moments Percival stood up and looked over to Lottie. "Thank you," he said sincerely.

Lottie smiled just on the cusp of laughter, "No problem. Well anyway I must get going now."

"Of course," Percival said.

Lottie walked out of the door with Lupe and began making his way to training. He would get the chance to talk to Percival again after his training when the whole household was going to witness one of his speeches.

After his training, he walked into the courtyard with Lupe at his side when he saw Gilpin's head above the crowd waiting patiently for the speech to begin. There were around three hundred people there and every single one began to part the way as the giant wolf walked beside him. It was a usual occurrence, people tended to fear creatures that could tear their limbs from their bodies with one bite. What they didn't know was that Lupe only followed Lottie's command. If Lottie were to say it, Lupe would kill every person in the crowd tearing them apart limb by limb.

"Hey El," Lottie said casually to the beautiful blonde as he approached the group standing in the front of the crowd. They were on rocky terms at the moment, and he didn't want to do anything to set her off again.

"Hey Lottie," she said smiling, "How was training?"

"It was good, oh and by the way, can I talk to you about something after all of this?" Lottie asked.

"Sure," Ella said as Percival walked up to the makeshift stage that rose some half a meter from the ground.

Percival cleared his throat as he prepared to speak, "Hey everyone, how are we all doing today."

"Good," the whole crowd said in unison.

He laughed, his pearly white teeth shining in the light of Randint Cavern, "What an interesting time to be alive am I right." Seeing their faces, Lottie knew this was a group of people unaware of the prophecies and wolf god and really anything. They just go to and from work every day, this would probably be their only time out this week other than to get food. Lottie envied them; their ignorance only served as less of a heartbreak to them.

Percival continued. "Well, I am sure many of know the history of Randint Cavern and the Lupens, so I won't go over it too much. Long ago, there was group of Athonians cast from society because of their belief in the one true god Albalupius. The group crossed the Chein Mountains and settled above our very heads in the fief they now call Norhall. They stayed there for many years before a new nation, Anjagor, attacked. The fighting was intense, and it looked as if the Lupens would win until a ruthless masochist named Outin Ryder, massacred hundreds of women and children in the name of Anjagor. The Lupens were eventually forced into a small cavern under the surface of Norhall where they expanded and created what you see today."

There was a murmur of resentment in the crowd, most people knew the story already, and even thinking about all that their ancestors lost, that they had lost, set their blood boiling. "First, we were repudiated, and cast from society simply for our beliefs. Next, we were driven from our homes and new society based on our sole existence in a place Anjagor deemed belonged to them. But I am here to tell you that we can get our revenge."

There was another murmur from the crowd, but this one was of disbelief. Moments passed before someone finally spoke. "HOW?" A man shouted from behind Lottie.

"Pardon?" Percival asked the anonymous voice.

A man pushed through the crowd, Lottie looked over to him to see a built man in his early forties, a farmer by the looks of him. "How do you plan to take our revenge? I mean Doran promised us revenge as well but look where he is now," He said loud and clear; there was a mass agreement from the crowd, all asking the same question. Lottie's rage was festering, how could these people resent Doran after all he had done for them. *Ungrateful buffoons.* Ella slipped her hand in his already sensing what he was feeling. That siffled his anger slightly, but only slightly.

"That's a simple question with a very complicated answer, and to explain would go far into the night. So let me just show you instead," Percival said as he looked around the crowd. "Lottie, please come up here with your friend."

Every eye turned to Lottie and his wolf; he walked up to the platform, standing side by side to Percival. "This here is how we take our revenge," Percival said pointing to Lupe who sat casually by Lottie's side as a wave of confusion washed over the crowd, "For those of you unaware, this wolf here is the manifestation of the one true god Albalupius, and he will bring along what has been promised to us all. The death of Anjagor."

There was a roar of approval from the crowd. Applause rang through the plaza for several moments before Percival knelt and began worshipping the wolf that stood in front of him. Moments later all three hundred people in the crowd were kneeling before Lupe. Everyone except for Lottie, Gilpin, and Ella. Lottie looked over to Gilpin skeptically. He hoped the questions that raced through his mind were conveyed well enough through his eyes. What did he need Lupe for? Why was he already rallying the troops? What was his endgame?

An hour or so later the whole house and Percival sat patiently by the dinner table as Sylvia passed out the food. The plates were filled to the edge with an assortment of potatoes, bread, lamb, and greens. "There you go Lottie," she said as she placed the plate in front of Lottie who sat near the head of the table with Gilpin and Percival.

"Thank you ma'am it looks great," Lottie replied as he eyed his food hungrily. Sylvia smiled at him and took a seat next to Ella and the dinner began.

As Lottie stared at his food trying to decide what to start with he caught a glimpse of Percival with his head in his hands whispering to himself. "What are you doing?" Lottie asked.

Ella kicked his shins hard from across the table. "Oww," he said casually. He wasn't trying to be rude or anything, he was just asking a question.

Percival took his head out of his hands and smiled slightly. Lottie still couldn't get over the fact that his teeth were so perfectly white and straight. "Were you asking me?" Lottie nodded, "Oh yes, it was just a prayer. I do it before every meal, it helps to show thanks to Albalupius."

"That's cool," Lottie said. Lupe was not allowed anywhere near the dining table as per Sylvia's request. There were just a *few* incidences were he would steal a plate, or maybe two depending on the day.

"So, Percival," Sylvia said putting down her fork gracefully. "Are you a native born or did you move here."

Percival turned to her, "Moved here sadly. I didn't find out about this place but recently."

"What fief?" Lottie asked.

"Acrine."

"That far north?" Gilpin asked, "Surely you must have been freezing constantly."

"Actually, not really surprisingly," Percival noted, "The fine craftsmen up there make rather appropriate clothing for the climate."

"So, why'd you decide to move all the way to Norhall then?" Sylvia asked.

Percival paused, pondering the question. "I read about the wolf god in a book, and I read of the Lupen's story. When I read that you all went underground so long ago I decided to make a visit to see if the culture still existed. Of course, I found this place."

"And how long have you been here?" Sylvia asked.

"Three years give or take," Percival said. "I planned to go home, but the religion simply enthralled me and never let me go."

"Hmm," Sylvia said as she picked up her glass of wine, "That's interesting."

"Indeed," Gilpin added, "Did you know Doran well?"

Percival turned to Gilpin, "Well enough, we had a few chats at formal gatherings and stuff of that nature, but not enough to tell you of his favorite color."

"Yellow," Lottie said with a slight frown. "He loved the color yellow."

Sylvia laughed daintily, "That he did. He wanted to paint the house yellow, and he would have if I hadn't been here to talk him out of it."

"It's a shame really," Percival said, "he seemed to be a kind soul."

"He was. He really was," Lottie said.

They spent the next hour or so getting to know Percival better, but nothing sparked Lottie's interests. Soon they were finished eating and Keryn's childlike attention span grew shorter. As the minutes passed he grew seemingly more annoyed by the boring chatter and eventually forced Sylvia to let him go to his room. Soon after, everyone moved to do their own things.

About an hour later after everything had died down Lottie was sitting in his room staring at the ceiling once again. Memories of Ella and Jet laughing together during their ambush of the convoy flashed through his mind. He began to grow angry. However, he didn't know who to be angry at. Should he be angry at Ella for talking with the boy, or should he be angry with himself for allowing it to happen? Whatever the case, he had to talk to her about it, so he got up from his bed. Lupe got up also, but Lottie motioned for him to stay. "Sorry, this is something I have to do on my own buddy," he whispered to the wolf.

He walked into Ella's room down the hall and saw that she wasn't in there. He then walked to Gilpin's office and knocked on the door, "Come in," Gilpin said.

When Lottie walked in, he saw Sylvia and Gilpin sharing a pot of tea with Percival. It had been a good day for them. "Hey Lottie, come join us," Sylvia said kindly.

"Thanks, but actually I was looking for El, have you seen her?" He asked her mom.

"I think she went to the training area, she said she was rusty or something along those lines," Sylvia said. Lottie thanked her and practically ran out of the door and out of the mansion.

When he reached the hidden door to the arena he heard voices inside. One belonged to a male, and the other, a female. When the door slid down from its original spot

Lottie walked in hurriedly. In the center of the arena were Ella and Jet sparring and laughing the whole time while Tomas and Tyson sat resting against the wall. "Uh oh," Tomas said getting up as he noticed Lottie's frantic entrance.

Ella noticed Lottie's entrance and signaled Jet to stop their spar. Lottie was walking over to them when Ella said, "Hey Lottie, what's up?"

"Hey, El, can we talk?" Lottie said.

"Oh yeah sure, but can we finish this spar really quick?" Ella said clearly not hearing the urgency in Lottie's voice.

"It's kind of urgent," Lottie said.

"Okay… well can we finish the spar first," Ella said. Lottie didn't understand why she just wouldn't talk to him.

"No, I need to talk to you like now," Lottie said as he glanced over to Jet who was watching Lottie carefully.

"Why can't you just wait a few minutes Lottie, I mean we were just about done," Jet said as he drew a little closer to Lottie and Ella.

"Why don't you just stay out of it," Lottie said, "Now can we please talk Ella." He reached for her arm, but he grabbed it harder than he intended to. She yelped and flew back, "Oww Lottie."

Lottie immediately grabbed his own arm as if it were something out of his control, "I'm so sorry El, I didn't mean to," he said as he went to comfort Ella. However, before he could do that Jet pushed him to the ground. "I think you've done enough," he said.

Lottie got up red with rage, who was this man to carry himself the way he does? Who was he to try and replace Lottie in every aspect of life? Jet threw his guard up ready for a fight, but it wouldn't be necessary because at that moment Lottie heard Ella say. "Please don't Lottie, I beg of you."

All of the anger that Lottie held instantly vanished and he rushed over to Ella who was still clutching her wrist. "I'm sorry El, please forgive me."

Ella put her head on Lottie's shoulders and started crying. She knew just as he did, that Lottie would have killed Jet right then if she hadn't said anything.

"Please leave," she asked Jet, Tomas, and Tyson, who were all standing over them now, "Lottie and I have to talk."

"Are you sure?" Jet said almost refusing to leave.

"Jet, let's go," Tomas demanded.

The three of them walked out of the training area leaving Lottie and Ella alone.

"I'm sorry El," Lottie said as he heard the rock door slide closed.

"You stopped, you didn't even fight back, but you always fight back. What changed?" Ella asked.

"You asked me to tame my anger, and I am trying my hardest to every day," Lottie replied.

"Thank you, so what did you want to talk about that was so important?" Ella asked.

"It doesn't matter anymore. I can trust you and I realize that now," Lottie said.

"Of course you can dummy," she said still clutching her wrist carefully.

"Here, why don't we have someone take a look at your wrist?" Lottie asked as he helped Ella to her feet, and for the first time in a long time, he felt calm.

CHAPTER

9

Again, Haran dreamed of the girl and the flower cove. Every time he had the dream he began to feel more immersed in his surroundings. He could sense the crisp sea air's thickness and taste the salt of the ocean breeze. The small path leading to the flower cove was covered with autumn leaves. The sunset was pinkish with just the hint of orange on the horizon. The sound of waves crashed against the rocks that surrounded the inlet. Everything was just so... perfect.

He woke up again slamming his fist against his bed, why couldn't he just stay there forever he thought to himself. Haran had yet to talk about his dreams with anyone. He had never experienced such reoccurring dreams before, and they have only been happening since the battle. He thought it would be best to talk about his dreams with Orion. After minutes of staring at the wall thinking of the best possible way to approach the topic he got up. He decided that it would be best if he were to say it simply and explain accordingly.

He walked out of his room and down the hall where he saw Orion was sitting at the table reading what he thought was a report of some kind. Haran stood at the entrance to the living room, waiting for a minute. However, before he could even gather enough courage to approach his master. Orion, without looking up, said, "Come and sit Haran, something must be wrong."

Haran did so, pulling up a chair beside his master. He paused, trying to find the words, "Uhm yes, actually something is. Well, you see I have been having these dreams recently…"

"Dreams you say?" Orion asked curiously, looking up from the paper.

"Yes. Well, no not dreams per se, more of visions. I can feel them. I am in them," Haran said recalling his two drastically different dreams. The first made him terrified, and the second, euphoric.

"Visions you say," Orion asked, "Visions or dreams it doesn't matter much, either way they seem to be getting to you. Are they reoccurring?"

"Yes," Haran said.

"Can you describe the visions?" Orion asked. Dreams had the potential to tell of events past and future, but something that can leave Haran as blank faced as this must be bad.

"The first vision is of the battle," Haran said, "I recall the events, but I see everything, almost as if I am watching from five meters above the battlefield. I see King Nigel kill Doran. And then I see you beat Gilpin, Cassius free Lyra. I see the battle between Lottie and I, all taking place almost simultaneously… I see the fight between Shiva and the wolf, but something is different… This time the wolf doesn't stop on Lottie's command. He kills Scarlett, and then he goes on to kill Shiva, you, Lyra, Cassius, King Nigel, and all that's left is me to fight everyone. The wolf walks beside Lottie who turns into, someone else… something else. Something. Dark. A black suit of armor with spikes jetting out from every direction, it's terrifying. I am pushed back to the canyon's edge, my feet barely keeping me from falling in. And then the ground crumbles beneath me and I fall into an abyss only to wake up drenched in sweat." The emotion was so apparent in his voice that it began to crack as he finished. Orion got up and hugged his apprentice.

After a few more minutes, he asked, "you say that was your first dream? What of the second?"

Haran composed himself enough to tell Orion the second dream. "I am on a path in a forest with orange leaves. There is a young girl, maybe five, running ahead of me. She turns back and calls me her father. She says we are heading towards 'the Flower Cove'…"

Lyra, who had apparently been listening carefully from the hallway the entire time, interjects, "Wait. The Flower Cove you say?"

Haran turned around, "Yes, do you know of such a place?"

Lyra walked over to the table. "The Flower Cove that I knew was beautiful. A small inlet surrounded by rocks; flowers were abundant in the field leading down to the cove. Many times, I would plunge myself into the flowers and not come out until night arrived. However, the most beautiful thing in the cove was the sunsets. The orangish pinkish sun came down beautifully between two rock formations. It was breathtaking. " Lyra said recalling her childhood.

Haran looked shocked, she had just perfectly described his dream, even up to the point where she ran into the flowers. Haran had his suspicions before when he saw her hair and eyes, but he had no doubt now. Lyra was the girl in his dreams.

"I've never heard of such a place in all of Anjagor, where is it?" Orion asked carefully choosing his words.

"That's because it isn't in Anjagor… it is in Athon," Lyra said regretfully.

"Athon? Why would you have been there?" Haran asked skeptically.

Lyra grew quiet and her eyes fixated on the ground, "I may have hidden some of my past from the two of you."

Orion now spoke, "Go on Lyra, its ok, I already know."

"Ho- How do you know?" Lyra asked her master.

"Know WHAT?" Haran asked as he got up quickly from his chair in frustration,

"Tell him," Orion said to Lyra.

"Haran, my name is Princess Lyrissa of Athon, and I am the true heir to the Athonian throne," Lyra said regretfully.

Everything around Haran shifted slightly. The floor began to move in snakelike patterns and the walls began to spin rapidly. The roof was pushing down on him suffocating him. What did she mean she was the true heir to the Athonian throne? She was Lyra, his rough around the edges companion. His best friend. How was she the princess of Athon? Haran was so shocked that he had to take a seat once more, "I don't understand. You're a princess? But you are you. You could never be a princess. You are too rough around the edges."

"Thanks. I think? and I wanted to tell you many times, but I figured it might put me at risk," Lyra said.

"Put you at risk of what? My anger because it didn't help to tell me later," Haran said.

Lyra sighed deeply, "Haran some ten years ago when I was but a small kid my uncle, King Werneck, killed my mother and my father and took over the throne of Athon. I was gracefully spared when one of our main servants took me out of the castle and got me to Norhall safely. I stayed with her for many years in hiding learning of my heritage. All the way up until she died last year. And now, somehow, I am here with the two of you." She then turned to Orion. "What I really want to know is how you knew?"

"You have black hair and eyes, signature Athonian traits. When I first met you, you carried yourself completely contrary to that of an orphaned child such as Haran," Orion said. Haran didn't know whether to be offended or not about what his master just said, but he didn't have time to really question it as Orion continued. "Oh, and you have a tiny burn on your elbow, like someone had marked you. It's just the same as the one King Nigel has and Doran had," Orion said.

"That's the mark of royalty, I didn't realize the Anjagorians did that as well," Lyra said starstruck by Orion's masterful reasoning.

"Apparently," Orion said.

"Wait I am still confused," Haran said, "Can we go back? So, when Athon invaded Anjagor, it wasn't for power was it, they were looking for you weren't they?"

Orion was the one to respond this time, "That is what I believe the main purpose of the invasion was."

Lyra nodded as well. "I was too young at the time, but I wouldn't doubt it if my uncle started a war just to see to it my *entire family* was dead."

"But you beat them Orion, I thought you killed Werneck in the Battle of the Anvil," Haran said to his master. then he turned to his friend. "Then why are you still here? It's been ten plus years since then, and if the Athonian throne is yours for the taking as you say, then surly you should be there, you know, on the throne."

"No, I can't. Uncle Werneck had a son, Theos, not much older than I, but still older. Therefore, he is technically the rightful ruler of the throne. Plus, the people of Athon would never rally behind a woman when a man was already on the throne." Even as she said them Lyra's words stung like sharp knives in her chest. Even though Theos was an inconsiderate fool who didn't deserve the place, it was law, and it shouldn't be broken.

Haran was still confused; how did this relate to the dream about the Lily Cove and the dream of the battle at the canyon. "I don't understand. Surely the dreams must mean something then. I mean I haven't even been to this Lily Cove place, yet I dream about it just as Lyra described. So, what is so important about these two dreams."

Orion shook his head; he had no idea. However, Lyra was the one to interject. "So, the first dream is a dream of the battle, right?"

"Correct, but the wolf is uncontrollable and kills everyone," Haran said as he thought about the dream.

Now it clicked in Orion's head, "And the second dream is in Athon, the birthplace of the supposed 'wolf god' right?"

"Correct," Haran said, the pieces not yet clicking in his head.

"So if your first dream is of an uncontrollable being and the next night you dream of the place of the being's birth. Therefore, the dreams are trying to tell you something. Then where do you think we need to go?" Orion said, breaking it down for Haran.

"Athon," Haran said dismally. He had always subconsciously known that Athon was where he needed to go, he just didn't want to admit it to himself.

Orion nodded with conviction. "Yeah, so it's settled then—"

"We have to go to Athon to figure out how to kill the wolf god," Haran said firmly clenching his jaw.

CHAPTER

10

Haran began packing for the trip immediately; they would leave by the end of the week at the latest. Orion figured they would be gone two weeks at the least so Haran was packing the little clothes he had. His cloak, three pairs of black slacks with slight rips in them, and three dark green shirts he had from his castle days. Haran smelled one of his shirts and instantly regretted it. It smelled of sweat and leaves, neither one mixing in a way that could have ever smelt good. It was time for him to wash them.

TAP-TAP-TAP. He turned around to see that it was Lyra who had knocked on the door frame. "Hey," he said, "done packing already?"

Lyra shook her head, "That is actually what I came to talk to you about. You know I can't go with you right?"

Haran looked at her a little shocked, she had done everything with him since the day he had become a Recon, "What do you mean you can't go with us?"

"Haran, if Theos finds out I am in Athon he will surely hunt me down and kill me," Lyra said.

It was reasonable Haran thought, but he needed her with him on their journey. If it were only him and Orion things would get boring and fast. He drew in closer to Lyra, touching her arm in the process, "You will be with me and Orion, we can protect you."

Lyra pulled away slightly from his touch, "I know that, and I appreciate the offer, but Orion and I have already talked about it, and he also believes I should stay here. Not just to protect me, but there also needs to be an Outryder here while he isn't, even if it is just a Recon."

Haran had to sit down; he hated the thought of going into dangerous territory without his companion by his side. "I don't think I can stop him without you."

"Who?" Lyra asked.

"Lottie," Haran replied.

Lyra sighed and took a seat beside him, "Why do you want to beat him so badly? I mean I know you two have history, but still."

"I don't want to beat him Lyra," Haran said, "I want to stop him. He was bearable before, but with the Lupens he found this new sense of rage that drives him to be so…dangerous."

Lyra nodded and said, "I understand, but you don't need to worry about that right now. I believe that you will win when the time comes. For now, though lets have some fun."

Haran smiled and stood up. "Sure."

"How about some good old detective work then?" Lyra asked.

"Sounds like a plan. I am following you," Haran said.

"I might need you for this one after you found out that Terence was a spy so quickly," Lyra replied facetiously.

Haran laughed and punched her in the arm as he was walking out. "Alright, so what are we doing then?"

"We are finding out what happened to your father," Lyra said.

"What do you mean?" Haran asked. "He died soon before I was born. I know nothing about my parents but from the note delivered alongside me on the Baron's front door."

"But people don't just die with no one who remembered them. I mean doesn't that seem odd to you?" Lyra asked. Haran had to admit that she brought up a good point. He always wondered why no one seemed to remember his father at all. Everyone knew Heide's parents, and some knew of Lottie's father, but Haran's parents, nothing. Lyra continued as they walked out of the door. "I have asked around town many times for anyone who remembered your parents, every time they knew you well, but no one knew of your parents."

"How long has this investigation been going on for exactly?" Haran asked.

"Since the battle I guess," Lyra said, Haran looked at her quizzically. "It helps ease my mind from what happened."

Haran thought about the way Scarlett the fox died. He could still hear the cracking of the creature's bones and the small cry she let out as her flesh was being ripped from her body. Chills went down his spine. He pushed the memory deep down in his mind as something new took its place. Who was his father? Who was he?

"Fine, let's get going then," Haran said. "Where are you taking me anyway?"

They both hopped on their respective horses when Lyra said, "Baron Ligate."

Haran groaned and rolled his eyes. "I have already asked him many times Lyra. He claims to have never known my dad or my mom."

"He has to know something Haran. Trust me," Lyra said as she pressed further ahead on her horse.

TAP-TAP-TAP

"Come in," Baron Ligate replied through the thick door. Lyra cracked the door slightly and then fully opened it. Baron Ligate was sitting at his desk with piles of papers around him. "Ah if it isn't my favorite two Outryders," he said gesturing for them to be seated which they did readily.

They talked to the Baron regularly while letting him know of the ongoings in Norhall, so they were friendly enough. Though Outryders stayed to themselves most of the time. At least that's the way Orion does it, so that was the way that Haran and Lyra do too.

"Ah but what of Orion. Surely he should be your favorite?" Lyra asked playfully. All three of them knew that Orion could be a pain sometimes. Well, most of the time.

"Ehh, Orion can be a bit of a hardhead at times and has grown even colder than I thought possible in his many years of service," Ligate said. He had known Orion for over a decade and the man had always been distant and cold, but he just assumed that was the Outryder way. "However, you two are fresh and lively enough."

"Thanks…I guess," Lyra said with a smile.

"So. What brings you here today?" Baron Ligate asked, "Did something else happen with the Lupens?"

"Not that I am aware no. Actually, we have come to ask you about Haran's parents—" Lyra was interrupted by a knock on the door.

The Baron held up a finger, "Come in," he said. Haran caught Lyra's eyes; Ligate had just brushed them off.

The door opened to reveal a face that Haran would have never expected so far from the capital, General Lee. The man was heavily built with basic chain armor on and had a highly decorated longsword at his waist. The last time Haran saw General Lee Orion condemned his fatherly ways and essentially denigrated him in front of the king, but now he was here.

"General Lee," Baron Ligate exclaimed as he stood reaching for his hand, "So good to see you."

"Yes, yes you too my friend," General Lee said seemingly distracted by the two Outryders in the room. General Lee took the position from Ligate once he became a Baron, so it was obvious that they would be close friends.

Baron Ligate let go of his hand and sat back down. "Have you had the pleasure to meet Haran and Lyra yet? They are—"

"Orion's pets," General Lee said intentionally disrespectful, "Yeah, yeah I've met them."

Lyra was about to retort, but Haran stopped her, "Nice to see you again general. I hope you got your boy straight since we last met."

The general looked to him with a hint of a smile, "I heard about your tragedy at the canyon. I can't imagine what it would have been like to lose so handedly."

Haran met his eyes, "I won my fight," he said.

"Ahh but you lost the battle," General Lee said, then he turned to Lyra, "Can you still hear the sound of the little creature's bones snapping?"

Haran saw Lyra fill with anger from head to toe. He too was angry at the pompous general, but they both knew they couldn't do anything about it.

"Vividly," Haran said dryly answering for Lyra. He could already see the tears beginning to well up in her eyes. *Bastard*, he thought.

The general only grunted and turned back to the Baron, "Anyways Ligate, as requested I took a look at the new training regimen for the Battleschool since that bastard Gilpin left. It looks great apart from a few untrained men, but Battlemaster Finnretts will get them into shape soon enough, he's one of the best in the business."

Baron Ligate nodded, "Well, thanks for taking a look over it for me, it really does mean a lot."

"No problem Ligate," the general said, "I trust dinner is still on then?"

Baron Ligate simply nodded and General Lee left his office with a giant smile on his face.

Baron Ligate sighed heavily and turned to Haran once more, "Sorry, what were you asking me?"

"His father," Lyra exclaimed. "Who was his father?"

"Oh yes," Baron Ligate said not noticing the tear that was forming in Lyra's eyes, "Well as I have told him many times, I knew nothing of his parents, or how he even ended up at my front door."

Haran shook his head at Lyra. The stone floor quickly caught his attention. She had given him a slight sign of hope to figuring out who his father was, but it was quickly squelched. "I told you Lyra, this was pointless, we should have never come Baron. We'll get going now"

Lyra shook her head in sheer disbelief, wiping her eyes slyly. "No." She then turned back to the Baron and said,

"There must be some records kept of everyone in Norhall, otherwise how is the king supposed to tax?"

The Baron looked at her with a new sense of interest. Not even he thought about the records. Everyone that lived in Norhall for the past twenty years would be on those records. "There are and I suppose I could grab them for you. However, there would be no faces put to the names, so how would you go about even finding Haran's parents?"

"I will figure it out, for now, I need the records from the year Haran was born in which would be…" Lyra turned to Haran for the answer.

"Seventeen years ago," Haran said softly. He was growing older and older now and hated the idea. It felt like just last year he was barrel roll racing with Lottie across the Wolf's Tail, sharing laughs and having fun without a care in the world.

"I will get someone to get that to you right away," Baron Ligate said, snapping Haran out of his daze. "It may take a few days though to get them to you."

"Haran. It looks like we have a lead," she said as he turned to her with a hint of hope in his eyes.

Lottie looked up to the ceiling from his bed. He realized he was doing this a lot since the battle. TAP-TAP-TAP, he heard on the door to his room. Lupe looked up and stared intently at the door to see who caused the disturbance. "Come in," he said.

Lupe growled softly as he saw Percival walk into the room. Lottie looked over to his wolf. *That's odd,* he thought. *Lupe never growls at anyone.* "Relax Lupe, it's just Percival."

Percival smiled, "Please, call me Percy."

Percival had just moved into the mansion in the room down the hall from Lottie, so he was still getting accustomed to the layout of the mansion. Gilpin asked him to move in so he could be closer to Percival's action in regards to Lupism, as Percival now deemed the worshipping of Albalupius. Of course, they still had plenty of spare rooms for him to stay in, even after Lottie and Ella moved in.

"Well, what's up Percy, what do you need?" Lottie asked as he sat up on his bed.

"Gilpin told me to fetch you and Ella," Percy said as his eyes fixated on the wolf at Lottie's side. "So yeah I am fetching you. Do you know what room she is in by the way?"

Lottie got off his bed and moved closer to Percival. "One down on the right. But what does Gilpin need? I have to be at training in an hour or so."

"No idea, he just told me to get you and Ella and join him in the office, it sounded rather urgent." It seemed Percival was just as lost as Lottie himself, so Lottie figured it best to just go see for himself.

"Oh ok, I will be there in five," Lottie said as Percy went out the door to fetch Ella.

Lottie and Lupe walked into Gilpin's study where he saw Gilpin sitting at his desk with Percival and Ella standing in front of the desk waiting patiently. "Good you're here now please close the door," Gilpin said seriously.

"What is it Gilpin," Lottie asked, "What's going on?

Gilpin looked to Lottie and more specifically towards Lupe. "It seems as if your friend Haran is making his way to Athon with his master as we speak."

Lottie relaxed his tense shoulders. "And?"

"And?" Gilpin asked in return. "We are going after them."

"Why would we go after them?" Lottie asked. "They are probably just going on a diplomatic mission for the king or something."

"Or—" before Gilpin even finished his sentence Ella interrupted with a hint of sadness in her voice. "They could be looking for a way to stop Lupe."

"Exactly," Gilpin said, "Which means we have to stop them before they can do that."

Lottie shook his head not understanding. "What do you mean? Lupe has no weakness; you claim he is the one true god. The god of destruction."

"God of chaos actually," Percival corrected him and continued to speak. "And while it is very true that Albalupius is god. Lupe isn't Albalupius' true form, the god is only working through Lupe. With Lupe's body being sort of like a catalyst for Albalupius' power."

"Wait so that means Lupe can die?" Lottie asked shocked. Doran had told him that Lupe was indestructible and everything that had happened at the canyon made him think that much. He saw three knives thrown into the wolf's back and Lupe didn't seem to feel a thing. Yet now he was supposed to believe Lupe could die? Impossible.

Percy nodded his head, "At least from what I can gather; however, how? I have no idea."

Lottie was growing angrier by every word the man was saying and by the time Percy was finished he was red with rage. He moved closer to Percival until their faces were only ten centimeters apart. "What do you mean 'I have no idea'? Are you not supposed to be the one who knows these things?"

Percy stayed calm under the overwhelming anger from Lottie, "Listen, everything I know comes from the books we have in Randint and in Norhall. And they aren't the best sources of information. That is probably why the Outryder's are going to Athon, to get information from the best source. Which is why I have to go as well." He was looking at Lottie but talking to Gilpin.

Lottie backed off as Gilpin thought over it for a second, "No… you have to stay here. Lottie, Ella, and I will go. You have to keep this country running while I am gone."

Without a moment's hesitation Percival said, "Fine, but you have to promise to get some writings or something for me."

"WHAT NO! Not *fine*," Ella protested. She tended to stay silent in these heated debates because she hated conflict, but apparently this was different. "I never agreed to this. They have done nothing to us since the battle at Calcore, and yet we continue to attack them repeatedly. I'm sorry, but I cannot join you on your quest."

"El? What are you talking about of course your coming?" Lottie said softly to Ella.

Ella looked to Lottie with tears in her eyes. "Lottie, you promised me that you wouldn't go after them again unless provoked. Do you really plan to break that promise?"

"El, this is different…Lupe's life is in danger—" Lottie said trying to reason with the girl, but Ella interrupted him.

"There is no difference Lottie!" Ella said raising her voice. "You can go all you want, but don't expect me to follow behind you like a sheep to her shepherd." At that she walked out of the door, slamming it behind her dramatically.

The three men stood there for a moment or two before Gilpin finally spoke up, "You are in deep trouble there mister, but it will have to wait until we get back. For now, you pack, we leave in one hour's time, and bring the wolf for both our sakes."

CHAPTER

11

Haran and Orion had been on the road for about three days now and were only a few hours away from Ediv Pass. Ediv Pass was the only way in between the two countries of Athon and Anjagor. Each country had respective guard posts on their sides of the pass just in case the other decided to invade.

The sun was setting now; Orion brought his horse, Nova, to a stop when he spotted a small clearing fifteen meters from the road leading to Athon. "Let's stop for tonight, we will reach the post early tomorrow morning," Orion said as he walked his way down to the clearing with Nova following close behind.

Orion made food after they got down to the clearing and set up their camp accordingly. The food was stew cooked from a rabbit he killed on the outskirts of the clearing while gathering firewood. Haran looked up from his second bowl of stew, he was about to speak, but soon went back to eating. "Got something to say?" Orion asked noticing the movement.

Haran shook his head no but then spoke anyway, "Yes actually, why did you convince Lyra that she needed to stay?"

"Why does the grass grow? Why is the sky blue?" Orion asked. Haran looked at him confused so the man continued. "Why do you care? The things are the way they are meant to be, she was meant to stay home for this adventure, and she's okay with that. Why aren't you?"

"I guess it's because I feel, if I am not by her side, that means I couldn't protect her, and she could get hurt. Then it would be my fault, just like—" Haran said trailing off. But Orion finished it for him. "Just like in Randint Cavern"

Haran nodded and realization dawned upon him, he blamed himself for the events that happened in Randint Cavern. He blamed himself for Lyra getting captured. For her having to stay weeks in captivity with Doran as her warden. For letting Orion down on the only task that had ever been asked of him. And for the eventual death of Scarlett the fox.

"Haran, no one blames you for the incident," Orion said as he finished off his bowl of stew. "Not King Nigel, not me, and especially not Lyra. It's just the way things go sometimes. Sometimes we lose sometimes we win."

"But we are the good guys. I mean surely the good guys have to win right?" Haran said shook by his teacher's words.

Orion laughed, but it wasn't one of pleasure it was more of an incredulous laugh. One that told Haran that Orion was a little more than skeptical. "That's the problem Haran. In the end...Who really are the good guys?"

"What do you mean?" Haran asked.

"I mean, in their eyes they are the good guys," Orion said as his smile faded and he stared blankly into the fire. "In our eyes we are the good guys. In the end, no one is truly good. Everyone is just different shades of bad."

Haran was very confused by his master's thoughts but decided it best not to say anything else on the matter. "Anyway," Orion said getting up and moving to his bag, "here, put this on." He handed him a dark green shirt with multiple rips in it. It looked as if it had seen years of constant war and smelled like it too.

"What's this for?" Haran asked as he fluffed out the ripped-up shirt.

"How did you think we would get across the border Haran?" Orion asked testing his apprentice.

"I assumed we would sneak through," Haran said as he began to take off his cloak and put on the dark green shirt. "I mean we are Outryders after all."

"That is true," Orion replied, "and we probably could sneak through the hundreds of meters of flat land that is Ediv Pass. However, there is no need. We will simply walk through the Athonian guard post tomorrow."

Tomorrow came quickly as Haran slept like a baby through the night with Shiva curled up in a ball beside him. Just before sunset, Orion woke him, and they got on their way again. As they neared the pass Haran started smelling the water in the air from the Hermirtha Sea. The smell of leaves and greenery that he was so accustomed to was now being tainted by a smell that was very foreign to him in

Norhall. Salt water. He hated salt water. He thought back to a time when he and Lottie snuck to Dalhurst for a few days to see the crystal blue water of the Hermirtha Sea that they had always heard about. He recalled briefly entering the frigid water only to be overcome by both the awful taste as the water entered his mouth and the burning sensation as he stupidly opened his eyes under the water. "Haran look," Orion said snapping him out of his flashback and into reality once more. Haran looked ahead as they emerged from the woods only to be greeted with an open field that had a singular guard post on it.

"The guard post," Haran said to Orion, "it must mark the start of Ediv Pass." Orion simply nodded as Haran pushed Spirit to greater speeds.

Ediv Pass was a small piece of land in between the Chien Mountains and the Hermirtha Sea. The pass was only about 100 meters in width and a few hundred in length. On the Anjagorian side of the pass there was a small outpost that contained ten to fifteen guards at a time on it. The guard post was small, but the guards could see everything within a kilometer's distance all around as they looked for any signs of attack.

Orion and Haran, as they drew closer and closer to the guard post, were eventually stopped near the post by an Anjagorian guard. The guard had the classic grey colors of Anjagor on. "State your business travelers," he said crassly.

Not having their signature Outryder cloaks on, Orion went back to his bag, and took out a small amulet. Haran had never seen the necklace before. However, he recognized the symbol on it, for it was the same symbol on the satchel he was currently hanging to his side. The symbol was the exact same with the same calligraphic R surrounded by a circle. "The name is Orion of Norhall," he said as he showed the guard the symbol.

The guard didn't seem to recognize the amulet, so he went inside to bring out his captain.

The captain appeared in the same regulation dress of an Anjagorian soldier with the red badge pinned on his left sleeve marking him as a captain. He immediately recognized the symbol. "Ah, an Outryder, we don't see many coming this way, especially without those signature cloaks of yours, so excuse my guard for not recognizing you."

"Not a problem; however, we really must be on our way, we have important business in Athon," Orion said hurriedly.

"Of course, go ahead but might I add that that beast right there is rather terrifying" the captain said as he moved out of the way of the road. "The Athonians will not let an Outryder go through the border, especially one with something like that hanging from their side."

"Dually noted," Orion said dully. Haran realized now why his master made him wear such horrible smelling clothes. He didn't plan to cross as an Outryder. He planned to go as a logger.

The Outryders went on their way down the road, the sea crashing against the rocks about fifty meters to their right causing a rather large amount of spray. And of course, the sheer face of the rocky Chien Mountains was to their left. Haran thought it was a rather imposing scene being trapped between a sheer mountain face and a sheer cliff face. He laughed slightly as he thought of how bizarre geography could be.

After a few hundred meters they came across the Athonian guard post. The guard was wearing almost the same exact uniform as the Anjagorian one other than the fact that it was blue in color. "State your business traveler."

"The name is Owen Lightfoot, and this is my son Herald, we come from Anjagor seeking business in the uncertain times," Orion said.

"What sort of business is it that you seek in Athon," the guard said skeptically.

"Simple loggers we are sir," Orion said, "but there is too much competition where we live, so we decided to branch out."

And what is that?" The guard asked pointing to Shiva who was lying in the specially made pack saddle.

"Just a little pet cat to help him get through the hard days," Orion said pointing to Haran.

"That thing isn't little or pet like, but fine, come through I suppose. As long as you can control it," the guard said as the Outryders went past him. However, the guard captain was watching everything very observantly from his post some ten meters away. He could barely make out a symbol on the side of the younger man's satchel, easily recognizable as the symbol of the Outryder.

Some ten minutes after they left, the guard captain called all the guards into the guard post for a meeting. Some fifteen men gathered in their small living quarters. The room consisted of a small kitchen for cooking, a small table for eating, and eight beds that lined the free walls. None of them were usually in the room all at the same time, so they didn't need much more room than that. Each had their own small cubby where they sat their things for the many months that they stayed at the guard posts, but other than that they really didn't have much to complain about. The Athon guard posts were always the most uneventful places to be in the military. Athon hadn't been to war in many years, and the guards had become lazy at best.

However, Captain Virden always remained alert and ready for possible attacks, which he believed was coming soon. "It seems as though we have forgotten what the responsibility of a guard at this post is supposed to mean," Virden said threateningly to the other men. "We as border guards must protect the country from potential outside threats coming in." He then turned to the guard who let Haran and Orion through the border, "Now Tobin, what is it that the two men who just came past here said they did?"

"They said they were loggers sir," Tobin said terrified.

"They did look a lot like loggers didn't they Tobin. I mean who other than loggers would carry two very sharp axes, have green clothes on, and wear a satchel with a R on it?" Virden asked rhetorically.

Tobin shook his head and smiled. "I don't know sir. A traveling minstrel with a particular knack for axe throwing perhaps." The guards around him laughed but were quickly silenced by Virden's steely gaze.

"Perhaps," Virden said, "However, have you ever heard of something called an Outryder Tobin?"

Tobin's face immediately shifted down and his eyes locked to a piece of dirt on the floor. "I have sir."

"Ok then, now that you've realized what you've done, you are going to do something for me," Virden said. "You are going to ride to Athon and tell King Theos that you have let two fully armed Outryders into this country and that he should watch for them."

"Surely you can't be serious," Tobin protested. "It will take a week to ride to Athon and even when I arrive he will have my head for the action."

"Better than him having mine. So go Tobin, warn the king of the consequences of your actions. Let me know how that turns out for you. Actually, never mind you probably won't be alive to tell me." Captain Virden laughed. However, the other guards did not join in this time. For them, this was no joking matter.

CHAPTER

12

Lottie and Gilpin walked through the checkpoint on the Anjagorian side just as easily as Haran and Orion had. They cross the hundreds of meters of plains between the two sides and onto the guard post on the Athonian side.

As Lottie crossed he thought of how cool the scene was. Water sprayed like a continuous fountain, crisp and unforgiving. The sheer face of the mountain seemed to slowly be encroaching upon him as he walked through it as if it were a wall slowly closing in, trapping him. The guard captain approached the two as they rode up on their horses. The darker shade of blue he wore as well as the pin he wore on his right arm marked him as a higher rank than those guards in the lighter blue. The captain was in his early thirties, which was fairly regular age for a captain. He was dark eyed and dark haired with a very basic face structure. Nothing was particularly spectacular about this man; he was average in almost every visible way.

Lupe stopped beside Lottie as he got off his horse. "State your business warrior," the captain said. They put no effort into hiding they were fighters. Their swords hung proudly from their belts as signs of great confidence.

"I actually come to ask you a question before we move on our way," Gilpin said to the guard captain.

"Oh yeah? Ask away," The captain responded not daring to deny the fully capable looking warriors. Lottie saw the fearful look in the captain's eyes as he looked to Lottie's side at Lupe. He didn't blame the man really. The wolf tended to have a rather imposing appearance.

"Did you happen to see two rather short men riding rather unkept looking horses wearing green pass by here at all?" Gilpin asked already knowing the answer, but he wanted to see how far ahead the Outryders were.

"Yes actually," The guard captain said. "Not but two days ago, they said they were loggers. They had a strange animal, looked like a big cat by my guess. It was almost the size of that one there by the boy. The name is Captain Virden by the way, what's yours?"

"My name is Battle—" he stopped himself, "Gilpin, and his is Lottie." He pointed to each respectively. "Do you know which direction they went?"

Captain Virden pointed to the road that started after the guard post. "Last I saw they were heading down the main road south."

Gilpin nodded; they weren't that far behind he thought. "Ok, thank you," He said as he went to move past the guard.

However, Virden moved in front of his way. "As you can understand sir, I cannot let two very powerful looking, fully armed warriors in our country. Especially Anjagorian ones." Lottie saw the dozen or so other guards move behind Virden as they realized there was trouble. Lottie sighed, he really hated to have to fight all the time.

"I really suggest you move out of the way. It has been a long few weeks, and I need to go after those *loggers*," Gilpin said squaring off with the captain. Lottie knew that there was nothing that was going to stop him from getting to Orion, especially not some half trained Athonian guards.

"Go after them?" Virden asked feigning ignorance, "What is wrong with a few loggers?"

"Let's just say they are enemies in every sense of the word, and we have to stop them from getting important information," Gilpin said, "Now. Move."

"They are enemies you say?" Virden asked, "I thought Outryders were well respected in your country. Surely an Outryder would be a bad enemy to have?"

"Ahh so you knew they were Outryders huh," Gilpin asked catching Virden in his lie.

Virden silently cursed to himself. "I have heard stories of legendary feats from the Outryders. So I find it hard to believe that you two could ever compete with an Outryder."

"You will believe it soon enough," Gilpin said. "Now I won't repeat myself again. Move."

"Sorry sir, but I can't let you go past," Virden said sternly. He held his ground bracing for any attack to come his way.

"Oh. That's where you are mistaken. It's not about letting me... it's about stopping me. " Gilpin said turning around as if he was going to leave. However, he only got about a meter away before he unsheathed his sword with lightning speed and launched an attack at the captain's neck.

Before the captain could even react, the sword sliced his neck clean in half. The captain's head fell casually from his body and rolled over the ground. Blood poured from the captain's neck and his body fell limp to the ground beside his head.

Seconds later, after processing what they had just saw, the thirteen other guards jumped on the two warriors. Lottie, drew his swords and easily deflected a downward stroke from one guard and push kicked him, sending him crashing some two meters away. He had no time to focus on that guard however as three more came up behind him.

He jumped out of the way and killed all three at the same time with a perfectly timed cut across their torsos. By this time, Gilpin had dispatched two of his own and the one that Lottie kicked got up and ran down the road towards Athon. Lottie, seeing the movement gestured to Lupe. The wolf understood what his master was asking and took off after the guard, taking him to the ground and killing him only fifteen meters away. Seven more guards remained, but Gilpin, Lottie and Lupe made quick work of them.

Lottie looked around in the aftermath of the fight, there were fourteen bodies and fourteen pools of blood. There were no survivors. "Did we really have to kill all of them?" he asked to his master.

"No, I suppose not, but they made me mad," Gilpin said as he got onto his horse.

"I mean they were only doing their job Gilpin, surely we could have worked something out?" Lottie said.

"Yeah, well, for some reason that man knew Orion was an Outryder and lied about it," Gilpin said. "Meaning he must have already sent a messenger to warn the king that the Outryders were here. Which also means we can put all

the blame on the Outryder's shoulders for this massacre."
It made sense now to Lottie. Gilpin planned to make it out
as if the Outryders killed these men so the Athonian king
would think the Anjagorians killed his border guard.

"Surely this will start a war between the two nations
don't you think?" Lottie asked.

"What do I care? They don't even know where to find
the Lupens in Randint, and a war between the two would
probably be a good thing," Gilpin said turning to Lottie.
Seeing the confusion on his face he decided he had to clarify.
"A war could weaken Anjagor making it easier for us to take
Norhall when the time is right. Now, let's get going, we are
not very far from the Outryders."

As they rode down the dirt road, thoughts of Percival's
speech raced through Lottie's mind. The man brought
up his wolf and had him worshipped like a god. *Wait*, he
thought, *he is a god.* Or was he? He had seen three knives
thrown directly into the wolf's heart and the wolf barely even
flinched. However, if he were a god how could Lottie control
him with just simple words. If he were a god did that mean
Lottie could control gods? *Impossible.* How could he control
a god when he could barely even control his own emotions?

"Gilpin?" he asked as his master nodded his head slightly
in acknowledgement. "Do you think Lupe is an actual god?"
Surely there must be something else to explain why the wolf
followed his command so willingly.

Gilpin shrugged, "There was a point in my life when I
thought gods were nothing but simply ways for people with
great imaginations to cope with the tragedies of the real
world. However, now I think they are real enough, even if I

don't believe in them. So, to answer your question, yes I do think Lupe is an actual god."

"But it doesn't make sense," Lottie said as he looked to his wolf sleeping ever so peacefully in the side of his packsaddle. "If Lupe is a god, then why does he listen to me? Why would a god follow a simple human like me?"

"To be honest, I don't know," Gilpin said. "Maybe we should do a little research of our own in this god forsaken country." Lottie smiled, for the first time in his life he liked the idea of doing research.

Two days passed since Haran and Orion had crossed the border to Athon. The small dirt road that they had been traveling on up until this point slowly diverged into two roads, one headed north, and one headed south. Haran looked to the west to see the sun slowly setting through the trees. "Alright," Orion said, "let's set up camp for the night."

The two Outryders moved to a small clearing that Orion noticed some hundred meters from the road. Haran set up both his and Orion's small one-man tent while his master went to collect firewood and start the fire for their dinner that night.

After he finished setting up, Haran went with Shiva to find something that they could eat for that night. They had been eating rabbit stew for the past three days and he was getting rather tired of the taste of the small mammal. Haran was searching for about an hour when he came across the tracks of an animal he had never seen before that sank very visibly in the muddy ground. They were much the same size as a horse's hooves if not slightly smaller. However, unlike horses, the hooves were longer and curved inward.

Interesting, Haran thought as he followed the tracks deeper into the woods. After about ten minutes or so of following the tracks he heard a snap of twigs behind him. He turned around to see nothing was there, when he turned back to Shiva he saw that she hadn't even noticed the sound. *Odd*, he thought, Shiva was usually far more observant. He continued walking, listening for the sound again. About thirty seconds later he heard another twig snap. He whipped around with his throwing knife in hand ready to kill whatever it was that made the noise… but there was nothing. Not a single bit of movement.

Almost instantly he felt a presence behind him. He whipped back around to see that it was the black suit of armor that he had dreamed about. He tried to throw the knife, but his wrist was seized instantly. The wheezing figure's ironclad hands gripped him firmly, almost ripping the tendons in his wrist in the process. Haran looked to Shiva beside him who simply sat watching in front of them as if she couldn't see what was happening. Haran began to fold under the dark suit's death grip but brought up enough courage to fight back. He tried to hit the hand gripping his with his free hand, but the suit simply grabbed that hand with its other hand. Haran could feel his tendons start to rip apart as he was driven to the ground in pain. However, he made one last ditch attempt to get free as he jumped up and kicked the suit with both legs. The suit flew back, letting go of both his wrists. Terrified, Haran took off running the opposite way of the black spiked warrior. Shiva did also. He ran for several minutes through the thinly wooded area, heart racing with every step as he looked behind him to see the black suit chasing him.

After several minutes of running Haran was met with a small river too wide to jump across. He looked back to see the suit wasn't far behind. He turned back to the river trying to decide whether or not to risk the jump. Eventually he decided to stand and fight the dark man, but as he turned around and withdrew his axes, the black suit was no where to be seen.

He stood confused at what happened for several moments as Shiva looked at him curious at why he had just made her run. "You couldn't see him?" he asked the large cat. There was no response. *How? It felt so real.* He thought to himself as he shook off his wrist painfully.

His heart still raced with panic, but after realizing the dark suit was gone he took a drink from the river. When he looked up and looked to his left he saw what he had been tracking before drinking from the river some twenty meters away.

It was… well Haran had no idea what it was. It was just over a two meters in height and about three meters long. Its brown coat shined perfectly with the light from the waning sun. It had horns that branched out like one would see on a tree, but the horns were made of bone. Haran counted ten different points on two different horns where the main bone branched outward. Whatever it was, the creature was majestic. It moved gracefully through the woods as it maneuvered around trees and overgrowth. Haran followed it, curious to what the creature was. As he got closer he saw Shiva tense her hind legs preparing to pounce. He held his hand up for her to stop. How could he justify killing such a majestic creature? Especially when he could not eat all of its meat.

He watched it for several more minutes as it moved gracefully through the woods. He tried to follow it closer, but as soon as he came within ten meters the creatures head turned and he met eyes with the animal. As Haran looked into the creature's dark eyes he saw nothing but innocence and gentleness. They locked eyes for several seconds before the creature eventually pranced out of sight.

When Haran arrived back at the camp he described to Orion what he saw as they shared a bowl of rabbit stew. He excluded the part where he got chased by a figment of his imagination for almost ten minutes. He thought telling his master he is going insane wasn't the best option for a promotion to a fully-fledged Outryder.

Horns you say?" Orion asked as Haran gave the creatures physical description.

Haran nodded. "Yes, like antlers of sorts."

"Must have been a deer then," Orion said as he finished his first bowl of stew and went for more.

"A deer?" Haran asked. "What is that?"

Orion looked to his apprentice. "It's an animal that's nearly extinct in Anjagor. Its massive antlers provided some sort of a trophy to many poachers that lived some twenty years ago."

"They killed them just for their antlers?" Haran asked as his blood started to boil in his body. Orion nodded. "Didn't the king try to stop them? I mean surely he could have gotten them all arrested or something."

Orion sighed, "He passed a law that forbade their killings, but there were just far too many poachers. They continued until eventually the entire species was extinct.

The king tried his best to import deer from Athon, but all the ones he imported were eventually wiped out as well."

"Why must people be so evil?" Haran asked as he stared into the fire that was now nothing more than embers. "When I looked into its eyes I saw nothing but innocence. How can they kill such a creature just for sport?" Orion didn't reply, he simply continued eating his food.

Haran got up and walked towards the road to clear his head, he emerged at the crossroads and looked up and down the worn-down dirt roads. He looked down to Shiva who was at his side. "Don't worry Shiva," Haran said to the big cat, "I won't let anyone poach you." The lioness purred as she rubbed up against Haran's leg.

When Haran arrived back at the camp he sat down and asked, "Where are we going anyways?" He hadn't really thought about where they would go, he just simply followed his master.

"Gora," Orion replied between mouthfuls of soup.

"What is that? I thought that the capital was called Athon," Haran asked. Similarly, to Anjagor, the capital of Athon was named after the country. *Or maybe it was the other way around*, Haran thought.

Orion set down his bowl for a minute, "It is. However, Gora is the actual centerpiece to everything Athonian, including the Athonian religion which is what we came for. Also, it helps that Brios lives there," Orion finished and picked up his bowl again to resume eating.

"Brios? Who is that?" Haran asked not familiar with the name.

Orion put his bowl back down, "One of the three Outryders assigned to Athon." He picked his bowl up once more.

"Three?" Haran asked.

Orion put the bowl back down getting rather annoyed by his apprentice's questions, "Yes, as you know, there are 35 Outryders in Anjagor and 35 spread out throughout the known world. Athon is a big nation, so it needs three Outryders to cover the whole thing."

"Where are they located?" Haran asked.

"One is in Gora which is in the exact middle of the country. One is in Athon, the capital at the very south of the peninsula, and one in a city on the north border to Galak called Selia," Orion said, not picking his bowl back up this time.

"Have you ever met Brios?" Haran asked anxiously.

"No, but I am sure he is just as peachy as I am," Orion said.

Haran opened his mouth to ask another question, but Orion stopped him, "Haran."

"Yes?" Haran said wondering why his master had stopped him.

"Let me finish eating please," Orion said as he picked up the bowl and started eating once again.

CHAPTER

13

The Outryders woke up the following morning and took the road to the south. They stayed on that road until noon when they came across another intersection. The intersecting road was very obviously the main road for travel in the country as it was well paved with gravel. The paved road was around twice the size of the dirt road and far more populated. There were horse-drawn carts coming to and from the city of Gora. Haran nodded to every single one, but he didn't even get a glance in return. That's when he realized that Athonians were not as polite as their Anjagorian counterparts.

After another ten minutes' travel, the city came into view. Gora was in the middle of a plain and in the center was a reasonably sized hill which held the castle on its top. It was quite the sight; between the soaring towers of the castle and the rows upon rows of buildings and houses beneath the hill it looked rather majestic. However, the main thing that attracted Haran's eyes as they approached the city was the giant river just on the edge of the city as well as the subsequent port and boats going to and from their destinations. Haran assumed that the river wrapped around the whole city, but he wasn't close enough to see for sure.

There was a raised wooden bridge so that the ships could sail clearly under, and people can exit and enter the city as they wished. Without even having to ask the question Orion simply said, "Creight River leads from the Hermirtha Sea and stops right here. It took years for them to wrap the river around the whole city, but it does make for a wonderful sight and is quite easily defendable."

"What about Bianet Raiders?" Haran asked. The seafaring people of Bianet tended to raid the coastal areas but have been known to travel up rivers to raid villages further inland. "Surely they see this city as a gold mine, especially since the river wraps all the way around."

Orion scoffed. "The Bianets would never attempt to make it through the river. They would be spotted too easily, and they simply don't have enough manpower to take the city for their own."

Haran nodded and moved from that question onto the matter they were there for, "Do you know where this Brios is? I mean this is a huge city. Surely he could be anywhere. How do you plan to find him?"

"We have to cause a scene," Orion said pointing to the castle at the top of the hill.

They arrived at the castle gates at just past midday, the towering stone walls loomed over their heads as they rode through the main gate. The inside of the walls was a regular enough design on its own, the stables to the left side, the garrison quarters to the right side, and a rather imposing fountain with an Athonian god spewing water from its mouth in front of the inner ward. They walked through the courtyard with ease; however, as they made their way to the door to the inner ward two large, well armored guards stopped them. "State your business," one guard said.

"We are but simple loggers from Anjagor come to talk to your lord about our stay in his humble city," Orion said.

The guards laughed in their faces which Haran thought was quite rude. The guard to their left spoke. "Argo speaks to no one. Especially not loggers now leave before I have to make you leave."

Orion turned around casually, not even daring to argue back. However, as they were exiting the main gate Haran asked, "What was the purpose of that, surely you knew they were going to turn you away?"

"They know we are here now, and that we want to talk to their lord." Orion said. "So, what do you say we go grab a drink to celebrate the successful day." Haran was very confused by what his master was planning, but before he could ask a question Orion pushed his horse Nova to greater speeds leaving him behind.

They entered The Hawk's Beak Tavern shortly after sunset, leaving their animals in a stable just across the street. As the two entered, they caught the eyes of many of the locals who were wondering who these two figures dressed in green were. Orion led the way to a table in the very back of the tavern. Haran heard hushed whispers of prejudice as they walked past the tables in the tavern.

"They know we are foreign," Haran whispered to Orion as they sat down in the back of the tavern.

"Good," Orion said, "draws more attention to us."

Within five minutes of sitting, a barmaid approached; she was rather pretty with her raven-colored hair and hazel brown eyes that made for a contrast quite appealing to most men. "What can I get for you fine gentlemen today?" she said perkily.

"Just a water is fine," Haran said.

"Give me some ale, and hurry up with it," Orion demanded loudly while slurring his words almost drunkenly. The barmaid nodded and went to making their drinks.

While she was gone Haran looked at his master, "What are you up to?" he asked curiously. Orion simply gave a hint of a smile.

The barmaid came back after two minutes or so and set the drinks on the table in front of them. "Here you are," she said to which Orion replied with another slurred, "About time."

The woman simply smiled as Orion went to sip from his ale. After taking a sip of the ale he spit it out on the barmaid as if he had tasted a mouthful of cinnamon. "You call that ale? That's a sorry excuse for water if anything. Honestly, are there no good taverns in this whole city."

"So sorry sir, it's my fault," the girl said apologetically.

"No not you girl, this whole city is terrible, and that bastard Lord Argo is responsible for it."

That seemed to draw the wanted attention to the scene, so Orion continued, standing up on the table and speaking very loudly, "Argo. What kind of pretentious fool do you have to be to be called Argo? His mother must have been knocked in the head when she was young to name her child Argo. You know. I heard his mother slept with a horse once…" That was where the people in the bar drew the line, they could be jailed if they let such heresy go on for too much longer. At this point Haran had his head in his hands, he knew Orion's plan and he hated it.

It took four grown men ten minutes to get Orion down from the table. He kicked, bit, screamed, hollered, he did everything he could to make him seem drunk and by the time they eventually got him down, the watch was there to take both him and Haran to the castle dungeons. However, before they were able to restrain Orion he managed to slip a small bag of silvers in the girl's pocket. He figured it was the least he could do after spitting in her face.

The castle dungeons were much like those in Norhall. There were two cells on each wall; however, these cells had metal bars on the front opposed to the wooden ones at Norhall's dungeons. Whatever the difference the goal was still the same, to keep people in captivity for an indefinite amount of time and not let them out.

They had left their horses and Shiva with their weapons and gear in a stable close to the Hawk's Beak. It had been Orion suggestion seeing as he knew they would eventually end up in the dungeons. No one would think to steal them due to the fact that a giant, ferocious cat was sitting in the stall with all of their goods.

After the guards shoved Orion and Haran in two cells across from each other, they locked the door and left the Outryders in a dark and damp room that reeked of a combination of wet dog and sweat. "So, you plan to talk to this Argo person tomorrow then," Haran asked trying to figure out their plan of escape.

"Yes actually, I have a sneaky suspicion on where Brios could be," Orion replied.

"Care to enlighten me?" Haran asked just a little ticked off that his master never included him on his elaborate plans.

"No," Orion replied.

"Of course not." Haran scoffed, "You never do. You just expect me to go along with whatever ruse you have going on that second, day, or even week."

Orion stood up taken aback by the sudden hostility of his apprentice, "What is wrong Haran."

"Nothing, I am fine," Haran said as he sat down against the wall. "I just like how Lyra and I are expected to follow you blindly without any say in the plans."

"This is about me sending the two of you to Randint Cavern isn't it?" Orion asked, guessing it immediately.

Haran nodded slightly, and then spoke, "How could you let us go in there without backup? If we hadn't been captured, none of this would have even happened." They had yet to talk about what happened at Randint. He spent multiple days in a hostile country with no sign of backup. After he was captured he was tortured for information, but eventually let go to deliver a message. And Lyra. He couldn't imagine what Lyra went through. What he went through was nothing compared to the weeks that Lyra spent in their captivity.

Orion paused for a second to think and then he hung his head in shame, "That is one action of many in my career that I cannot defend. I thought you were ready, but

I was wrong, and no boy should have to experience that at your age."

Haran thought back to his experience in the cavern. "No," he said, "It's not your fault. I was not prepared to face such challenges. However, when you asked I foolishly said I was, so I am to blame for what happened after. I am sorry. I am just so angry that Lyra had to go through what she did because of my failures."

Orion nodded, "You managed it just fine and so did she. She is quite the lady don't you think?"

"Quite the lady indeed," Haran said as he thought about the raven-haired girl hundreds of kilometers away.

The next day they were awoken by the same two guards that had put them in the cells, "Get up you two, Argo will see you now."

They led the two up the stairs from the dungeons, down a dimly lit hallway, and into the great hall.

The great hall was very grand in design, with towering pillars of marble edged with gold. In the center there sat a giant golden throne that looked godly. However, in the chair was no god. There was a small man; his legs swung well off the floor and his body was half the size of the throne itself. He sat upright and looked to be rather angry with the two Outryders.

There was a man beside him who Haran assumed was a chamberlain; however, he was a little bigger than Haran and well defined, so not what he expected a chamberlain to look like. The man had a steely gaze much like the one he saw in Orion. Even from a distance Haran saw the man flinch slightly when they came into view. At this point he had figured out Orion's plan. That man was no chamberlain, that man was an Outryder.

"Leave us," Argo said to the two guards who had taken Orion and Haran to the great hall.

After they walked out Argo turned his attention to the senior of the two Outryders, "How dare you come into my city and talk bad on my family name." His voice was almost higher than birds chirping.

"Oh, I dare," Orion said meeting the lord's eyes.

"You bumbling imbecile. You piece of worthless Anjagorian garbage. What kind of arrogant buffoon are you?" Argo said.

"Arrogant?" Orion asked, "You are literally sitting on a throne coated with gold."

"This is not coated *logger*, its solid gold," Argo said in protest. Orion simply coughed.

"Hey, Argo was it?" Haran asked trying to take this mission into his own hands. He looked to Orion who nodded and let him do so. *It would be good experience for the boy*, he thought.

"That's Lord Argo to you child," Argo said as he turned to the younger man in green.

"Oh yes of course. Well anyway Argo. We really must speak to your chamberlain, so if you don't mind could you take a step outside," Haran said and glanced sideways seeing Orion smiling slightly.

"You want me to what? Do you know who I am?" Argo yelled, his face turning red with rage.

"Yeah you are Argo," Haran said confused by the question. "Come on I thought we went over this. Now, can you please leave so I can speak to your chamberlain."

"Why you disrespectful little runt of a boy, you know I can have you beheaded for such talk." He tried getting up from his chair, but before he even got a meter the chamberlain punched him in the back of the head, leaving him unconscious immediately.

He then moved to greet Orion and Haran, "Quite the show you two put on there, but what else can I expect from the legendary Orion."

"You must be Brios then," Orion said.

"Yes indeed. That was quite the risk you took there, getting yourself arrested just to talk to me. How did you know it was me anyway?" Brios asked.

"I knew you would probably be in a position where you can get the most information about the ongoings in Gora. And that position is one of chamberlains," Orion said.

"Well, whatever the reason, it was a beautifully executed plan," Brios said as he looked over to shake Haran's hand.

"Hey, it was his plan, but it was my execution," Haran said smiling as he shook the Outryder's hand.

"And you must be his Recon," Brios said endearingly.

"It's Haran sir, pleasure to meet you."

"You too, so why have you two come all the way from Norhall to speak to me?" Brios asked.

"We need information on a certain wolf god Albalupius," Orion said.

"Ahh, the forbidden god. Quite the tricky one he is, but I think I know of someone who can help you out. He lives in the woods just northeast of Gora, but the path is tricky, so it'd be best if I took you. Meet me on the northeast bridge at midnight and I will take you to him. However, for now I must take care of this fool," Brios said finally as he gestured to Argo on the floor some two meters away.

"How do you plan on doing that?" Haran asked curiously.

"Well, I'll put him back on his glorified baby seat and when he wakes up and asks about what happened I will tell him it was all a dream," Brios said, "He will think nothing of it, after all, he is not the brightest in the bunch as you can tell."

"Clearly," Orion said, "Oh, and one more thing. How do we get out of a fully manned castle unseen?"

Brios simply laughed and said, "Follow me, I know the way."

Brios led them out of the great hall where they passed by the same two guards as before. "Hey," one of the guards said, "where are you taking them?" Haran's heart began moving at a rapid pace as he thought of a way to escape if things got dangerous. These two guards they could take care of easily, but without his weapons it would be almost impossible to escape from the castle with his life.

"None of your business, it's on Argo's orders," Brios said threateningly.

The other guard simply waved it off and began walking to where they were initially heading. "Close one," Haran said as he wiped his brow.

They saw no one else on their way outside and stopped at the castle gates. "Well," Brios said as he went to shake Orion's hand, "I will see you tonight then."

"See you then," Orion replied.

CHAPTER

14

After saying goodbye to Brios, the two Outryders headed into town to collect their belongings from the stables they left them in. As they walked in they saw that Shiva and their horses were still there, it was expected. No one would dare steal the horses while Shiva was sitting in there with them.

Haran figured Spirit would be hungry after not eating for a whole day, so he fed him some oats and an apple from his satchel. He then hopped on Spirit and rode out into the markets with Orion. The markets were livelier than any Haran had ever seen. They were in the center of the city that was in the center of the country. *Quite poetic*, he thought to himself.

The markets were colorful, vivid, lively, and also very loud. To his left he saw a group of girls playing a game and screaming at the top of their lungs. To his right there was a man in the stalls banging pots together to prove their solidity to a customer. To his back were hooves clopping on the ground, and to his front there were two young boys laughing flirtatiously at the girls.

Haran could barely hear himself think as he rode through the rows. There was no end in sight as they rode in between rows and rows of stalls. The stalls themselves had everything from silks to fresh food to jewelry, and it was like at every stall Haran saw someone of different skin, hair, or eyes.

"Quite peaceful isn't it?" Haran yelled to Orion who was only riding a meter away.

"Yeah about as peaceful as a leaf can be in a hurricane I suppose," Orion replied.

However, as they were riding through, Haran saw something in a rather rundown booth that caught his eyes instantly. A pendant gleaming in the afternoon sun. He tapped Orion's shoulder and gestured for him to stop so he could take a closer look. And so, they did, dismounting their horses and making their way to the stall.

The closer he got to the necklace the more he realized why it had caught his eye. The necklace was in the shape of a fox head and looked much like Scarlett. It was simplistic in design with a silver-colored head and two of the most beautiful rubies he had ever seen for its eyes. He knew immediately that he had to get it for Lyra.

"Quite the necklace, isn't it?" The vendor asked.

"Yes indeed, a friend of mine loves foxes and this is simply breathtaking," Haran said, "How much for it?" He was willing to pay anything after all Lyra had to go through at Randint Cavern.

"300 silvers." The vendor said.

"Are you insane?" Orion asked through his clenched teeth. Those three hundred silvers were all they had left for the trip.

"We will take it," Haran said as he made eye contact with his master.

Orion gave him a death glare. "You owe me." There was no doubt in Haran's mind that his master would make sure of it that he gets his money back.

"Of course," Haran said as he went to Orion's horse to get the money. He came back with bags of silvers and gave them to the vendor. In exchange Haran got a small necklace with a foxes' head on it; it was a worthy trade to him. He put the necklace carefully into his satchel and began mounting Spirit. "Thank you," he said as he looked between Orion and the vendor. If he were honest, he didn't even know which one he was thanking.

They scanned the market until midnight; there was a slight decrease in people when the sun went down, but when the torches came out some more people showed. Orion found well-crafted saddles to replace their old, tattered ones. They were dyed light brown and beautifully engraved with Ushayian symbols that probably meant something that Haran couldn't read. However, they couldn't afford them due to Haran previous purchase.

At midnight they began heading towards the northeast bridge where Brios was already waiting on his own horse. They greeted each other and then rode out of the still lit city and into the dark woods just northeast. The woods were not nearly as dense as Fuestres Woods, but the darkness and the movement of random animals in the forest left a foreboding taste in Haran's mouth.

A few hundred meters down a winding game trail— much like the one that led to their home in Norhall—they came into a clearing. In the clearing there stood a rather sizable building and between the soaring ceiling and the design of the outside, Haran realized that it was a library. They decided to leave their horses with Shiva at the entrance of the clearing and approached the front of the library very cautiously. When they walked into the building they saw rows and rows of books to the ceiling, a small hearth in the center, and a small wooden rocking chair. Back and forth it went as the person in it—who didn't seem to hear their entrance—sat reading.

"Ahem." Brios cleared his throat as he approached the man.

The man practically leapt out of his chair and whipped around to see what the noise was, "Ahh, Brios, lovely to see you again." The man was short, a head shorter than Orion who, on his own, was short. His head was covered by maybe a half a centimeter of grey hair on either side of his head with the middle being bald completely. Both the hair and the light grey eyes blended perfectly together to mark him as ancient. And his black pajamas and fluffy slippers marked him as a man who seldom walked outside of the library. His speech was thick and lifeless, drawing out every syllable in a way that only an old man could do.

"Hey Holland, nice to see you again too," Brios said sighing.

"I see you've brought some friends huh?" Holland said as he turned his attention to Haran and Orion.

"The name is Orion of Norhall fief in Anjagor, and this is Haran, my apprentice," Orion said.

"The name is Holland, but wait you already know that," Holland said with a little laugh.

Orion didn't even smile and said, "We've come to ask you an important question about the wolf god."

"Ahh, Albalupius, yes, quite the controversial god these days. What do you need to know?" Holland asked as he moved to a shelf across the room. The Outryders followed his movement.

"We need to know how to kill it," Orion said stoically. Holland shot a worried glance over to the Outryder.

"Then you have come to the wrong person. No human can kill a god, and even if they could I could serve no role in it," Holland said as he made his way back to the fireplace. Orion looked to Brios, his eyes saying many things at once.

However, before he could speak, Haran interjected. "Please Mister, I have had terrible visions of the wolf tearing everyone I love apart limb to limb. I cannot just sit and watch this if it were to take place, there must be something you may tell us. Or do something that can help us kill the wolf."

"Fine," Holland said, "But I will just tell you the story of the god of destruction. I know not the way to kill him."

Haran nodded his understanding and Holland went back to his chair next to the fireplace. The three Outryders followed him, taking a seat on a rather comfortable couch next to the old man's rocking chair. "Ok so as I am sure you are well aware by now; the gods have the ability to take form in the mortal plane. Manifestation is the term. Usually, they come in the form of animals such as a wolf as in Albalupius' case or as a hawk as in the case of his father. Or, in the case of his mother, a dove. Or in the case of his sister a—"

Orion knew where this was going so he decided to stop the old man in his tracks. "Holland. The history please."

"Oh yes yes," Holland said stopping his pointless rant. "Well, as the story goes many millennia ago the god of time called Cuthar fell in love with the goddess of creation, Nala. They had many children but the first two were twins, Albalupius and his sister Felashiva. And even though they were bound together by birth, these two were opposites in every way. Albalupius was born the god of death and destruction, and Felashiva born the goddess of life and restoration. However, they did both have one thing in common; the absolute desire to be called the god of order. Each struggled for millennia trying to one up each other in attempts to prove themselves worthy of their parents' attentions. However, only one could be given the title, and that winner was Felashiva. However, as appropriate to their births, their powers were forced to balance out. Therefore, the title of the god of chaos was granted to Albalupius. In rage the god snapped on his parents and was the first god to ever pass over to the mortal plane. In doing so he landed here, in Athon, and thus began the worshipping of Albalupius as the one true god. However, Felashiva followed Albalupius down here and after a fierce battle that destroyed half the country, she sent him back to the godly realm. Ever since then he has been imprisoned and Felashiva has been his warden. But now it seems that he has escaped as prophesied, but that also means that Felashiva must have followed him down here. And that spells out the end to the world itself."

Haran was confused at the end of Holland's speech. Felashiva, the name sounded familiar to him, then it clicked, "What did you say Felashiva took form as again?"

Holland looked up confused by the question. "A lioness. Why?"

Haran and Orion locked eyes. Shiva was a lioness. Haran had always known that Lupe was far bigger than a normal wolf, but he always just assumed that Shiva was a regular size for a lion. However, now that he thought about it, it made sense, he had found Shiva right around the time when Lupe was born and the only thing that seemed to be able to hurt Shiva was Lupe himself. Could it be true? Could Shiva be a goddess?

CHAPTER

15

Ella woke up in her bed again, it had almost been a week since Lottie and Gilpin went after the Outryders. She was still furious with Lottie for even pursuing his rival. He had nothing to prove to her or to anyone. Well, no one except for himself. However furious she may be, she could see now why the boy had done it. He was trying to prevent from more conflict happening in the future.

In their absence Percival continued doing what he had before, rapidly converting agnostics to Lupism as he referred to the religion as. Ever since the revealing of Lupe as Albalupius those associated with Lottie and the wolf were treated with the utmost of respect as to avoid the wrath of the god.

Percival had another speech planned later in the evening which everyone in the entire cavern would be forced to attend. To accommodate for all the people, he would be making the speech from the balcony of the house. This meant that everyone in the house would have to stand dutifully beside him as he made the speech. *Figures*, she thought when she was told to be at the speech, *we are nothing more than symbols to him.* She nearly threw up at the thought of being a part of someone's trophy family.

Standing supportive by the side of someone she knew so little about frightened her. However, if it was necessary for the country to remain in one piece while Lottie and Gilpin were gone she would do it.

The speech was scheduled in three hours' time so Ella figured she could go get some training in before then. She weaved in between the very busy looking residents as she moved down the main gravel street of Randint Cavern. She passed close to a hundred houses, the courtyard, the clock tower, and the crop fields as she made her way to the training area. Inside the training area Ella saw Jet training alone in the center of the sand pit. He was practicing his sword strokes on a wooden dummy when she approached him, "Where is everyone?"

"We have already had training today, so they've gone home," Jet replied stopping what he was doing.

"And why haven't you?" Ella asked casually.

"Nothing better to do I suppose," Jet replied.

"What about your family? Where are they?" Ella asked.

"My mother is in another country," Jet said, "and my dad, well let's just say my dad is no longer around anymore."

"He's dead isn't he?" Ella asked. She knew that glimmer of sadness that filled his eyes. The slight twinkle of happiness as he recalled his father's face, but the eventual change to sadness as he realized he could never see it again. And that every time he looked in the mirror he would only see his father. She knew because she too experienced the same thing every time she spoke about her father.

Jet nodded. "He was murdered ten years ago while... visiting Norhall." He turned to Ella as her face shifted into a frown, "You lost your father too didn't you?"

"Yes," Ella said, "In the Athonian invasion. He fought off dozens of soldiers letting me and my mother run to safety, but eventually I saw him murdered in front of my eyes."

Ella saw Jet shift uncomfortably from where he was standing. An awkward silence passed between them before Ella eventually said, "Wait, if your mother is alive then why aren't you with her?"

Jet's black eyes shined off the radiant crystals in the walls leaving a hint of light in their never-ending darkness. "I am searching for someone. A relative of mine. She's been lost for a long time."

"Interesting," Ella said diverting her gaze from Jet's relaxing eyes. "Do you think I could help you find her?"

"I think you can yes," Jet said as he moved to sheath his sword. "In fact, I think you can help me more than either of us realize."

Ella was confused but she continued the conversation. "So how long have you been here in Randint?"

Jet pondered on the question a little and then replied. "A month or so." Then he smiled. "Hey, I got a question. Would you have noticed me if not for Lottie?"

"Oh definitely, you are hard to miss." Ella laughed slightly. "You stick out in here like a sore thumb."

"I can't tell if that's a good or a bad thing," Jet replied.

"It's definitely good," Ella noted, her cheeks turning light pink, then she began to move to the door. "Well, I might want to go get ready for the speech later."

"Oh yeah, I forgot about that," Jet said as he moved to the door with her. "Well. Look out for me there. Shouldn't be too hard since I 'stick out like a sore thumb', as you so kindly put it."

Ella laughed and said her goodbyes. She saw the boy leave with a renewed sense of interest. He was an enigma and she would make it a point to get to know him better in the coming weeks.

By the time the clock struck one, the entire nation was standing in the streets just below the mansion. Thousands of citizens filled the streets as they all waited nervously wondering why Percival had called them there.

Ella, Keryn, and Sylvia were preparing for the event when Percival walked in as dashing as always. He wore a bleach white suit with a black tie and black shoes unintentionally matching the marbled floors of the house in a satisfying way. Keryn wore much the same clothes as Percival other than the fact that the suit was a size too big on his small body. Ella and her mom both wore basic peach-colored dresses with a simple green broach on their chest, but they both pulled them off gracefully. Ella also wore her pearl necklace that her father gave her before his death. She wore it every day, but it was usually covered by her clothes. Now the necklace was visible and shining brilliantly off the illuminating crystals of the cavern.

"Quite the crowd don't you think?" Percival said as he walked over to sit on a chair beside Sylvia.

"Yes. Quite," Sylvia said as she finished fixing her hair in the clear mirror on her wall.

"Well, I needed a big stage for my next announcement and what better the stage than that of an entire country," Percival said convincedly.

Ella noticed his words and asked a very simple question, "What announcement?"

Percival smiled and got up from his chair, "You'll see... come now let's get going, my people are waiting for us."

My people? Ella thought, Percival was only acting as a leader in Gilpin's absence, but he referred to the Lupens as his people? What was his game? She pushed the thought out of her head and walked out onto the balcony behind Percival.

Percival was the first to emerge onto the balcony then Sylvia, next Ella, and finally, Keryn. They walked out to deafening applaud that lasted for many minutes before it died down. In those minutes Ella scanned the crowd for the dark-haired boy. She saw him almost immediately. He was standing in the front of the crowd looking directly at her; his eyes bored deeply into her sending a wave of anxiety yet bliss down her spine. She waved him a second hello of the day and smiled at him.

When the applause died down Percival took the advantage to speak. Loud and clear he spoke, his words ringing off the walls of the expansive cavern. "Dear people of Randint Cavern, as you know we have suffered greatly since the birth of the Lupen kind. We were persecuted for our beliefs, pushed out of our country, and when we were heinous enough to simply try and find another home; we were invaded and driven underground. However, it does not end there, after some 100 years of somewhat peace between our invaders and us, Anjagor's king ruthlessly murders our leader for simply existing out of the purviews of their tyrannical reign. Now. That being said I am pleased to announce that we are done bending the knee for that wicked king and his iron fisted Outryders. For just this morning we began making plans to take Castle Norhall within the next few weeks. And we will take it for the glory of Albalupius. We will take it for the glory of the Lupens."

As Percival finished there was a resounding applause from the audience below and a chant began to form, "Lupus Vivat- Lupus Vivat- Lupus Vivat- Lupus Vivat- Lupus Vivat"

When the chant died down Percival spoke again, "That being said which of you valiant men would like to join me in this task?" Almost every man in the crowd raised their hand. This is where Ella snapped, she turned and stormed inside, slamming the door behind her.

After everyone dissipated from their doorstep, Ella made her way down the hall and into Gilpin's office, which Percival had now claimed for his own. Which infuriated her even more. Without even knocking she opened the door and stormed into the office. "How dare you make a decision like this without Gilpin present, when he gets back I will make sure you are beheaded for treason on the highest degree. Who are you to make these decisions anyway? Oh, and don't get me *started* on trying to recruit men who have probably never held a sword in their life. They are not sacrifices to your god or whatever cause suits your needs. They are people with families and lives."

"Are you finished yet?" Percival asked and Ella nodded relentingly, so Percival continued, "Ok then, well first of all, Gilpin told me to go ahead with his plan while he was gone and secondly these men willingly signed up for the siege, and there is no doubt that they will serve the cause valiantly and courageously."

Ella's faced turned from red to purple, "You have brain washed these people into thinking you are some type of altruistic and capable man, but you are not, you are a phony who just wanted a spot at the table. Why would Gilpin ever give you so much power as to move pawns like a leader of men?"

"I can tell you why. Failure," Percival said, he saw Ella's face switch from anger to confusion so he decided it would be best to explain. "You see everyone has a motive that can drive them to do crazy things. Gilpin wants to make up for his failure to Doran. Lottie wants to prove to you and to himself that he can best his rival. Perhaps that desire can lead even to the point of killing him."

"He would never kill Haran," Ella said convincedly.

"How can you be so sure about that?" Percival asked, "From what I have heard King Nigel killed his own brother to protect his country; who says Lottie won't kill a rival to protect you? You see everyone has something that makes them tick, and I can figure all of them out. I mean without even meeting him I know that the boy Haran wants so desperately to live up to the expectations that comes with being Orion's apprentice. And Orion wants to protect his apprentices at all costs because he feels he failed someone in the past. However, you are different Ella Frenger. I can't pin you down quite yet. Maybe you can enlighten me?" As he was speaking Percival got up and walked over to the bookshelf where he grabbed a sizable book.

Ella looked at him dazed, she actually didn't know what to say to that, and he was so charismatic in his approach, "I don't know. I feel kind of useless right now if I am honest..." she said trailing off.

"Then perhaps, instead of fighting me, you can join me," Percival said.

Ella snapped out of the daze instantly, "Never."

Percival tutted in disapproval, "It really is a shame then."

Ella looked at him confused, "What do you mean? You ask for what makes me tick. What if I asked the same?"

What makes me tick?" Percival asked, Ella nodded. She saw the man pause for a second as if he were trying to think of what to say next. "I want to serve my god as best as I can, and sometimes that means… well chaos," Percival replied as he blitzed across the room.

Ella tried to draw her sword as she saw him move towards her, but Percival smacked it out of her hand with the heavy book he picked up. He then wrapped his arms around her and put his hand over her mouth, "Now now now, we wouldn't want your mother to hear your screams now would we. You see I can't kill you right now because I would surely get caught, but I swear to you. If you speak a word of our conversation today to anyone, I will make you watch me kill your entire family, and then when Lottie and Gilpin get back, I will make you watch me kill them too. Understood?"

Ella nodded her head, but as he eased the pressure she broke free from his grasp and dived for her sword on the floor some two meters away. However, he grabbed her by her foot while she was in the middle of the air and drug her across the hard wood floor. He picked her up and clamped her mouth shut once more. With his free hand he pulled his knife from its sheath at his side and said, "Hopefully this will make you understand." He slowly slid the knife down her left cheek leaving a shallow cut about a few centimeters long down her face.

He let go and said, "Now leave, you will not speak a word of this to anyone."

She grabbed her sword and walked out of the office, head down. Utterly defeated.

CHAPTER

16

Haran came back inside with Shiva. "Could this be your god?" he asked.

Holland crouched and studied the animal for a short while and eventually said, "Oh dear, there is no doubt that this is her."

"Are you sure?" Haran asked. "I found Shiva months before the wolf was even born. And if it is true when you say that she followed the wolf down here, shouldn't she have been born after?"

Holland thought about it for a second then said, "Well to be honest I don't have an answer to that question, but this is her I am sure of it. Those eyes match the drawings perfectly."

"So, what do we do now then?" Haran asked.

"We find a way to kill that wolf," Orion said.

Holland looked around at the three Outryders in front of him, "I can't help with your research, but if you are determined to find a way. I have plenty of books in here if you would like to take a look at them."

Orion looked at Haran and back at Holland, "Thank you sir, you have no idea what it means to us. We will sleep outside for however long we are here."

Holland nodded his appreciation and Orion turned to Brios, "I guess this means you will be on your way then?"

Brios met his eyes and offered his hand, "I suppose. I must get back to that bastard Argo before he realizes I am gone. Be careful you two."

"We will," Orion said as he met his colleague's hand.

Brios nodded and walked out of the door to resume his undercover life. "You Outryders are quite the breed aren't you," Holland said as he saw the door close.

"They really are amazing," Haran said with a small frown. *They?* He was an Outryder as well, but why didn't he feel like it? Ever since Lyra brought up finding the identity of his father he felt so… lost. She had reminded him that of who he really was. Nobody. An orphan boy pretending to be something more than what he was worth. Nothing.

That night they set up camp in the clearing. Camp was a small fire and two one-man tents, anything more would just take too long to set up. They sat around the fire casually watching the logs in the fire slowly dwindle to nothing more than ash. As he looked into the fire he thought about Brios. The man was so assertive and competent, yet in the presence of Orion he was deferential to man's opinions. Haran looked up from the fire and said, "It is crazy how even an accomplished Outryder like Brios still looked up to you as if you were a superior."

"Yes I suppose," Orion said. "Respect is a hard thing to earn, and even I shouldn't be as revered as I am today."

"How do you mean?" Haran asked. Orion's name held weight behind it in Norhall and presumably the whole country. He was known as the most dangerous man in the

Outryders with his legend even rivaling that of the founder himself, Outin Ryder.

"You know my plan at the Battle of the Anvil?" Orion asked.

"Of course," Haran said recalling the events that transpired. "You led the Athons into a trap as they were forced to attack the Anjagorian army and then led a surprise force to the rear of the Athons leaving them between a metaphorical hammer and anvil."

"Well, those weren't my plans, actually, they were the plans of a brilliant man. They were the plans of your father," Orion said deciding it was about time he told Haran what he knew.

Haran shot up instantly. "You knew my father?"

Impossible. No one knew his father, not Baron Ligate, not the townsfolk, not anyone. He had asked around for years with nothing but a satchel to prove his father's existence. His father was a ghost.

Orion shook his head, "Very well. Actually, I would even go as far to say he was my closest friend."

Haran had so many questions flowing through his head, but the first of them were, "So, what happened to him? How did he die?"

"His death was the product of the worst of my failures," Orion said, "The day before the Battle of the Anvil, your father and I were getting set up for our plan when unexpectedly he decided to go on a walk and asked me to accompany him. On our way back to the camp, we were ambushed by three dozen Athonian soldiers. Now your father was an even better fighter than myself, but we were greatly outnumbered. Back-to-back we fought off the endless stream of soldiers that is until I got cut…" He paused and pulled down his shirt to show a long gash from his shoulder to right below his chest. "I collapsed to the ground in pain leaving his back exposed. However, he still fought, beating them back until there were only five left, but the fatigue had set in for him, and all of his adrenaline dumped. He missed one parry from a side stroke and collapsed to the ground beside me. Red with rage I picked myself up and finished the job, but it was too late, he was dying at my feet. He told me to lead his troops into the battle, and to take care of his wife and son. Unfortunately, I failed him again on the second account, your mother was taken during the war, and you were left an orphaned child on the floor of a wrecked house."

It was difficult for Haran to process what he had just been told, all of his questions had been answered except for one, "So who was my father then?"

"Your father was Atticus Ryder, son of Roman Ryder who was the son of Outin Ryder," Orion said.

Haran's world shifted at the mention of the name. "The Outin Ryder? Like the founder of the Outryders?" Orion nodded his head yes. His head began to spin in on itself. Everything he assumed about his heritage was wrong. He thought his father was a nobody a nothing, but he was an icon. A legacy. "So that means… Outin Ryder was my great grandfather."

"Oh yes indeed my boy, you are pure of blood. Outryder through and through," Orion said.

Haran thought for a minute, he was no longer the orphan boy he had once been only minutes before. He was a legacy. The last of the Ryder blood. He was no longer a speck of dirt in a field; he was the field. He smiled to himself slightly. "Huh, Haran Ryder, it's got a ring to it don't you think?"

Orion fully smiled for the first time since Haran became his apprentice. Orion truly smiled.

The next morning, they woke up at dawn and got straight to work on their researching on how to kill Albalupius. There were many books in Holland's library, but the ones essential to their research was in the religion section in the back right corner of the expansive library. The religion section consisted of about five rows with about twenty books in each. *This will take a while,* Haran thought. Holland had already set up a table and two chairs to better accommodate their stay, but as he said the night before, he would not associate with killing a god. The first book that Haran picked out was a book called *The Athonian Pantheon,* once he opened it he realized that it was entirely written in the Athonian language, "Hey Orion, this book... I can't read it."

Orion looked up from his book that was also written in Athonian, but apparently, he was well versed in the language. "Here take this," he said as he handed him a book that translated every word in the Athonian language to a word in common tongue. The book was thicker than Haran's head, and wider as well. Haran sighed softly, so much for getting home within a few weeks, this was going to take them months at best.

After translating the book word for word all day, he only read some ten pages in. Haran figured out that a pantheon was the collective amount of gods from a certain religion. In addition, he learned that the Athonian Pantheon started when Cuthar, the god of time, overthrew the three most powerful gods called Titans. After he overthrew the Titans a civil war broke out among the gods and Cuthar wiped half of them from existence. Cuthar then reversed time to when the world first began and met the goddess of creation, Nala. They then began replenishing the pool of gods among those including: Albalupius, the god of chaos, Felashiva, the goddess of order, Khilo, goddess of wisdom, and Zircon, god of fortune. There were many more, and the book went into detail into how each one's powers affect the mortal world. However, after scanning through the section on Albalupius he discovered no new information, so Haran put the book down for the day and passed out on the hardwood table.

The next morning Haran woke up and continued reading the book about the pantheon. He thought maybe there would be something worth the read in there. However, when he was nearing the end of the book all that he learned was how expansive the pantheon of the Athon was. With fifteen major gods and roughly a hundred minor ones, the Athonian Pantheon contained so many strange names that he thought his head was going to explode. Frustrated, Haran slammed his head on the desk, instantly regretting it, and went to find a new book.

The book he picked out didn't have a title and was shorter than all the other ones. The cover was just a piece of tattered leather that looked as if it had been through many years of severe weather and journeys. Turns out it had because when he opened it, it was not a book at all. It was a journal, and it was written in the common tongue. The author was a researcher during the time when Albalupius first arrived, and he had many notes on his findings. In the light from a wax candle, Haran read the first of these entries:

"6/6, 1232

I caught a glimpse of the wolf last night. He ripped through the small town of Revit destroying everything in the process. Women and children fled from the scene frantically as the men fought desperately to hold off the wolf and his master. His master was olive in skin, but his face was pale, almost as if he was scarred. He was a giant man, but very quick with the sword, and the few men that got past the distracted wolf were easily dispatched by the master swordsman."

A few entries later, the author wrote:
"6/19, 1232

The wolf was in Selia yesterday with his master when a big cat came out of nowhere and attacked to wolf. From my research, it looks like the cat comes from the plains of Afros, but I can't be sure. It is strange though because both animals seem to have an unnatural connection to their masters; the cat's master is rather small, at least compared to the wolf's master, but he is equally skilled. They fought for several minutes before the wolf retreated with his master. They seem to slowly be making their way to the capital, and Gora stands the only obstacle for them to be stopped at. I am heading there now trying to arrive before the wolf and his master."

Haran thought for a minute, Gora was the city they were in, maybe that's why this journal was here. He continued reading:

"6/22, 1232

I reached Gora this morning and talked to many citizens who have heard of the white wolf causing terror through Athon. They claim it is their forbidden god Albalupius and that he came down from the heavens to torment their lives. Now, I don't believe much in gods, but it would explain his sudden appearance and his seemingly infinite strength. I asked them about the cat as well and they claim it is also one of their gods called Felashiva come to stop Albalupius."

Haran thought the journal was getting boring now, and that no new information would be in it, but on the last page he read:

"8/19, 1232

It's been almost two months since Albalupius and Felashiva disappeared. After the death of the wolf's owner, both the gods disappear. I have a theory that the gods were tied to their owners somehow as well as each other. I have concluded that when one of the owners died, or even as far as when the connection was broken, both the gods returned to the godly realm."

Haran read it repeatedly. *When one of the owners died... both the gods returned to the godly realm.* He found it. He found how to kill Albalupius. He discovered the cracked code. "Orion come here now."

Orion got from the other side of the table stepping over Shiva, who was laying down at Haran's feet, and looked at

141

the journal entry and back at Haran. "That's it Haran, that's how you kill Albalupius."

After the initial excitement wore down, Haran stuffed the journal into his satchel and hung his head. *Wait,* he thought. If he was Shiva's master and Lottie was Lupe's master that meant… That meant either he or Lottie had to die to kill the god.

He saw the realization dawn on Orion's face as well as they were both thinking the same thing. After a moment Haran shook his head no to his master. *No,* he thought, *I can't kill Lottie there has to be another way.*

Orion look switched from hopeless to tense as he saw a light outside. Haran heard Spirit's neigh outside. It was a warning; someone was out there. Gesturing for Haran to be silent, they both moved towards the door. Holland and Haran hid behind the shelf closest to the door with Shiva sitting to Haran's right. Orion approached the door and saw the light coming through the crack. Silence filled the room as Orion came closer to the door… three meters… two meter…one meter… BOOM. The door flung open and off the hinges knocking Orion to the ground. And in the doorway Haran saw two dark figures illuminated by two torches.

Gilpin and Lottie had arrived.

CHAPTER

17

J ust over a week after Haran and Orion left for their trip to Athon Lyra received the records she had hoped would lead her to figure out who Haran's parents were. Even the records from a single year filled up half the room with boxes. The first few boxes consisted of the names and addresses of every citizen of Norhall during that year. She read through the names thoroughly although she knew they would be little to no help. She saw familiar names like Ligate, who at that time had been a general in Norhall's army. She also saw a familiar name to her, Hartfell, Heide's family name. However, there was nothing that could point to Haran's parents. The next few boxes were of income and tax revenue of citizens during that year. That also served her no purpose other than hours of combing through numbers.

And finally, the last five boxes were of troop movements and Outryder reports during the times of the Athonian invasion.

The tactics of the battle were simple, the forces of Norhall and adjacent fiefs were to hold their ground in Norhall fief while Anjagor prepared more troops for reinforcements. However, the Outryder at the time, a man by the name of Atticus Ryder made plans to stop the invasion in its tracks and prevent further loss of life. *Atticus Ryder*, she thought, could he be related to Outin Ryder. Surely it couldn't be a coincidence that their family names were the same. She continued reading, apparently to stop the invasion Atticus brought together ten Outryders and three hundred of Norhall's men and hid them in the trees in Fuestres Woods. The reports continued all the way up until the day before the final battle when they stopped for good. She flipped through the papers frantically trying desperately to find out what happened to Atticus, but there was nothing.

Nothing except for a small parchment drawing at the bottom of the last box of two man dressed in the green drabs of the Outryder. The man on the left she easily recognized as Orion, although his partially grey hair was significantly more blond. The connection between Orion and Atticus wasn't strange in any way; Orion *was* most renowned for his part in the Battle of the Anvil. That was until she looked at the man on Orion's right. Atticus Ryder. His sandy blond hair and sea green eyes looked so familiar to her. The man looked so much like Haran that she began to think she had found Haran's father. Her suspicions were proven correct when she saw what Atticus wore at his waist; a brown satchel with a small rip in the front of it likely from getting caught on underbrush and right beside the rip…a big R surrounded by a circle. That was no random satchel, that was Haran's satchel, and it belonged to a Atticus Ryder.

She practically jumped from where she was sitting on the floor. *Haran's a Ryder. Haran's a Ryder.* She repeated in her head. It made no sense, but there was no doubt; that man in the drawing was Haran's father. she had to tell someone about her discovery. However, Haran wasn't there. *Why isn't Haran here* she thought, cursing to herself slightly. He would be ecstatic over the news.

She pocketed the drawing and ran out of the cabin and onto her horse, Ranger. Riding him out of the woods. She thought about who she would tell as she was riding into town. Who would be close enough to Haran so that his heritage doesn't get out to the public? The first person to come to mind was Baron Ligate. However, she ruled him out due to lack of trust. There was only really one person she could tell, but she dreaded doing it. She had to go talk to Heide and fast.

She walked into the courier "school" shortly after midday. School was a loose term, it was little more than a classroom. It was situated in the middle of town to the right of the bakery and to the left of the inn. The building wasn't very big, at best being able to hold twenty people if you squeezed them in tight. The inside of the building was just one big room where the master courier, Anna, would teach her students the ways of diplomacy. It was a highly respected position even if the teaching area wasn't the largest. When Lyra walked in she saw Anna handing out papers to the girls in the class. As the door shut loudly behind her, all eight courier heads turned to her. Lyra wanted to look down to hide herself from their judgmental faces, but she kept her head high. She was an Outryder after all.

"Ahh, an Outryder walks into a courier school. Sounds like the start of a really bad joke," Anna jested. The couriers in the room laughed politely.

Lyra glanced around not daring to crack a smile. She hated couriers, they were all so gracefully perfect and full of themselves in the worst kind of way. They got what they wanted when they wanted and from whomever they wanted. *Or maybe that was just Heide,* she thought.

She caught a glimpse of Heide's scarlet hair sitting at the front of the room, "Don't mind me sorry, I just needed to talk to Heide about something very important."

"Oh wonderful," Anna said as she handed out the last of the papers. "You know, I just gave her an assignment and she lacks proper protection. I was going to ask one of the Battleschool boys, but you are here now. So will you accompany her?"

Lyra clenched down on her jaw. She could hardly say no to the master courier in a room full of her apprentices. "Of course, when do you need me to do it?"

"Now preferably," Anna said.

"Fine with me,' Lyra said. In fact, it was not fine, just the idea of spending the entire day with Heide was something she dreaded. She turned to the redheaded girl in the front of the room, "let's go Heide." Heide got up ever so gracefully and followed her out of the building and onto the gravel streets of Norhall.

"Where are we going?" Lyra asked as she got onto Ranger. Heide followed suit.

"Randint Cavern," Heide said hopping on Ranger as well. "Anna asked me to try for peace with them once more on the king's orders." Lyra flinched slightly as she heard the destination. *Randint Cavern.* It hadn't been long since she was last in the giant cave, but she had not wish to return ever again. She recalled sitting in a dark, damp room for what felt like an eternity. She recalled going to bed every night wondering if she would wake up the next day. She recalled hearing that her best friend had abandoned her leaving her to the whims of their captors.

"Are you sure you want to go down there?" Lyra asked mainly talking to herself.

"Yes. If I can make even the slightest bit of difference to prevent a coming war, I will do it unquestionably," Heide said. Lyra looked at her with a renewed interest. She thought the girl was nothing more than a coward, going through each day taking what she wanted when she wanted because she was perfect. However, now Heide was claiming she wanted to help? What was her angle? What did she want?

"Then I shall follow your lead," Lyra said.

They entered Randint Cavern through the shack on the edge of town. There were two guards posted there, they nodded their recognition to the Outryder and moved swiftly out of the way. "Watch the horse will you?" Lyra asked the two guards who simply nodded.

The layout of the shack hadn't changed since she and Haran had last been in there, it was expected seeing as few had entered or left the shack since then. She stuck her finger in the small hole feeling her way to a small button and the rock door slid down the adjacent wall. She walked through and did the same on the other side of the door; the door slid loudly back up. "So odd," she whispered to herself as she grabbed a torch off the wall and struck it with the flint she had in her pocket.

They walked in silence down the tunnel for half an hour until Heide spoke. "So, you wanted to talk to me?"

Lyra reached into her pocket and pulled out the small drawing. "Yes, it's about Haran."

"I thought he was in Athon. Is he okay?" Heide asked. *Of course he told her,* Lyra thought, *why wouldn't he?*

"He is with Orion. I am sure he is fine, but no. I actually need you to take a look at this," Lyra said as she handed Heide the drawing.

Heide looked over the drawing for a minute and then spoke. "Wait that is Haran's satchel, and those are Haran's eyes, but who is the man?"

"His name is Atticus Ryder, and I believe he is Haran's father," Lyra said.

"Ryder. Like Outin Ryder?" Heide asked voice peaking with curiosity.

"I believe so yes," Lyra said.

"Lyra, you know what this means right. It means you figured out who Haran's father was," Heide said with just the slighted hint of envy in her voice. "He will be so grateful." Lyra nodded her head, she sure hoped so. Haran would never admit it, but Lyra knew how lost he was since the battle at the canyon, and she hoped that such news will bring him a new sense of wonder to his life.

They walked into the cavern and were immediately met by two rather odious looking guards. They met the newcomers with a sense of distrust, but after Heide explained the situation they ever so kindly led the two women to the mansion at the top of the cavern.

When they entered the mansion, they were greeted by a woman that Heide apparently met last time, Sylvia. Lyra thought she looked much like Ella between the silky blond hair and the crystal blue eyes. Then she recalled Ella mentioning to her many months ago that she had reunited with her mother. This Sylvia must have been her. Sylvia led them up to the top floor and to the last door on the left. Inside sat Ella to the right and a stunning man to the left. The man had a chiseled jaw and shining blue eyes; his sandy brown hair faded perfectly into his neatly trimmed beard. His eyes and nose aligned in the most perfectly symmetrical way that Lyra couldn't help but stare. Lyra quickly picked her jaw from off the ground and diverted her attention to Ella who gave her a weak smile.

Sylvia swiftly exited the door and left the four of them alone in the room. Heide was the first to speak, "Wait, where's Lottie and Gilpin?"

The man stood up, his muscles bulging from his light blue shirt as he went to shake their hands. "The name's Percival Woodberg. And to answer your question, they are otherwise preoccupied."

Lyra locked eyes with Ella and knew immediately where they were, Lottie and Gilpin had gone after Haran and Orion. She worried slightly for what happened when they met, but she trusted them to make it back in one piece.

"Well then, I assume you were the one put in charge here," Heide said to Percival who just simply nodded his head.

They began introducing themselves, but Lyra wasn't interested in that, for when she looked over to Ella once more she realized the girl had a very fresh scar on her left cheek. She interrupted the small talk between Heide and Percival. "Ella, what happened to your cheek?"

She noticed the slightest glance from Ella to Percival. "Oh, it was a sparring accident, it has been a while since I have held a sword and I got cut." Lyra simply nodded, immediately knowing it was a lie. That cut was not one of a sword, but it was of a small knife. A very sharp knife, and she was starting to think that this Percival guy had done it.

"Aw I am sorry Ella; it looks like it hurt," Heide said.

"I'm sure she is fine," Percival said with a smile. His teeth gleamed perfectly in the dim lighting of the office. Lyra looked at him skeptically, something about the man was odd, but she couldn't quite pin it. "Now, where were we miss Heide." They returned to their small talk, but again Lyra wasn't paying much attention. She was far too busy paying attention to Ella's foot behind the desk. The lamp on desk created a very apparent shadow of Ella's foot. TAP-TAP-TAP, the foot came up and down on the hardwood floor.

There was a three second pause. TAP-TAP.

Another three seconds passed. TAP.

Another pause. However, this pause was longer, five seconds. TAP.

TAP.

She kept going repeating the cycle. TAP-TAP-TAP. Pause TAP-TAP. Pause TAP. Longer pause TAP. Another pause TAP.

Lyra recognized the patterns. It was one that her foster mother taught her. It was a communication method they used to keep her identity as the princess of Athon a secret. Each letter in the alphabet had a corresponding number of taps and pauses. Taps signified some letters, while other letters had pauses in them. One second pauses meant they were on the same letter and three second pauses meant a change in letters. She knew the code well. However, one thing she didn't know was how Ella knew of it.

Whatever the case, the word that Ella spelled out with her taps left more questions in her head. S-I-E-G-E. Siege.

She looked around wondering if there was anything she could use to respond. There was no light pointed to her so she couldn't use shadows, and she couldn't just stomp her foot on the ground that would be far too obvious. She had to think of some way to respond and fast. The conversation between Heide and Percival was well under way.

She leaned forward acting as if she was trying harder to focus on the conversation. She then put her hand over her mouth as if she were pondering a difficult question. It would be obvious if Percival knew the code, but she hoped that Percival didn't as she tapped on her cheek.

TAP then she paused for five seconds. TAP-TAP-TAP. Three seconds passed, TAP. Another three seconds passed. TAP slight pause TAP. Then another three seconds passed. TAP.

She repeated this over and over again. Spelling out W-H-E-R-E.

Where?

She stopped when she saw Ella's foot start tapping again. The taps and pauses of Ella's foot spelled out H-O-M-E.

Home. She knew immediately that Ella was referring to Castle Norhall, so she tapped back W-H-E-N. When?

Three taps of Ella's foot signified that she estimated three weeks before the siege on Norhall. At this realization Lyra paused. *Three weeks?* She didn't even know if Haran and Orion would be back in three weeks. What if they weren't? What would she do? How would she be able to handle planning for a siege? She pushed the thoughts out of her head and sat back in her chair.

The conversation between Percival and Heide was coming to a close and within two minutes Heide stood up gracefully to make her exit. Lyra followed suit. "Well thanks again Percival," Heide said as she bowed slightly to the man. "And I understand that you do not have the power to sign such treaties. However, I would like to show my gratitude for you being respectful unlike your leader Gilpin."

"Oh yeah, he can be a real pain at times; however, I will treat no courier such as yourself in any other way than that of respect. You two have a great evening," Percival said.

After Lyra and Heide walked out of the mansion and onto the exit of Randint Cavern Heide turned to her, "Lyra you felt it too didn't you?" She saw Lyra's confused face and continued, "Percival. He had this strange glow about him he was almost too perfect."

"Yeah," Lyra said. She hadn't paid much attention to their conversation, but she could feel it in the air. That man had something sinister about him. "Ella's scar," Lyra added, "I think he caused it."

Heide pondered the accusation. "Why?"

"Because, Ella, she sent me a message," Lyra said, seeing the confusion on Heide's face she continued, "She said that they were going to siege Norhall in three weeks' time."

"Really?" Heide asked her voice raising a few decibels, "I didn't see her move at all, how could she have possibly sent you a message?"

Lyra smiled, "I have my ways."

CHAPTER

18

Orion flew back from where the door was kicked open by Gilpin. Both Lottie and Gilpin stood in the doorway with torches in hand while Lupe sat to Lottie's side. Haran stood up from where he was crouched behind a bookshelf. Questions flew through Haran's head. How were they here? How long had they been following them? He pushed the thoughts aside as he saw his master clutching his side some three meters away. Although Orion was visibly hurt he shot up almost instantly, taking his axes out of their sheaths. Haran followed suit.

"It looks like we've found you," Gilpin said menacingly.

"Looks like it, so you ready for round two already then?" Orion asked. "I mean after I dispatched you with such ease last time, surely you would think twice."

"Last time I was distraught, this time I am angry," Gilpin said as he tossed aside his torch and drew his weapon. Lottie did the same. Gilpin's torch landed on its head to where it was snuffed out quickly, but Lottie's torch landed next to the curtains around the windows. It took only a few seconds for them to catch fire and within just minutes the whole house would be in flames.

Gilpin attacked Orion with a renewed vengeance delivering near bone shattering blows with every swing of his sword. Haran and Lottie stood by as they watched their respective masters duel it out. There was no room in this place for more than one battle to take place at once.

Haran looked over to Holland who was in shock as he saw the fire raging ever closer to his precious collection of books. There was nothing he could do but stand there paralyzed. "Go," Haran said to the old man, "get out through the back door now."

"But my books. I can't let them burn," Holland said back frantically.

"It's either they burn or you do so GO," Haran said. Hesitantly Holland shuffled to the back door. Haran turned his attention to Shiva, "Follow," he said. Shiva followed Holland out the back door, he decided it best not to keep them both in here if it meant they might get hurt.

After Holland and Shiva went away it freed up the necessary wiggle room for Lottie and Haran to start fighting. When Haran turned around, he met a front kick from Lottie that sent him reeling into the bookshelves. His satchel went flying from his shoulder in the process. Haran's back slammed against the hard wood bookcase sending a jolt of pain down his whole spine. He got back up instantly, but his back still writhed in pain at every slight movement.

"This is it Haran, it ends here," Lottie said.

"If you kill me here, you lose, so no, I don't think it does," Haran said. Lottie launched a side cut at Haran's left side, but Haran barely got there to stop it. His back was stinging with the effort, but Haran still fought. He was barely holding his on with the stronger, and now faster,

Lottie. He had to think of something. He could try to use Contrium, but with the smoke that now filled the room he knew he couldn't pull it off. Lottie hit Haran with another front kick sending him flying through two more bookcases that crashed to the ground like dominoes. Haran struggled to get back up from the sheer pain that shot through his back, but he soon did and continued to be pushed back through the bookshelves and onto the only wall that had yet to catch fire. An idea popped into his mind, but he knew it would be risky. Between all the smoke in the air and the constant pain in his back, he was unsure if it would work. However, it was the only thing he could do, for the wall was approaching fast now.

Time slowed as he grew closer to the wall. He stepped to the side and ducked under Lottie's side cut. He could see both of Lottie's swords whiz past his nose as his back bent at such an unnatural angle. A new wave of pain shot up his back as he went back to a straight up position. He grimaced in pain, but he knew he couldn't stop now, he had to succeed, or he would surely die. He spun around Lottie to where Lottie's back was to him, and he front kicked him into the blank wall. In that instant he launched two knives in quick succession at the boy's clothes. The knives pinned Lottie's shirt deep into the wall on either side of his arm. *It worked!* Haran thought, *it actually worked.* He knew it wouldn't last forever though as Lottie was already struggling to get free from the wall.

He ran back through the fallen bookshelves, and, through the thick smoke, he saw his satchel on the ground some two meters away. However, as he moved to pick it up Lupe, who had been sitting in the doorway ever so patiently up to this point, moved in between Haran and his satchel. The wolf's beady blue eyes met Haran's eyes warningly. Lupe moved to pick up the satchel and held it in his mouth; it was a challenge for Haran to take it. Haran grunted, *of course,* he thought. Although the piercing blue eyes of the wolf was terrifying, Haran didn't dare break eye contact with the wolf. If he did he was all but dead.

Out of the corner of his eye he could see his master was still fighting dauntlessly through the heavy smoke. By this point Gilpin's initial rage was growing quieter and Orion was getting the upper hand. He noticed Haran's hesitation and said, "This is no place for a fight with that thing Haran, run, hide, I will be right behind you."

"No you won't," Gilpin said as he sent an overhead strike directly at Orion's skull to which Orion skillfully dodged.

Haran looked at the satchel in Lupe's mouth and then to Lottie pinned against the wall behind him. Lottie was wiggling his way free now, and it would only be a matter of time before he was pincered by both Lottie and Lupe.

No, he thought pausing, *I can't leave. They have my father's satchel.* The wolf was slowly approaching Haran who was paralyzed in indecision, "GO HARAN," Orion yelled as he parried a rather strong looking side stroke.

That seemed to snap him back to reality and, even though he hated to do it, he turned away from the wolf and looked to the exit. In the state his back was in there was no way he was winning the fight. So, he ran, leaving his satchel in the burning house. The satchel that contained the journal, Lyra's present and more importantly the satchel that belonged to his father.

When he got outside he whistled for Spirit who came galloping around the burning building. He got onto his horse and saw Holland some ten meters away crawling towards the burning house. He crawled about a meter before Shiva drug him away from the fire once more, "My books," he yelled. "They are all burning. Everything I have worked for. Everything is gone."

Haran rode over to the man at the edge of the clearing, "Holland, they are gone, please, let's just get out of here." Haran offered the man his hand.

"You don't understand. Those books are my legacy, without them who am I?" Holland asked desperately.

Haran paused for a second. He too had been asking the same question. He once defined himself on his family, nothing. However, now he carried the weight of generations of excellence. How could he compare. Who was Haran without the Ryder at the end? The answer started pouring out of Haran before he had more time to think, "You are *you* Holland. There will always be more books, but if you go into that fire there will never be another you." Holland stopped struggling against the lion and looked at the boy with a hint of gratitude in his eyes and took his hand, getting on to Spirit.

"Wait what of your master," Holland said, "you left him in there alone with those psychopaths?"

"He will be fine, he's an Outryder and the best of the best at that," Haran said as he urged Spirit to a gallop out of the woods with Shiva following directly behind them.

He rode until he reached the main road that broke off and led to his rendezvous point with Orion. They decided it best to have a meeting point in case they got in trouble soon after reaching Athon. It was Orion's idea of course, he thought that being in a foreign country to which Anjagor was on the brink of war with would put the two at threat. He was right on that account. Although they didn't imagine the threat would be coming from their homeland.

When Haran rode into the small clearing he saw no one there. "Are you positive your master would have survived? That was a bad fire, and he was in the middle of an intense fight."

"He'll show. He has to," Haran said convincedly.

They waited for hours in the foggy clearing until sunrise. Haran paced back and forth through the fog worriedly, *surely Orion should have been here by now*, he thought. Had his master actually died in the flames? If so, what would he do now? What would he do if Orion died?

Luckily that question remained unanswered as Haran saw a figure materialize through the fog. Soon after, the clop of horse hooves echoed through the trees. Haran stopped pacing as the figure got closer. Orion emerged from the fog on Nova covered in blood and soot.

"Orion!" Haran exclaimed as he went to hug his master, he smelled of thick smoke and looked worse for wear, but at least he was alive. "I had begun to think you died."

"Well, I was closer than I would like to admit unfortunately," Orion replied.

"How did you get out? Between Lottie, Gilpin, and the wolf, I thought you would be overwhelmed."

"I was up until the roof collapsed from the fire. The beam cut me off from them and I was left to freely escape through the back," Orion said.

Haran looked over to Shiva and saw that she was still there. The words from the journal flew through his head. *When one of the owners died… both the gods returned to the godly realm.* He turned back to Orion, "So I assume they are alive also?"

"Yes, they chased me out of the woods, but once I hit the flat ground Nova here blew their big horses out of the water," Orion said as he patted his horse.

"So what took you so long to get here then?" Haran asked. It had been some five or six hours since they arrived at the clearing.

"I had to deliver a message to Brios," Orion said getting off of his horse. "A warning, although there isn't much that he can do about it now."

Haran nodded and looked sternly at his master, "Orion. They have my satchel. I have to get it back."

"I know Haran. I know," Orion said. He knew how much the satchel meant to Haran, and he also knew that the boy wouldn't stop until he got it back. "However, I don't think they are giving up on their chase quite yet. In fact, I think I know where they will strike again, so be prepared for another fight."

"So where do we go then?" Haran asked.

"Home."

CHAPTER

19

Ella sat on her bed just after the meeting with Lyra and Heide. It was a risk using the code to warn Lyra of the siege. If Percival would have known it she would have surely been found out.

Ella was genuinely surprised when Lyra tapped back to her, she thought it was a miracle that Lyra also knew the code. She briefly pondered how the girl knew it, she recalled Lyra saying that her parents died in a Bianet raid a few years back, but she assumed that was a lie now that she knew the Outryder type. *Very secretive.* Whatever the case, the girl knew the code, and she now knows that Percival plans to siege Norhall which Ella saw as payback for the scar now slowly forming on her cheek.

Ella had been taught the code by her grandfather. They used it to talk behind her dad's back when he was still alive. *When.* She sighed slightly at the thought of her dad. He was so perfect, she thought. He was kind, loving, and strong, everything a man should be. Lottie was great, but no man could meet her expectations of a man, and she knew that, but something still bugged her about Lottie. First he was acting strange ever since she started hanging out with Jet. Was he jealous of their friendship? If so, why? Ella only knew Jet because of Lottie, if not for the attack on that convoy they never would have met in the first place. Surely Lottie should know that she only had feelings for him. Or did she? He abandoned her while he was out for revenge with the Outryders. Even after he had promised to not go after them unprovoked. Worst of all, he left her with a psychopathic cult leader who planned to take over Norhall within the coming weeks, and she had no idea how to stop it. She didn't even know if Lottie would be back before the siege even happened.

As the thoughts flew through her head at the speed of light she felt herself slowly drifting to sleep. *No,* she thought, *can't sleep. What if Percival comes in?* She had been on edge ever since Percival revealed his true intentions. How could she sleep in the same house with a psychopath that had given her the scar that still stung on her cheek? She lied about the origin of the scar. She lied to Lyra. She lied to Heide. Most importantly, she lied to her own mother. Why did she lie? Why was she so scared?

She didn't know the answers, and, after pondering it for many more minutes, she decided it best to get up and get some training in. Maybe training would distract her mind. Her mother was sitting on the couch reading a book when Ella waved her goodbye and walked out the door and onto the training area.

After walking inside, she saw Tomas and Tyson sparring, Tomas with his spear and buckler, and Tyson with his club. They were evenly matched in the most part. Tomas was small and fast, but Tyson was also very fast for his size, so he would occasionally land a strike. And when he did, it was devastating. The most recent one, one that Tomas was still recovering from, had sent Tomas across the whole sand pit and face down in the dirt.

Tyson also had his fair share of injuries; he was clutching his side from where Tomas kicked his exposed ribs. He also had a bruise on his bicep from the blunted weapon.

She was still impressed at how Lottie had bested both of them with the relative ease he did; she always knew he was a natural, but now she realized that there were levels to the sheer skill. They noticed her entrance after a few more minutes and then waved her over and say their hellos.

"So, how often do you two practice together?" whe asked. It was like every time she went to train they were there. She knew they had practice with the blue group four times a week, but that was only for a few hours' tops.

"We try to come in here for at least four hours every day. I mean there is no other way we are going to catch up to Lottie and Jet if we don't," Tomas said as he wiped the blood from around his lip. "Speaking of Lottie, where did he go?" Tomas asked. "I haven't seen him here in a while?"

"He's in…" She paused, thinking whether or not to tell them, "He's being Lottie. He's doing what Lottie thinks is best for Lottie, and sometimes that means he goes against the wishes of his ever so loving girlfriend." She noticed the two boys share a glance and saw their eyes get wider. "What?" She demanded.

Tomas and Tyson shared another glance to which Tyson just simply nodded to, Tomas spoke, "Well, he would never tell you this, but recently I don't think you've been acting so *ever loving* as you so boldly put it."

Ella's face scrunched in confusion and her tone became sharp and cold, "What exactly do you mean by that Tomas?"

Tomas flinched slightly under Ella's steely gaze, but he still spoke, "I mean for the past few weeks you have been treating Lottie like a second thought. I mean if you were so *ever loving* you would wake up and wonder if he's okay not resent him for leaving. He just wants to feel cared for Ella, and you haven't been providing that."

Ella grew angry now, "What do you know about mine and Lottie's personal lives?"

"It's not that hard to see Ella. He has it written all over his face if you would just pay attention," Tyson interjected.

Ella was taken aback by the sudden realization, had she really been distant with Lottie recently? I mean if both Tomas and Tyson picked up on Lottie's feelings before she did, what does that say about how much she cared? She spoke again but her voice was one of defeat, "I think you might be right. I have just been so distracted since the battle at Calcore to even consider him."

Tomas spoke this time, "One more thing. Don't give excuses for your actions, that's cheap just do better from here on out."

Ella heard the door open up behind her and unsurprisingly she saw Jet emerge through, she ran up to him and hugged him tightly, "Hey Jet. I have been wondering where you were. Do you still need help with finding that person?"

"Yes actually that's why I've been looking for you," Jet said, "I think she may be somewhere in Norhall. Care to come look for her with me?"

"Of course, why don't we go now?" Ella asked.

"Sure," Jet said as he moved his way to the door. Tyson and Tomas simply sighed as they both walked out the door. They tried.

Ella and Jet walked out of the tunnel that let out at Calcore Canyon around midday. According to Jet, all the other entrances were blocked off by Norhall soldiers, but it seems they were unaware of this one. "So, do you have any leads on where your family member might be?"

"I have an inkling, but nothing exact, I just need some information is all," Jet said as he walked up the steep path of Calcore Canyon.

"What is she to you exactly? Sister?" Ella asked.

"Cousin," Jet said distractedly. "Do you know where I can get information in this fief?"

"Hmm, I am sure the tavernkeeper in town knows something, everyone who travels here goes through there," Ella said as they emerged at the top of the canyon. She looked over some ten meters away where the battle took place just over a month ago. She could still see the skid marks on the ground from that night and the accompanying blood that stained the ground.

She shuddered slightly at the thought of the battle. Jet seemed to notice, "What's wrong?" She told him of the battle that took place, but only of the battle between Haran and Lottie. Out of precaution, she decided it best to withhold the important information.

"Sounds terrible. I can't believe there is another that can best Lottie in a fight," Jet said.

"Another? Who's the other?" Ella asked curiously, as far as she'd known Lottie had only lost to Haran in a fair fight.

"Me of course," Jet said as he pushed forward toward the town.

Ella laughed and jogged slightly to catch up. "You think you can beat Lottie?"

Jet simply smiled, "I know I can beat Lottie. He's great and he is a definite natural, but he stands no chance against me."

"Oh really now because I seem to recall I beat you pretty easily," Ella chuckled.

Jet grew defensive, "I let you win so you could join us on the mission."

"I'm sure you did mister hotshot, but if you can't beat me, I believe it is *you* that stands zero chance against *him*," Ella said as she rushed past him and entered the town.

The White Tail Tavern was mostly empty when they walked in apart from the middle-aged man who was cleaning the tavern. "Hello, are you the tavernkeeper here?" Jet asked the old man.

"Why yes, the name is Jasper. What can I do for you?" the tavernkeeper said as he was struggling to pick up an oak table.

"I am looking for a girl, slightly younger than me," Jet said as he moved to help the man. Ella followed suit. "Have you seen any girl with black hair come through here?"

The three of them easily moved the table to the intended location. "Thank you," Jasper said. "In fact there was one about two months ago that wasn't a regular, her name was

Leida Lightfoot I believe. However, I haven't seen her since then."

Ella flinched slightly at the name, *Leida Lightfoot, why did that ring a bell?* Then she realized it was the alias Lyra used to sneak into Randint Cavern.

"Leida, you say? Well thanks sir for your information." Jet pulled out a small bag of silvers and threw it on the table. He then walked out of the door while Ella followed behind him.

When they got outside Ella whispered, "Why would you pay him that much money?"

"What do you mean? He gave me information; I was just being courteous," Jet said.

"Well, the information led you nowhere, Leida was the name Lyra went by to sneak into Randint Cavern and spy on us," Ella said.

"Lyra. Who's Lyra?" Jet asked almost too curiously.

Ella sighed, "It's a long story," she said.

"I have time." Jet said smiling as they began heading back to the entrance to Randint Cavern. Ella looked at the boy, his face was so ruggedly asymmetrical in a rather appealing way. His eyes shined like obsidian in the waning sun. His smile matched the sparkle emitted from her pearl necklace.

Ella smiled back and blushed slightly. Now is when she told him everything. "Okay so it all started when I began looking for my mom..."

CHAPTER

20

Two days passed since Haran and Orion met up in the clearing; however, they were now coming up on the Ediv Pass. After weeks away from home Haran was excited to be going back. Still a nagging sense of doubt was left in his mind. Lottie still had his satchel. What if Orion was wrong? What if Lottie didn't come after them. If he were to leave Lottie in possession of his father's satchel what son would that make him? What Outryder would that make him? What man would that make him?

"You say you know where they'll attack next. Are you sure?" Haran asked his master who was riding next to him. Holland was asleep behind Haran and Shiva was walking alongside the horses.

Orion thought about it for a minute. "They chased us over one hundred kilometers and into a dangerous country. They obviously want to kill us. However, that will be quite difficult when we aren't surrounded by a raging fire."

Haran shook his head, it was bad enough that Orion had not answered his question, but he had left him with many more in the process. "Why do they want to kill us?"

"Because they are scared," Orion replied simply.

"Why are they scared?"

"Because we are getting closer," Orion said.

"Closer to what?"

"Winning," Orion said as he pushed his horse to greater speeds. Haran sighed and gave up the hopeless task. Finding answers to questions Orion didn't want to give you an answer to was impossible. He'd have to just figure it out himself.

When they were some hundred meters away Haran thought it was odd to see no guards vigilantly scanning the area for any intruders. And the smell. For some reason the gentle breeze that smelled of salt earlier now smelled of rotten corpses. However, when they came up onto the actual post itself, he figured out why. Fourteen bodies laid strewn across the ground in front of the post.

"What happened here?" Haran asked his master who was knelt over the bodies.

"I think this is how Lottie and Gilpin got into Athon so easily," Orion said cautiously.

"By massacring over a dozen soldiers, are they insane?" Haran asked with rage building in his throat. Orion simply nodded. Haran went to investigate further while Shiva followed behind him carefully. The man furthest from the guard post had his head dislodge from his body in one of the cleanest cuts Haran had ever seen. The name tag on the beheaded body read *Captain Virden*. By the footprints in the wet ground Haran could tell there was a pause just before the others pounced on Lottie and Gilpin. *They hesitated.* He moved to where he saw three guards in a row were lined up all with a cut to the torso. *Correction*, he thought, *two cuts. Two swords. Lottie killed three people with just one movement?*

He moved over a few meters where he saw two more bodies stacked on top of each other with cuts to the chest. *Those must have been Gilpin's kills.* The next two had bite marks in them, apparently the wolf got in on the killing as well. Five more bodies lined the ground with five dried pools of blood soaking the grass. Haran walked over to a body some fifteen meters from the others. The body was covered with bite marks and a piece of the man's calf was ripped off. Apparently that man had tried to run away.

Orion came upon where Haran was looking at the body. "One is missing," he said stoically.

Haran looked up confused. "Missing, how do you mean?"

Orion looked around to the fourteen bodies, "When we first walked through here I counted fifteen heads, and three horses tethered to the building. Now I count fourteen bodies and two horses tethered."

"So you think one escaped?" Haran asked trying to see what the big deal was.

"No. This guy here tried to escape and look what happened to him. Lottie and Gilpin would never be that sloppy," Orion said stating a fact that Haran had pointed out when he discovered the spy from the caravan. If Lottie was going to kill, he was going to make sure no one was alive to tell the tale.

"So what are you suggesting then?" Haran asked.

"The fifteenth man left after we left, but before they arrived," Orion noted. "Which means, somehow, they saw through our disguise as loggers and sent a messenger to inform the king that there were Outryders in his country."

Haran gasped slightly, if the king were to see this massacre after just being informed that Outryders had crossed into his lands it would be reasonable for him to assume that the Outryders killed these men. It would be an act of war. "So what can we do about it?" Haran asked worriedly.

"Nothing," Orion said plainly, "but I think that was Gilpin's plan all along, get us in a war with Athon while they take Norhall for themselves. Quite smart of the man, perhaps I should have given him more credit," Orion said as he walked back to his horse.

"How can we stop their plan though, surely there must be something? Can we send a diplomat or something just to inform the Athonian king that it wasn't our doing?" Haran asked. If Athon got involved their war with the Lupens would be all but lost before the year was up.

"That's not going to work, he would never believe you. All we can do now is inform King Nigel and hope he musters some semblance of a plan," Orion said. "For now though we have to get through this pass with our lives."

Apparently Holland had woken up while they were talking because he spoke tiredly as Haran got back onto his horse. "Quite the scene. I wonder who did this."

"Trust me you will find out soon enough," Orion said as he turned to the old man, "Holland, as we make our way through this pass you must do everything I say ok. If you do not I will not hesitate to send a knife between your eyes." Haran snickered slightly, he knew Orion was lying, his master would never kill an innocent old man.

Holland, however, was not aware of that fact and shifted away from Orion, "The both of you saved my life, and with however long I have in it, your wish is my command."

They began making their way through the tall grass of Ediv Pass. Haran scanned the pass anxiously, Orion said Lottie and Gilpin were likely to surprise them somewhere in the pass, and Haran wasn't too keen on that idea. The pass was ruggedly imposing between the jagged face of the Chien Mountain range to their right and the sheer face of the cliff overlooking the Hermirtha Sea to their left. They stayed in the exact center of the pass, any further left and they were subject to the cold, foamy spray that shot up from Hermirtha Sea as the water slammed against the jutting rocks below. Any further right would see that they were at risk of being crushed by the random boulders that fell down the rocky mountains.

They decided against riding the horses through the pass, Orion figured if they were on their horses their reactions would be limited at best. He wasn't wrong, they were struggling through the tall grass of the pass already, so Haran knew it would be far worse on their horses.

When they reached the halfway mark there was a slight clearing where the grass was at their ankles, and that is where Orion suddenly stopped. Out of the side of his mouth he whispered to Holland, "Get on the horse, when they are distracted gallop away." Holland nodded his understanding and hopped onto Nova. Hearing this Haran tied the ropes of Spirit to the ropes of Nova. Now, whenever Holland led Nova away, Spirit would follow along.

"Show yourselves, or I will send two knives directly between your eyes," Orion yelled out. Haran had not yet seen the two ambushers, but he could sense them. And bluffing is Orion's sharpest tool in his arsenal.

Lottie and Gilpin revealed themselves some five meters away in the tall grass at the edge of the trimmed clearing. "Very perceptive in your old age aren't you Orion?" Gilpin asked rhetorically. Orion was an Outryder, and one of the best at that, he wasn't expecting to surprise the man.

"Well, when you are bumbling around like a buffoon it's not that difficult to hear you," Orion said. Haran was surprised, he had heard nothing, and he typically was very aware of even the slightest of sounds. *No*, he thought. they didn't make a sound, but somehow Orion knew that they were there. How?

Before Gilpin could respond in their childish game of insults, Haran spoke up, "I assume you killed those men back there." He pointed fifty meters behind him to the fourteen rotting bodies. He saw Gilpin nod slightly, but he also saw Lottie's head lower. *Did the boy actually feel the guilt he should for slaughtering those men?*

Whatever the case, he would still pay for those fourteen lives they took, and the turmoil he caused since joining the Lupens, "You have something of mine," Haran said looking at the satchel now residing on Lottie's shoulder.

"I do, and actually, it fits quite well. Excellent craftsmanship." Lottie and Gilpin chuckled. However, Haran didn't find the joke funny in the slightest, he bit down on his jaw in anger.

"Give it back. Now," Haran demanded.

"Come and take it then," Lottie challenged as he stepped into the clearing, Gilpin followed. Now is when Lupe revealed himself from his hiding in the tall grass to which Shiva growled softly. *That's right*, Haran thought, *the last time the two of them fought he injured her badly and killed her friend, maybe she wanted payback of her own.*

Haran unsheathed his weapons. The sheer wall of the Chien Mountains loomed over them in the rising sun, and to his left, water from the Hermirtha Sea smashed violently up against the rocky cliff sending a violent spray of water down onto the pass. Even through the tense air Haran couldn't help but admire how epic the scene was for the battle.

The three pairs stood in the center of the clearing in a stalemate. Neither side dared to make a move because of their knowledge of their opponents' skill. However, after what felt like an eternity, Shiva actually made the first strike. She pounced on Lupe viciously. The two animals weren't holding back, Lupe was biting ferociously at any part of Shiva open, but Shiva was clawing relentlessly at the wolf's head, scratching him multiple times. The two were fighting with all of their weight on their hind legs, it was almost strange how humanlike they fought.

Haran snapped back to Lottie just in time to see a side stroke coming rapidly to his left side. He barely avoided the attack by somersaulting out of danger. "Pay attention Haran. I don't want to end this too soon," Lottie said. Haran simply grunted and responded with an overhand cut. Out of the corner of his eye he saw that Gilpin and Orion had begun fighting also.

Over the growling of the animals and the clashing of metal-on-metal Haran heard hoofbeats. Holland had made his escape, *good*, he thought.

Haran and Lottie exchanged blow after blow, each blocking, parrying, or dodging the others attacks. There seemed to be no end in sight for the fight seeing as both of the fighters were still in peak condition.

Orion and Gilpin's fight was more one sided as Orion was demonstrating how much better than Gilpin he was. Gilpin was a master swordsman and strategist, but one thing was clear, he was no natural like the other three, his skill came from hundreds of hours of practice and hundreds of millions of sword swings.

Orion was pushing Gilpin to the edge of the clearing now and to the start of the waist high grass. However, Gilpin refused to give up, he had a score to settle, and no matter how he did it, he was going to win. "Fine," he said as he parried an attack and threw down his sword and shield, "I surrender, there's no chance at beating you." He got onto his knees, an obvious sign of his surrender.

Orion rose his axe up for a final deadly blow but held it back, "Tell me. Why should I let you live? Those fourteen men over there were shown no mercy. Why should I show it to you?"

"Those men fought valiantly until the end, a sign of their bravery. This, killing me would be a coward's move," Gilpin said as he hung his head in anticipation of the finishing blow to come, but it never did. Orion relaxed his muscles and turned around angrily. In this moment Gilpin saw his opportunity, he took out the knife he had lodged deep within his boot and tried stabbing him in the back.

Haran saw the movement out of the corner of his eye and yelled a warning out to his teacher. However, the warning wasn't necessary, his master was already in the process of sweeping his opponents legs from under him sending him crashing to the ground once more. "No, *that* was a coward's move," Orion said as he took Gilpin's knife and searched him for any more weapons.

Lottie saw that his master had been defeated and slacked slightly on his offensive. In doing so he gave Haran the opportunity to take the advantage, he slammed the blunted part of the axe hard against Lottie's left side cracking his ribs in the process. Haran then front kicked Lottie some two meters away to where Orion was watching ever so carefully. Lupe saw his master in trouble and took a momentary pause in his fight with Shiva to come by to his master's aid. Shiva did the same. "Now let's try this again, give me what's mine," Haran demanded.

"Never," Lottie said as he barely got up from the pain in his ribs.

"I will not fight you in this condition Lottie," Haran said. "Just hand me the satchel and come with us."

"How about you go fetch it then," Lottie said as he threw the satchel off of the pass and into the Hermirtha Sea.

Without hesitation Haran jumped off the side of the cliff and caught the satchel in midair. However, now he was well past the edge and some ten meters above the rocky waters of the Hermirtha Sea.

CHAPTER

21

When he hit the frigid water, it felt like he had just fallen on the hard ground. Waves of pain shot through his body. First it went through his chest, taking the breath from his lungs in the process. Then it went to his back sending a new wave of pain to his already injured spine. And finally, to his legs as they seized under the cold. He couldn't move, he was paralyzed by the pain. *Why would you do that?* he thought to himself, but there was no answer.

He was under the water for barely a minute, but the cold had already enveloped around him. Everything froze, hours passed in seconds as Haran looked at himself from out of his own body. He could see the raging sea slamming against him as he sank lifelessly into the currents. He could feel his heartbeat slowing as the freezing cold slowly found its way through his veins. He thought of everything that had happened up until this point in his life, all that he had experienced, all that he had gone through...

He snapped out of his death accepting daze and a new feeling of warmth coursed through his body. He pushed his body to its limits and resurfaced from his premature deathbed. The cold was somewhat bearable after he surfaced, but seconds after he did he was hit with a wave that sent him under the water again. It was a vicious cycle that would ultimately lead him to being smashed against the rocky side of the cliff. He surfaced once more and looked around for any hope of him getting free from the cycle, but to no avail. He didn't know which would be his death, the freezing water, or the rocky cliff that was imminently approaching. "Haran!" His master yelled from twenty meters above as he pointed to a curved rock sticking out of the cliff a meter or so from the surface of the water.

Haran understood, if he were to hook the strap of his satchel on the rock before being slammed into the cliff by the waves, he could avoid any real injuries. However, if it were not timed to perfection, Haran would be slammed with his ribs exposed to the sharp rock wall. It was risky, Haran thought, but he might as well try it. If he didn't he would surely die. The next wave hit, and he was pushed just out of reach of the rocky outcrop. "Three . . . Two . . . One." The next wave hit Haran and in that instant, he swung his satchel to where the strap could land directly on top of the flat rock. The strap caught, and he used his legs to brace against the rock wall, greatly reducing the damage done to his body.

He took a moment to appreciate his father's taste in fine craftsmanship, for he was supporting almost all his weight from the one strap. However, he knew if he were to keep his weight there for an extended period the strap *would* snap. Therefore, he grabbed onto the rock with his right hand and held himself up. Slinging the satchel back onto his shoulder with his left.

Luckily for him, he had been climbing since he was old enough to remember, so making his way up the rocky cliff was simple enough other than the fact that his body ached with even the slightest of movements.

By the time he reached the ledge Lupe, Gilpin and Lottie were long gone. Lottie had caused the perfect distraction that allowed them to escape to their horses. He rolled tiredly onto the ledge and stared blankly at the clouds above. He lie in peace for a solid thirty seconds when Orion yelled, "You absolute idiot! What were you thinking!?"

"Uhh. I was thinking I needed to get my satchel back," Haran said shivering, cautious of his master's rage.

"So, you jump off a cliff?" Orion asked rhetorically.

"Exactly," Haran said.

"Well, that stunt just let the two people who have been chasing us for weeks go free," Orion said.

"Well scold me all you want but don't expect an apology because you won't get one," Haran said, he'd keep that satchel safe no matter what it took or how many times he'd risk his life to save it.

Orion met his apprentice's eyes and looked at them for a minute or so, "Fine, but it's you who's going to have to fight him again."

"I beat him twice now, if he wants to go again, I am ready," Haran said confidently.

"Don't get too confident son," Orion warned him. "Both times the boy got distracted. If not for that, the fights could have just as easily gone to him."

Haran knew his master was right but didn't want to admit it, so he simply nodded. Rolling onto his side and eventually sitting up, Haran called Shiva over to him. Up until now she had been watching the tall grass carefully, perhaps waiting for Lupe to return. He patted her head gently and hugged her softly. She had held her own against the wolf god, and might have even beat him under different circumstances. That was something to be praised.

"Do you think they'll attack us again?" Haran asked his master as he dried off in the hot sun.

"Not until after they get back to Norhall and Randint Cavern," Orion said.

Haran thought about how they let Holland take both of their horses from the area for his escape. "Does this mean we have to walk home now?" It took three days on horseback to travel from Norhall to Ediv Pass. It would take almost three times that long on foot, and he dreaded the walk.

"I'm afraid so," Orion said as he began walking on the long trek to Norhall.

When they reached the Anjagorian guard post Orion gestured to the guard captain that he met with weeks ago. The captain walked over respectfully, "Ahh the Outryders is it? Glad to see you are back."

"Yes indeed. Who have come past this point today?" Orion asked, he already knew the answer, but he decided to feign ignorance.

The guard captain spoke, "There was one old man on two very shaggy looking horses, and not long after there were two Anjagorian warriors on two battle horses. Both galloped past. I figured the two warriors were chasing the old man, but they went separate directions, so I don't know."

"Which direction did the old man go?" Orion asked. The road from the guard post-split into two directions, the road to the northwest went to the fief of Osmole and eventually onto Norhall and the one to the southwest led to the fief of Grien.

"Just down the main road there into Grien," The guard captain said as he pointed southwest.

Orion nodded his acknowledgement and just as he was about to leave he asked, "Does that road there lead directly to Grien Castle then?"

"It does," The guard captain said, "That's where we go to get supplies for the winter."

"How far is it then?" Orion asked.

"Some ten kilometers down the road," The guard captain said.

Orion nodded. It wasn't that far of a walk at all, and it was worth a shot to see if Holland was there. He went on his way past the guard captain and onto the road leading to Grien. Haran followed behind slowly limping from the brute force his legs had taken when he was smashed against the cliff.

The walk to Grien Castle was long and painful and by the end of the two hours Haran was sick and tired of seeing wheat and mustard. As Orion said soon after they entered the fief, Grien was composed of mainly fields and provided much of the food for those fief's further north that couldn't farm their own. It wasn't a powerhouse fief like Norhall or Millstone, but it was almost as valuable to the overall economy of Anjagor. As Orion put it, "If Grien stops producing crops for the northern fiefs, the production of everything from the north stops. Most importantly, their iron production."

The castle wasn't very impressive in design or structure like Norhall or Anjagor respectively. It was in the shape of a square on the top of a hill like almost every castle. However, the height of the castle was only some ten meters tall which paled in comparison to Norhall's twenty-five-meter-high walls or Anjagor's thirty-five. If any enemy were to attack, it would be easily scalable by ladders.

The entrance was a wooden gate reinforced with iron; it would be very easy to break through if the enemy saw it necessary. They were greeted at the gate by two guards, the one on the left side of the gate spoke, "What is your business here?"

"Have you seen an old man come through here today maybe an hour or so ago?" Orion asked the guards.

The right guard was the one to speak this time, "We have. He was riding a horse with another tied behind it. He said he needed to speak to the Baron."

"Good. Take me to your Baron then," Orion said as he began walking through the wooden gate.

The guards cut him off before entering the gate, "Hold it. Where is your manners old man? What is your name?"

"Orion of Norhall, and if you don't start leading me to your Baron right now, I will make sure the both of you begin working the fields by week's end." Haran didn't know if it was Orion's name that did the trick or the threat to their lively hood, but either way the guards were now taking them to the keep in the center of the castle.

Grien's keep was very basic. Like every keep, it was at the very top of the central building of the castle, the inner ward. It was quaint in design with a suite of rooms for the Baron, his family, and any guests he had. However, it was nothing compared to Norhall's keep that held half a dozen suites and a dozen more rooms.

When they made their way to the Baron's office the first guard knocked gently on the door, "Sir, a man named Orion from Norhall wishes to speak with you."

"Send him in," Baron Sinday replied.

When the two Outryders walked in they saw Holland sitting at the front of a hard oak desk calmly. Sitting on the other end was an interesting looking man in his mid-forties. The man was not handsome at all, his hair was wild and unkempt. His face was long, and his nose was sharp. In fact, the only real redeeming factor of the man's appearance was his crystal blue eyes; as Haran looked at them, he could tell that they commanded respect from any man that were to look at them.

"Orion of Norhall huh?" Sinday said carefully choosing his words. "And you would be?" He turned his friendly gaze to Haran.

"Haran sir."

"Well, I assume you are *the* Orion right," Sinday said, "The Outryder?"

"We are Outryders yes," Orion said carefully.

"Lovely to see that green cloak again, it's been a while," Sinday said sadly.

Haran was confused by the statement, so he asked, "What happened to the one stationed here?" Every fief had one fully capable Outryder in it, so the Baron of the fief *should* see them at least once a week.

Sinday glanced down sadly, "A few weeks ago we lost him suddenly in his sleep."

"His name was Rendall wasn't it?" Orion asked. He had recalled seeing the name on a monthly report sent out by the king. Apparently, the man was alive and healthy one day, but dead the next. Orion thought it was intriguing, but with everything happening in Norhall he put the thought aside.

"It was, but everyone called him Ren. He hated that nickname so much. He was a great Outryder and an even better man," Sinday said. "We have still yet to receive a replacement for him; however, I am sure whoever comes to replace him could never live up."

"Probably not," Orion said, "replacements rarely do. But how about this, I will personally tell the king that this fief needs a man as capable and generous as Rendall. Deal?"

"Thank you, Orion," Sinday said with a smile. "It means a lot."

Haran saw Orion shift uncomfortably and smiled inwardly. He knew his master hated praise and recognition. "Well, we really must be heading back home now," Orion said as he gestured for Holland to get up. He did so with great effort and shuffled his feet to the door.

"I hate to lose you so soon," Sinday said to Holland, "Perhaps we can talk again my friend."

"Of course," Holland said as he exited the door. Haran followed him out.

"One more thing," Orion said after the two others walked out. "You see I can't tell you the circumstances, but could you send any spare food over to Castle Norhall as soon as possible. I give you my word that it will be repaid with interest."

"Of course," Sinday said, the word of an Outryder went a long way in Anjagor, especially one as legendary as Orion.

Haran noticed the extra minute Orion stayed in Sinday's office; however, he knew now not to question his master. "That man was quite interesting," he said casually.

"Quite interesting indeed. Now let's go home," Orion said as they made their way out into the courtyard, onto their horses, and onto Castle Norhall.

CHAPTER

22

Lyra nocked on Baron Ligate's door at dawn. "Come in," Baron Ligate said.

She walked in and took a seat in the cushioned chair in front of the Baron's desk. "Lyra? Why are you here, our meeting isn't scheduled for another three days?"

Lyra nodded, "Yes Baron, but I have discovered something rather pressing I would like to inform you of."

"What is it?" The Baron asked as he sat upright in his seat.

"The Lupen's. They plan to assault Castle Norhall in three weeks' time," Lyra said.

Baron Ligate nodded. The siege was expected, but he didn't expect it for another two months at least. "And you are sure of this?"

"I am."

"Well, I assume your master hasn't returned yet seeing as he hasn't reported in is that correct?" Ligate asked.

"I don't believe he has yet sire," Lyra said.

"All the same I suppose, as long as he is back before the siege. I knew it was far too quiet for far too long," Ligate said. "Well, I suppose I will have to contact the king to ask for even more reinforcements."

"Is there anything I can do to help?" Lyra asked. If she were honest, she had been feeling rather useless recently and was wanting something, anything to do to help.

"Yes, we need men and supplies, but we have to do it discretely so that we don't alarm the Lupen's of our knowledge of their plans. I trust you can handle that until your master comes home?" Ligate asked in a demeaning way.

"I will do whatever it takes to defend my fief, but I will not be belittled by an equal," Lyra said. Her rank as a Recon, or apprentice Outryder, marked her as equals to every Baron in the country. She only needed to serve her master, and the king of course. "It's always good to work in close association with the Baron of the fief you serve, but never let them think they control you." It was one of the first lessons Orion told her, and—as always— he was right.

"You are just like your master. Well then if you would like to help that is what you can do," Baron Ligate said lightheartedly.

"I will do it," Lyra said as she walked out of the Baron's office.

Four days passed since her meeting with the Baron. Lyra had been working tirelessly to rally troops in Norhall and gather food for the siege. It was a rather tedious task, but it could mean the difference between a victory or a defeat, so Lyra did so without complaint.

Lyra had just arrived at a small farm at the edge of Norhall at noon. The farm was quaint with a few animals and rows and rows of crops. The house itself was surrounded by a painted wooden porch that blended perfectly with the whitewashed side paneling. She walked cautiously up the porch not trying to be intimidating in anyway. She decided to leave her cloak and weapons behind knowing that many people thought Outryders were people to be wary of. She knocked on the door. TAP-TAP-TAP. There was no response. She waited several seconds and knocked again. TAP-TAP-TAP. Still, no response. However, she did here a noise coming from inside the house. A hushed whisper of caution from a mother to a child. She sighed; it had been like this for several days since she began recruiting. "I hope you know I can hear you."

A brief moment passed, and the door crept open. A disheveled looking woman in her mid to late thirties opened the door. Her hair was frizzy, and her dress was ripped in many places, it looked as if she had been crying, "What do you want from me? Come to take my boy as well?"

Lyra looked at her confused, "What are you talking about mam?"

"My Daniel," the woman said, "they took my Daniel. One moment he was here in my arms and the next he was gone with them."

"With who?" Lyra asked.

"The soldiers from the castle," the woman said, "they took him to fight in some siege. Daniel hasn't wielded a sword in his life."

"Who is it mommy," A child's voice came from behind the door. "Is papa home?" The child quickly rounded the door and caught eyes with Lyra. The boy was young, maybe four or five. The boy was holding a small stuffed bear and had a rather warm looking blanket on his back. Lyra smiled softly at him. "You're not papa," the boy said.

"No bud I am not," Lyra said, she could already feel her throat closing and the tears coming up.

"I want papa!" The boy screamed at the top of his lungs clutching on to his mother's side. "Where is papa!?"

The mother looked down to him with a tear rolling down her cheek, "I know baby I know, but your father is away right now."

"The bad men," the boy said, "they took him away."

"Your father went willingly," the mother said as she got down to comfort her son. She was feigning strength, but Lyra could see through the façade. The woman was hurting far worse than she would ever show her son.

"I want papa," the boy screamed again. Lyra quickly wiped away a tear. "Sorry," she said, "I shouldn't have come. I will get going now."

The mother looked up from where she was comforting her son, "That's probably for the best."

Lyra walked off the porch and back onto Ranger. She rode out of the farm with her head held high, but as soon as she was well out of range of visibility she hopped off her horse and collapsed to the ground in tears. The boy's face of disappointment when it wasn't his father at the door played over and over in her head. What kind of person was she to want to rip someone from their family just to get them killed in a siege? How was that fair to anyone?

Hours later Lyra rode into Fuestres Woods, she spent an hour or so on the ground crying before she eventually picked herself up and carried on home. On the ground outside of Fuestres Woods she noticed horse tracts that she knew were not there before. Seeing as few people even knew of the path, she assumed that Orion and Haran were back and urged Ranger into a gallop.

Her suspicions were confirmed when she hit the clearing and saw Haran outside playing with Shiva and Orion on the porch watching contently. She basically jumped off her horse and tackled Haran to the ground excitedly. "Oh wow, a bit aggressive don't you think?" He said laughing as he pushed her off him.

"Not at all. It's been a long day. I'm so glad to see you. I have so much to tell you," Lyra said as she helped him to his feet.

"Same, but first, let's go eat," Haran said as he walked Lyra inside.

They ate dried beef and bread for dinner. It was a very basic dinner for them, but you couldn't go wrong with it. "So," Orion said between bites of bread, "What happened when we were gone?"

"Well to start off," Lyra said as she pulled the drawing out from her cloak. "Haran, through about a week of digging through those records we requested, I figured out who your father was. You will not believe it."

"Atticus Ryder," Haran said with a slight smile.

Lyra was taken aback, "How do you know?"

"I told him," Orion said casually.

"You knew?" Lyra asked angrily. Orion simply nodded. "So, the whole time Haran has been looking for who his father was, you knew the whole time?" Orion simply nodded again, there wasn't much he could say. Lyra grew angrier now. "How could you hide that from him?"

"Relax Lyra its fine," Haran reassured her. "He has his reasons for everything, and I am sure they were well intentioned."

"What happened between the two of you while you were gone?" Lyra asked. Before Haran had been slightly annoyed at Orion for his lack of sharing important information to the two of them. Now he seemed okay with it.

"I just realized that he is who he is going to be and no amount of angry looks from us will change that," Haran said.

"Haran you are a Ryder," Lyra said practically glowing, "That is insane, you were basically destined for this job. Your great grandfather founded it. Quite the legacy you have to live up to isn't it."

"Says the princess," Haran replied jokingly, but Lyra's words still sat deep in him. He always wanted to find out who his father was, even if he didn't realize it at the time. However, now that he found how who his father was how could he live up to that legacy? "Anyway, what else happened?"

Lyra told the two of her journey into Randint Cavern and of the code Ella used to communicate her warning of the pending siege of Norhall.

"A code you say?" Orion interrupted her explanation.

Lyra nodded. "Yes, I was taught it in secret to communicate with my adopted mother after I arrived here. It's a series of taps and pauses used to communicate letters in the alphabet."

"The code you speak of is called Basili's Code," Orion said. "He was a rather eccentric Athonian scholar who created the code to communicate with ghosts. However, the Outryders use it as a means of secret communication. I wasn't going to teach it to you until you got more Outryder training, but it seems like you already have it mastered."

It was silent for a brief moment until Haran spoke, "Why was Ella helping you?"

"That was my question," Lyra said, "but I assume it has to do with the Percival guy."

"What was he like?" Orion asked trying to build a profile for the man.

"He was radiant and seemingly altruistic, but I felt something sinister in his presence," Lyra said. "And she had a newly forming scar on her left cheek, it looked like it was done after an altercation with a small knife of sorts."

"Do you think he caused it?" Haran asked. Lyra simply nodded. "Well, then I think it's safe to assume he was the one who called for the siege while Lottie and Gilpin were gone." He looked to his master who nodded his agreement.

"Well, how was your trip. Did you find out how to kill the wolf god?" Lyra asked.

Haran explained everything from their ploy to reveal Brios as an Outryder to his eventually leap off the cliff to save his father's satchel.

"Where is the old man now?" Lyra interrupted the story to ask about Holland.

"I left him with Baron Ligate, he should be fine now, there are tons of new books for him to read in the Norhall library," Orion said casually.

Lyra nodded and turned back to Haran, "Also you absolute idiot!" She said it in the same way that Orion had. "What would possibly possess you to jump of a cliff."

"I had to save it Lyra, it's the only thing that my father left to me. Also, it contained two rather important things acquired on the trip," Haran said.

"Important enough to risk your life? Let's see them then," She demanded as she pointed to his satchel.

The first item Haran pulled out of the bag was the journal. It was slightly water damaged, but it was still readable. He flipped to the back page and showed it to Lyra who read it carefully.

She seemed to make the same realization Haran had when he first read it, "But that means." She caught herself from saying it. It was better left unspoken. For Albalupius to be killed, Haran or Lottie also had to die. "Haran that's an impossible decision to make."

"You really do have a knack for point out things I don't want to think about," Haran said jokingly, but he was telling the truth. He didn't want to think about having to live up to his family name, or the decision between whether he or Lottie had to die.

Lyra smiled slightly, "And what of the second item?"

Haran glanced at his master who quickly made his way to his office and shut the door. Haran reached into the bag, but before he pulled out the necklace he said, "Promise me you won't get mad."

"Haran just show me," Lyra demanded.

"Fine." Haran said as he pulled out the silver fox necklace.

Lyra gasped at the sight of the necklace. Even in the dim light of the sunset the ruby eyes of the fox pendant were gleaming entrancingly in contrast with the silver of the necklace. "It's beautiful. Where did you get it?"

"Gora. When I saw it, I immediately knew that I had to get it for you," Haran said.

"Haran. I don't know how I could ever repay you," Lyra said.

"It's not that big of a deal," Haran said, "I mean it's just a necklace."

Lyra's eyes were watering now, and she hugged Haran, "Did I ever tell you why I saved Scarlett from the canyon?" Haran shook his head no, all he knew was that Lyra had saved Scarlett from a pack of wolves, he didn't know the reason. "It's because her face reminded me of my family."

Haran was confused, "What do you mean?"

"My family crest. It is a fox head. It looks exactly like this necklace," Lyra said as she began crying for the second time that day. Haran thought the necklace must have been made for the royal family before their deaths, and somehow the vendor got his hands on it. Maybe the necklace seemed to be calling him to get it for Lyra because it was made for her in the first place.

"Oh, Lyra I didn't mean to upset you with it," Haran said as he tried to take the necklace back from her, but she yanked it away from him.

"No Haran thank you. I love it," Lyra said as she gestured for him to put it on her. He did so and she turned to him, "How do I look?"

"Like a troll who has a very beautiful necklace on," Haran said jokingly which got him a stiff punch to the chest. It was worth it. This time he hugged her tightly. They stayed there for several minutes before Haran pulled away sadly. He thought about Heide and what she would do if she saw them like this.

He cleared his throat and walked to the door, "I should probably go train, it's been a few weeks."

"The sun is down," Lyra said.

Haran stopped on his way out, "I can start a fire."

"Care if I join you then?" Lyra asked.

Haran paused slightly, "I think I just need to clear my head." Lyra nodded sadly and Haran walked silently out of the door.

CHAPTER

23

After they made it back into the fief of Norhall Lottie and Gilpin had to sneak their way into Calcore Canyon's entrance to Randint Cavern. It was a long process, but after a day or so they found their way at the entrance. Seeing as there was no way to get them into the cavern, they had already tethered their horses to the hidden stables in the woods just next to Randint Cavern.

They stayed there with most of the Lupen's horses under strict care of a few Lupen stable hands. Currently, they were working on digging a hole right above Randint Cavern and adding a pulley system so that they could lower horses into and raise them out of the cavern. However, that was a long process seeing as where they were digging the hole was in Malen Plains, a frequently busy place due to its proximity to the Battleschool.

After they entered the tunnel that led to Randint Cavern Lottie took out something he got Ella as an apology for leaving abruptly on her. It was a blue stained-glass rose, Ella's favorite flower. He found it in the Gora marketplace while they were hunting for Haran and Orion and thought it would be the perfect gift for her. He felt Gilpin's gaze avert to it when he pulled it out, "You think she will like it?" Lottie asked quietly, there was no reason to, but he still did.

"She will love it Lottie," Gilpin replied with a smile. "It's quite beautiful."

"It is," Lottie said.

They reached the cavern in just over an hour, Lottie didn't know what he was expecting when he came back, but whatever it was it wasn't militantism. As he overlooked the cavern from the entrance at the top of the hill, he saw what looked to be a thousand men at the bottom. He couldn't quite make out what was happening, but he knew it wasn't good. "What is that?" Lottie asked.

"I don't know, why don't we go see?" Gilpin said as he jogged his way down the hill to which Lottie followed close behind.

When they reached the bottom they heard the booming voice of Supreme General Norman, "Men of Randint Cavern, you have made a choice to serve our people valiantly and take back our ancestral lands. That being said, you have a lot of training to do before we can stand a chance in a siege, and we only have three weeks to get it done. So, let's begin. First, you have been given a number each. Numbers 1-300 see General Jaron to my left. Numbers 301-600 see General Feris to my right. Finally, numbers 601-954 come see me."

The men made their way to their respective generals, but Gilpin and Lottie made their way to Supreme General Norman himself. Gilpin walked up to him and said, "What is going on here Supreme General? The siege isn't scheduled until months from now."

Norman looked confused, "Sire, Percival said that under your orders we were meant to siege Norhall in three weeks' time."

"Oh, did he now?" Gilpin asked, his voice raising several octaves in the process. "That's news to me."

"Would you like us to stop the training Sire?" Norman asked Gilpin.

Gilpin pondered the question for a little bit, "No, the men are fired up for revenge, so let's give it to them. However, I would like to know your battle plans immediately."

"Yes Sire," Norman said as he bowed deeply.

"Now excuse me while I go talk to the man I left in charge," Gilpin said annoyed.

Gilpin stomped his way up the hill once again and into the mansion at the very top. Lottie followed close behind to make sure Gilpin didn't kill the man. Usually, it was Gilpin who stopped Lottie from getting angry, so he felt he should be responsible for when the opposite happened.

Gilpin bolted up the spiral staircase taking three or more steps at a time. He then made his way to his office that once belonged to his best friend Doran, but now it had a conniving snake in it. By the time Lottie entered the room Gilpin already had Percival against the wall by the collar on his shirt. "How dare you make a decision so big without waiting for me to return! After everything I have done for you. You little deceiving power hungry bastard's son. Do you have no concept of respect?" Gilpin yelled at the man.

"Gilpin. Let me explain," Percival croaked calmly. At this point the yelling made everyone else in the house intrigued and now Ella, Sylvia, and Keryn were all standing in the doorway with Lottie.

Gilpin refused to let the pressure off the man's collar and was choking him. "Gilpin," Lottie said. "Let him explain himself."

Gilpin growled and let the pressure off of Percival's collar, "So. Explain."

Percival gasped for air for several moments before he finally spoke, "He knew."

"Who knew what?" Gilpin demanded.

"The king, he knew we were going to attack Anjagor in two months. He's been sending supplies secretly not just in big convoys," Percival said. There was a small glance over to Ella, only she knew he was lying, but if she outed him out here, he would hold his promise to kill everyone.

Gilpin relaxed slightly, "So you wanted to attack before they could get enough supplies and defenses."

"Exactly."

Gilpin fully relaxed now, "Mmm. Go over my head again and you are done, okay?" Percival simply nodded, "Now get out of my office. I have to go help train a thousand untrained men in just two weeks."

Percival walked out of Gilpin's office with his head held high, catching Ella's eyes warningly. He didn't even speak, but she knew exactly what he was saying. *Say something and they are dead.*

After everything died down and everyone was back in their respective rooms, Lottie knocked on Ella's door. "Come in," she said with a quivering voice.

Lottie walked with his hands behind his back holding the flower to see her trying to quickly dry up her tears.

However, she was failing tremendously, "What's wrong," he asked immediately.

"Nothing, you're here now," Ella said trying to gently smile.

Lottie noticed the scar on her cheek that, up until now, she had been desperately trying to hide with her hand. "What happened here?" Lottie said as he touched the scar gently.

"Bad sparring is all. I'm fine," Ella said lying twice in the span of six words. Trying to change the subject she gestured to his hands, "What is that?"

Lottie moved to sit down on her bed beside her, "Oh it's something I picked up for you while I was gone." He pulled the blue glass rose from behind his back.

Ella gasped at the sight, "Its beautiful Lottie . . ." There was a knock on the door. Ella looked sideways to Lottie who was frowning now.

"Come in," she said.

Jet came through the door looking at the gleaming black swords in his hands, "Hey Ella you want to go train? I just bought some new swords and I want to try them out." By this point he noticed Lottie as well, "Oh hey Lottie. Good to have you back."

"Hey," Lottie said dismally.

"What is that?" Jet asked.

Ella looked away from Lottie now, "It's a blue rose, Lottie got it for me. I used to pick them outside of Blackrock Village in Osmole and give them to my mom."

"Oh that's cool, well, I am heading there now if you two would like to join me," Jet said.

"I'll be down in a little Jet," Ella said as Jet walked out of the room. She gave it a few seconds and then turned to Lottie. "I'm so sorry Lottie." Jet had just interrupted their moment.

"It's fine," Lottie said.

"No it's not," Ella said, "I love the rose it's very beautiful. Thank you." She leaned in to hug him, but he stood up instead of hugging her back.

If he were honest with himself he really didn't want to look at her at the moment. "I will talk to you later Ella," he said and walked out of the door.

"Ella?" she whispered to herself. Ever since she had known him Lottie had called her El. It was *definitely* not fine.

Lottie walked to the bottom of the hill to go train. He had to clear his head, and training as the way to do that. After wading his way through the thousand of those training outside, he made his way to the less cramped blue training area.

Inside were a few of the other blue group, Jet, Tomas, and Tyson. As he noticed Lottie's arrival Tyson ran over to Lottie and gave him a bear hug. The giant held Lottie so tightly that he was crushing Lottie, "Aww Lot you are back I have missed you so much buddy."

"Thanks," Lottie croaked, "But can you please let me down now."

"Oh yeah sorry," The giant said sympathetically. By this point Tomas walked over and shook his hand as well. "Good to have you back buddy." Jet watched carefully from a distance which Lottie was okay with.

"Good to be back. Now, can we get to some training, I am told we have a siege coming up and I am rather rusty," Lottie said.

"Actually, you and I have a meeting with the Supreme General soon," Tomas said.

"What for?" Lottie asked.

"He wants us in charge of the blue group during the siege," Tomas said.

"All three hundred of them?" Lottie asked.

"Seems so."

"Why would he trust us with that?" Lottie asked.

"How about let's go and find out," Tomas said as he moved out of the blue group's training area and into the main area and onto the Supreme General's office at the very back of the facility.

As they walked in, they saw Percival, Supreme General Norman, and Gilpin all there in Norman's war room. Five chairs were spread out around a map of the fief of Norhall. On the map he had ten figures all grouped around the spot in Malen plains right above Randint Cavern. "Ahh yes, please join us," Norman said as he gestured to the two empty seats. They did so reluctantly, and Norman continued, "As I was just explaining to Gilpin, Baron Ligate has roughly five hundred well trained men at his disposal currently. However, by the time that we begin the siege I expect him to have rallied some seven hundred more men giving him a total of thirteen hundred men. We currently have three times that much at our disposal. Now I would have liked to have at least five times more than them because Norhall is a very sturdy castle and we've no equipment."

"Couldn't we build some?" Lottie asked.

"We could, but that would take far too long," Norman argued. "Also, we don't need it because the drawbridge will already be down by the time our army arrives at it."

"How do you plan to do that?" Tomas asked.

"Well, that's where the blue group will come in. You see when we first built this place, the Lupens placed five entrances. The first was the Battleschool here," he said as he pointed to the middle of Malen Plains. "The second was from Calcore Canyon. The third was from Fuestres Woods. The fourth was from Norhall village." He pointed to each respectively. "The main army will use the exit at Calcore to get all of our men out of Randint Cavern, but the fifth entrance was in Norhall Castle itself. That's the entrance you are going to use." As he said it, he moved nine of the ten figures to Calcore Canyon and one to Norhall Castle.

Lottie was understanding the plan now, they would use the fifth tunnel to sneak into Norhall Castle and drop the drawbridge giving the rest of the Lupens free reign on the castle. However, he still had one more question nagging his mind. "Why us? Why put us in charge of such an important mission."

"Well. The blue group contain our best fighters and Tomas is the captain of it," Norman said.

"And what about me?" Lottie asked.

"I chose you because you are our best fighter Lottie, and I trust you can handle whoever you come against up there," Norman said.

Lottie's heart sank, if he were their best fighter and he lost to Haran for the third time then the siege would surely fail. If he lost again then he would let down everyone and get thousands killed. "No pressure though," Percival said with a slight smirk as if he were reading Lottie's mind.

CHAPTER

24

Haran lie patiently in the tall grass of Malen Plains for several minutes. He was stalking something although he himself knew not of what it was. Whatever it was, it was injured by Shiva as it tried to enter the woods outside of their clearing. Haran assumed it was something rather foreign to the area seeing as everything around the forest knew that if they entered the clearing it would be killed by Shiva. He found the blood trail at the edge of the woods early that morning and had a hunch he might need to track it. Haran continued tracking it now on the slim chance it was the wolf god Albalupius. It was improbable, but Haran didn't weed out the possibility. He moved silently to some three meters ahead of him when he heard a rustle in the grass behind him. He whipped around with a throwing knife in hand ready to kill whatever dared sneak up on him, but as he did, he heard a sad whimper. The whimper was made by a dog. A brown and white pointer dog to be exact. The dog had a scratch mark down the length of his side that was quite obviously made by Shiva. Haran knew the dog well enough, it belonged to the goat farmer that lived some three kilometers away from Fuestres Woods. The dog has been around since Haran could remember, always out exploring the fief as Haran once did.

Haran assumed the dog must have wandered off and somehow ended up in their clearing to where he was attacked by an overprotective Shiva. "Aww you poor thing," he said as he took off his cloak and bandaged the gash on his side.

He carefully picked up the injured dog who flinched as he tried to do so, "Relax buddy it's okay," Haran said soothingly to the dog who relaxed slightly.

He gently carried the dog to Spirit who he left twenty meters behind while tracking the animal. He laid the dog very gently into his side bag that Shiva would lay in when they traveled. "Come on buddy let's take you to your master."

He rode slowly for about half an hour before reaching the outside of the farmer's cabin. "Hello?" Haran knocked rapidly on the door.

There was no response so Haran beat on the door, "HELLO?"

This time the farmer's wife opened the door, "Who is making all this fuss," she asked crankily. The woman looked to be in her mid to late fifties with the white hair to match. Her eyes were blue, marking her as Anjagorian.

"Sorry madam, but I believe I have found your dog. He was injured in Malen Plains," Haran said kindly as he went to grab the dog from the saddle and give him to the woman.

"Oh my poor Missy. Yes, we lost her last night. We thought she was dead. My husband is out looking for her now. Do you know what happened to her?" she asked.

"I did not see what happened to her no mam," Haran said cringing unnoticeably. Technically he didn't lie, he just withheld the truth.

"Oh. Well thanks anyways for your kindness," the woman said as she took the dog from him.

"Honestly, it's the least I can do," Haran said. He felt bad for what Shiva had done to the poor dog and wanted to make up for it in any way necessary. The old lady thanked him again and he went on his way back to Fuestres Woods.

Haran walked into the clearing in Fuestres Woods slightly after noon. He had returned just two days before and had been training like crazy ever since. It had been weeks since he properly trained the hours he should be to perfect his crafts and he could already feel his skills fading. His knife throwing especially was becoming increasingly dull which was already below par before his trip to Athon.

He spent the last two days trying to get back up to par. It was both tiring and boring to stand in the sun for hours at a time throwing his knives into the wooden dummy some fifty meters away. Lyra would filter in and out throughout the day to join him which helped the boredom, but only slightly.

After returning to the clearing and putting up his horse Haran, was greeted by Shiva, "Heyy girl," he said as he patted his lion's head, "Quite the damage you did to that dog earlier wasn't it." Haran knew the lion couldn't hear him and it had been hours since she had attacked the poor dog so there was no need to scold her. He gently said, "Shiva," she sat down in front of him. "Promise me you won't kill anything that isn't hurting me." He held out his hand and Shiva met it with her paw. She shook on it.

Haran moved to practice his knife throwing once more with Shiva following close behind him. However, before he even started practicing Orion called him inside.

In the cabin Haran saw that Orion had a message sitting on the dining table. "What's that?" Haran asked as he took a seat at the table next to Lyra who was rubbing the necklace he got her while entranced in deep thought.

Orion, who was currently putting out the fire in the fireplace, said softly, "A letter from the king, he wants us to go to Anjagor to discuss what to do about the approaching siege."

Haran looked to his master shocked, "That's going to take a week at the very least. Yet there is still so much to do. First we must find out how many men they have for the siege and what their plans are. And we must keep training, I am already feeling the effects of the trip to Athon."

Lyra realized the same thing, "And we still have to find out where that fifth tunnel that you discovered leads. I mean it could lead to somewhere essential to their plans."

"I know all of these things that we need to do, but we have to make a choice. Do we go to the king in hopes he can be of any help to us in the event of a siege, or do we go on our own and find out as much information possible about the situation?" Orion asked. Haran knew it was an impossible decision to make. If they went to the king and he couldn't help them in time, then they would walk into the siege blind and likely lose. However, if they didn't go to the king, but also didn't find out their plans for the siege they would also likely lose without any hope of reinforcement.

"What if we split up again," Haran suggested to solve their dilemma. "Orion will go to the king and Lyra and I will get information on the siege plans." However, before he could continue he saw Orion shaking his head no.

"I will not leave the two of you alone here to get information, you could be caught again and ransomed, or even worse they could just kill you on the spot," Orion said.

"So what do we do then?" Haran asked. If Orion made the wrong choice there was a good possibility that Norhall Castle would be taken and the fief itself would fall prey to the Lupens. Norhall was not prepared for a siege, nor was Anjagor prepared for a war. The country had spent the last ten years in relative peace and the army was now both complacent and weak compared to its former glory.

Orion stared into the small cinders of the fireplace for several minutes before saying anything, "We have to go to Anjagor in hopes that the king will be able to help us."

Haran sighed; he didn't like the idea of leaving behind his fief in such dire situations. However, he also knew that the decision Orion had made was a correct one because his gut was saying the same thing.

"Are you certain?" Lyra asked still rubbing the necklace thoughtfully.

"Nigel caused this problem with his brother so I trust he will fix it," Orion said.

'Let's go then," Haran said as he moved out of the house and onto the porch where Shiva was waiting patiently outside scanning the woods for any signs of intruders. "Come," he said as he patted his leg and went to their small stables to the left of the property. Haran saddled up Spirit and Shiva jumped into the side bag that was hanging gently from its side. When Shiva was in the bag it slowed Spirit's gait significantly, but the horse still carried the weight without problem, so Haran still used the side bag. If they were ever in an event that they were being chased Shiva knew by just the tap of Haran's leg to get out of the side bag. At that point Haran would pick the bag up from Spirit's side and Shiva would run alongside the horse. She was not nearly as fast as the horse in long distances, but Shiva could keep up with Spirit for a solid five hundred meters, well enough time to outrun any pursuers.

Orion and Lyra walked up behind him and saddled up their own horses. After doing so, Orion looked hard at his apprentice, "Where is your cloak?" he asked.

Haran looked down to see that he was wearing his tan shirt that he often wore under his cloak. He thought for a second of where his cloak went, then he remembered that he had used it to wrap around the dog he had saved this morning. Haran smiled brightly, "Hey, can we make just one stop before heading to the capital." Orion simply sighed and rode out of the clearing.

Haran knocked on the door of the goat farmer's house to which the farmer's wife opened the door yet again. She opened it frantically as if she had been waiting by the door expecting someone. Haran met her eyes, there was a small tear rolling down her cheek when she looked at him. "What's wrong?" Haran asked immediately. He wondered if the dog had died from her wounds.

"My husband, he's not home yet," The woman cried out loud. The sun was going down now. Haran assumed the man would have given up his search for the dog by now, and apparently she thought the same.

Haran looked at the woman crying before him. "Maybe he's just running a little late is all. I'm sure he will be back soon," Haran reassured her.

"I don't think so sir. I can feel it, he's in danger," The woman said it with so much conviction that Haran thought it must be true. How could she tell though? He thought to himself. Was it a thing that came with love? If so, would he ever experience such a connection. Haran shook it off, that didn't matter right now.

"You're an Outryder right?" the old lady asked as she held out his newly cleaned cloak.

"I am," Haran said.

"Then I beg of you. Find him," she said as she forced the cloak into his hands. Something switched on inside Haran's head. He would find this man no matter what the cost. He took the coat gratefully, nodded his head and walked calmly over to where his master and Lyra were waiting on their horses. Lyra noticed his face immediately, it was focused and determined, it was bright but also eager. Lyra recognized the face; it was the one she had seen when he first started training with her. "What happened?" She asked.

"Her husband, he's lost. I am going to find him," Haran said it with one hundred percent conviction. The woman had just trusted the life of the man she loved in his hands. He couldn't fail.

Haran looked to his master for permission although he had already made up his mind. Orion noticed the determination written on his face. He also realized that there was nothing that he was going to do to convince Haran that they needed to get to the capital. "Fine," The scruffy man said, "Find the man and then ride like hell to catch up."

"Thank you, Orion," Haran said.

After Orion and Lyra left the farmer's house Haran approached the man's wife. "Do you know which way he could have gone?" Haran knew that he couldn't track the man in the dark, but he also knew that if he were to wait until morning the man could be dead.

"Well usually when Missy gets lost she heads to Calcore Canyon. I don't know the reason. Maybe it has something to do with wolves. Oh my, there are wolves in that canyon. What if Rex gets caught by them?" The old lady asked worriedly.

Haran assumed the old man's name was Rex. "I will find him mam I promise you," he said as he rode off towards the canyon some four kilometers away, and he never broke his promises.

When he arrived at the canyon he heard nothing, not even a slight breeze or a loose rock falling. The silence was so deafening that Haran forced himself to stop breathing for several seconds just so he wouldn't break it. He could sense the air getting colder and thinner; as he breathed out all he saw was a puff of white smoke rise from his mouth. "What is happening?" he asked himself. As he looked around, he realized where he was, he was in the same spot where they had their battle months ago. In fact, he was in the exact location that the wolf god mercilessly killed Scarlett the fox and almost killed Shiva. He could sense the death and anger that took place there, and it sent chills down his spine.

He shook the feeling off and began making his way down the canyon. He left Shiva at the top of the canyon with Spirit so that if anyone thought they were going to steal his horse they would be gravely mistaken. When he reached the bottom, he hugged the left side of the canyon's walls. There were multiple reasons for this, the first was that the center of the canyon had a small river running through it. It only just recently began raining again as they were entering the summer months, so Calcore Canyon was once again filling with water. The second reason was that if any wolves were to attack him while he looked for the old man, he could easily climb his way up the canyon and out of danger.

He continued making his way to the end of the canyon and about halfway through he heard a howl in front of him. He moved quicker now but remained as silent as possible. Although that task was rather pointless due to the wolves' keen sense of smell. Whatever the case, he wouldn't take any chances. After moving some ten more meters down the canyon he saw what had made the earlier howl and why.

The alpha wolf of the pack was waiting at the bottom of the canyon wall looking up to something halfway up the wall in the darkness. The howl must have been a warning to the other wolves that there was something there or someone.

Haran couldn't see in the darkness, but he assumed it was the farmer. He got a little closer to the wolf but not close enough to risk getting caught. He then climbed some twenty meters up the wall to about the height he estimated Rex to be at and moved laterally the rest of the way to the man. It was a long process and rather exhausting, but eventually he reached the point where he could see the ledge that the wolf was howling at. His suspicions were confirmed when he saw the man bundled up on the ledge.

He moved a little bit closer to the man to where he was about two to three meters from the ledge, "Pst." The man didn't budge. "PSSSTTT" Haran did louder. The man looked to where the sound was coming from.

"Who's there?" he asked the darkness.

Haran thought about what to say, the man didn't know him so it would be no help identifying himself, "Your wife, she sent me after you. Can you please move over so I can get on the ledge with you?"

The man shuffled over ever so slightly, and Haran moved over to the ledge. He got onto it with a sigh of relief for his aching muscles.

"You're an Outryder," The man said trying to move as far away from him as possible.

"I am," Haran said noticing the slight shift in the man as he caught a glimpse of Haran's cloak.

"Well then I think you should go back to where you came from because I aint leaving with you," the old man said.

Haran sighed; many people had problems with Outryders although he saw no reason why. Maybe it was because Outryders tended to be somewhat reclusive and a tad bit irritable at times. However, they did a lot for their fief, and they received nothing in return, not even the slightest bit of recognition. "Listen your wife is worried sick about you and if you don't help me help you then I will tell her that you died because of your own pride." Haran saw the man's face shift slightly, "Now, will you let me help you."

The man nodded slightly and shifted a little closer to Haran. "Fine, but you wont see me thanking you when I get out of here."

"Wasn't expecting it," Haran said, "Now, here's what we are going to do. Can you climb?"

The old man unbundled himself to reveal a nasty bite on his left thigh. The old man had smartly cut off circulation to it to avoid blood loss, but if he would have stayed all night he would have surely died. "No."

"How'd you get up here?" Haran asked confused. There was no other way to get onto the ledge without climbing.

"Fear drove me up the wall, but now I can barely move," Rex said. Haran grunted he had really been hoping it would be easy. He maneuvered his satchel from his side to his front. Luckily for the both of them he had been stranded in Calcore Canyon many times in his life and he knew what it took to get out of there with his life. He brought a rope out from the satchel and tied it to the man's waist and tightened it. He also tied the other end to his waist. "Hold tight when I reach the top I will pull you up. What you are going to do is climb up the wall with your arms as I pull you up. That way even if you slip you will not fall," Haran said to the man calmly. In another stroke of luck, the old man was rather skinny, and Haran figured he would be able to pull him up the thirty meters or so with some help from him.

He began climbing up the wall face with the rope tied around him, so he had both hands free. He was exhausted as he climbed up the sheer face. About ten meters up the canyon his left hand slipped leaving him hanging on just the right hand. He held himself, but if it had baen his right hand that had slipped, he would have come crashing back down to the ledge. "Phew," He sighed as he continued his climb. He made the rest of the way up without incident and rolled over the edge of the canyon.

Haran then began pulling the old man up the sheer face of the cliff. At around five meters in the man slipped leaving all of his weight squarely on Haran's shoulders; he held the rope up just barely and the man caught his balance. "Just because I said you don't have to worry about slipping doesn't mean it's fun," He called down to the old man who simply grunted without care. He made it up about ten more meters and then slipped again. Haran only grunted with strain this time. There was no point in complaining twice.

After some five more minutes of struggle, Rex made it to the top. Haran was breathing heavy when he rolled over the edge. "Ok old man remind me to never save anyone else as long as I live."

The man only grunted and sat down on the rocky ground. Haran sat down beside him, "The name is Haran Ryder in case you cared to know."

Ryder," the old man said with an ironic smile, "of course your family name is Ryder. I assume your father was Atticus then?"

"That's what I am told," Haran replied, "Although I never knew him."

Rex looked at the boy beside him, "You know he saved my life once too right?"

"Really? How?" Haran asked. He had been told so much about his father from Orion. He was known as the best in the Outryders even with carrying the weight of three generations of secrets and expectations squarely on his shoulders. *How did he do it?* Haran asked himself, *how did he live up to the Ryder name?*

"It was turning spring some many years ago and the entire country were on edge because the Athonians were wiping out town after town in the invasion. One day I was serving as a lookout on the road for Athonian troops when me and those who were serving with me were ambushed by the Athonians. Now we were no trained fighters mind you, we had only just been called into the military because they were in desperate need of men. We were destroyed in seconds as twenty trained men surrounded me and half a dozen men. However, as one of the soldiers rose his sword to finish me off, a knife came spinning out of nowhere and slammed into his chest. Not even two seconds later five soldiers that were around me all fell from a knife in their chest. Then, out of nowhere, your father appeared in the same green cloak you have on now. He fought everyone with those two axes of his, tearing through everyone that dared come near him. It was honestly terrifying to watch, it was like he was possessed by some god of war. I have never seen a man that could fight like that again and I probably never will."

"He sounded awesome," Haran said, but then he thought back to when the man shifted away from him when he first arrived on the ledge, "So why don't you like Outryder's then?"

The man got up and took Haran's hand, "because two years after that the current Outryder Orion took my first-born son's life."

Haran gulped and took Rex's hand standing up exhaustedly, "Sorry for your loss, what was his name?"

"Vincent, but we just called him Vin," Rex said. "He was a bandit and made many poor choices in life, but he was still a good kid at heart. That was until Orion came along."

Haran sighed, no one blamed the logger for felling trees or the farrier for trimming hooves or the farmer for harvesting crops, but everyone blamed the Outryders for doing their jobs. Everyone blamed the Outryder for saving lives.

After limping their way to Spirit the two of them rode to the farmer's house silently. After arriving Haran supported Rex and walked him to the door. Without even having to knock the old woman opened the door and hugged her husband. "Thank you," she said on the verge of tears. "Thank you."

"No problem," Haran said. It was all worth it in the end.

"Is there anything we can do to help you?" She asked.

Haran shook his head, "Nope I am totally fine," he said as he walked over to Spirit. However, before he could even get on the horse he passed out from sheer exhaustion.

CHAPTER

25

Haran woke up in a small room on a rather comfortable bed. The sun was beaming through the window violently. He grunted trying to think what had happened, but before he could think he heard a voice from the doorway. "Wait wait young man you need to rest." Haran looked up to see the old woman was the one that spoke. Now he remembered, he had just returned the farmer from the canyon, he must have passed out and the couple must have moved him to this room. "Where's Spirit and Shiva? I need to get going Orion and Lyra are probably already at the castle. How long have I been asleep?" Haran asked.

"Almost fourteen hours," The woman said.

"Fourteen?!" Haran exclaimed. Haran sat up on the bed although every bone in his body protested it. "I have to get going."

"No son you have to rest. You are exhausted, have bruises all over your body, a sprained ankle and are running a fever you have to rest for at least another day or maybe even two," the woman said. However, Haran ignored it and got out of bed, an instant regret. His legs gave out from under him, and he fell on to the hardwood floor below. "Oww," he groaned.

"You insolent boy I told you that you need rest now get up," the old woman demanded.

Haran struggled greatly to his feet. "Fine, twelve hours," he said with a sigh as he sat back down on the bed. "Whose bed is this anyway?" he asked as he fluffed the pillow. It was the softest bed he had ever felt.

"My son's, or it was his," the woman said sadly.

"Vin's?" Haran asked assuming that was the son she was referring to.

The woman noticed his change in tone, "No, no, Vin died many years ago. This was my second son's room."

"What happened to him?" Haran asked, "Did he die too?"

"Oh he's fine. He is all cozied up in Norhall Castle right about now. He's a guard there," she explained.

Haran sighed with relief as his shoulders untensed. "What's his name?"

"Akin," she said with a smile.

"That's a cool name," Haran said tiredly. He visited the castle a lot, maybe he met her son already.

"Thank you. Now please rest son. You need it," the woman said as she walked out of the door.

Haran didn't dare refuse her request. As soon as she walked out his head hit the soft pillow and he passed out.

Some eight hours later he woke up and was able to limp into the living area. After a rather lovely dinner, Haran made his way out of the door slowly. He thanked the couple for their hospitality and moved over to Spirit who was tethered to a wooden post some five meters away. Shiva, who was laying down beside the horse, noticed Haran's movement and ran over and tackled her master to the ground playfully. "Mmm," Haran groaned painfully. He laughed at the thought of how the old couple possibly could have drug his unconscious body away from the overprotective Shiva. It must have taken hours at least.

After getting up he hopped onto Spirit and waved the couple goodbye.

He started at sunset and rode Spirit hard to catch up to Orion and Lyra. He saw no one on the road to Anjagor, but it was a given. He reached the border of Anjagor just after midnight and stopped to give Spirit a rest for a few minutes. He was quite bored on his journey. The only sound was that of Spirit's hoofbeats and an occasional rustle from Shiva, but other than that there was nothing. Not even a slight breeze, it was just calm. "Interesting," Haran said as he sat on a log just off the road and watched the stars above.

He waited in that spot for just under ten minutes and began moving again. At the pace he was moving, he would reach Anjagor by noon on the next day.

It was about sunrise when he finally saw someone on the long road to the capital. The man looked like a trader of sorts. He had the classic Anjagorian features and was driving a wagon stuffed with various fruits and vegetables. Haran thought it was smart to be on the roads before the sun came up. The bandits and lurkers wouldn't be out yet, so there would be no attacks against him. They waved to each other kindly and went on their way to their destinations. The man was so much different from the people he had passed by in Athon. There, every time he waved he only received a scowl in return for his friendliness.

Haran passed many more people on the way to Anjagor Castle. They were making their way to their respective jobs and tasks. It was a very good possibility that they could be going to war soon, he thought with a frown, but now they were cheerful and smiling. Could he keep it that way?

He reached the bottom of the gentle slope that led to Anjagor Castle. The castle was on a rather big hill that plateaued out at the top. A big ravine cut a scar down the middle of the plateau leaving one side with the gentle slope to its side and the other with a steep two hundred meter drop off on the other. The ravine itself was made by thousands of men mining for the necessary stones of the castle. Haran didn't know if they mined it like such to serve as a defensive tool, or if it was coincidence, but whatever the case, the ravine served as the best defensive tool of the entire castle.

A stone bridge loomed over the thirty-meter scar. About ten meters of that was a removeable wooden piece. Therefore, if any attacker were to approach from the side with the slight slope the defenders could simply remove the wooden centerpiece of the bridge. And if anyone were to try attacking from the backside of the castle, they wouldn't be able to get an entire army up the sheer face of the plateau. The placement of the capital was remarkable and was probably how Anjagor remained in its earlier years as a country.

After making his way up the slope the bridge came into view. He had seen the bridge three times now and every time it amazed him how they managed to get the bridge to span such a long gap and how deep the plateau's scar really was. As he looked down it and couldn't see the bottom chills shot through his spine. He passed a man going away from the city, he had a large frame and large hands, it looked as if he were a fighter of sorts. As the man passed by, his blonde hair and light grey shirt quickly turned into a black suit of armor with jutting spikes coming out of it in every direction.

It was a quick switch, but a terrifying one. Haran's heart raced as he thought about his dream of the canyon, and how the black suit of armor drove him into the bottomless pit. He looked to the edge of the bridge. *No*, Haran thought, *I can't let that happen.* He whipped around taking a knife out of his sash in the process. However, as he turned around the black suit of armor was a man again, a very confused man, "Hey son," he said reaching for his sword. "Put that knife away before you hurt yourself."

Haran took double take, blinking his eyes repeatedly before he eventually put his knife away, "Sorry sir, I thought you were someone else."

"It's okay son," the man said, "just try not to pull knives out on random people from here on out."

Haran looked to the man confused. "Will do sir I am sorry. Have a nice day," Haran said as he turned around and took a deep breath. *What just happened*, he thought. One second the black warrior was there, and the next he was gone. What was wrong with him? Why was he seeing this warrior so much? He shook the thoughts out of his mind as he entered the castle.

Castle Anjagor was set up in a two-wall concentric system where the outer wall held the city of Anjagor itself and all of the residents and the inner wall held the barracks, the keep, and many other important buildings. That's where he headed now assuming Orion and Lyra were already waiting for him with the king. After making his way to the inner wall and putting up Shiva and Spirit in the stables, he heard a familiar voice call his name. He whipped around to see Cassius, the Outryder commander, standing a meter behind him, "How long have you been following me?" he immediately asked.

"Oh, only about the ten minutes or so since you first entered the city," Cassius replied.

"I only noticed you some three minutes ago," Haran said. "So not to bad I don't think."

"No not really I suppose, what gave me away?" Cassius asked as he walked casually into the castle.

"You were upwind. I smelled your scented perfume that you wear," Haran said, the first time he visited Cassius he noticed the rather poignant scent of lavender that the man wore. He didn't think much of it when he first smelled it, but now it was easily recognizable as his scent.

"That wretched wife of mine, always spraying that stuff around me," Cassius defended himself, "I keep telling her that it is a detriment in the field."

"Interesting. Where is Orion and Lyra?" Haran asked to which Cassius' initial reaction was one of confusion. Haran had assumed the two Outryder's would have been here by now, but it seems he was wrong. They must have stopped for the night somewhere whereas he carried on through.

Cassius walked up the castle step with Haran right behind him. "I haven't seen them," Cassius said. "Why aren't you with them?"

"It's a long story," Haran said, "but let's just say I got caught up in a different situation entirely."

"Oh, got it," Cassius said, "Well they shouldn't be too far behind in any case."

Haran nodded and stopped, "Well, actually, since we have time, can you help me with a little something I have been struggling on?" Cassius was the Outryder commander, so he figured if anyone other than Orion could help with his throwing it would be him.

"Sure, why not?" Cassius said as Haran led him into the courtyard below.

In the courtyard there were many hay targets that the archers of the garrison would use for practice. They were all empty now due to how early it was in the day. In a few more hours he was sure there would be many archers and infantry there to hone their skills. However, for now, he figured that would be a good place to throw into. He lined up to it, counted twenty meters away, judged his distance, took a throwing knife from his sash, put the knife between his pointer finger and his thumb, and released it smoothly yet with great power. It spun through the air beautifully and hit the target three centimeters over the bullseye. The throw was great, but Haran still missed his target. He looked over to Cassius who was watching carefully. "Once more," the commander said.

Haran threw another knife. It spun through the air with the same gusto, but this time it hit the target some five centimeters below the bullseye. Neither were bad throws by any means, but the target was stationary, it would be much different if the target were charging at him erratically.

"Again," Cassius said.

He threw another with nearly the same results. However, this time Cassius didn't ask for it a third time, he simply took a knife of his own out and sent it flying toward the target. The fluidity of the movement was like water in a stream. He grabbed the knife, put it in between his thumb and his palm and put his pointer finger down the hilt, drew his hand back to his cheek, and released at the point where the knife was roughly one hundred and twenty degrees from the turning point on his wrist all within the span of a second. The knife sliced through the air gracefully, almost as if it were moving in slow motion. It struck the dead center of the bullseye with so much power that it knocked the target off its resting place. However, there was one very important thing that Haran noticed, "there was no spin." Every time he has seen Orion throw his knives spun through the air majestically and struck the target just where he wanted it, so he had been trying to replicate that.

"Very good," Cassius said, "You see there are two ways an Outryder throws a knife. The first is with spin, that's what Orion uses. The second is with no spin. Neither way is easier than the other, but somehow only half of the Outryders can perfect one and the other half can perfect the other."

"Why is that?" Haran asked.

"To be honest, I really don't know," Cassius said, "Maybe it has something to do with the person's personality, or brain function or something, but all I know is that you are a no spin thrower."

Haran struggled to wrap his mind around the idea of personality affecting use of a weapon. It was plausible, but was the assumption accurate? Both Lyra and Orion could throw their knife with spin, why were he and Cassius different? "Wait so what was my father then? Spin or no spin?"

Cassius was taken aback that Haran knew his father was an Outryder, but then he reasoned that Orion must have told him and answered honestly, "Atticus Ryder was a spin thrower."

Haran grew even more confused. If his father was a spin thrower, then why was he different. Cassius saw his look and said, "Don't get caught up on how it all works because you will just drive yourself insane, how about I just teach you how to throw without spin?"

Haran nodded and Cassius began teaching him how to throw the knife with no spin.

It took about an hour for Haran to even hit the target using the technique of putting the knife between his thumb and palm and controlling the release with his pointer. Learning it new was significantly harder for him seeing as he had already been practicing on the spin technique for so long. However, after countless times of the knives helplessly bouncing off the hay target, he finally stuck one in solidly.

They continued to practice for another hour as the courtyard filled with people practicing before Cassius whispered, "Stop." He moved smoothly to the shadow casted by the castle walls.

Haran followed suit. "What are we doing?" Haran asked confused by the sudden change in the commander.

"Orion's horse," Cassius whispered back, "Its here."

It was hard for Haran to think through all the noise in the courtyard. Between the clanging of swords, the releasing of bow strings, and the clopping of horses' feet, the noises were deafening. He whispered back, "How can you tell?"

"It walks at a slightly slower gait than every other horse," Cassius said. "Which may or may not be my fault," he added.

Haran couldn't even hear himself think, yet Cassius could differentiate between the gait of hoofbeats from the dozens of horses outside the walls? He had a lot more training before he was on that level.

Cassius snuck to the gate that Orion and Lyra were about to come through using the shadows of the wall; Haran copied his actions. Cassius hugged the castle wall in front of the gate. Haran could hear the hoofbeats approaching. Cassius took out an axe from his scabbard with his right hand and held up three fingers. . . then two . . . then one . . . and zero. Orion emerged from the gateway seemingly unaware of his surroundings. However, Haran knew him better than that and he already knew that Lyra was somewhere waiting for her time to strike.

Cassius swung the blunt end of his axe at Orion's side, if it made contact it would probably crack a rib but not do any significant damage. However, before the swing even got close to Haran's master, Lyra came from the shadows behind Haran and tackled Cassius to the ground.

"You can't surprise me Cassius, I can smell your lady perfume everywhere," Orion said.

It's not *my* perfume," Cassius grunted as Lyra helped him to his feet. "You sent her in here when I was teaching him how to throw right?"

Orion simply nodded.

Lyra turned around to Haran, "How did you get here already? And what happened with the farmer is he alive."

"He is alive and well," Haran said, "If not a little mortified."

"What happened—"

"Alright, chit chat can resume later," Orion interrupted, "We are on a time crunch here, and it's time to see the king."

CHAPTER

26

The four of them walked into King Nigel's office together. "Four Outryders enter in a king's office," Nigel said beginning to start a really bad joke. "You know what the oldest one says?"

"You know I get sick of your jokes Nigel," Cassius said.

"Right on the dot," Nigel jested, "How does he do it folks?"

Haran laughed alongside him and thought about the last time he saw Nigel. He was in a broken state at that point; he just had to make a choice between killing his only brother or protecting his country. There's no worse decision to make, but Haran believe his decision was the right one. However, apparently going home to his family had helped him significantly over the past two months since then.

"Haha so funny," Cassius said, "Now can we please get serious, Norhall is at risk here."

"You are no fun," Nigel said, "but fine, I suppose we can get serious." Almost instantly Haran saw a change in King Nigel as if he had flipped a switch that turned him serious.

"Alright so Orion," he said. "I hear you took a hiatus in your duties as an Outryder to go on a vacation to Athon is that correct?"

Vacation? Haran thought, he had risked his life multiple times on their trip to Athon only for them to come back and for King Nigel to refer to it as a 'vacation'. *Unbelievable.*

"I wouldn't refer to it as a hiatus or a vacation my lord," Orion said defensively. "We went to Athon to research how to kill the wolf god."

"And? What'd you find?" King Nigel asked.

Orion gestured for Haran to show him the notebook. Haran took it out of his satchel and flipped to the last page showing it to King Nigel. "Ahh, I see," he said as he looked over the page several more times. "Show that to Cassius if he hasn't seen it yet."

Haran showed the journal to the Outryder commander who also read over it multiple times; each time reading it he grimaced slightly more.

"So who is the wolf's owner?" King Nigel asked.

"Lottie," Haran said.

Cassius looked up from the journal and seeing the confusion on King Nigel's face he added, "You remember the boy who almost took your life at the canyon?"

"A boy?" King Nigel said, "We have to kill a boy to stop a god?"

Kill? Haran thought, *Surely they didn't plan to kill a man in cold blood?* Haran had his fare share of spats with the boy, but the thought of killing Lottie never crossed his mind. It was barbaric. There had to be another way.

"Lottie may be young," Orion said, "But don't underestimate him. He *would* be very tough to kill."

Haran was flabbergasted by his master's acceptance of the idea. "No one is killing anyone," Haran said convincedly. "We are going to find another way."

Cassius and Nigel looked over hopelessly to Orion who said, "Haran, there is no other way."

"What gives you the right to think that?" Haran asked, "We have barely even researched the concept, yet you three are willing to take a man's life on a chance."

"Haran the fact is that we have simply run out of time," Orion said. "He will be at the siege, and if there is a chance we have to take it."

He looked to Lyra for support but was simply met with a shrug. Everyone was against him. He paused, not daring to break eye contact with his master, "There's another way Orion. I promise you, there has to be another way."

Moments passed as everyone's eyes fixated on Haran. After a minute or two King Nigel sat up in his seat agitatedly, "Ok so what is it about the siege that you know?"

Lyra spoke this time, "We know when they are attacking."

The king sighed disdainfully, "Is that it? What about tactics, manpower or equipment."

"As of now we do not know any of those three," Orion said.

"For crying out loud Orion," King Nigel exclaimed as he threw a stack of papers from his desk. "Is it not your job to know these things?"

"It is my lord, but-"

"But what?" King Nigel demanded, "I don't need excuses, I need you to do your job."

Haran looked over to his master who was stone faced as ever. He knew Orion wanted to argue back, but for some reason he did not, he just sat helplessly under the king's scrutiny.

"Excuse me King Nigel," Lyra said clearing her throat. All the tense air in the room shifted to her, "But we came to you in Anjagor instead of doing the reconnaissance work."

"Yeah," Haran interjected relieving even more of the tension from Orion, "We could have gotten the information, but you asked us here. We decided to come here because we thought you would be able to help us not for you to yell at us."

The king was about to speak before Lyra interjected again, "Plus, your brother is the one who caused this all to begin with. Orion is simply cleaning his mess."

Haran saw King Nigel grow angry for a split second, but soon the anger turned to shame. After a brief time and eventually hung his head in contrition, "I am sorry Orion, you have done more than your fair share of work. Now it's time for me to do mine." He gestured to the door, "Cassius can you grab General Lee from his office for me?"

"Yes my lord," Cassius said as he walked out of the office.

They waited in the room for some time before Cassius came back with General Lee. The general was a big man, at least a foot taller than Haran, he had emerald eyes and blond hair. At his waist he carried a five-foot longsword that was encrusted with rubies. "You called me my lord?" He said after taking a long look around to the four Outryders in the room. As he caught eyes with Orion, Haran could feel the tense air that was once there rekindle. The last time they had met, Orion had denigrated his son to his face and embarrassed him in front of the king, so it was reasonable to assume that he still harbored ill feelings.

"Yes I want you to take five hundred of our finest men and make your way to Norhall Castle right away," King Nigel said.

"Five hundred?" General Lee exclaimed. "That's almost the entire garrison. What are you going to do in the event of an attack?"

"There will be no attack on this castle," King Nigel said. It was true, even without the majority of the garrison, Castle Anjagor could hold out indefinitely. "However, there will be on Castle Norhall in two weeks' time, so you need to get there and fast."

"But my lord it will take at least three weeks to move that number of troops to Norhall," General Lee said, "Surely you must be joking?"

"You have two weeks general. Might want to get moving," King Nigel said. At that, General Lee exited the door and went to rally five hundred men.

"My king," Orion said. "The siege is just over a week from today. If Lee shows up in two weeks' time we could be long dead."

"I am sure you can stall just a little bit Orion," King Nigel said tiredly. "I have done all that I can."

Orion nodded, "Thank you my king."

"Of course," the king said. "Now please leave, Cassius and I have a long-awaited chess game that I would like to finish."

Orion nodded and walked out of the door with Haran and Lyra following suit.

They were all downstairs and in the courtyard before they dared to speak a word. "Orion," Haran said, "Why didn't you defend yourself back there?"

"There's no point, he's right."

"What do you mean he's right?" Lyra asked.

"Nigel, he's right," Orion said, "I have been too focused on keeping you two out of danger when I should have been doing my job."

Haran was confused, nothing he had done since the canyon was pointless, everything they had done was to prevent from further pain and suffering. "Well, that's not fair," he noted, "We are your apprentices, so it is technically your job to protect us too."

"Exactly," Lyra added, "Besides, Orion, don't worry about us, we can handle ourselves."

"I know," Orion said, "But I don't know what I would do if I lost the two of you, especially if I made the call."

Haran was jarred to the core, did Orion just kind of admit he cared about them? Surely it must have been a joke. Orion would never admit to such a thing.

Lyra turned to her master, "Whenever we follow you it's because we trust you Orion, not because your our master. We trust you will have the answer we don't because you are you. Orion the magnificent," she said it with an echo as if she were announcing a stage magician.

Haran laughed and said, "Shut up Lyra."

"Why don't you make me with those floppy ears of yours," Lyra replied.

Haran subconsciously felt for his ears, "They aren't that big you bug eyed freak."

"Enough," Orion said with a hint of a smile as they hopped onto their horses and made their way back to Norhall.

Their ride back was fairly quiet, Haran talked about what happened with the farmer in the canyon and his conversation with Cassius about the two different techniques.

"Oh yeah sorry about that," Orion said, "I meant to say something when we came back from Athon, but I guess it slipped my mind."

"So your father threw differently than you throw? Lyra asked, "How does that work?"

"I have no idea," Haran said, "Cassius theorized that it was based off of personality traits, but I don't know how accurate that is."

"Very actually," Orion said.

"How so?" Haran asked. It made no sense, how could personalities affect your ability to throw a knife?

"You'll have to figure that out on your own," Orion said.

Haran scoffed, Orion was always like this, always avoiding questions that he knew the answer to. "Can't you just tell me, it's easier that way?"

"If I told you everything then you would never know the satisfaction of figuring it out yourself," Orion said. Haran conceded to the point and continued his ride in silence.

When they arrived back in Fuestres Woods they had exactly one week to prepare for the siege. "Do you think we should try and investigate the fifth tunnel?" Haran asked as they rode into the clearing.

"There's no point, we have no time left," Orion said, "For now you have to keep up your training, especially your throwing Haran, and rest up before the fight of your lives."

"What will you do Orion?" Haran asked.

"Well, I have to go to Baron Ligate and figure out what he thinks we are going to do during the siege, and I have to figure out how to stall the Lupens for at least a week."

"I thought Outryders didn't take other people's battle plans," Lyra said smiling. It was an idea that Orion commonly espoused along with other very *insightful* quotes that essentially doubled their workload.

"That's why I said, 'what he thinks we are going to do' not what we are actually going to do," Orion said.

"We will get you one day Orion," Haran said jokingly. He and Lyra had been trying to get Orion to contradict his words since the week Haran started, but they still hadn't succeeded. The man was abnormally consistent.

"Not a chance in the world," Orion said as he rode his horse out of the forest and onto Norhall Castle.

After Orion left Haran went straight to his training, he thought about their conversation with the king and how easily everyone else was willing to kill Lottie simply because they could not think of another way to kill the wolf god. And maybe there wasn't another way to kill Lupe, but he would never kill someone in cold blood. Maybe Orion was right, maybe there were no good guys. Including himself.

CHAPTER

27

Lottie woke up in his bed just as the clock struck six, he lie there for a few more minute staring at the marbled ceiling. Eventually he drug himself out of bed and got himself dressed. Lupe, who noticed the movement, soon came over to his side, "Hey buddy," he said as he pet the wolf, his ever-constant companion.

He walked outside the house and down the hill to begin training. He only had a week and a half before the siege and if he were going to beat Haran he would have to train like a madman. The last two times they fought Lottie got distracted, this time that wasn't going to be the case. Nothing would distract him during the siege. Nothing. Almost in that same instant he heard someone call his name. He turned to see who it was to find Tyson and Tomas walking up to him from the top of the hill. "Hey guys," Lottie said, "What are you two doing down here already, we don't have mandatory training for another two hours."

"Umm actually we came to talk," Tomas said.

"About?" Lottie asked.

Tomas paused for a while and looked to Tyson who simply shrugged, "Mhm. Fine. Lottie when you were gone we started noticing Ella and Jet hanging out a lot. We tried telling her that it was getting weird, but she ignored us, so we wanted to let you know before you found out too late."

"Thank you boys, but I am not too much worried about that whole thing right now." Lottie said which was technically the truth. All he was focused on was winning the coming fight against Haran. If he could just win he might regain his dignity and be able to face Ella as a man, but as of now he would come before her as a trembling little boy.

"Fair enough," Tomas said, "Want to go train then?"

"Of course, can't have yall dying on me during the siege now can we?" Lottie said as he ran down the hill to begin his intense training.

They spent two hours training hard before the entire blue group showed up for their actual training. As Supreme General Norman requested in their meeting, Lottie and Tomas were to lead all the blue group's trainings until the siege so that they could gain the respect of the group.

"Alright," Lottie bellowed over the roughly three hundred voices in the room, "First item of business. Who amongst you do not think Tomas or I am qualified to lead you?" Roughly fifty people rose their hands immediately, and some fifty more followed shortly after. The rest would have seen either of them in battle, or at least heard of their skill.

"Alright then, which one of you would like to take our spots?" Lottie asked.

All one hundred of those who had their hand up immediately put them down. Leading a group of three hundred people on a mission that could make or break a siege was a daunting task, and none of them were eager to try their hand at it.

"That's what I thought," Lottie said, "So now let's begin."

Lottie split the three hundred people into groups of thirty seeing as that was how he planned for them to enter the castle. They would go in thirty at a time in waves until eventually they overwhelmed the defenders. His group would be the first thirty in, those would be the most skilled and deadly fighters. This was because the first group would face the most opposition in the beginning part of the siege. The rest would pour in soon after and they would all be able to hit the defenders in their expose flanks. At least he hoped they would. There were many flaws in the plan, but it was the best they could do on such short notice.

He paired the ten groups off and they began practicing working together with their respective teammates. It was a crude form of training, but it was effective to say the least. After some six hours of the training, he could already see the groups' teamwork beginning to strengthen.

"All right, that's enough for today," Lottie said, "You boys go home and be prepared for training tomorrow."

That night Lottie was laying on his bed staring at the ceiling when he heard a knock on his door. "Who is it?" he called to the door.

Ella barged through the door quickly, "Alright Lottie, I have something to say, and you aren't going to interrupt."

"Go for it," Lottie said.

"Ok, so I feel really bad for the other day when Jet interrupted our moment. I really really really love the rose." Ella caught her breath. "And we haven't talked for days, and I really miss talking to you and you haven't even told me about what happened on your trip, and I really don't know what I did wrong."

"Are you done with all your reallys?" Lottie asked with a smile.

"Yeah really sorry," Ella said. Then she realized what she had said and cringed slightly, "Ok I am done."

"Ok," Lottie said as he told her the story of him and Gilpin's trip to Athon. He told her everything from when they killed the guards at the guard post to when he threw the satchel off of the cliff.

"Gilpin murdered that many people?" Ella asked surprised, "For what reason?"

"He said it might start a war between Anjagor and Athon, but I couldn't tell you," Lottie said.

"Hmm and you burned down the library? Why?"

"I honestly didn't think of the fire burning when I threw the torch down, but it served rather useful, and the old man lived so it was ok," Lottie said.

"And what was so important about that old man that led them there?" Ella asked.

Lottie thought about it for a moment, "I don't know, but I assume it had something to do with something in Haran's satchel. I mean he jumped off a cliff for it, so it must have been special in some way."

"It's his father's," Ella said as she recalled the time when she asked Lyra why he carried the thing around and that was her exact response.

"I know," Lottie said, "But something isn't right. I think something was in the satchel. But El...I lost again."

Ella sighed and sat slowly on the bed, she had told him multiple times that she didn't care about all that, but he would never listen. "Lottie. How many times do I have to tell you that you don't have to beat him."

"But I do though El, he took my dignity at the battle at the canyon, and I *have* to return the favor," Lottie said as he met Ella's eyes. "He must feel the shame I felt as I knelt beneath his mercy and the feeling of impending death I sensed at his every slightest movement."

"Lottie I hope you don't mean that you plan to . . ."

"Kill him? Of course not, but he *has* to feel it El. He has to feel my fear," Lottie said.

Ella got up energetically, "Well then I will help you, so what's the plan?"

Lottie smiled and laid down on his bed, "First things first we get a good night's sleep and tomorrow you can train with us."

"Those are few and far between these days," Ella said rubbing her eyes tiredly.

"How so?" Lottie asked. He had noticed how tired Ella had looked since he got back from Athon, but he figured it was because she had resumed her training.

"I can't sleep," Ella said, "what if he—" She paused, stopping herself from further speech.

"What if what?" Lottie asked confused by Ella's sudden pause in speech, "who is he?"

"No one," Ella said, "Nothing. Good night Lottie." She began to walk out the door as Lottie looked at her confused. However, she turned as hand felt for the door, "Oh. It wasn't sparring by the way."

Ella walked out of the door leaving Lottie a little more than confused. *It wasn't sparring.* What did that mean? Who was he she was referring to? Did she mean the scar on her cheek? If so, what had happened, and why was she being cryptic about it?

He lay thinking on her words for an hour or so until he eventually heard another knock on her door. He immediately shot up thinking it may be Ella. "Come in," he said.

Percival entered the door casually, "Hey Lottie."

Lottie looked away slightly disappointed; Percival noticed the action. "Not who you were expecting huh?"

"No," Lottie said honestly, "Not really."

"Fair enough," Percival said as he strutted across the room, "Well I wanted to say thank you for saving me from Gilpin's rage and I wanted to tell you I heard about the trip."

Lottie assumed the man was talking about his and Gilpin's trip to Athon. "Which parts?"

"All of them," Percival said, "Quite the bold move of you two to go after the Outryders don't you think?"

"I suppose," Lottie said, "but I don't think that it paid off."

"How so?"

"Well, I mean we don't even know if they learned anything that will help them kill Lupe," Lottie said, "And if they did, we certainly didn't stop them as I had hoped."

"Stop them? Are you referring to your loss at the cliff to the other boy?" Percival asked casually, "What's his name again?"

"Haran," Lottie said after pausing for a few seconds.

"Ahh, Haran you say? He must be quite powerful to defeat you in combat," Percival said.

Lottie shook his head, "He's strong definitely, but I shouldn't be losing to him. However, every time I go to fight him I always seem to come out on the losing end, and I don't understand how."

Percival shook his head, "Lottie, you see I subscribe to the notion that every person in this world including yourself has exactly one other person that seems to be able to beat them at everything they do. Everything from horseback riding to fishing to fighting they will always beat you. A person that you've often known for what seems like many lifetimes. A rival of sorts."

"Many lifetimes?" Lottie asked, in fact, it did feel like he had known Haran for longer than he had known anyone else. Could he have known him in a past life? *No.* He thought, *impossible. But wait, that's what I said about gods too.* He looked over to Lupe who at the foot of the bed eyeing Percival carefully

"Yes lifetimes," Percival said. "Well in that case just the word rival is a bit reductive. How about eternal rival?"

"Eternal rival you say?" Lottie asked. If he were honest, the idea wasn't too farfetched as he thought about it. If he and Haran were eternal rivals then Doran and the king were most likely eternal rivals. Could Gilpin and Orion be eternal rivals? Who was Ella's eternal rival, or Jet's, or Tomas'? All of these questions left him with just one he could ask that the man could answer. "So, then who is *your* 'eternal rival'?"

Percival grimaced slightly, "A man by the name of Byron Redcliff. He was the bane of my existence. He was perfect in every way, the perfect house, the perfect children, the perfect wife . . ." He trailed off. Lottie noticed the switch.

"His wife. You seem attached to her. What was your relationship with her?" Lottie asked, he knew nothing of the man in front of him other than the fact that he worshipped Lupe. So he pried deeper into the little he knew about Percival Woodberg.

"We were together before I got put into a coma by a bucking horse," Percival said. "When I woke up six months later, Byron had my job, my misses, and my entire family on his side."

"What'd you do after waking up?" Lottie asked.

"Well, I turned to books for answers to my problems before I eventually found that no problem can be solved by words. So, I took matters into my own hands. However, I did come across a book that talked about a wolf god who, much like myself, had been cast out from his family," Percival said. "And after researching him in depth, I found out about the Lupens, and I found out about this place."

"How did you beat him? Byron that is?" Lottie asked.

"I soon realized that we humans manifest everything we do," Percival said, "So when I looked deep within me, I realized that in fact, Byron was no better than me at anything and I could finally live my life after I left."

Lottie took in his words carefully, but Haran was better than him at everything. He was a better fighter, a better person... a better man, "What if your eternal rival *is* better than you."

"Trust me son," Percival said, "that is only in your head. You are better than you could possibly imagine."

"Maybe you're right," Lottie said. *Maybe.*

There was a slight pause before Lottie spoke again. "Have you seen Byron since you left?"

"I have been back home a few times, but Byron wasn't there," Percival said.

"What happened to him?" Lottie asked.

"Unfortunately, he and his entire family died in an explosion shortly after I left," Percival said.

Before Lottie could ask his one last question Sylvia knocked from the doorway, "Gilpin needs you in his office right now."

Lottie shot up from his bed and followed Percival and Sylvia into Gilpin's office. Ella followed closely behind Lottie. As they all entered the room Sylvia shut the door behind them.

"What seems to be the problem sir?" Percival asked Gilpin.

There was a slight pause before Gilpin replied, "The tunnel exits. They have all been exploded."

Lottie flinched as he heard the news. If the tunnel exits had been exploded, then there was no way that they could use them in just a week's time for the siege. It would take at least twice that long to dig them all out again, postponing the siege by at least a week.

Lottie cursed slightly under his breath. They had been outsmarted once again.

CHAPTER

28

It had been a week since the Outryders blew up the tunnels of Randint Cavern. It was Lyra's idea to use gunpowder to explode the tunnels to postpone the siege, and it seemed to be working rather efficiently. The siege was scheduled for the next day and there were no Lupens to be found.

Since Cassius had shown him the new throwing technique Haran had been putting in hours and hours of practice to perfect it. However, his training had to stop for now, and he was still far from perfect. He hoped that the siege wouldn't have him use them, but he knew that it was a good possibility.

For now, Haran, Orion, and Lyra were all starting the process of moving every resident of Norhall village into the castle itself. They didn't expect the Lupens to get free from the tunnel for another day or so, but they went ahead and moved the residents to be safe.

The Outryders gathered every resident of the village and moved them into the castle in just under a day's time which was pretty good for the five hundred residents they had to move.

After moving everyone into the now cramped castle, Orion went up to Baron Ligate's office to plan leaving Haran and Lyra to do whatever they please. Haran walked into his old room in the keep. It was much the same as he left it, there was an oak table with four oak chairs, a fireplace with chairs in front of it, a small kitchen, and a very comfortable bed in the far-left corner. It was a very cozy room that held many memories of his life as an orphan.

Haran recalled the day when he and Lottie ceased to be friends and how bad he felt for not being able to help Lottie when he fell from the canyon. But what could he do? He was just a little kid far too weak to pull his friend out of the canyon. And now, he and Lottie tried to kill each other every time they could. However, Haran thought, each had multiple chances to kill the other, but neither went through with it. Could Lottie be redeemed? There was a slight chance. He thought about how Ella told them when the siege was happening. Why did she help them? The thoughts ran through his head rapidly, giving him a headache trying to think of the possible outcomes of the siege. He didn't know what would happen, but one thing he knew for sure was that he would try to get Lottie onto their side. No matter what it took.

There was a knock on the door, "Been a while, hasn't it?" Heide's voice came from the doorway.

Haran didn't know if she was talking about how long it's been since she's seen him, or since he's been in the room. He went with the former and hugged his oldest friend.

"Yes quite," Haran said.

"Are you ready for the siege?" Heide asked.

"As I'll ever be," Haran said. If he were honest with himself, he didn't really know. But it helped if he lied to himself.

"Do you think Lottie will be there?" Heide asked.

"Most definitely," Haran said. "And he'll come after me with everything he has." That he did know.

"Good luck then," Heide said, "he's an admirable enemy."

"Rival," Haran said with a smile. "He's an admirable rival." With everything that they had gone through together, Lottie deserved Haran's respect, and he realized that now.

Heide picked up on the meaning. "Don't underestimate him Haran. He's dangerous."

"Yeah," Haran said, "Well so am I."

"Very true," Heide said, "Well, I will leave you to it for now, I am sure you have much to do."

He, in fact, did have a lot to do. He had a theory about where the fifth tunnel led, and he was determined to prove it right. After Heide walked out he headed down the stairs and made his way into the castle library. After a brief conversation with his old teacher Lady Usrea, Haran found out where the blueprints for the castle were. He was most interested in the blueprints for the centermost building in the castle. The inner ward. The building that held the great hall, the library, the keep, and, most importantly, the dungeons.

His theory was predicated on when bandits attacked the Fuestres clearing months ago. Somehow, they escaped a well-guarded dungeon and made their way up and out the castle undetected. Something else they said didn't sit well with him, "We got a little help from a higher power."

The bandits knew exactly where the Outryders lived and there was no way they could have known that unless someone told them. And only one of the Lupens could have possibly known that.

Gilpin.

Which must have meant that the fifth tunnel was in the castle. However, he couldn't quite figure out how the bandits escaped from the castle, or more importantly, where they escaped from.

"How are you feeling son?" A gentle voice said from behind. Haran jumped slightly. He was so focused on the blueprints that he tuned out his surroundings. He turned around to see Holland standing behind him with a stack of books in his hands.

Haran exhaled. "Nervous. What about you? How are you holding up with the move?"

Holland smiled in only a way that an old man could, "I am doing great, the woman over there. Usrea, I think her name was, she showed me your entire library. Its rather quaint."

"Well, that's good Holland," Haran said, "Oh and I truly am sorry for what happened to your home, we had no idea they were tracking us."

"Thanks son. It means a lot that you gave me a home here," Holland said.

"It's the least we could do," Haran said. They had unintentionally led two dangerous men to his house and let them burn it to the ground. Of course, it was the least they could do.

"Why the nerves though son?" Holland said as he sat next to the boy.

Haran looked to the old man anxiously, "A siege is coming near, and I know Lottie, the boy that I fought in the library, will be there. We have fought many times, but somehow this time feels different. Everyone wants me to kill him, but I don't think that's a good idea. What if he can change?"

"Ahh," Holland said, "Is it a rivalry built on hatred?"

Haran was confused by the question, so he responded with, "Huh?"

"A rivalry built on hatred is like a house built on sand," Holland said, "Someday it will crumble beneath your feet, and someone will get buried in the rubble. But a rivalry built on respect is like a house built on stone. You will only serve to build each other up. So, I ask you again, is it a rivalry built on hatred?"

Haran paused taking a moment to think about his past encounters with Lottie. He didn't respect Lottie when they fought at the tournament so long ago. In fact, he hated Lottie for bullying him all those years. He didn't respect Lottie until after the fight at the canyon's edge. He respected Lottie now, but did Lottie respect him? "To be honest I don't know," he said to the old man.

"Once you find the answer you will know the truth," Holland said, "until then do what you feel is right, or it might be *you* who is buried in the sand." The old man walked off leaving Haran to ponder his words. However, after several minutes of thinking he pushed the thoughts out of his mind and went back to looking at the blueprints.

He didn't know what, but something was off about them. He panned the dimensions of the walls and the floors of each room of the castle, but he couldn't find the missing piece. He looked them over meticulously for what seemed like hundreds of times, but he simply couldn't find what he was looking for. He knew the fifth tunnel had to be in the castle, but where was the question.

The sun was rising four days after he asked that said question. There was still no answer. Time just seemed to have passed quickly between training and preparing for the siege. General Lee was scheduled to arrive in just a day's time which would bolster their numbers significantly. The courtyard was lined with tents from residents of the village, and everyone waited anxiously for any signs of the enemy. Haran was sitting on the ramparts looking over the southwest wall towards Calcore Canyon. Shiva was sitting quietly to his side. He heard the giant clock on the inner ward wall ticking the seconds down slowly.

Lyra approached him from the side. "Quite the scene isn't it. Everyone on edge like this I mean."

"Yes, it's very picturesque I would dare to say."

"Picturesque?" Lyra asked with a laugh.

"Well yeah," Haran said, "I mean the sun is rising on a new day gleaming off the castle that holds hundreds of people worried for their safety that we have sworn to provide. Very picturesque."

"Hmm." Lyra paused, "You are such a weirdo."

"Weird is such a strong word," Haran said, "More like unique."

"More like idiot."

"Maybe so, maybe not. Whatever the case, I am smarter than you," Haran said.

"Oh yeah," Lyra said with a scoff. "You? An orphaned boy, smarter than a princess?"

"Do I have to remind you that you are an orphan much like me?" Haran asked.

"No. I don't think I will ever forget," Lyra said.

"At least you remember your parents some," Haran said. Lyra laughed and then they grew quiet for several minutes. "Do you think he was a good person?" Haran asked as he diverted his eyes from the sunrise to the cobblestone ramparts.

"Your dad?" Lyra asked. Haran shook his head yes. He had been told countless stories of his dad and of his impact, but was he good to the core, or was it nothing but appearances? "I think the apple doesn't fall very far from the tree."

Haran smirked slightly, "I have no idea what that is supposed to mean. I guess you do learn something from Orion."

Lyra laughed slightly but didn't clarify her point. She figured it was best to leave it not understood. Haran was far too simple for that.

"What were your parents like?" Haran asked. He had always wondered what it felt like to be so unconditionally loved by anyone, especially by parents.

"They were great," Lyra said, "My mother was kind and gentle, but firm in her beliefs, and my father, well he was much like you in a way. Determined, but loving. Great, but modest. Powerful, but vulnerable."

"See that's where you wrong," Haran said as he looked into the sunset once more. "I am none of those things."

As he looked out he saw something in the distance. It was quickly approaching. Five hundred meters. Four hundred. Three hundred. Two hundred. One hundred. He could see what it was now, a cloud of dust created by a horse's gallop. The rider was coming straight from the canyon. He was yelling something, but Haran couldn't make it out. He looked over to Lyra who was looking to him worriedly. Orion came up behind Haran, "The spy," he said. Haran almost jumped out of his shoes.

"You people have to stop doing that," Haran said.

"What do you mean 'the spy' Orion?" Lyra asked.

"We sent a spy to check on the entrance at Calcore. That's him there." Orion pointed toward the rider.

"A spy?" Haran asked, "I thought that was our job?"

"Well, spy is a very loose term in this sense," Orion said, "Seeing as we were all busy, Baron Ligate sent a garrison member to keep an eye on the canyon entrance to Randint."

Haran nodded his realization and gritted his teeth. "But if he's back, that could only mean one thing."

Orion nodded. "The siege has started."

CHAPTER

29

L ottie walked into the training area yet again. It had been almost a week since the tunnels were exploded and men were working diligently to reopen them. When he first heard the news that the tunnels had been exploded and they had been outsmarted yet again he didn't take it well. However, after Ella talked him out of his rage he realized that the opportunity could be good for the blue group.

If the siege had taken place on schedule the blue group would have been uncoordinated to say the very least, and most likely would have failed the mission. However, three days have passed since the siege was supposed to happen, and the blue group was looking far more coordinated. However, that didn't mean they were perfectly synchronized either.

They could perform in tandem with others in their twenty-man group, but any person beyond that was like fighting alongside a complete stranger. *Whatever the case*, Lottie thought to himself. They were making progress. Gilpin told him the tunnel wouldn't be cleared until the next day or two. Therefore, they had very little time to play with.

When he walked into the room the entirety of the blue group was lined up waiting patiently. Tomas agreed that they should split the blue group in half with Lottie taking one hundred and fifty and Tomas taking one hundred and fifty. Of course, when the siege started they would be in the same group of the twenty best fighters. However, for the short time they had this way was far easier to maintain such a number. "Alright boys," Lottie bellowed. "We don't have much time now before the siege starts, so let's get to work. Group 1 you are fighting group 14. Group 2 you are fighting group 13. Group 3 you are fighting group 12 and so on. Group 15 put up your weapons and come with me."

Lottie had been taking one group to the side each day and testing them for their strength, endurance and skill. The best one on of the group would join him, Ella, Jet, Tomas, and Tyson in the leading group. He had already gone through fourteen of the fifteen groups, carefully picking who he believed would give him the best possible group as the lead.

He led the group into the streets of Randint Cavern, "Alright boys. Let's have us a good old fashioned race why don't we."

He paused to test their reaction which bordered on confused. "The first of you to touch the bell on the top that water clock in the center of the cavern. Gets the final spot on the leading group during the siege."

The men of group fifteen let out an excited whoop, Lottie smiled slightly, "Oh I forgot to mention, you will also be competing against me." He took off sprinting down the main gravel path that led to the clock tower sending little rocks flying at group fifteen. They took that as an insult and took off after him.

Lottie knew that to reach the clock tower some two hundred meters up the slope he could not take the main road. It would be far too crowded for any type of fast paced running, and he didn't want to put anyone in danger by the group of stampeding warriors.

He cut left down the back alleys of Randint Cavern. When he looked back he saw what he estimated fifteen of the twenty men following him. It was good enough. He continued running before he eventually came across a pile of empty barrel stacked alongside a tavern wall. After running past them he stopped briefly and pushed them away from the wall and scattered them across the alley, blocking the entire alleyway. He made a mental note to pick those up afterwards and continued running.

By the time he reached the tower he already saw two people fighting to get onto the ladder that led to the top. By the time he got to the ladder one of the men had been knocked off and was out cold and the other was beginning to climb the ladder quickly. However, Lottie caught his foot as he was going up and quickly drug him to the ground disabling him for the time being.

Lottie began to climb the tower now, but only got about three rungs up before someone grabbed onto his leg and slammed him against the hard rock floor as well. His head slammed against the floor the hardest bouncing off the rocks and slamming down once more. He felt the concussion coming along, but he got up still, groaning in pain in the process. He looked groggily over to the ladder when he saw five blurry figures fighting to get on it. *The ladder is impossible*, he thought as he pondered another way to get up the massive tower.

By this time, all twenty men were in the courtyard that had just been emptied due to the fighting taking place. Lottie sprinted around the tower looking for some other way to climb the tower when a fist came flying from seemingly nowhere. Lottie ducked the blow barely and swept the attacker's leg. When he looked to see who it was, he recognized the red-haired boy as someone he had his eye on for the past week or so. He was younger than Lottie by a year or two, but he was skilled with the sword, and followed instructions well.

Lottie popped up instantly and got into a fighting position. He wanted to fight, but he knew he didn't have that kind of time, so he simply pushed the boy away far enough to where he could run freely. As he came upon the back end of the clock tower, he saw a rope that led straight to the top. He had no idea why it was there, or if it was even securely tightened to the top, but he decided there was only one way to find out. He began climbing the rope, dragging himself up one hand at a time. The tower was some twenty meters tall and by the time he was about a third of the way his hands felt like they were bleeding on the coarse rope. His head still throbbed from when it was slammed against the hard rock floor, but he continued to move up the rope. After a few more meters he felt the rope start to shake violently as he was holding onto it slamming his shoulder against the wall. That hurt worse than all of his injuries so far as he wasn't prepared for it.

When he looked down, he saw the red-haired boy from before. He cured slightly under his breath and continued climbing, if he fell now, he would be severely injured if not outright killed. He held onto the rope with a grip of steel as the boy below repeatedly slammed him against the rock wall. After he climbed another five meters or so, the shaking stopped.

Lottie looked down to see if the red-haired boy had finally given up. However, to his surprise, the boy was actually climbing the rope after him.

"Kid's got heart," he grunted to himself as he kept climbing.

Lottie knew he wasn't the best climber in the world, but he could climb faster than most. However, the boy below seemed to be catching up to him quickly. Too quickly. Lottie still had two meters to go, and the boy was only that far below him.

He climbed faster now, using his leg muscles to propel himself even farther, if he let the boy catch up to him before he reached the top, it was a certain death for both of them.

Luckily for them both, Lottie's adrenaline kicked in overtime, and he reached the top of the tower and rang the bell before the boy could catch up. He looked over the edge to see the rest of the boys on the ladder had given up. Lottie won the race. However, the red headed boy was only seconds behind. When the boy climbed over the wall and into the open bell part of the clock tower he started breathing heavily. When he caught his breath he said, "Sorry for trying to kill you back there."

"Oh, don't worry about it," Lottie said rubbing his shoulder, "It's scarily common for someone to try and kill me."

The boy laughed. "The name's Fynn."

"You got guts Fynn, and where'd you learn to climb like that," Lottie asked.

"I've spent years climbing these walls," he said pointing to the walls of Randint Cavern, "but I have never actually climbed a rope before, so I was a little slower than usual."

"Slower huh?" Lottie scoffed. "Well, Fynn you could come in handy during the siege, you can be our twentieth man."

"Really? Thanks."

"No problem," Lottie said, "Now, let's get down from here. I am rather terrified of heights."

Fynn laughed and they climbed their way down the much easier ladder.

Lottie woke up in his room early the next morning to a knock on his door. Gilpin entered the room. His eyes were heavy and the bags under his eyes were a clear indication that he had been getting no sleep. "Get up," he said.

Lottie groaned in protest, but eventually followed the man's instructions. By the time he was up and ready Gilpin was already walking out of the door. Lottie struggled to catch up to the man as he made his way out of the house and onto the empty street below. "Where are we going?" Lottie called from the doorway.

"Shh," Gilpin said in a hushed tone.

Lottie did so, but he also wondered why Gilpin was being so secretive.

They made their way to the dungeons under the clock tower. No one was inside; in fact, the only people Lottie had ever seen in there was Haran and the Lyra girl after they captured them spying on Randint Cavern. Gilpin stopped in the center of the dungeon and started pacing worriedly.

"What is your problem?" Lottie asked.

"It's him Lottie, he's a menace," Gilpin said.

"Who?"

"Percival," Gilpin said.

"Wait what? What did Percival do?" Lottie asked.

"He's the one who got Doran killed. He's the one who caused it all."

Lottie looked confused at what his master was saying, "Gilpin, Doran was killed by King Nigel. You were there when it happened. Are you ok?" His master was starting to act more and more insane by the second. What did he mean Percival got Doran killed?

"Yes yes I know that Lottie. However, Doran was acting strange long before his fight with his brother," Gilpin said, "Our plan was never to fight Nigel one on one, we were going to take Norhall with the help of the Battlemaster at Osmole fief. It was a perfect plan. However, something changed in Doran shortly before the battle at Calcore. He was rushing into the plans and totally out of character, but I went along with it because I thought we would still win. But now I realize what I was too blind to see before."

"What are you talking about Gilpin? What did you realize?" Lottie asked. He too noticed the slightest of changes in Doran after they captured the Outryders many months ago. He had always planned to take Norhall with a siege, but suddenly changed tactics and asked for a fight to the death with his brother.

"It was Percival," Gilpin said, "Percival told Doran something that put him on edge enough to go after his brother immediately. Somehow Percival knew that Doran would die in the battle and that I would take his place. He also knew that I would choose him as the priest. He knew everything Lottie. He's outsmarted us all."

"Wait, slow down, you are saying that Percival made Doran get killed by his brother and he knew that you would recruit him as the priest," Lottie asked, Gilpin nodded. *Impossible*, Lottie thought, *no one thought that far ahead*. How could he have known have any of that would happen? How did he even know Doran in the first place? It didn't make sense. "But why, what does that give him?"

"Power, enough power to begin a siege weeks before the planned date," Gilpin said, "How could I be so naïve?"

"You're saying he rushed the siege on purpose? Why?" Lottie asked.

"Because he's a sadist Lottie. He wants to see the world burn," Gilpin said.

"If your right that means we left Ella with him all alone for weeks," Lottie said. Then he recalled what Ella had said a few nights before. "It wasn't sparring." Could it have been Percival who had caused that scar on her cheek?

Slow claps rang from the dungeon entrance behind them, when Lottie turned around, he saw Percival standing in the doorway. His eyes somehow shined brightly off the dim lights of the dungeons. "Quite the detective you are Gilpin. Although I am sad that you figured it all out before our big siege."

"You," Gilpin said dryly, "You killed Doran."

"Oh yes that, well killed is a very strong word," Percival said. "All I did was provide him a with a solution to his growing desperation, he did everything else himself."

"How did you even know him?" Gilpin asked, which was one of the top questions in Lottie's mind.

"Mmm, a word or two here and there and he came to me begging for help with his problems," Percival said moving ever so closer as he spoke. "I simply told him to tackle his problems head on. Actually, it was the same advice I gave you Lottie."

Lottie saw his master look to him disappointedly. His eyes said so much more than his words could say. They were filled with so many emotions that Lottie could tell which one shined the brightest, they weren't full of jealousy or anger. They were full of defeat, failure, sorrow. He felt replaced by his apprentice. But his eyes soon switched to compassion and then anger as they turned to Percival, "You manipulated him, you manipulated everyone."

"Yeah," Percival said with a shrug. "I'm sorry it's just what I do. In fact, I even manipulated you to get you here."

Gilpin reached for his sword. "What are you talking about?"

"A small seed of doubt formed in your head when I launched the siege without your permission," Percival said rubbing his neck from where Gilpin almost strangled him to death. "Ever since then I stuck to you like glue giving you the illusion that I was everywhere. That's why you came to these dungeons right? To make sure I wasn't there."

Gilpin grunted, the man was right, he had felt like if he told Lottie inside the house that Percival would have somehow been there. Somehow heard.

Percival smiled and put his hand on his weapon as well. "I mean it wasn't hard really, you truly are a simple creature Gilpin. All I had to do was get you out of that house. So now when I kill you and Lottie here, Albalupius won't be here to smite me before I get the chance to kill the both of you."

Lottie blinked and Percival had already drawn his sword from his sheath and was upon them. He launched his first attack on Lottie who had barely been able to pull one of his swords out in time to parry it. Percival then turned his attention to Gilpin who had unsheathed his sword also. He launched a blistering fast overhead strike to Gilpin that he barely stopped.

Lottie tried to stab Percival in his expose ribs, but somehow the man saw the attack and dodged out of the way. Percival kept bouncing back and forth between the two of them easily. He would block one and attack the other in almost the same movement. *So good*, Lottie thought, he had never even seen Percival do as much as unsheathe his sword much less train with it, yet he was a master, how was that so?

They continued their attacks to no avail for two minutes straight before Percival put more pressure on. He began focusing on Gilpin now, blow after blow he was getting faster and faster. Lottie tried his best to attack Percival from his exposed flank, but the man's sword always seemed to stop his own. Gilpin struggled to stop the sheer speed and precision of Percival's blows for almost a minute before he was eventually deeply cut on his upper arm. He instantly dropped his sword and fell to the ground clutching his arm. Lottie saw the blood flowing out of his master's arm and something in him switched. He didn't care anymore if he was hurt or even killed fighting Percival. Tonight, he was going to stop Percival and have him answer for what he had done. He filled with rage, more rage than when Doran was killed, more rage than when he lost to Haran, more rage than he had ever felt in his life. But it was controlled, he could see clearly, his eyes grew sharper. and his muscles tensed in anticipation. He finally learned to control his anger, and it was exhilarating. As Percival's sword came above his head to deliver the final blow on his master everything slowed. He moved from Percival's side to Percival's back. And just as Percival was about to end Gilpin's life, Lottie pushed Percival into the wounded Gilpin. Percival's sword flew from his hands, and he unintentionally put all of his weight on the wounded Gilpin. With Percival doubled over Gilpin, Lottie push kicked Percival from behind sending them both flying into the hard stone wall a meter away.

Percival took the brunt of the damage from hitting the wall headfirst and was unconscious by the time he hit the ground. The resounding thud left Lottie with a smile on his face. However, Gilpin didn't get away without a scratch, he had also hit his head pretty hard and was still bleeding profusely from his arm. Lottie's smile faded as he saw his master in serious pain and hurried over to Gilpin, ripped off his shirt sleeve, and tied it on the wound to stop the bleeding. "Sorry Gilpin," Lottie said, "It was the only way I could think to stop him."

Gilpin coughed, "You saved my life and all I got was a headache, no apologies needed."

"What do we do about him?" Lottie asked gesturing to the unconscious man on the floor.

Gilpin pointed to the rope hanging on the cell door, "Tie him up and stick him in the cell for now."

Lottie did as Gilpin told him to, double checking the knot to make sure they were securely tightened and shutting the metal gate behind the unconscious man. After locking the door, he helped Gilpin to his feet slowly. However, as they were walking out of the door they heard the bell directly above them sound. DING-DING-DING.

The bell was rung three times Lottie thought. It was daytime now and the tunnels were open once more. The siege was about to start.

CHAPTER

30

Orion, Lyra and Haran all headed down the walls of Norhall Castle and into the inner ward and eventually up to the keep and Baron Ligate's office. The messenger was already in the office talking to the Baron about what he saw when the Outryders walked in. "The tunnel opened just past dawn. I stuck around to see how many men we were going to be dealing with, but I was spotted soon after, so I came back here. However, I can tell you this, the whole canyon was filled by the time I left, and there seemed to be more on the way."

"Good work Marcus," Baron Ligate said. "Now go and join the ranks, you could be needed sooner rather than later."

After the boy Marcus walked out of the room Baron Ligate put his head in his hands and sighed deeply, "You three actually think we can win this?"

"I know we can," Orion said. Haran looked at him with a smile, Orion wasn't the type for hopeful optimism, so he must have one hundred percent believed himself.

"You better be right Orion," Baron Ligate said. "If we lose I will be to blame."

Haran envied his master's conviction, but the Baron was right, if they lost the castle to the Lupens, the king would place the blame squarely on Ligate's shoulders. He would be cast from his rank and most likely banned from ever holding another position of power again. That Haran did not envy.

Orion took a seat in the cushioned chair in front of the desk. He met the Baron's eyes. "If we lose neither of us will be alive to be blamed…So, let's hope I am right.

Roughly an hour later a horn blasted out from the tower walls. It was a signal, the first of the Lupens had been spotted by the castle guards. The three Outryders and the Baron got up from where they were sitting in the Baron's office. They made their way down the stairs and into the packed courtyard. No one cheered for the Baron as they usually did as they made their way to the southwest wall, no one even batted an eye, everyone was so focused on the horn that had just blasted across the courtyard. That horn could spell out the end of their lives. That horn could mean the death of everything they have known.

Now that the first of the Lupens had been spotted, each wall held about one hundred archers each and one hundred infantry each. There were more men in the towers, but there wasn't enough room on the walls to hold them as well.

He let the others go ahead, and after retrieving Shiva from the stables Haran pushed his way up the stairs and onto the southwest wall. Haran then pushed his way through dozens of shuffling bodies and onto where Orion, Lyra and Baron Ligate were standing.

Ligate spotted the guard captain after a few minutes and motioned him over. The young, muscular man walked over to the Baron and shook his hand firmly. He gave a slight nod to the Outryders beside Ligate and said, "Look towards Calcore my liege, they are headed this way now."

Haran looked over the edge of the wall and to the direction of the canyon. It took a little while for him to see the Lupens, but when he did his heart sank. A kilometer away bobbed what had to be thousands of heads moving slowly towards the castle. "Like ants," Lyra said as she peaked her head over the wall.

"Has to be at least five thousand of them," Baron Ligate said. "Where did they get all of these men?"

"I don't know," the guard captain said, "but I can tell you one thing. We are in for a fight to our lives today."

They stood and watched the slow approach of the Lupen army for several minutes until they eventually reached a spot one hundred meters from the base of the wall. The archers on the wall drew their bows back. The army continued to advance slowly. "What are they doing?" he whispered to himself, Haran had expected them to stop just out of the archer's range, but they didn't.

When they were within eighty meters of the castle wall the twang of a hundred bow strings let out. The archers of Norhall Castle weren't master archers by any means but firing into such a mass killed some seventy people. The rest of the arrows now resided deep in the Lupen's shields. The Lupens back out of range quickly, but the archers got one more volley off killing fifty more.

"Why would they do that?" Haran asked turning to his master.

Orion looked over to his apprentice, "Best I can assume is they aren't accustomed to fighting against bows or even using them down there for that matter."

Of course, Haran thought. Bows were mostly used for hunting and long ranged combat, neither of which Randint Cavern provided the means of doing. Haran was still confused, surely one of their generals must have been privy to the information of Norhall's use of bows. However, before he could ask another question Lyra chimed in. "That's a blessing in and of itself."

"We got lucky this time," Orion said. "They won't make the mistake again."

Haran sat and watched for an hour and a half before he realized that no order had been given from the commander in the center and not a single man moved the whole time. Apparently, Lyra noticed the same thing. "Why are they just standing there?"

"You've never been a part of a siege before have you Lyra?" Baron Ligate asked. Lyra shook her head no, so the Baron continued. "Well ninety-nine percent of it is just this. Sitting and waiting. Patience, they will come."

Haran looked out again to see that nothing had changed, "Surely they would be setting up camp by now though?" No one responded. He had a point of course, if they were really trying to wait the defenders out, they would have set up camp and gotten out of the hot sun.

About another hour passed and the army began to move away from the southwest wall and to the main gate just out of range of the bows. The main gate was in between the northwest and northeast walls. There were shouts of fear from the guards on the wall, but they were drowned out by the deafening sound of thousands of boots moving in unison. Haran followed their movements and moved to the gatehouse pushing through the guards on the wall.

By the time he reached the gatehouse he saw that the Lupens lined every street and alleyway in Norhall village just out of range of bowshot. However, after every Lupen was in the village not a single one moved a muscle. Haran thought they moved to the village to burn it down, but they just stood silently. *Strange*, he thought, their movements reminded Haran of a dead man, it was almost as if their minds were connected, and they knew exactly when to move and exactly when to stop. Their blank stares and absolute silence sent chills down his spine as he watched. Lyra came up behind him now and watched also.

Ten minutes later the five thousand Lupen started making a sound all at once. Haran couldn't make it out from so far, but it was slow and methodical almost like a chant. Haran listened closer, it was a chant, and it was one that he had heard only once before.

Lupus Vivat- Lupus Vivat- Lupus Vivat- Lupus Vivat- Lupus Vivat

Shiva growled at the chants. Haran looked down to her curiously, Shiva had only growled like that one time before, and it was when she saw Lupe at Ediv Pass.

"What are they chanting? I can't make it out," Lyra asked from beside him.

"Lupus Vivat," Haran replied, "Whatever that means." It was words in an ancient language that dated back long before Anjagor was formed. Haran recognized it but couldn't piece any of the words together.

"Long live the wolf," Lyra said as she looked over the ramparts. Without even having to look to him she already knew Haran was giving her a face of confusion, "Its ancient Athonian, I kind of *had* to learn it since I was born."

It made sense, but Haran was still starstruck at how much Lyra knew about her culture. She hadn't been there for even a decade and even when she was there her brain was far too young to process anything, yet she seemed to know so much.

"That's rather terrifying." Haran heard an archer beside him say to another.

"Truly," The other said. "I had expected to come here for a siege not a séance."

"You don't think they have actual gods on their side, do you?" The first archer asked worriedly.

"Of course not," the other said, but then hesitated in his words. "At least I hope not."

The conversation between the two ended there as the Lupens began to move towards the castle once more. "Not again," the archer said as he raised his bow up for a shot.

When the Lupens came within eighty meters the twang of the hundred bowstrings sounded and five seconds later some sixty men were dead. The Lupens pulled out slowly again but continued to chant. *Lupus Vivat-Lupus Vivat- Lupus Vivat.*

Why? Haran asked himself. Why would they go in again just to be shot down? It made no sense. What could they possibly gain from going in repeatedly?

"They're stalling," Orion said from directly behind him almost as if he were reading Haran's mind.

Haran leapt up and into the air letting out a high-pitched yelp in the process. "You have to stop doing that. Where'd you even come from?"

"You have to stop being a little baby. I just walked over here. Focus up son," Orion said.

"What do you mean they're stalling?" Lyra asked entirely focused on the mass of Lupens slowly making their way back to the village.

Orion looked over to the Lupens that lined the village. "They are waiting for something to happen. Something that will give them the go ahead in their plans."

"What is it?" Haran asked as he calmed his heartbeat.

"I don't know," Orion replied. *This is bad,* Haran thought, if even Orion didn't know what was going on, then they would surely lose the day.

After returning to their positions the Lupens didn't move once more. After thirty minutes passed the Lupens launched their attack again. This time an ear-ringing horn blasted as they approached. They put their shield up when they were within, and the archers let go another mass of arrows. Haran couldn't tell how many died this time, but it was definitely less. Most likely around three dozen. However, this time, the Lupens didn't retreat they simply continued to move forward. The archers released shot after shot after shot into the mass of Lupens, but they continued forward chanting *Lupus- Vivat Lupus- Vivat.*

Hundreds of Lupens lie punctured on the floor like ragdolls, but the others simply stepped over them harmlessly.

It was like they had no care at all for their fallen comrades. Haran was confused at why the Lupens continued to move towards the gate like they were. The drawbridge was up and if they continued to move towards the gate, they would eventually have to stop due to the presence of the moat. Maybe this siege would be easier than he expected.

However, as they neared the other side of the moat to the drawbridge, Haran heard a deafening snap below him.

As he looked down, he saw something he had never expected, the drawbridge was crashing down across the moat and onto the other side where the Lupens waited patiently. The bridge broke in half vertically as it came down to the other side, but there was still plenty enough room for the Lupens to cross at least ten at a time. "What just happened!?" Lyra asked.

"Lottie," Haran said as he took off running to the tower of the castle and down the stairs, he could hear the sounds of clashing swords near the drawbridge entrance. When he reached the bottom of the tower and looked to the mechanism that controlled the drawbridge, he saw Norhall guards in a heated battle with a group of three people. And of course, at the lead of the group mowing through countless guards was Lottie. Haran stood on the staircase and even as Lottie was fighting he met Haran's eyes.

You've lost, they said as Haran saw Lottie's face crease into a smile.

CHAPTER

31

Lottie walked with the blue group through the fifth tunnel for what seemed to be hours. The smell alone of the three hundred men in such a small space nearly made Lottie throw up multiple times. Ella actually did throw up, but that was due to her claustrophobia more than anything.

Everyone cheered by the time they reached the end of the tunnel and poured out into a large, open room. The room was just big enough for all of the blue group to move around in. By the time they all came through the rock wall closed behind them leaving them in the complete dark. Lottie struck a torch and began lighting the sconces on the wall. The others followed suit and in just a minute the room was fully lit with torches. The big room was empty apart from one ladder on the far wall that led up to the castle. It was lucky enough that he left Lupe to guard Percival he thought, because there was no way he was getting that giant wolf up that tiny ladder.

Lottie had never used this tunnel before, so he had no idea to which part of the castle the ladder led to, nor was he told. All that was said regarding their part was to drop the drawbridge at any cost and that's what he planned to do. However, they had to time it perfectly. If they went too soon then they would be easily overwhelmed by the defenders and the bulk of the army would be left to die to the arrows. However, if they went to late, the bulk of the army would be getting picked apart outside and have their numbers cut in half. In addition, if they failed to lower the bridge entirely then the whole siege would be ruined, and thousands will be massacred outside the castle walls.

Lottie heard the shouting of orders above clearly. The ladder led up to a trapdoor only three meters above, so he figured he must be only that far under the ground. He climbed the ladder to hear more clearly, but he only heard the pattering of footsteps above.

Ten minutes later he heard a horn blast from above. He figured the defenders must have only just spotted the Lupens on the move from the canyon, so they had at least a few hours to wait. He climbed down the ladder and said, "All right you all can relax for a little bit, we are going to be here a while." The blue group, who was waiting patiently for his instructions at this point, eased up and sat on the hard rock floor of the room.

Lottie walked over to where Tomas was standing some five meters away and whispered quietly enough for only him to hear, "I am tempted to peek above and try and see where we are at. What are you thinking?"

The assignment to drop the drawbridge was just as much Tomas' as it was Lottie's; Lottie had only taken the leadership role because Tomas pointed out that he grew up in the castle so he would know it better. "I think we should wait for the signal. The risk of getting caught up there is far too high."

"Good point. I would like to know how much we are going to have to fight before reaching the drawbridge though. " Lottie said.

"Hopefully it won't be much, plus most of them will be distracted by the main army anyway," Tomas said.

"True, anyway, I better get some rest before, wake me when you hear the chanting start," Lottie said. It would be hours before their part came into place, and he was sleep deprived to say the least.

He slumped against the wall right next the ladder his back ached as he slid down the wall. Even though it only lasted a few minutes, that fight with Percival was finally taking its toll on his body. After a few minutes of resting his head on the hard rock wall Ella came and sat beside him. He leaned his head on her shoulders and was almost instantly out cold.

He woke up about two hours later to a tap on his shoulder from Tomas. His eyes creeped open to see Ella still beside him looking around.

"Hey Lottie, the chanting started," Tomas said. They were told that soon after they heard chants outside the castle walls they would hear a horn blast as a signal for them to begin their siege.

Lottie rubbed his eyes and got up from where he was laying. He stretched slightly and began the process of waking up the blue group. Apparently he wasn't the only one who hadn't gotten much sleep the night before because half of them were passed out cold on the rock floor. It took about thirty minutes for everyone to wake up and get into their positions once more. Lottie climbed to the top of the ladder and said loud enough for everyone to hear, "Alright guys, now I am not one for big speeches or motivational words, but one thing I can say is that if we do everything right then nothing can really go wrong right?"

Everyone laughed below him. He hadn't intended to be funny, but he shrugged it off and said, "Alright boys get ready for-"

He was cut off by voices above, he couldn't quite make out what they were saying but they were close. Personal conversations between the blue group were growing progressively louder now and he didn't want those above to hear them. Unluckily for him it seemed those above had already heard when Lottie was making his speech because the trapdoor above him flew open and light poured through the opening. Lottie looked to the guard above and simply sighed, "Of course it's you."

Grew stood above the entrance. Grew was one of the most annoying people that Lottie had ever met in his life. He was short and stocky with freckles across his face. He and Lottie shared a bunk together at the Battleschool and he would stay up all night talking about his make-believe girlfriend from the adjacent Dalhurst fief. They had gotten into a fight one time when they first started in the Battleschool. And now look where they were, Lottie thought, the boy had the potential to ruin their whole mission by just one word. "Lottie?" he asked.

"Grew hey buddy, how's it been?" Lottie asked as he climbed up the ladder casually motioning for those below to climb up as well. They would be a little early than intended, but it was the last resort.

"Good, but where have you been for the past six months? You kind of just disappeared on us. Battlemaster Gilpin too."

Lottie was up and out of the hole now and looked around to find that he was in the bottom of the northwest wall, not far at all from the main gate. With its unique design, Castle Norhall's designer was forced to build essentially double layer the castle walls for support, but there was still a two-meter gap in between the walls. The guards of the castle took advantage of this and use the space in between as a direct and easy trip from tower to tower. When he looked around he saw he was surrounded by guards just waiting for their time to get into action. "Oh yeah, well Battlemaster Gilpin had some uhh family business to take care of and asked me to come along, but I am back now, and just in time it turns out. What's going on in here?"

"Our very first siege, we are waiting for the attackers to make their move now, and when they do we will chop them up real nice," Grew said as he swung his sword around clumsily. Tomas opened the trapdoor and climbed out. He reached for his sword instantly, but Lottie motioned him to stop.

Lottie saw his confusion, "Ahh my *good friend* Grew, have you had the pleasure to meet Tomas here?" Lottie said as he motioned Tomas to meet his hand.

"I have not," Grew said as they shook hands, "good to meet you Tomas."

Tomas eyed Lottie skeptically but eventually said, "Ahh I see, good to meet you too Grew."

By the time Jet opened the trapdoor a high-pitched horn sounded from outside the wall. "Finally," Lottie said as he punched Grew in the face knocking him unconscious.

The other guards were too busy focusing on the attackers advancing outside that they didn't even seem to realize what he had just done. The more Lottie thought about it, the more he reasoned they probably just didn't care. It was only Grew.

"Thank Lupe that is over," Tomas said. "Where are we going Lottie?"

Lottie turned to his right towards the main gate, "You two come this way, we can't afford to wait for everyone else."

Tyson climbed up the ladder as the three pushed through the guards to the main gate. He shrugged it off and began attacking everyone in his vicinity. Lottie heard shouts of confusion from the guards behind him and hoped that the confusion would give the others enough time to get up before Tyson was killed.

There was no time to worry about that now Lottie thought as he entered the bottom of the north tower. He turned right onto the main gate and saw that Tomas and Jet were still closely behind him. They moved quickly to the pulley that raised and lowered the drawbridge. It was drawn up by a pully connected to a wooden handle on both sides so that it only took two men to raise such a heavy piece of wood.

The chain that lifted the drawbridge was currently locked in place by a stop at the top of the now vertical wooden bridge. He knew there was no way to break the chain in such a short time. He cursed to himself quietly, if he would have just waited for a few more minutes he could have had his whole group, but in particular Fynn. The redheaded boy would have scaled the wall faster than Lottie ever could. However, the decision had already been made and he had to deal with it. He pushed his way through the mass of people and onto the pulley system guarded by a dozen or so men.

He decided at this point to stop the charade and pulled out his swords. Tomas and Jet did the same. He attacked the man closest to the wall with a deadly overhead strike. The man, oblivious to what was happening, died instantly with eyes wide open in shock. The guards around Lottie saw this and began to withdraw their own swords.

Tomas and Jet protected his back as he pressed forward towards the wall that the pulley was on. A dozen bodies lay dead on the ground before Lottie reached the wall. Tomas and Jet had his back covered, but there were more guards coming so he quickly sheathed his swords and began climbing slowly.

The top of the wall was about twenty meters high and the pully for the drawbridge was at the very top. It took him two minutes just to get halfway and he looked down to see that Jet and Tomas were already being overwhelmed. He pushed himself to greater heights and in just a minute he reached the very top of the wall. He climbed laterally to the pully and looked at the system.

The stop was holding the chain firmly in place so that it would not bring the whole bridge crashing down. To lower it down the people at the wheel on the ground would have to tug the chain just enough to where it gets free of the stopper, but not enough to send the whole bridge crashing down at once. They had the wheel there to control the descent of the bridge. However, Lottie didn't have time for all of that nonsense. He simply took out his knife from his boot and began hitting the stopper hard with the hilt. The first hit didn't do any damage to the stopper, so he hit it once more, still nothing. The third time he hit it however, the entire stopper came flying from its place and sent the wooden drawbridge crashing to the ground outside. He winced at the sound it made as it hit the ground. The sound of boards snapping hurt his very soul, but he hoped that it was intact enough to cross at least.

He quickly began descending the wall and within a minute he was on the ground with his swords drawn and ready to support his friends. He charged into the group of defenders dauntlessly. He had done his primary goal today and that was to lower that bridge. However, as he looked up to the staircase ahead, he caught eyes with his secondary goal, Haran.

He took off after the boy on the staircase motioning for the others to stay behind. The army was crossing the drawbridge now, so they wouldn't be fighting alone for much longer. He parried strokes from swords easily as he rushed towards the boy on the staircase. Haran, seeing that Lottie was charging him, ran down the stairs the rest of the way and began running in the opposite direction from Lottie.

Lottie must have pushed through hundreds of guards as they made their way to defend the main gate. They ran past where the blue group was fighting valiantly near the trapdoor. The group had pushed out from the trapdoor in either direction about five meters or so and were holding the area down well enough. Haran pushed through the blue group without much resistance. Everyone simply watched as he passed by, not even realizing the cloaked boy was an enemy. Lottie caught a glimpse of the giant boy Tyson as he ran through the blue group. *Good*, he thought, *he's still alive.* He stopped for a brief moment looking for Ella anywhere in the group. However, he saw no hint of her blond locks anywhere, what he did see though was a tinge of red in the center. He ran over to Fynn and yanked the boy to him, "Follow me."

After a moment of confusion about what happened to him, Fynn began following Lottie as he pushed through the tons of people fighting.

By the time they reached the west tower the crowds began to thin, and Lottie could actually see what was going on. He saw Haran dash up the stairs of the tower three steps at a time. Lottie and Fynn followed directly behind him. They went up the twenty meters high staircase in just under a minute's time and burst through the doors leading out to the southwest wall. Haran continued to run on the now abandoned southwest wall before he turned around and launched a knife towards Lottie's leg.

Lottie saw the boy draw back his hand and knew was knife coming so he easily leapt out of the way. Haran continued to run until he reached the south tower where he stopped and sheathed his axes. Lottie was some five meters behind him when the boy started scaling the wall of the tower.

"Yes," Lottie said. He knew when he had grabbed Fynn that he would be needed for something, he just didn't know what. "Fynn, get him to me."

The redheaded boy sprang into action at Lottie's command, sheathing his sword and climbing the tower after Haran. From below Lottie could see that Fynn was a slightly faster climber than Haran and was gaining ever so slowly. There was no way Haran was making it to the top before Fynn caught him.

Apparently Haran had noticed this too because he stopped climbing the tower and held his ground. By the time Fynn reached his foot level Haran began to kick at the boy's hand holds. Three kicks was all it took. The first kick Fynn held on tightly with both hands. The second kick left Fynn hanging on with only his left hand. And on the third Fynn's grip slipped, and he began falling to the hard rock of the castle walls.

The fall would have likely killed the boy if Lottie hadn't caught him. He braced the boy just enough to where he could crack his skull or back open when he it the hard rock, but the boy still hit his head against the jutting rock merlon leaving him unconscious. Lottie looked up to see that Haran was looking down terrified that he had killed the boy.

"He's not dead," Lottie reassured him. He didn't know why he did, but he felt it was the right thing to do.

Lottie heard Haran's sigh of relief from ten meters above as he shifted the boy gently into a more comfortable position against the crenellations. Lottie cursed slightly under his breath as he looked up to see Haran climb the rest of the way up the tower and roll over the crenellations easily.

CHAPTER

32

Haran peeked over the side of the crenellation at the top of the tower. He saw Lottie tending to the boy he had just sent to his premature death. He hadn't intended for the boy to fall; he just wanted the boy to get away from him. Haran was terrified, he had been running from Lottie for the past ten minutes and in a moment of weakness he almost killed a man in cold blood. Luckily Lottie was there to catch him, if not he would have surely died, and it would have been entirely his fault.

Haran sat down for a minute or so to take a breath of fresh air. He first ran from Lottie to get him away from the main fighting. He knew that Lottie could put a huge dent in the defending armies, and he didn't necessary like that idea seeing as their numbers were already smaller. However, after the first few minutes of running it was more for his own protection than anything. He didn't regret his decision to run, but that didn't make it a good one. Haran peeked over the edge once more to see that Lottie was still at the boy's side. He turned back around and slumped against the crenellations once more.

Through all the exploring he had done in Norhall, he never thought that the top of the south tower would be the most magnificent sight. The sun was slowly descending onto the horizon to his right, the high grass of Malen Plains swayed gently in the wind to his left and, even from so far away, he could see the edge of Calcore Canyon straight ahead. In that moment all he wanted to do was sleep. To let go of all his worries and responsibilities and fears and just… sleep. His muscles began to relax, and his eyelids grew heavy in the beaming sun.

Shiva. He thought as his eye flew open once more. Where was Shiva, she had been next to him before the drawbridge went down and he figured she would follow him. However, she didn't, he began to worry, but then he reasoned Orion and Lyra had would keep her safe and he closed his eyes once more.

He might have actually fallen asleep if not for the nagging quote running through his head. *A rivalry built on hatred is like a house built on sand…Someday it will crumble beneath your feet.* Was his rivalry built on hatred? If so, who would be the one to suffer the consequences.

Lottie. He thought, Lottie was still down there. He forced his eyelids open and peeked over the crenellations. Luckily he did because Lottie was climbing up the wall to him.

"Since when can Lottie climb?" He asked himself; he had never seen the boy climb in his life, and now he was doing it effectively. Whatever the case, he was doing it now, and that could only lead to one thing. They were going to have to fight once more. Or maybe not. Maybe he could convince the boy to join his side.

"Aren't you tired of fighting Lottie?" Haran asked the air.

There was no response for several moments until Lottie finally made it over the crenellations. "I will only be done when I get what I want."

"And what is that?" Haran asked not daring to take out his weapons. He had a chance to get Lottie on his side, even if it was a small one.

"For you to feel how I felt as I was kneeling before you at the canyon's edge," Lottie said. "The humiliation. The fear. I want you to see the pitiful look from the woman you love most in the world as you kneel before the man you hate the most."

Haran was speechless. He had so many questions, but not a single one came out of his mouth. He just sat there looking, not being able to make a sound.

Moments passed between them when Haran finally said, "You do not hate me Lottie as I do not hate you. You've had twice the amount of chances to kill me than I have you and yet you haven't yet. Maybe that is a good thing. Maybe we weren't meant to be fighting each other."

"Maybe so," Lottie said, "but this rivalry has to end one way or another and I don't plan on losing again. Now kneel and maybe we can be friends one day."

Haran hadn't thought of the impact of his victory at Calcore or how it would feel to have to make the choice to kneel before a man or to die. Now that he did he realized, "Orion was right. He said there was no good guys, only different forms of bad. I didn't understand him then, but I think I do now. I *truly am* sorry for how I made you feel. However, I will not kneel to you or any man for that matter, so if we must fight, then I am ready." He unsheathed his axes from his back.

Lottie did the same and in that same instant he launched his attack. A blistering fast side stroke came from the boy which would have cut Haran clean in half in he hadn't shot his body backwards. Haran tried to retaliate, but he was off balance, so Lottie simply parried the strokes.

Lottie launched attack after attack on Haran that was barely stopped each time pushing the boy off balance even more he tried to throw another shot out, but it was fell flat without a proper footing. Haran continued to be pushed back slowly to the edge of the tower.

Haran got his footing enough to launch an overhead strike against Lottie, but he brought his sword up to parry just in time. They held where they were for a few moments exchanging blow after blow until Lottie eventually push kicked Haran off balance and started pushing Haran back again.

Haran's heart raced, if Lottie pushed him back to the crenellations then he would be cornered and eventually lose. He cursed himself for choosing such an impractical spot for fighting and began thinking of ways out of the situation. He couldn't spin around and wedge Lottie's clothes into the wall as he had done in Holland's library because the crenellations were made of stone and not soft wood.

He couldn't perform Contrium as he had to win at Calcore because Lottie had two swords still. How would he beat Lottie? He was so much faster and stronger than when they last fought.

He pushed the thoughts on how to defeat Lottie out for later, for now he had to figure his way out of his current situation. He was a meter from the edge now and it was quickly approaching. Then he thought of something, he had never done anything like it before, and it probably wouldn't work, but he had to try.

When he was a half a meter from the edge he tossed his axes in front of him, jumped up and sprang from the crenellations with so much force that he knocked a stone crenel free from its lodging on the wall.

He somersaulted off of Lottie's head who, luckily, was not in an overhead strike. The force of Haran's somersault almost pushed Lottie through the now empty space of the crenel and onto his death. Luckily enough he caught himself on the rock merlons right beside the empty space and remained in the fight.

Haran didn't fare much better than Lottie did; after he somersaulted over the boy's head, he landed hands first into the hard rocks of the tower leaving him with badly scraped hands and an injured shoulder.

He scrambled to pick up his weapons, but Lottie was already ahead of him and kicked them through the gap in the crenellations. Lottie began laughing heavily as he held his sword to Haran's neck. Days passed in a second's time as Haran's entire life flashed before his eyes. *Is this how I die*, he thought. *Impossible.* Moments passed as he met Lottie's eyes. He paused, a feeling overwhelmed him, almost leaping out of his chest. *This is what he felt,* Haran thought. *Failure.* They stayed like this for many moments before Haran saw the glint of anger in Lottie's eyes fade. No, not fade, but subside. Lottie threw down his own swords and looked to Haran's badly scraped hands. "This is where the fun begins," he said. "Get up."

Haran looked up to the boy standing in front of him menacingly. His hands were bleeding now, but he still used them to help position his body enough to sweep Lottie's legs from underneath him. The boys' eyes grew wide as he fell heavily to the ground alongside Haran.

Both the boys struggled to get up from exhaustion. Neither had gotten much sleep in the past week and both had been fighting for going on ten minutes now. They both got to their knees and eventually to a squatted position, but at almost the same exact time as they both rose to their feet they both passed out onto the hard rock floor from sheer exhaustion.

Lyra ran down the stairs after Haran, but when she reached the bottom she saw him running away from Lottie. She shrugged, he could handle himself, for now she had to focus on the dozens of attackers slowly pouring through the main gate of the castle. Orion stayed at the top of the castle saying he had a plan. She knew best not to question her master because she knew how Orion loved to not share things. For now, she joined the defenders in pushing back the attackers. If only they could push the Lupens back through the gate they would have a very good chokepoint so that only a handful of the Lupens could attack at one time.

She stood at the top of the stairs and let a knife go from her hand killing a Lupen in the front in the middle of his attack. She let six more go in the span of twenty seconds targeting the Lupens in the front; each landed perfectly on target. After another two minutes all but one of her knives had landed directly on target. The last one she threw missed because the man moved just in time, so it hit the guy behind him.

When her knives ran out she unsheathed her axes and charged into the mass of people fighting. After pushing her way to the front of the line she began attacking the closest Lupen to her. By the looks of the middle-aged man, she could tell he had little experience with the sword he was using. His swings were sloppy and wild. She felt bad for the man, whoever was in charge had just sent him to his death.

She blocked his pitiful down stroke and swept his leg from under him. "Run," she said to the man. There was no need for the man to die today, and she didn't plan of delivering the final blow.

She backed up into the bulk of the defending army and looked around to realize that most of the attackers here were swinging the same way. She figured they must have only been trained for a few weeks tops whereas the defenders at Norhall had been chosen after *at least* a year's training. However, there was over five times the number of attackers as there were defenders. Would their superior skill be enough to best such a volume?

She pushed the question out of her mind, the best that she could do now is try to take out as many as she could. However, she would not massacre those who barely knew how to use a sword.

She ran to the stairs once more to get a better view of anyone with some competence with a sword when she heard more swords clashing to her left. She ran down the northwest wall corridor when she saw defenders being pushed back by a group of Lupens.

How did they get over here?" she asked to herself.

She pushed her way through the defenders once again to see a giant man slamming a two-meter cudgel into a very unlucky defender. She noticed the giant had a blue armband on, the same one that Lottie wore. One hundred attackers stood behind the man with the same armband not daring to get into range of the cudgel. Among those attackers stood a familiar face to Lyra. The one that had told her of the siege in the first place. Ella.

She caught eyes with Ella questioningly; Lyra was confused. Ella had told her about the siege, but she was also participating in it. It made no sense. What was going on in her head. She snapped out of her questioning daze when she saw a giant club coming down at her head.

She barely rolled out of the way in time as the cudgel came crashing down shaking the floor as it made contact. By the time she had recovered the giant was already taking another swing at Lyra. She dodged it yet again and jumped out of the cudgel's range. She sheathed her axes and cursed herself slightly for being so liberal with her use of throwing knives. Now she had none to throw at the giant in front of her. She sighed and charged the giant who was already coming down with another swing of his massive club. She rolled under the blow and through his legs.

The giant bent down to see where she went only to find that she was on his back. She grasped onto the giant's neck as best as she could as he began bucking like a bull.

She held on desperately for almost a minute before he threw down his cudgel and his hands eventually found her, seizing her by the wrist. He ripped her off his back and threw her across the ground like a ragdoll.

As soon as she hit the ground Lyra knew she had broken a rib or two. She began to wheeze heavily, her left side felt as if someone had just stuck a sharp dagger into her side and every time she breathed it felt like her whole chest was going to explode. She struggled to her feet wheezing heavily as she got up. She caught eyes with Ella who had her hands over her mouth in a long gasp. Lyra began to charge the giant once more clutching her side as she went. Apparently he had picked his cudgel back up as she was getting up because as she was charging the giant came down with the cudgel for the final blow.

"Stop," Ella yelled, but it was too late. The giant was already in the swing.

Lyra painfully rolled under the strike. Every bone in her body protesting as his cudgel came crashing down to the rock floor. However, this time as she ended the roll, instead of getting onto the giant's back she simply swept his legs out from under him.

The giant came tumbling to the ground beside Lyra as his cudgel flew out of his hands. She withdrew her axes once more and put them to his neck. She didn't say anything to the man because she couldn't, all she could do was sit and wait until he surrendered as she pushed the sharp end of her axe deeper into his neck. Three seconds passed and blood was flowing out of the boy's neck when she heard Ella behind her say, "We're leaving Tyson."

Lyra released the pressure off the boy's neck enough for him to say, "Ella. We can't. Lottie's plan."

"Lottie never planned for any of this, but the job they gave Lottie is already complete," Ella said looking to Lyra, "Enough of us have already died can we just go home?"

Lyra nodded. "Let them go," she croaked to the guards who were slowly approaching now that the giant was seen to.

Ella thanked her, opened the trap door some two meters away and began descending the ladder. "The fifth tunnel. Of course," Lyra said to herself as she watched the rest of the blue banded Lupens climb down the ladder.

By the time they were all down the ladder Lyra slouched against the wall. Now she could rest for a short while.

CHAPTER

33

Haran snapped awake on top of the south tower. He looked over to see Lottie was still unconscious beside him. He smiled slightly at the boy beside him. He had lost to the boy fairly, yet he didn't feel like a loser. He saw the change in Lottie's eyes as he held the sword to Haran's throat. Lottie had the chance to kill him, but he didn't. Maybe he couldn't, just like Haran couldn't when they battled at the canyon. However, there was one thing he knew for certain. Their rivalry was always built on respect.

He began to descend the wall once more. He still wasn't at one hundred percent, but he felt a lot better than he had before.

When he reached the bottom of the tower he retrieved his weapons that Lottie kicked onto the top of the wall. He walked through the tower and onto the southwest wall. The redheaded boy he had almost sent to his death earlier was leaning against the crenellations painfully. He tried to move away as he saw Haran coming, but by the time he got up he collapsed right back on the ground.

"Hey," Haran said as he approached the boy, "I am sorry for almost killing you back there. I was scared, but that's no excuse."

"What have you done with Lottie? Is he—"

"Dead?" Haran finished his question. "No, he is not. We both passed out before the fight even really started."

The boy let out a sigh of relief, "What's the history between the two of you? Why did he chase you with such intensity?"

"Lottie and I were once friends," Haran said, "then we turned enemies and now all I can say is that we are the greatest of rivals."

The boy nodded in understanding and Haran took off towards the main gate where the fighting was taking place.

By the time he reached the west tower he decided to go down the spiral stairs and make his way to the gate on the ground floor. As he exited the spiral staircase and made his way down the northwest wall corridor he saw Lyra leaned against the wall in the dim light clutching her side painfully. As soon as he saw her he sprinted to her side. "What's wrong?" he asked as he held her free hand up.

"Nothing. I'm fine," she said as she tried to walk away from the wall. She got about three steps before she fell to her knees.

"You are very clearly not," Haran said, "What happened?"

"Club wielding giants and blue banded Lupens, that's what happened," Lyra said.

"Blue bands?" Haran asked, "Like the one Lottie wears?"

"Exactly."

"How many were there?"

Lyra tried to stand back to her feet for a moment using Haran as a crutch. "A lot, but they left with Ella after I beat the giant."

"They left? With Ella? Was it an actual giant?" Haran asked in rapid succession. All of this was hard to digest. All that he knew was Lyra was badly injured in front of him and that she got it from a fight with a supposed giant with a blue armband like the one Lottie wore. It made no sense. "What hurts?" Haran asked finally.

"My ribs. I think I broke a few," Lyra said.

"Ok, will you be alright here for a little while, or should I stay?" Haran asked.

Lyra shook her head, "No. Go. I'll be fine."

Haran nodded and began to move away from the girl. "Good. Don't die on me."

"I should be saying that to you," she croaked as he ran to the main gate. He was well out of earshot by then and as he ran further away she said. "That boy."

Haran rounded the corner of the north tower and turned onto the main gate. If he were honest, he expected worse than what he saw. The defenders were holding strong against the constant outpour of attackers, in fact they were even pushing them back through the main gates. Haran didn't see Shiva or Orion, so he figured his master was still on the top of the castle walls concocting a plan.

Haran ran into the thick of the fighting trying desperately to push the attackers back through the gate. Blow after blow the poorly trained Lupens fell beside him as if they offered no more offensive threat than dirt itself. However, the guards weren't fairing much better. Many of them were also poorly trained farmers rallied throughout the fief with only a handful of the defenders having formal training in swordsmanship.

Haran made a dent into the left side of the attacker's line, but it still felt like they were moving no closer to the gate itself. When he looked around he found out why. Two boys stood back-to-back cutting through the defenders like butter. Haran easily recognized the tidy bun and deadly spear of one of them as Tomas, the boy he had bested in a spar during his first visit to Randint Cavern. The second though he had never seen before, yet he looked very familiar. He had jet black hair and was wielding a sword almost as good as Lottie did. *Almost.*

He began fighting his way slowly over to the boys on the right-hand side of the attacker's line. He didn't know if he could beat them both at the same time especially since he wasn't one hundred percent, and his hands were still a little busted up from his fight with Lottie. However, it had to be done to take the gate back.

By the time he fought his way over to the two boys Tomas spotted him. Tomas tapped on the other guy's shoulder and said something too quiet for Haran to hear. He assumed it was something along the lines of "get us room" because the other guy began to charge the defenders pushing them back. The push freed up some space for Haran and Tomas to fight, but only some.

"So," Haran said, "I assume we have to fight now."

Tomas shrugged his shoulders, "I mean we don't have to; you could always kill me with one of those knives across your chest."

Haran looked down to his sash full of throwing knives, "But that's no fun." In fact, he hadn't even thought about using them yet.

"True. Plus, I want a rematch from the last time," Tomas said.

Haran was about to speak when someone charged him from behind. In one swift movement he took out one of his knives, turned around, and launched it deep into the attackers left leg. The man yelped out in pain and collapsed on the ground a meter away from Haran. "Maybe we could fight somewhere else huh?"

Tomas was about to respond when a loud explosion rang from outside the castle. Haran heard screams coming from the Lupens outside. Tomas looked to Haran skeptically. He shrugged; he had no idea what that was. A minute passed and another explosion rang out and more Lupens screamed. "What is happening?" Tomas asked.

Orion. Haran thought. This must be his plan. "So sorry we couldn't finish our fight," Haran said as he sent a knife into Tomas' calf. He began to make his way to the north tower until he saw the black-haired boy still fighting valiantly against the defenders. He sent a knife into his hamstring. As he ran past the boy he heard him say, "You'll regret that Ryder." His voice was so cold and steely that it sent chills down Haran spine as he ran by. *Ryder*, he thought as he continued to run to the stairs. *How does he know my family name? Was it a mistake? Who was that boy anyway?*

When he reached the top of the stairs and looked at the wall above the main gate he saw Orion and Shiva at the part of the wall above the gate entrance. He saw his master throw something that resembled a ball of sorts and ten seconds later another explosion shook the walls.

"Orion," He called as he approached his master. Shiva snapped up as she heard her master and ran over to him, tackling him to the ground and licking him. "Ok Shiva, that's enough get up." She did as he said, and Haran got up wiping the lion saliva from his face. "What are you doing? What is that?" He asked pointing to the ball in his hand.

"That is an explosive bomb that Holland and I have been working on for the past week or so. It seems to be working don't you think," Orion said gesturing to the ground below. Haran looked over the crenellations to see Lupens scattered all over the ground and three rings of destruction from where Orion threw his first three bombs. The ground where he had thrown the bombs was covered in flames and burning body parts from those unlucky enough to have been within the blast radius.

"It seems so. Can I try one?" Haran asked.

Orion handed him the bomb, "Sure, but be careful. This is the last one."

"Where should I throw it," Haran asked.

"You see that group in the back of the lines over there?" Orion said pointing to Haran's left.

Haran looked and realized why he had chosen that spot. The man in the exact center of the group was Gilpin. However, the former Battlemaster was far away from Haran especially for a throw.

He brought his arm back to his ear and threw the spherical bomb as far as he could to try and reach Gilpin. It exploded some ten meters away from him. Haran cursed to himself. He had hoped to take out the man with the throw.

"Its alright, I already took out the rest of the bridge with the first one," Orion said.

Haran looked down not even realizing that the drawbridge was completely destroyed now. He let out a whoop of joy. The attackers couldn't cross anymore, they had won the siege just like that.

"Don't get so happy," Orion said, "Over half of them have already infiltrated the castle, only about two thousand of them remain outside."

Haran's smile faded, "Why didn't you drop the bombs earlier then?"

"Because I had to find Holland and get the bombs from him," Orion said, "He only just finished that last one when I found him barricaded in the library."

Haran saw three sets of fifty Lupens outside the castle begin to pick something up from the ground beside them. Haran squinted his eyes to see what they were picking up only to see wooden rungs of a ladder. "Oh no," Haran said mainly to himself. "Where did those come from?"

Orion's voice grew steely, "I don't know, they weren't carrying them when they first arrive."

"You don't think they were put there before the siege even started do you?" Haran asked. "Surely they couldn't have thought that far ahead?"

"It's a siege boy," Orion said. "You have to prepare for everything."

So, what do we do?" Haran asked.

Orion looked away from where the attacking army were moving closer with the ladders to Haran, "I have a plan, but it requires three people. Where's Lyra?"

"Currently indisposed in the southwest corridor," Haran said.

"What happened?" Orion asked.

"I don't know, something about a giant," Haran said trying to recall what she said about her injury. *Not much.*

"Well, I guess we will just have to make do," Orion said. "Wait until they get the ladders hooked on and follow my lead."

Haran did as his master said and waited until the ladder hooked down on the crenellations in front of him. He saw his master move to the next ladder over as the Lupens began to climb the ladder. Orion unsheathed both of his axes and began chopping at the hooks now.

Haran understood and followed his movements. They couldn't simply throw the ladders from the wall because they were hooked over the crenellations. Therefore, Orion was chopping the hooks off entirely. It would be a long process, but if it were completed before the attackers reached the top, the ladders would be rendered utterly useless.

Haran knocked out one hook of the ladder when the first Lupen was halfway up. As soon as the hook was shattered all the weight on the ladder tilted to the left. Haran heard screams from below as the Lupens desperately held onto the ladder.

He peered over the crenellations to see that the Lupens were still climbing up the ladder even as it was tilted ninety degrees. *Relentless*, he thought as he moved to the next hook.

After a minute or so of chopping he heard screams from the ladder Orion was working on. *He must have got it down.* However, even though they had gotten one down, the Lupens on the third ladder were closing the top of their ladder. Haran chopped faster and within another minute those on his ladder also fell to the ground with violent screams and death threats. He peered over the crenellations once more to see that most of them hadn't died in the fall, only gravely injured. Some even landed in the brownish water of the moat.

At least they're alive, he thought as he whipped around to see the few Lupens that had made it up the third ladder were already engaged in a fight with Orion. He rushed over to his master's aid hitting the Lupens like a ton of bricks. The two of them easily delt with the few Lupens and began to deal with those climbing the ladder.

Orion threw knife after knife down at those on the ladder in quick succession to try and delay the Lupens advances. Seeing this Haran began to work on one of the hooks of the ladder. "I'm out," Orion said after about a minute, yet Haran wasn't even close to being finished with just the first hook and the Lupens were still making their way up the ladder.

At the exact time that the first Lupen vaulted over the crenellation, Haran snapped the first hook of the ladder. Orion push kicked the first Lupen back over the crenellation. However, more and more poured over the wall. "Leave it Haran," his master said as Haran was moving to take out the second hook. Haran did as his master said and started helping him push back the endless hoard of Lupens.

CHAPTER

34

Haran and Orion fought for about ten minutes straight. Haran's arms were tiring from the weight of swinging his axes around and he saw no end in sight. Wave after wave the Lupens poured over the crenellations just to be kicked over the edge or gravely injured with an axe. Haran estimated that they must have killed at least a hundred Lupens just based on the half a meter high pile of bodies that lie in front of where they fight. Shiva was beside Haran as he fought, protecting his exposed flank from the constant flow of Lupens.

Haran parried a blow from a Lupen and kicked him off the wall and to the ground twenty meters below. He didn't even have time to breathe as another two Lupens attacked him from the side. He parried the first two strokes and cut one of the Lupens deeply in the upper arm. And almost as if he became possessed, the other came forward with a blistering speed that Haran hadn't expected.

Surprised and tired, Haran couldn't bring his axe up in time to parry the blow, but he did have enough time to move the bulk of his body out of the way. However, the sword still slashed through his cloak and sank deeply into his arm. He let out a sharp cry and fire shot up his arm painfully. He dropped his axe from his bad arm sending it crashing to the courtyard below the wall. An unnatural feeling warmed in his heart as he stood near the edge of the wall, a feeling of bliss, yet also overwhelming terror. His arm grew warm with blood. *I'm about to die aren't I?* He thought.

"Haran," his master called out as he rushed to his aid. Haran saw nothing but a flash as his master's axe came upon the Lupen's head. The head came clean off the Lupen's body, both crashing to the ground helplessly. He caught a glimpse of Shiva defending the two of them through his pain fogged eyes. He silently thanked her, for if she hadn't been there he would have surely died.

"Haran," his master said again as Haran's knees buckled beneath him. Orion held him up and ripped off a piece of his cloak, tying it quickly to his arm to stop the bleeding. "Don't do it. Don't let me down as I let your father down. You are a Ryder boy. You are better than me. Now focus."

It felt like Haran was underwater as he heard his master talk. *Father. Ryder. Focus.* Haran repeated in his mind. *Father. Ryder. Focus.*

A horn blast snapped him out of his painful daze and unbuckled his knees. A newfound energy coursed through Haran's veins as he wondered what the horn blast was for.

Orion looked at him with a slight smile, "That's the boy. Haran Ryder. That's my boy." Orion began to fight once more as Haran went to check where the horn blast originated.

Hundreds of horsemen coming from the main road through the village in a gallop. *General Lee*, he thought, *finally*.

The siege started just after dawn, and it was well past sunset now. General Lee was hours late, but he was just on time for the glory.

Haran let out a small whoop and began to fight one handed against the Lupens. *Even if I die here. We win.* Haran thought as he charged into the Lupens. *And that's all that matters.*

As Haran kicked a Lupen over the crenellations he felt a presence behind him. He whipped around with a side stroke only to find that it was Lyra who was standing behind him. She blocked the stroke easily. "Whoa," she said, "No need to get angry. Just trying to help."

"Sorry," Haran said as he parried a stroke from a charging Lupen. "How's the ribs."

"Good enough," Lyra said as she kicked the same Lupen off the wall. Her eyes shifted to his bloody arm. "Haran. Your arm."

"It'll be fine," Haran said as he sent a knife into a Lupen Orion was fighting three meters away.

Haran heard cries of pain from the Lupens on the ground below as General Lee's reinforcements slammed into the unsuspecting Lupens trying to climb the ladder. It wouldn't be long now before there would be no more endless hordes of Lupens on the walls for them to fight. They had won the day.

The three Outryders thinned the number of Lupens on the wall in a matter of minutes and they moved to the ladder hooked on the wall. Some more came over the crenellations, but they were easily delt with.

Of course, the last one to swing over the crenellations was none other than Gilpin himself. When he hit the ground and looked up to see the three Outryders in front of him he simply sighed, "Well," he said as he held out his arms in surrender.

Cheers of joy rang from the Great Hall that fateful night. Guards of the castle and residents of the village sang, danced, and ate to their hearts' content. The long dining tables were filled with various meats, fruits, and vegetables prepared by Norhall's finest chefs.

Baron Ligate sat at the table at the front of the room looking out among the crowd of joyous people. General Lee sat by his side in his full shiny clean armor laughing as the constant stream of people thanked him as a savior.

"Look at him," Haran said to Lyra and Orion from where they sat overlooking the joyous affairs from the balcony. Shiva sat beside Haran happily as he pet her. "Being celebrated as a hero after doing basically nothing to deserve it."

Neither Lyra nor Orion said anything, they just simply watched contently from their position of seclusion high upon the balcony.

Haran saw Baron Ligate stand up from afar. His purple robes cascaded down the chair and to the ground haphazardly. "People of Norhall," he said, his voice echoing off the walls of the Great Hall. The music ceased and the dancing stopped. Once he realized that every eye was on him Baron Ligate continued, "Today is a very joyous day indeed. For weeks we lay in fear of this siege. We thought it would surely be the end to Norhall as we knew it, but did it end?"

"No!" The crowd shouted from below him.

"No is correct," Baron Ligate said, "We are still alive today because of you, all of you doing your part in the cause. Just as there is no wall without stones there is no victory without you."

An applause rang out from everyone in the room for several minutes until Baron Ligate held up his hands to continue, "Now we have lost many lives today. Friends, family, loved ones, but their sacrifices were not in vain. We have won the day and deserve to celebrate in their honor. Now, I would like to acknowledge someone very crucial to the victory of this siege." Haran edged forward in his seat as he waited for Baron Ligate to continue, "This man saved the day single handedly with his wits, his expertise, and his skill. I would just like to humbly thank... General Lee for his crucial role in the victory today."

Haran scoffed disdainfully. If anyone were crucial to the victory against the Lupens it was Orion. Lee just simply cleaned up the stragglers. "That's outrageous," he said to Orion over the deafening cheers, "You were the one who blew up the bridge and single handedly took down hundreds of Lupens."

"Haran," Orion said to his wound-up apprentice, "I had your help also."

"Ok and he had five hundred men's help," Haran said. "He doesn't deserve such recognition. He barely did anything." Haran began to walk towards the stairs of the balcony. Shiva got up and followed closely behind him.

"Where are you going Haran?" his master asked.

"To tell them who the real hero of the day is," Haran said as he reached the stairs.

"Oh my," Lyra said with a sigh.

A knife came flying from nowhere and stuck into the wooden railing where he was about to move his hand. "Come back here son." Haran heard Shiva growl from beside him. "Shh," he said, "its ok."

Haran moved back over to his master and met his master's eyes as he spoke, "You deserve the fame Orion. You are the true hero of today."

Orion sighed, "Haran, one day you will realize that there is more to life than glory. I did my job today and I did it well, but I deserve no fame for it. We are Outryders son. The shadows are where we belong."

Haran's head was getting cooler now as he realized that his master was right, "I know, but he doesn't deserve to be treated like a hero."

"No one does," Orion said, "but that's the way it goes. Now sit."

Haran did as he was told and sat in his wooded chair overlooking the festivities. Shiva sat down beside him once more, but this time she kept her eyes fixed on Orion. The cheering had died down now and Haran caught the back end of Ligate's speech, "and we have captured the man responsible for such heinous crimes against Norhall."

Guards entered the Great Hall through the front door escorting someone to the Baron. Boos and familial death threats rang out from the crowd as Gilpin was led to Ligate. Even from so far away, Haran saw that the man had already been beaten beyond recognition. His face was a mess of cuts and swellings, and his arms were blue from nasty bruises. "This man, who was once the Battlemaster at this very fief, respected and loved by all who encountered him, has committed the highest form of treason imaginable. So, what punishment do the people want?"

"Give him death. Give him death. Give him death." The crowd began to cheer.

Baron Ligate held his hand out in silence, "It looks like the people have spoken," he said to Gilpin.

Haran turned to Lyra and Orion in utter terror. "This can't happen," Haran and Lyra said simultaneously.

"Yeah, you're right," Orion said, "It can't."

CHAPTER

35

The next day Orion entered Haran's room in their cabin in Fuestres Woods. After dinner the night before Orion said that they could return home. They had been staying in the castle for over a week now, and Haran was glad when he reached his own, much softer, bed. His dreams about the battle and about the Lily Cove had subsided after their trip to Athon. Maybe that *was* the message they were trying to send. "Get up," Orion said kicking his leg, "We have bodies to clean."

"Bodies to what?" Haran said groggily.

"To clean. From the siege," Orion said, "now get up, they have to be done before they start to smell."

"Why do we have to do it?" Haran asked. The Outryders were a group of highly respected warriors only subservient to the king, so he felt cleaning bodies from the siege was a little demeaning to say the least.

Orion sighed, "Everyone is doing it including us, so get dressed and head to the castle."

Haran groaned in protest as he got up. Every muscle in his body ached from the constant running and fighting from the siege. The bandage that Lyra had put on the night before was bloody now from the irritation caused by his constant turning in sleep. He got her to rebandage it and walked outside into the cool autumn air. He left Shiva in the cabin to sleep. It had been a long few days for her also.

He walked over to Spirit, took out a packet of oats from his satchel, and fed it to him. "It's been a while buddy," he said to the horse as he began to saddle him up. If he were honest with himself, he had not been taking care of Spirit like he used to. The horse hadn't had anything to eat but grass for a week while he was gone, so he handed him two handful of oats. "There you go." He said as he gave him the second handful, "It's our little secret." Haran couldn't tell if the horse had sneezed or if it was a thanks, but whatever the case he hopped on and began making his way out of the woods.

As he heard the crunch of the autumn leaves beneath Spirit's hoofbeats he realized that it had almost been a year to the day that Haran had first started his journey as an Outryder. It felt so much faster than that, and the first half he had spent just learning how to become an Outryder. He sighed and made his way out of the woods and onto the castle.

As he approached the castle he saw wheelbarrows full of the dead as people moved them from wherever they died to where they were separated at the edge of Malen Plains. As the Baron said the night before, they would bury all their dead in Malen Plains in individual graves out of respect. However, the Lupen's would be buried in one big grave to save time and resources.

As Haran rode to the gate, he saw the aftermath of General Lee's charge. Hundreds, if not closer to a thousand bodies lay dead on the ground that was now painted crimson with blood. He crossed the moat on a makeshift bridge that could hold maybe three people at a time at best. The remaining pieces of the drawbridge floated in the moat beside him as he crossed, along with dozens of dead bodies of those that had tried to escape General Lee's charge. The water shared the same color as the ground beside it. He rode through the opening when he saw many people working to clear the bodies near the main gate. He caught a glimpse of Heide dragging a body arduously to a wheelbarrow beside him.

He quickly got off Spirit, pushed the wheelbarrow to her side and helped lift the body into it. "Thanks," she said as she wiped the sweat off her glistening forehead.

"How long have you been out here?" Haran asked, with the amount she was sweating he figured a long time because he had never seen Heide sweat so much in their lives.

"Five? No six hours," Heide said as she leaned against the wheelbarrow.

"Six hours?" Haran exclaimed, "it's a quarter till ten. You've been out here since four?"

Heide nodded her head, "Give or take yeah."

"Are you stupid or just dumb?" Haran asked. She had already been out there for six hours, and he knew she would be out there for at least six more.

Heide laughed tiredly, "It's the only way I can think to help. I mean yall did all the hard work fighting. I might as well do something too. Oh and hey, I checked where they were holding the prisoners and Lottie wasn't there."

Haran smiled slightly. *Good*, he thought. Lottie must have gotten out before the siege was over just as Ella did. Baron Ligate planned to ransom all their prisoners off except for Gilpin of course, and he knew that if Lottie were captured he would join Gilpin at the gallows. "Great, so did they say when the hanging was taking place?" Haran asked as he moved to put the next body in the cart. He knew that Heide and the couriers were the first to know of all information in and out of the fief, and by proxy, the castle itself.

Heide shook her head, "Sadly no, between all the celebrations last night and the cleaning up I haven't been able to ask around. But I assume you have about a few days or so since they still have to build the gallows."

Haran nodded. It wasn't long, but they had a little wiggle room to convince the Baron to rescind his decision to hang Gilpin. He didn't know why, but the thought of seeing Gilpin die in such a cowardly way drove him mad.

They worked in silence, moving body to body, putting them in the wheelbarrow and moving to the next until. When they reached the limit is when they took them to the pile in Malen Plains.

The guards of Norhall each had a pin with their name and rank on it. Haran tried his best to remember each one he moved. However, by the thirtieth one they were all just a jumble in his brain. He continued trying as he moved to the next body. *Beauregard: 2nd infantry*

He was young, maybe a year older than Haran, yet he was already second infantry. That alone impressed Haran. As far as he knew it took some people five years just to get that far. He threw Beauregard's body into the wheelbarrow and moved to the next body.

The face on this body was beaten beyond belief, but Haran could tell that he was once a very attractive man. *And rather good with a sword* he thought as he looked around and saw only his body amongst a dozen dead Lupens.

Akin: 3rd infantry

Haran saw the name tag and did a double take. *Akin.* He had heard that name before, but it had been a brief conversation. He racked his brain as he tried to recall where the name was mentioned and when he finally realized he fell to his knees beside the dead boy.

"What's wrong?" Heide asked seeing the movement.

"This boy," Haran said as a single tear fell from his face, "he was the son of a farmer I rescued in Calcore a few weeks ago. His mother was so kind, she even let me sleep in his bed. She mentioned that he was a guard in the castle, but I didn't think much of it. And now—"

"Now he's gone," Heide said finishing the sentence she knew he wouldn't be able to.

Haran sat for a moment mourning then turned to her with a tear running down his cheek. "Come with me. We have to tell them."

Heide looked at him skeptically, "Are you sure you want to do this?"

Haran nodded yes and threw the boy onto his shoulders and eventually onto the back of Spirit.

They rode in silence for the ten-kilometer ride to the farmer's house. There was much to talk about, but neither of them spoke. Haran found it more respectful to not speak on other topics without first burying the boy.

When they reached the small farm the pointer dog that he saved greeted him at the front porch. He pet her soothingly and she moved to get closer to him. The dog let out a sharp and playful bark to Haran.

"What's the matter Missy," the farmer called as he opened the door to see Haran standing at the base. "Ahh if it isn't my savior. What brings you here."

Haran creased his face and walked over to where the body of Akin was slung over Spirit, "I'm sorry," he said as he took the boy's body from the horse and moved him closer. "He died in the siege yesterday. When I saw the name I thought you might want to know."

The farmer's hand came over his face in a gasp as he saw his son's beaten and bloodied face. Tears started coursing in stream of water on his face that cut through the grime like a hot knife to butter. He fell to his knees cupping his hand over his eyes so that Haran wouldn't see. Haran moved to comfort him, holding him there for a moment before the farmer's wife walked out, "What is going on Rex?"

She saw her husband on the ground crying and looked over to the body in front of him. "Is that?" She walked over to the body to see that it was the bloodied face of the one she loved most in the world, her only son, her baby. "What did you do to him?" she asked Haran as he began to stand up to comfort her. He tried to speak but no words came out, so she repeated herself, "What did you do to my boy?"

"It wasn't him," Rex said through the tears.

"Who was it then, who killed my baby boy," she demanded from her husband.

Haran brought up enough courage to speak to the grieving woman, "He died in the siege yesterday, but he killed many of Lupens in his wake."

"I don't care how many people he killed," she yelled, "I just want my boy back. Give him back."

Haran nodded as she fell by her son's side, she sat there for many minutes crying over her son's body. "I assume it was that Gilpin man who led the siege?" she asked after a few minutes.

Haran shook his head, "Gilpin led the siege yes."

"Then he deserves a punishment much worse than hanging."

Rex looked up and dried his tears. He shook his head, "I knew Gilpin well before he disappeared. He used to come pick up milk for the wolves in the canyon. He was a great man if not a flawed one, but I don't think he caused all of this."

Heide, who had been watching quietly the whole time, looked at Haran, "Hey, let's leave them to mourn alone. I have an idea."

They said their goodbyes, climbed on Spirit, and began riding back to Castle Norhall.

After about a kilometer of riding Haran turned around to Heide behind him, "You said you had an idea?"

"Yeah," Heide said. "Something that old man said got me thinking. He said that he didn't think Gilpin was responsible for all of this and I can't help but agree."

"So, who do you think is?" Haran asked, as far as he knew Gilpin was solely responsible.

"When you went to Athon, Lyra and I went to Randint and had a meeting with Ella and another man. Percival."

"Yeah, she told me, that's how she found out when the siege was going to happen," Haran said not understanding her point.

"Well, the man, Percival. Something about him seemed off when I was speaking to him. He seemed almost too charismatic for his good, like he was putting on a façade," Heide said.

Haran was starting to realize now, "Oh, so you think Percival is responsible for this?"

Heide nodded. It was plausible, Haran thought, but that left one question burning in his mind, "But what does that do for us, the Baron is still going to hang Gilpin no matter what."

"Not if he thinks Percival is the real mastermind," Heide said.

"But how do we prove, that, how can we be even sure that he is a bad guy?" Haran asked.

"He's bad Haran," Heide said. "Trust me. You said Lyra and Orion were going to try and convince Baron Ligate to not hang Gilpin right." Haran nodded, she continued. "And Percival is the mastermind right?"

Haran understood fully now what he had to do and urged Spirit into a gallop. He had to get Baron Ligate to hang Percival instead.

CHAPTER

36

Haran bolted into Baron Ligate's office to find that Lyra and Orion were already in there along with General Lee. *Uhh not him again*, Haran thought. Everywhere he went it seemed like the full of himself general was there to critique their every move.

"Ahh," Baron Ligate said dismally, "All three of you are here now. Of course."

Haran caught eyes with Lyra questioningly, he hadn't expected them to be in here, only Baron Ligate. Her eyes said something, but they were far too complicated to understand.

"Anyways Ligate," Orion said, "as I was saying Gilpin deserves to spend his life in a very nasty prison. If he were to die today, he would only be seen as a martyr."

"While that is a possibility, it is a very slim one," the Baron said, "and as I am sure you heard last night, the people of Norhall have decided. The court of public opinion has cast its decision."

"Well, what if someone else was responsible for the siege," Haran chimed in quickly.

This time General Lee spoke, "Preposterous, of course the man led the siege, I captured him myself."

"But you just didn't, we did" Haran said sharply, he was fed up with the pompous general, and it was about time he was told off, "In fact you did absolutely nothing during the siege. Your armor still had the polished shine right after, and your sword had no blood stains. You didn't win the siege, you sat back while you ordered your men to do all the hard work. You are a coward who doesn't deserve your rank."

Haran heard Lyra's stifled laughter from his side as he saw the face of the general become ruby red. The man stood up and met Haran in his eyes, but Haran didn't even flinch, there was no need to. "You son do not speak to a superior like that," General Lee said. "My family has done more for this country than you or your family could ever do."

Haran saw Orion smiling out of the corner of his eyes and saw a slight nod, Haran smiled, *finally*, he thought, "First of all general you are not my superior, in fact as an Outryder you are inferior in rank to me, so I expect an apology. And second, my full name is Haran Ryder, my father was Atticus Ryder, and my great grandfather was Outin Ryder. So don't lecture me about familial accomplishments sir because you are greatly outmatched."

Haran saw the man hang his head in defeat and moved to walk out the door. "I'm sorry Haran, forgive me for my ignorance," he said as he shut the door behind him.

Haran smiled to himself and as soon as he heard the door shut behind him he let out a sigh of relief, he hadn't expected that to go over well. He turned back to the Baron who looked at him with a newfound respect, "Anyways, as I was saying Baron, I don't believe that Gilpin was the mastermind behind the attack."

"Ok then, who else could it be Haran Ryder?" Baron Ligate asked, "Enlighten me."

"A man called Percival," Lyra chimed in seeing where Haran was going with it. "He was left in charge of Randint when Gilpin and Lottie went after the Outryders. When we went down there I thought something seemed off with him, but now I realize. He's more responsible for the siege than Gilpin I just know it."

Baron Ligate grunted. "So say I believe you that this Percival is truly responsible, it changes nothing, the public have already decided to hang Gilpin. The crowd wants blood for their lost loved ones, and I am inclined to give it to them. What else can be done?"

"We could hang Percival in his place. The crowd will accept it if they know he was the mastermind," Haran said.

"Ok," Baron Ligate said with a hint of interest, "and what is to be done with Gilpin, do you wish for me to let a dangerous traitor go so that he can rebuild his forces."

"Of course not," Haran said.

"Ok so where do you propose we send him?" Baron Ligate asked. "I won't keep him in my dungeons for much longer."

Haran thought for a minute or two, but he couldn't think of a place, they couldn't give him to the Lupens for punishment for obvious reasons. And no other fief would want to take a treacherous criminal into their dungeons on fear of eventual escape.

"Irongate," Orion interjected.

Baron Ligate turned to the Outryder and looked at him warningly. "Are you sure?"

Haran looked to Lyra who looked just as confused as he was and asked, "What is Irongate?"

Baron Ligate turned to him. "Irongate is *supposed* to be a secret prison at the edge of Anjagor's frozen wastelands up north. It holds all the worst people from all around the world. For a fee of course."

"Other countries pay us to keep their prisoners locked up?" Haran asked. It seemed rather stupid concept to him, why spend money to imprison someone that you can imprison yourself.

"It must be quite the prison," Lyra added.

"I've never been there," Ligate said, "but from what I have heard its impenetrable and inescapable. I've even heard some who have seen it refer to it as 'the iron gateway to the underworld'."

The thought sent shivers down Haran's spine; he hated the idea of the underworld. Darkness, despair, agony, every bad thing imaginable in one place for eternity. He much preferred the idea of no afterlife at all. When he died he hoped that he would simply decompose in the ground like every other creature. It was much simpler that way.

"Alright, but let's go get this Percival guy before anything else," Orion said as he began to walk out the door.

Lottie woke up the day after the siege exhausted. After his fight with Haran, he was woken up at the top of the south tower by an injured Fynn to find the Outryder gone. He had let the boy live, the briefest of realizations hit him as he held the sword to his neck. He was in the same exact position Haran was when they fought at the canyon. He saw the terror in his rival's eyes and realized that he had gotten what he wanted. He finally beat Haran, he finally made him feel the same feeling he felt after losing at the canyon. The terror, the pain, the shame. He thought by making Haran feel how he felt would somehow give him back his dignity, but he realized now that he never lost it in the first place. Haran was an admirable rival and had only served to make him a better fighter and a better man.

The two Lupens climbed down the south tower and began making their way to the main gate only to find Tomas and Jet opening the trapdoor back down to the fifth tunnel. They were both injured from, as Jet explained it, "that bastard boy in the cloak." Lottie instantly knew that he was talking about Haran. They also explained to him that the drawbridge had been blown up and there were no reinforcements coming, they had lost. Lottie realized they were right and followed them back to Randint Cavern. When they made their way back, Lottie saw Ella and half of the blue group resting at the entrance to the fifth tunnel. They quickly greeted each other with an embrace and checked if they were ok.

"Gilpin?" she asked after the initial introductions.

Lottie shook his head. His master led the siege on the outside, he wouldn't doubt if he were captured or even dead.

He had no answer.

He walked out into the street the day after the siege, it was quieter now that thousands of people were presumed dead. Lottie noticed some Lupens coming home from escaping being captured, but it wasn't nearly close to the amount they started with, and none of them were Gilpin.

He walked into the dungeons under the clock tower and saw Lupe was still keeping watch over Percival. Everything was colder now, the feelings of anxiety and terror washed over him. "Good boy," he said as Lupe walked over to him to be pet. Percival's cell was the one in the far back of the dungeons and Lottie walked over to it stoically.

He saw Percival emerge from the shadows with a smile on his face, "Siege didn't go as planned huh?"

Lottie didn't respond, he saw no reason to, Percival was just trying to get a rise out of him. The man continued, "Did you fight the boy Haran?"

Still Lottie didn't respond, but his eyes did flicker at the question. Apparently Percival notice that so he continued, "You did. You couldn't kill him could you?"

"Shut up," Lottie demanded.

"You had him in your hands Lottie," Percival said as he rattled the cell door. "Everything you've ever wanted, but you let it get away from you. Why?"

"Because," Lottie said not wanting to give the man the reason why he had decided to not kill Haran.

"Because what son?"

"Because I was scared," Lottie finally snapped. "I couldn't kill him because I was scared to. He has only served to push me to be the better man and I realize that now. I wouldn't be here without him."

Percival smiled contently. Lottie realized that he had given him what he wanted, but he didn't care, he had to get it off his chest. "You fool," the man behind the iron bars said. Lottie scoffed, and he continued, "the Outryders have done nothing but harm us. You beat him because of me Lottie, *you beat him because of me*. Now let me go. I have so much left to teach you. We will rule this world with Albalupius by our side. We will fulfill his destiny; we will become chaos."

Lottie paused for a second looking to Lupe who was sitting on the ground beside him. "Not a snowball's chance in hell." He walked towards the door and motioned for Lupe to follow. "Come boy, he needs no warden, he is already a prisoner to his own twisted mind."

"You'll see I was right Lottie," Percival called as he was climbing the stairs to the exit. "There's a fine line that divides good and bad and if you continue to balance on it like this someone you love *will* die."

He walked into mansion where Ella was sitting on the couch talking to her mother. As he looked at her the words of Percival ran through his mind. *Someone you love will die.*

He stood for several minutes staring at her before she realized he was there, "Oh hey Lottie, I was just explaining to mom how you beat Haran."

"That's great Lottie," Sylvia added, "and you came out of it unscathed too, quite impressive."

Lottie smiled and hung his head embarrassingly, "Thank you Miss Frenger, it means a lot coming from you."

Sylvia laughed, "Hey I know some of those that participated in the siege have come back already. Has Gilpin come through yet or is he still missing?"

"No, he's still gone," Lottie said.

"Aww I'm sorry Lottie," Sylvia said. "I know he means a lot to you. I'm sure he is fine though."

Lottie smiled once more when he heard a knock on the door, he shot up instantly. *It could be Gilpin,* he thought.

He opened the door only to see Tomas standing before him. His calf was still bandaged from when Haran had sent a knife into it the day before. He limped inside hurriedly. "What's up?" Lottie asked.

"It's the Outryders," Tomas said, "they're here."

Lottie turned to Ella confused, she simply shrugged and got up to join his side, "Why?"

"Something about Percival and Gilpin," Tomas said, "I don't know, I was just doing my best to stop Jet from trying to kill Haran."

Lottie perked up at Gilpin's name, "Gilpin?" he asked, "Where are they?"

"At the entrance to the third tunnel," Tomas said. "Jet and I saw them dealing with the guards and walked over to see what they wanted. That's when Haran told me to get you."

"Take me to him," Lottie said.

Tomas took Lottie down the gravel streets to the far side of Randint Cavern. The third tunnel's entrance came out halfway up the cavern wall. A man-made wooden platform stood at the entrance adjacent to the wall. Wooden stairs also ran down the wall to make it easier to reach the platform.

Lottie saw the green cloaked heads of the Outryders as he was halfway up the stairs. He counted the three cloaked heads and a fourth head belonging to who he best guessed, Baron Ligate. *Odd,* he thought. Baron Ligate rarely left Castle Norhall, so seeing him this far out from the comfort of his home must mean something important was happening.

When he reached the top of the stairs he saw Jet and two guards on the far side of the platform from the Outryders. Even as far apart as possible, Lottie could still feel the daggers Jet was staring into Haran's soul. Lottie figured this irate feeling must have originated from what is now a knife sized hole in his upper left hamstring.

He heard a deep growl come from Lupe beside him as he looked over to see Haran's lion beside its master. Lottie tapped him on the head once and the growling stopped, but the death threatening gaze still was ever fixed on the lion.

Lottie diverted his gaze to Haran who gave him a small nod as he reached the top. Lottie scowled and said, "Why are you here?"

Haran continued to look to Lottie, refusing to break eye contact, "For the man called Percival."

Lottie gave him a questioning look. "And what is it that you want with him?"

Baron Ligate said, "He is responsible—"

"I was not speaking to you Baron," Lottie interjected with a piercing glare aimed at Ligate.

Lottie turned his gaze back to Haran as the Baron grew silent. "As I was saying, what do *you* want with Percival Woodberg."

"We know he is to blame for the siege," Haran said. "The people of Norhall want retribution for the death and destruction caused by the siege. Now, where are you hiding him?"

Lottie scoffed, "I am not hiding him anywhere, in fact, he is locked up right now by the virtue of trying to kill me and all of my loved ones."

"Well then it should be quite simple for you to hand him over shouldn't it?" Haran asked.

Lottie laughed, "You are joking right?" he said as he saw Haran's face was still stiff as a board, "What reason would I have to give you Percival?"

Haran opened his satchel and pulled out a small piece of fabric with an insignia on it. All Lupen's wore an insignia with just the face of the white wolf on their chest. However, this insignia was one of a white wolf standing on top of a rock. Lottie tensed as he recognized it as the insignia of the leader of the Lupens. The insignia once worn by Doran and the insignia worn currently by Gilpin. "We have Gilpin," Haran said, "and the people of Norhall want revenge. If we don't have Percival then Gilpin will be forced to the gallows and will be killed for his crimes. If you give us Percival you can see Gilpin again."

Lottie grunted angrily, he had just gotten the satisfaction of imprisoning Percival, yet he was already being taken away. However, to get Gilpin back, he would make that trade any day, "Fine," he said as he made his way back down the stairs, "follow me."

Lottie led the Outryders, Baron Ligate, Ella, Jet, and Tomas all to the clock tower in the exact center of the expansive cavern . The eight people and two animals descended the stairs and walked into the large dungeons. The dim lights of the dungeons and the trickle of water from the tower above was more apparent now to Lottie as the feeling of impending dread crashed over him like a violent wave. As they all reached the bottom of the dungeons Lottie led the way to the cell at the very end. The cell that held the man called Percival Woodberg. He walked towards the door with the key in hand. Percival emerged from the shadows once more with his hands still bound together, yet a smile still shined bright on his face. "Ahh, Lottie, you brought some friends this time." Percival looked around seeing everyone in the room dimly, his eyes focused on Haran, "oh no my boy you are teaming up with him? your eternal rival?" Percival tutted, "I told you what to do. You know what you have to do."

"What is he talking about Lottie?" Haran asked.

"Nothing," Lottie snapped. He then turned back to Percival, "Right now I am worried about getting Gilpin back." He turned the key to open the door to Percival's cell, cracking it open just a hair.

Percival began to laugh, a laugh that was filled with so much rage and darkness that Lottie could hardly handle the sound. A laugh that said it wanted everything and everyone to die in the most gruesome way imaginable, "He promised to give you Gilpin? You fool. Gilpin will spend the rest of his life in a prison far worse than death and giving me to them will only ensure that."

Lottie turned to Haran who looked at him stoically. Lottie just assumed that if he were to give up Percival that Gilpin would be returned to him safely, "Is this true?" he asked Haran.

Haran's face turned to compassion and pity, "Lottie, as you can imagine, we can't quite let Gilpin return here under the threat of another siege."

Lottie's head grew hot, and his body filled with an unnatural rage. "You said that I could have him back," Lottie said through gritted teeth. "You promised that I could have my master back."

"Lottie," Haran said speechlessly, "I never said that."

Before Lottie could push through the rage that coursed through his body, the iron gate of the cell flew open, knocking Lottie to the ground some two meters away. When he got up, he looked over to the cell to see that the door had been ripped from one hinge and was leaning heavily to one side. However, the most terrifying thing was the man in front of the cell smiling menacingly in the midst of eight skilled warriors and two gods with his hands tied behind his back. Through all those things Percival hung his head so confidently high that Lottie would think those fully trained warriors with weapons drawn beside him were nothing more than children.

This isn't good, he thought as he looked into the man's eyes. Percival Woodberg had escaped, and his eyes were filled with the embodiment of chaos.

CHAPTER

37

Haran stood with his axes drawn to the man called Percival's head. In fact, every weapon was drawn on Percival. They had all just witnessed the man kick an iron gate clean from its hinges. Lottie got up from where the force of the gate knocked him to the ground.

"Sorry about that Lottie boy," Percival said, "but I had to get out of that nasty cell. I mean there was an entire family of rats in the far corner. I mean I killed them of course, but it was disgusting."

"It's over Percival," Baron Ligate said as he drove his sword closer into the man's side, "You've lost."

"Ahh," Percival said to the man, "Baron Ligate isn't it? I've learned quite a lot about you in my time under Norhall. Your wife Teresa, she died in the Athonian attack so long ago didn't she? A rogue archer that was aiming for you hit her right? It's really sad and you can't blame anyone but yourself really."

The Baron let up the pressure from his sword, "How do you know all that?"

"I know a lot of things Baron," Percival said. "Like about the one you call Jet here—"

"Shut it Percival," Jet said.

"Ahh, touchy subject I see," Percival said. "Well then I'll just remind you that there is a knife sized wound in your leg and that you are standing right next to three people that have a sash of knives around their chest. Tell me, which one of them did that to you?"

Haran saw the black-haired boy beside him tense up and look directly at him, and then down to his leg. Percival saw the glance, "Ahh Haran was the culprit huh. Tell me. Do you recall the agonizing pain that was sent up the entirety of your left side as the knife was sent deep into your leg, tearing the tendons and muscles as it went?"

Jet's sword fell beside him as he grew angry at the thought. Haran looked to the boy and then to Lottie who had made his way beside Haran.

"Stop Jet," Lottie said. "We have to get Percival first."

Jet looked up from his leg, "Stop? Lottie I haven't even started." The boy launched a blistering fast attack at Haran who barely brought up his axe in a parry. Haran was thrown onto the defensive as the boy called Jet launched attack after attack at him. The others stood by and watched as the fight unfolded blow after blow. Haran tried his best to take the offensive, but the boy was too strong and far too fast. *He's good,* Haran thought as he was being pushed up the stairs of the dungeon, *really good*. With every blow his already injured arm grew weaker and weaker, and he knew that soon it would fail. When Haran reached the top he was forced against the door that led out of the dungeon. He kept pushing back, eventually landing a scraping blow onto the boy's arm, but he continued to press forward.

Haran stayed his ground at the top of the stairs not daring to back up any further. Jet's all out attacks were having a greater effect now and even his good arm was growing tired from the constant jarring of sword on axe. Though the boy was still attacking surprisingly fast, Haran notice he slowed slightly. He slowed just enough for Haran to front kick the boy down the hard wooden stairs. Haran grimaced as he saw the man roll down the stairs, seeming to hit each stair as he fell. *That had to hurt*, he thought as he ran out of the door and into the courtyard.

A minute later Jet emerged from the door rubbing his head angrily. The others followed them out as Jet stood in front of Haran. "You little rat—"

Lottie cut him off as he stood in between Haran and Jet, "Stop this Jet, back off, first we have to get Percival to Norhall."

"Percival," Orion said worriedly from behind Lottie. Haran looked around to see his master, Lyra, the Baron, Tomas, Ella, and the animals, but Percival was nowhere to be seen,

"Where'd he go?" Haran asked his master.

"I don't know," Orion said. "I had him when we came up the stairs, but now he's gone."

"I'm right here," the voice came from atop the clock tower.

"How did he manage to get up there with his hands tied," Lyra asked. No one had the answer other than some form of magic. He waved his hands at the group below showing that he had gotten free from the rope. *How?* Haran thought.

The man held up a vial in his hand. Haran could make out a yellow tint to the substance inside, "You see, the thing about these beautiful crystals that line the very walls of this cavern is that they are extremely explosive when exposed to a certain substance called sulfur." He paused waiting for some type of reaction, but there was none. "Oh well then, let me just show you." He threw the vile into the air as hard as he could. When it reached the ceiling some fifteen meters above Haran saw a small explosion as it came in contact with the crystals. Seconds passed and they stood silently as nothing seemed to happen. "Lame," Jet finally said.

Almost as soon as he spoke, a burst of fire emerged from the ceiling above. The explosion spread quickly across the area of the ceiling causing every crystal to have its own small explosion.

"Oh no," Haran said as he looked around to see the remaining residents of the cavern coming out of their houses to see what the noise was. He turned to the group of seven people behind him. "Get them all out of here. Now. Lottie stay with me, I think it's time we take this imbecile out." Everyone ran out of the courtyard and into the streets shouting commands to find the nearest exit. Lottie stuck by his side as they both saw Percival standing at the top of the clock tower laughing as the explosions rang out. Haran ran to the base of the clock tower and began to scale it. He saw Lottie do the same thing beside him.

When he was halfway up, Haran looked at the ceiling once more to realize that the explosions were stopping and that within just a few seconds, they would have died out for good. He smiled a little, Percival's plan had failed, they had won.

That's when the first chunk of ceiling fell, crashing into the small lake at the bottom of the cavern. Haran grunted in fear and began climbing the tower faster than before. When he reached the top he saw that Percival had several more vials at his feet. "Ahh, if it isn't Haran. Quite the spectacle huh? Care for some more?" he asked as he picked up a vial from the ground holding it as if he was about to throw it.

"Not particularly," Haran said as he threw a knife through the vial sending glass and sulfur dust harmlessly to the wood floor. In almost the same movement he sent three more knives into the other vials that lay at Percival's feet.

"That's not nice," Percival said with a frown. "In fact, that was so mean that I might just have to kill you now."

Percival tried to move to hit Haran, but Haran pulled out another knife and Percival stopped in his tracks. "Don't move another step," Haran demanded, not breaking eye contact with the deranged man. He could still hear the sound of rocks smashing violently against the ground and the screams. The screams. They pierced his very soul, all this agony caused by one man. All of this death, why shouldn't he return the favor, why shouldn't he kill the man called Percival.

"I know what you are thinking boy," Percival said, "Go ahead kill me." Haran eyed him suspiciously, but said nothing so Percival continued, "Look around you, I caused all of it. Everything is my fault, so why don't you just kill me. Send that knife through my chest and avenge these people's death."

Haran tensed up, ready to throw the knife at any moment before he eventually said, "No."

"And why not," Percival said, "After all I have done, all of the people I killed. Why not kill me right here right now."

"Because I can't change your decisions," Haran said. "But my decisions are firmly in my hands." It was something Orion said to him soon after they discovered that the Lupen's attacked the convoy of Millstone men. He didn't understand it then, but now he understood. He was a better Outryder than that. He was a better man than that.

"That's a shame then," Percival said as he hit Haran with a right hook before he even had time to react. He was sent into the hard metal bell headfirst, making a loud bang as he hit it. Dazed and dizzy, Haran saw two Percival's each coming at him with a nasty uppercut that sent him centimeters into the air. He groaned as he got up, the pain shooting through his whole body. "Bet you wish you killed me now," Percival continued, laughing maniacally, "I will make you regret even trying to stop me—"

"That all you got?" Haran interrupted, blood pouring from where he hit his head on the bell.

"What did you say boy?" Percival asked.

"A couple of weak punches and an evil laugh," Haran said, "Is that all you got? Because if so you are in for a world of trouble." Haran threw a sloppy punch that Percival easily dodged. Percival hit him with another right hook, this one far more devastating than the last. It sent Haran to the ground once more, but the boy still got up. Nothing would stop him from finishing this fight. Nothing. He was bleeding from his lip now as he threw a right hand at

Percival. It was better, but not great and Percival also dodged it easily. Haran followed it up with a left hook that Percival easily caught. He pushed against the fist, spinning Haran in a circle and sent a right hand to his nose when he finished the three-hundred-and-sixty-degree turn. Haran stumbled slightly but remained standing. "Don't you give up son?" Percival asked as Haran hobbled towards him.

"No," Haran said, tasting the hint of copper in his mouth as he spoke, "That's not my style."

"Everyone can change," Percival said as he let go another hook into Haran's ribs. Haran spit up blood onto the floor as he leaned over in pain, but he soon stood back up ready to fight. Percival sighed as Haran threw a cross that he dodged and a left hook that he caught. "Please just gi—"

The man was cut off by Haran's right hand landing square on his jaw. The man stumbled back but remained on his feet. Wiping a small bit of blood from his mouth, his eyes grew darker and more foreboding. However, Haran didn't care, he was going to win no matter what. Percival charged him sending a right hand followed by a devastating uppercut. Haran dodged the right hand barely, but the uppercut came too fast. He was sent flying into the air and smacked into the crenellations of the clocktower. Luckily they were there, otherwise he would have fallen to his death.

He lay on the ground trying desperately to get up, but it was over, he had lost. Everything he had done, everything he had accomplished, just to die in the hands of a maniac. He collapsed, utterly defeated as Percival stood above him. The man picked Haran up and held him over the edge of the clock tower. Haran squirmed in Percival's death grip, but eventually decided it would be best if he didn't.

Haran looked down to see the fifteen-meter fall below him. If he fell from that distance there was no way he would survive. *This is it*, he thought, *this is how I die*. Haran took a look around him. The whole cavern was collapsing in on itself. Boulders crushed entire houses. People were scrambling into the streets desperately looking for exits. Women and children shrieked in terror as they watched their entire world be destroyed in front of their eyes. Haran didn't make a sound as he dangled above his inevitable death. He felt it would be disrespectful to those who were losing everything. *What is the loss of one boy's life compared to the life of a civilization?*

Percival looked to him, his hair unkept and wild. His eyes were sharp daggers full of rage and fulfillment. "Now boy, do you see my plan. You could never beat me. Everything I have done has come to this. Has come to chaos—"

Almost as soon as the words came out of his mouth Percival was sent into the bell just as Haran had been, but this time it was by Lottie's left hook. Haran smiled as he fell to his immediate death. *About time*, he thought. He grabbed onto the closest crenel of the clocktower in just enough time to not fall to his doom.

He mustered enough strength to pull himself up just far enough to where his eyes were above the crenellations. He saw Lottie beating Percival closer and closer to the edge of the clock tower. Right cross, left hook, uppercut, Lottie threw every different type of punch he could think of and more. Percival had no retaliation; Lottie was both too fast and too furious to give him any room to breathe. He pushed Percival ever closer to the edge of the tower with one devastating punch after another. As Percival leaned bloody against the crenelations of the tower he paused looking to Haran. He walked over to where Haran was holding onto the crenel and offered a hand. Haran took it and Lottie drug him up with ease. Haran smiled inwardly, *of course this is how he saves my life,* he thought.

Haran rolled over the crenellations and onto his feet. He looked over to the bloodied Percival slumped against the far side of the clock tower. Lottie practically ran over to the man, grabbing him by his collar with an unbridled rage. "Lottie," Haran said warningly.

"Apologize," Lottie said to Percival. Percival sat smiling as he looked to Lottie. "Apologize for killing Doran."

Percival looked over to Haran and then back to Lottie. "Just kill me boy," he demanded.

Lottie's rage dimmed slightly as he dropped the man to the ground once more.

He turned around and looked to Haran with a defeated expression. "No," Lottie said, "You aren't dying today."

He began to walk towards Haran, but Percival spoke once more, "You are a coward. Just like Doran."

Lottie whipped around with a newfound anger. Without even hesitating he push kicked the man off the tower. The stone crenel that Percival leaned on helplessly flew from its resting place and Percival flew with it. Haran walked over just in time to see Percival falling to his death, grasping at nothing but air as he fell. Haran looked away as he hit the ground, but the image of the man's skull cracking burned into his brain.

"You know for someone of your size your pretty quick on your feet," Haran said recalling saying that to the boy once before.

Lottie smiled slightly, sighed and sank to the floor contently. Their job was done. Haran continued standing though, looking around to see giant chunks of rock were still falling freely from the ceiling, he saw one fall into a small cottage at the bottom of the cavern. He hoped that the family got out in time as he saw the rock split the house in two pieces.

"We caused this you know," Haran said. Lottie perked up to hear what he had to say. "It's our fault."

"How so?" Lottie asked.

"If we would have just not fought each other all of our lives then all of this could have been avoided," Haran said. "Doran's death, Scarlett's death, the death of thousands in the siege, and now we are here, watching as the world literally crumbles to pieces around us."

"You think?" Lottie asked letting the statement rest for a few moments, "You know, Percival had this idea that everyone had a rival so equal to them that they are what he referred to as 'eternal rivals.' I think that man was wrong on a lot of things, but that one I am sure he got right. We were destined to be rivals and nothing could have been done to avoid that."

"You may be right," Haran said. A brief second passed as Haran thought back to what it was like before the wolf cults and the Outryders. Back to when it was just him and Lottie log rolling across the Wolf's Tail River. *Good times*, he thought. That was until he let Lottie fall into Calcore Canyon and gave him scars.

"You know I always thought you were better than me," Lottie said with a laugh, "I tormented you for so long because I have always wanted your life."

My life? Haran thought, *Why would he want my life?* However, that question never left his mouth, "I thought it was because of what happened at the canyon so many years ago."

Lottie laughed once more, "You know that's what I thought too, but no. Now I realized that was just an excuse to be angry at you."

Haran grew quiet and sat on the floor once more, Lottie had wanted his life. Impossible.

He sat there staring at the rocks falling from the ceiling for what felt like a decade. The sound of rocks crushing houses was deafening to his ears. The repeated splashes of water from the lake at the bottom of the cavern also helped to create the effect of an ocean in his ears. "You know it's quite peaceful don't you think?"

"What?" Lottie asked, "The sound of rocks crashing to the ground?"

"No," Haran said, "the realization that you are about to die."

"Oh yeah," Lottie said. "That too."

Haran laughed and they sat again in silence for a minute or two before he eventually stood up once more. Haran saw several more houses get crushed as giant rocks fell onto their wooden frames. He saw Lupens below scrambling for the exits. Screams of pain rang out through the cavern. It was just what Percival had wanted, chaos.

However, through all the noise Haran heard something that snapped him out of his death accepting daze. Something so brief, but so powerful that he had to hear it again. He waited a few seconds and then he heard it again, it was the sound of a baby crying from below. Haran started climbing down the clock tower when Lottie said, "Where are you going?"

"To do my duty," Haran said.

By the time he reached the bottom of the tower the crying had stopped. *Oh no*, Haran thought, automatically assuming the worst. Shiva joined his side once more as he searched around to find where it was coming from, but without the continual noise it was impossible to find it

He felt a presence come up behind him, nervous as he was he whipped around taking out his axes in one fluid movement. When he completed the turn he was met with Lottie's big frame. The boy reached for his sword as Shiva growled at him. "I thought we were done with all that."

Haran let out a sigh of relief. "We are, you just frightened me is all." He motioned for Shiva to relax which she did so willingly.

Lottie let out a short laugh and said, "So, what are we doing?"

Almost as soon as he asked the question the baby let out another cry. "Ahh I see," Lottie said trying to find its origin. Haran too listened, but the cry stopped as suddenly as it had started.

A minute passed and the crying started once more. "Over here," Lottie said as he pointed to the house beside him. The house had a giant chunk of rock directly through the heart of the home. The two boys ran into the crumbling home to find the baby on the floor only a meter from the giant rock. Beside the baby was the mother, her legs crushed by the rock. "Please," she called to the boys. "Save her, save my precious Hazel."

Haran and Lottie met eyes. Lottie gestured for Haran to take the child. "You are better with children anyway."

Haran did as the mother asked and took the baby from the floor. The baby girl let out a loud cry as she heard another rock crash down to the road outside. "Shh," he said, "it is okay now. We are ok."

"Thank you," the mother said as her last words as she finally gave into the pain.

Haran met Lottie's eyes again as they both realized that this baby was now just like them, an orphan. "She's gone," Lottie said as he looked to the woman. Haran nodded.

They paid their respects for a second or two, but it wasn't the time nor the place for anything longer than that. As Haran and Lottie went to exit the door a loud snap made them both flinch. The noise came from the front of the house as the large support beam at the door finally gave way to the pressure of the falling rocks above. Apparently Lottie saw it first because he ran to the door as the beam slowly fell to cover their only exit.

He got there just in time, running under the beam and catching it from crashing across the doorway. Haran stood amazed behind the boy as he held up the beam. It must have been hundreds of kilograms in weight, yet he caught it with such ease. The beam bent around his arms, it wouldn't be long before they gave out and the two were trapped in the house. "What are you doing Haran," Lottie said through gritted teeth, "Go."

Haran looked to the boy with a hint of sadness. "No, you'll die."

"It's better than us both dying," Lottie said.

"I can help you," Haran said holding the baby, "Just give me a second to think."

"Haran please," Lottie said with great effort as the beams pushed down on his shoulders. "Just go, save the girl."

"No," Haran said, "I won't let you die down here. Just hold on while I figure out something to do." Haran racked his brain thinking of anything he could do to save the boy. *Nothing.*

"Haran I beg of you please. That girl deserves to live far more than either of us," Lottie said.

"I can't fail you again," Haran said on the verge of tears.

"You never failed me Haran," Lottie said. "I failed myself. Now go please. You are her only hope now." The beam cracked from the downward force. Haran didn't argue a fourth time. He saw no need. Lottie's mind was made up and there was nothing he could do to stop that.

He walked under the bending beam and through the exit. "Haran" Lottie called. as he held up the massive beam. "Tell El I said I love her and that I didn't break my promise."

Haran simply nodded. He knew the tears wouldn't let him form a sentence of goodbye to the boy. He turned away from the large boy, not daring to take a look back. He knew if he did he would try to save him instead.

"Oh, and Haran," Lottie added. Haran moved his head in acknowledgement, but still didn't turn back around. "You have been one hell of a rival."

Haran smiled to himself and said through the tears, "You too bud. You too."

And he walked away from the house. By the time he was ten meters down the road he heard the sound of the beam as it finally snapped from the force. The tears streamed down his face and soaked the ground as he walked away.

Lottie was dead. He looked to Shiva who had been sitting where he left her. She seemed to feel his pain, looking at him with compassionate eyes. And for the first time since he had become an Outryder he didn't know what to do. Everything around him was crashing and he stood broken in the center. Even his greatest rival had just died. What was he to do now? Where was he to go? Who was he to fight? Who was he without Lottie?

He sat paralyzed for several seconds before Shiva eventually nudged him. He looked down to the baby in his hand. *Hazel*. He had to get Hazel out of there. He sighed deeply and moved to the exit with Hazel in his arms.

As he stood at the third tunnel exit he was surprised that the platform and stairs leading up had remained intact. He looked to the cavern below to see all of the destruction he had caused, "I'm sorry," he said to no one in particular as he began to make his way through the tunnel and onto safety.

EPILOGUE

Haran emerged from the third tunnel with the baby in hand and Shiva behind him. The bright sun beamed off Calcore's walls blinding him for many seconds as they got accustomed to the change. He looked around to see hundreds of survivors sitting at the bottom of the canyon. "Haran," he heard Lyra say as he turned around to be nearly tackled to the ground by the girl.

"Be careful," Haran said gesturing to the baby in his arms.

"Oh my goodness, Haran," Lyra said. "She's so cute."

Orion walked up next and said, "I'm glad you are ok." Haran nodded his appreciation and handed the baby to Lyra who was reaching for her. Everyone else gathered around Haran now.

"Lottie?" Haran heard Ella's voice behind Lyra. She moved into view. "Where is Lottie?"

Haran forced his head down refusing to make eye contact with the blonde girl in front of him, "He's—"

"Don't you say it Haran," Ella said as tears started to well up in her eyes, "He can't be dead."

"I'm sorry," Haran said back.

"No. No. No. No. No. He is not dead. He is Lottie. Lottie can't die. Lottie is Lottie," Ella said as she fell to her knees in tears. Lyra handed the baby to Baron Ligate and knelt down to comfort Ella.

Haran looked to her. He was trying his best to act strong for the girl, but he wasn't after he allowed Lottie to die like that. "He was with me on the tower as we took on Percival. He saved my life and then we sat there for a long time. He told me—" Haran faltered, "It doesn't matter. Then we went to save the baby and the house collapsed in on us. He held up the beam to let me go free with the baby. I protested of course, but he begged me to tell you specifically that he never broke his promises."

"He said that?" Ella asked choking on her tears. Haran nodded, Ella shook her head in protest, "No. He can't be dead. Why would you let him sacrifice himself? Why did you let him die?"

Haran looked at her speechlessly, he had no response. What was there to say? It was his fault; he left Lottie in that building as he walked away scot-free. There was no way he survived that crushing impact of the beam unless... unless he got out from under it somehow. Surely he had to right? Lottie couldn't die.

"Look Haran." Lyra pointed towards where Shiva was sitting. Haran looked over to see that his lion was slowly turning into dust in front of him. It started with his paws and within a matter of seconds Shiva was nothing but dust. His constant companion, one that had saved his life more times than he could count, was nothing but a pile of dust easily blown away by the valley breeze.

"What just happened," Baron Ligate asked shushing the child.

"'When one owner dies'—" Orion said quoting from the journal they found in Holland's library.

"'Both the gods return to the godly realm.'" Haran finished his sentence. A tear coursed down his cheek. He had hoped somehow, some way that Lottie had gotten out of the cavern, but Shiva's dust confirmed it. Lottie was dead and no one was to blame but himself.

Everyone stood in shock as they realized the impact of what happened, "He's gone?" Ella asked. "He's really gone?"

They stood there for several minutes mourning the loss of Lottie. Lyra held Ella tight as she cried in his arms. Tomas was in the back saluting his fellow companion. Baron Ligate rocked the baby slowly to sleep as tears streamed down his face. Orion wrapped his arms around Haran as the boy stared up the canyon. He looked to the same spot that Lottie almost died so many years ago. The ledge was still broken, and the side of the canyon was still stained with the boy's blood as his arms were raked across its rocky face. He failed to save the boy twice while Lottie only served to save Haran's life. Maybe Lottie's belief about him was right, maybe he was weak after all.

Hours later they made their way up the canyon. Lyra helped Ella walk up the steep slope as Ella's knees were still weak from shock. When they reached the top of the canyon a horse came storming over the hill from Castle Norhall. Haran recognized the rider on it. It was the captain from Norhall Castle. Blood soaked his hands as he struggled to stay on the horse. He urged his horse to a complete stop in front of the Baron as he struggled to hold onto the reins. He grasped his side which seemed to be the source of the blood.

"Baron Ligate," he croaked helplessly, "So glad I found you."

"Captain Ryland," the Baron said, "What happened to you? Who did this?"

"A boy with jet black hair and eyes. He ambushed me and my guards on the road," Captain Ryland said groaning in pain.

Haran looked to Ella and said, "Jet."

Ella nodded confused, "Why did he attack you?"

"He wanted me to deliver a message to Ligate," the guard captain said, "he said, 'tell him that King Theos is here,' then he added, 'and I won't stop until Lyra is mine.'"

Everyone looked to Lyra confused, everyone except for Orion of course.

"I don't understand," Haran said. "What does that mean?"

Lyra was paralyzed in shock. "I thought I recognized his face, but he looks so different now. Everything went so fast I couldn't tell."

"Couldn't tell what?" Haran asked.

Orion's face turned to stone as he turned to Lyra and said, "I had my suspicions, but didn't know for sure."

"Know what?" Haran asked growing significantly more frustrated.

"The black-haired boy. Jet," Orion said. "He is Lyra's cousin. He is King Theos of Athon."